CRIMEUCOPIA

Dead Man's Hand

A Murderous Ink Press Anthology

****

CRIMEUCOPIA

Dead Man's Hand

First published by
Murderous-Ink Press
Crowland
LINCOLNSHIRE
England
www.murderousinkpress.co.uk

Paperback Edition ISBN: 9781909498280
eBook Edition ISBN: 9781909498297

Acknowledgements

To those writers and artists who helped make this anthology what it is, I can only say a heartfelt Thank You!

And to Den, as always.

Contents

* First appeared in the John M. Floyd collection *Deception* (2013)

** First appeared as a now-discontinued Outlaws Publishing project 2019

*** First published in StoryHack #4 August 2019

Your Horse Came Home Without You, and There's Blood on the Saddle...
(An Editorial of Sorts)

Is there such a thing as a 21st Century author working in the Wild West/Western genre?

With it's literary roots initially defined by the likes of Zane Grey and later Louis L'Amour – and with a respectable nod to the very British J. T. Edson – the American Old West wagon train still keeps rolling along, even in the 2020s.

It's a style of Adventure writing that has attracted successful crossover authors such as the late Robert B. Parker, Loren D. Estleman, the late Elmore Leonard and James Lee Burke – with alternatives such as the late Tony Hillerman, who gives a totally different, modern viewpoint with his Joe Leaphorn & Jim Chee Navajo police procedurals – yet another successful hybrid of Crime and Western fiction. His legacy is carried on with his daughter, Anna Hillerman, in her novels of his characters. And it's also good to note that there are more than just a few women writing in the genre – and winning the very prestigious Spur Awards from the Western Writers of America.

However, while there will always be a tendency for Hollywood to glamourise things – the Western 'movie' having gone through a boom, a slump, and a Spaghetti Revival – there have been relatively recent niche outings such as *No Country For Old Men*, and *The Sister Brothers* – neither of which could be said to be in the John Ford/John Huston style of story telling.

Not to be outdone, Australia has generated the remarkable *The Proposition* – a dark piece written by Nick Cave (so no surprises there) – not forgetting such unusual outings as *Tears of the Black Tiger*, or *The Good, The Bad, The Weird*.

But back to this collection.

The five writers here have very respectable track records in the Western genre, and are old hands when it comes to telling compelling stories.

John M. Floyd opens the proceedings with **Redemption.** Gunslinger turned private detective, Will Parker, is hired to find the missing daughter of Isaiah Dunn. However, all is not what it might seem, and Parker uncovers a deadly conspiracy, which has connections to his own dubious past.

From there, Alexander Frew gives us Book 1 of the Joe Flint trilogy, in the form of **Rebel Seed.** While on a cattle drive, William Shaw takes a shine to Joe Flint after hearing that the young man had been taken by Native Americans during a raid on his parents homestead. Now in his early 20s, Flint is confronted with Shaw's headstrong and impetuous daughter, Catriona Shaw, even though she's engaged to Rawley Henderson. Henderson does his best to deride, denigrate and bring down his rival. But with Native American Karankawa fire in his veins Flint fights back in his own unique way, sowing the rebel seed that will rule his life and his need to revenge those who have wronged him.

Jim Doherty's **For the Honor of the Family** puts the timeline in the early 20th Century. As the 1920's begin to roar, itinerant Texas cop Gus Hachette hires on as a field investigator for the Lone Star Cattlemen's Association, and finds himself swept up in a murderous blood feud between two wealthy ranching clans.

In Bruce Harris' **Murder at Bullet Pass** we have a sheriff, a mayor and a rabbi — but rather than it being the opening to a joke, in this western whodunnit, a peaceful town is turned upside down when a hotel owner is murdered. During their investigation, the sheriff, the mayor, and a visiting rabbi discover there is more than one killer in town.

And closing out this collection is Brandon Barrows' **Wild Yellow.** Railroad detective Clint Hagar never encountered an enemy he couldn't beat with bullets or fists - until he met the desert, alone and afoot. And though he survives, something inside of him has broken and he now he battles his own fear and self-doubt while trying to protect a small, isolated town from the outlaws who terrorize it.

Even though the Western may not be your genre of choice, hopefully there is something in this collection that takes your fancy, because in the spirit of the Murderous Ink Press motto: *"You never know what you like until you read it."*

Redemption

John M. Floyd

"I see you spent three years as a Pinkertons investigator," Colonel Dunn said.

Will Parker had turned in his chair to look at the rolling prairie outside the colonel's front window. Downhill and six miles to the south, a cluster of houses and buildings rose into view, a brown smudge on an otherwise featureless landscape. At this distance—and to Parker, who'd once spent four months on a cargo ship in the Atlantic—the town of Redemption looked like an island in a pale green sea.

He turned again to face the man across the desk. "That's right. A long time ago."

"Where?"

"Chicago and Washington."

"Why'd you leave the company?"

"A better offer."

Dunn kept his eyes on the open letter he was holding in his hand. Parker knew it was the one he'd written himself, in response to the colonel's wire.

"What'd you do afterward?" Dunn asked.

"Private security, for President Lincoln."

Dunn looked up. "If I recall, Lincoln was assassinated."

"Not while I was there," Parker said.

Colonel Dunn put the letter down, leaned back in his chair, and folded his hands over his belly. His white hair was neatly combed and his face had the pink smoothness of wealth and leisure, but his eyes looked tired, and hard as flint. Parker had no idea what Dunn had once been a colonel of, or why he preferred to be addressed that way. All Parker knew—all that mattered, really—was that this man was now his client. Depending, of course, on the outcome of this meeting.

"What happened next?"

Parker almost said *Rough times*, but didn't. "I came west. Ranch work, cattle drives, odd jobs."

"A hard life," Dunn said.

"It worked out. I've been in California two years now, at the agency."

The agency. As always, it sounded impressive. In truth, Parker Investigations consisted only of Will and his brother Robert, who had talked him into the venture. But he'd found that his Pinkertons training helped. He was a good detective. It was one of only two things he *was* good at.

Dunn seemed to read his thoughts. "Ever done any gun work?"

Parker hesitated. "I was a deputy for a while, in Arkansas. And security guard at a bank." He paused, keeping his face expressionless. "Guns aren't often required, in my current job."

"Yet you're wearing one. Why's that?"

Parker shrugged and asked, "Do you carry a pocketknife?"

Dunn sat motionless, watching him. "Matter of fact I do."

"Why?"

"In case I need it."

Parker nodded. "Me too."

A silence passed. The afternoon sun painted a lopsided yellow rectangle on the wooden floor near Parker's chair. Again he looked out the window. The pony he had rented in town stood where he'd left him, at the hitching rail beside the front porch. Parker watched him switch his tail at an invisible horsefly.

At last Colonel Dunn seemed to make up his mind. He sat up straight and tugged on both lapels as if about to make a dinner speech. Carefully he refolded Parker's letter and put it aside. Then he leaned forward, placed both palms flat on the desktop, and looked his visitor in the eye.

"Two months ago my daughter disappeared, Mr. Parker," he said. "I want you to find her."

*****

For the next half hour Will Parker listened to the colonel's summary of what had happened the night of June sixth. Parker never once interrupted, and didn't really need to. It was a well-rehearsed presentation of the facts.

According to Dunn, he and his daughter Elizabeth had lived here together for two years, ever since his wife passed on. A sweet but plain girl of seventeen, Elizabeth had few friends in town. This was by choice; she'd been schooled at home, and seemed content to do housework and sit on the porch and read, or occasionally ride one of the colonel's horses into Redemption to buy the fabric and thread for the clothes her mother had taught her to sew. She also had no beaus, except maybe one. The colonel said he would get to that later.

On the night in question, when Colonel Dunn had settled in with his newspaper after supper and Elizabeth was in her bedroom on the second floor, he heard the clear, flat sound of a gunshot. Under other circumstances he wouldn't have paid it much attention: some of his land was unfenced and so was his neighbor's, so drifters and hunters and drunks occasionally crisscrossed their property, and almost everyone carried a gun in these parts. But this had sounded like a pistol shot, and seemed to come from somewhere behind and west of the house, where there were no roads and no trails. He had checked his pocketwatch. It was nine o'clock.

The colonel rose from his chair, took his old fifty-caliber buffalo gun from its pegs over the fireplace, socked a hat onto his head, and stomped out the back door to investigate. The bunkhouse was empty and silent—all five of his cowhands were in town, probably the saloon—and only a sliver of moon lit up the countryside. For more than half an hour he wandered the low hills to the north and west but saw nothing amiss, and by nine forty-five he was back in his chair with his feet propped up and his concerns at rest, packing one last pipeful of tobacco before heading to bed.

And then he realized that he hadn't heard a peep from Elizabeth since he got back. She was never noisy, but he could usually hear her moving about upstairs. Was she already asleep? Surely not. She never went to bed until after ten. With a jolt he realized that he couldn't even recall hearing her *before* he'd left the house. Worried, he put down his pipe and hurried up the staircase to check on her.

She was gone. Her room was empty, the window open, the curtains moving in the breeze. A rose trellis had always hugged the side of the house below the window, but it had never crossed his mind that she might use it to sneak out. Had someone instead used it to sneak in, and kidnap her? He doubted that—there were no signs of a struggle—but what other explanation could there be? In a panic, he rushed back downstairs and out to the servants' residence behind the house before remembering that their maid had decided to quit a week earlier. There was no one else around to have seen or heard anything that might help him.

For the second time that night Colonel Dunn fetched his big rifle and set out on a search, but this time it was on horseback and in dead earnest. He remembered, all too well, the gunshot he had heard. Was there a connection? All he knew for sure was that his daughter was gone and he was terrified. Finally he rode into town, rounded up his men at the saloon, woke the sheriff, and spent the rest of the night combing the countryside. It was all to no avail. Elizabeth Dunn had disappeared without a trace.

Afterward, they found no footprints in the hard dirt at the bottom of the rose trellis—the whole county was dry as a bone—and the colonel verified that nothing seemed to be missing from her room. Whatever had happened, he knew she hadn't run away from home. But as the days and weeks passed, he also knew it was likely he would never see her again.

A few weeks ago, more than a month after Elizabeth's disappearance, he ran into an old friend who was passing through town, a friend who gave him a copy of a San Francisco newspaper in which he later found a small advertisement for Parker Investigations. He sent the wire that same afternoon.

"And that's what led to you and me sitting here today," Dunn said. His face looked even more weary and drawn than before.

The room had gone quiet. After a long pause Parker said, "I'm sure you understand, Colonel, that there is... well, there's very little chance that your daughter's alive."

Dunn just stared back at him.

"It's been two months," Parker added.

Dunn sighed, long and deep. "I realize that. But I need to know for sure."

Parker thought for a moment. "Are you certain about the times you mentioned?"

"Yes. Maude Fairley, my closest neighbor—well, relatively close—said she heard the shot also, and she agreed that it was at almost exactly nine o'clock."

"And what conclusions did the sheriff come to?"

"The sheriff doesn't know what a conclusion is," Dunn said. "He's out of his depth, in this matter."

"But you have conclusions of your own. Am I right?"

"I do, yes." The colonel lowered his head and studied the backs of his hands. "I believe a local young man, Jimmy Ray Smith, is the guilty party. I believe he either kidnapped or murdered my daughter—or both—that night."

"And why do you believe this?"

"Because of rumors that he and Elizabeth were seeing each other. I was told of these rumors but paid them no mind. In hindsight, I suspect that they were true, and that she did indeed have a beau, and that the two of them had been meeting at times when my men and I were away. Or even when I *was* here, because for several weeks she'd been going outside every night to use a telescope I bought her. I realize now that at least some of those stargazing sessions were probably to meet Jimmy Ray." He paused. "I know for a fact that they were supposed to meet the night she went missing."

"Excuse me?"

Dunn's face grew tight. "That next morning I searched her room, top to bottom. It felt strange to do that, to go through her personal things when I knew she might show up again at any moment—but I did it anyway. To try to find some kind of clue."

"And?"

"I found a note in her dresser drawer from young Jimmy Ray to Elizabeth, asking her to meet him the previous night, at nine o'clock."

Both of them fell silent. The colonel's fists were clenched on the desktop.

"And you only found out about this afterward?" Parker asked.

"The next day. If I'd known beforehand I'd probably have locked her in her room."

"May I see the note?"

"I tore it up and threw it away. That was stupid, I know—but I went into a rage. I'm still in a rage."

"Has the sheriff—has anyone—questioned the boy?"

A muscle had begun twitching underneath Dunn's eye. "He says he was nowhere near here. In fact two of his friends say he was with *them* that night, in the next county."

"And you think they're lying?"

"Yes."

"What does the sheriff think?"

Dunn shook his head. "I told you, he doesn't know what to think. We have no expertise here, Mr. Parker. That's why I sent for you."

Parker nodded and came to a decision of his own. "Good enough." He pointed to the letter on the desk. "I've outlined my usual terms—payment, expenses, and such. Are they satisfactory?"

"Yes. I'll pay your initial fee before you leave here today." Dunn seemed to have calmed down a bit. "But I have one requirement."

"What's that?"

"You must complete your investigation in five days."

"Five days? Why?"

"I have my reasons. Today's Sunday. I want your final report by this Friday at the latest. Is *that* satisfactory?"

"I guess it'll have to be." Parker picked his hat up off the floor beside his chair. "I'll need to see your daughter's room, Colonel, and I'll need a picture of her. I'll also require a list of her acquaintances, however few, in town."

Dunn looked relieved. "Of course. Her room's at the top of the entranceway stairs," he said, pointing. "I'll find a photograph and make the list while you take a look."

As Parker rose to his feet, Dunn added, "One more thing."

"Another requirement?"

"A question."

The two men's eyes locked.

"You're Charlie Parker, aren't you."

Parker sighed. It had once been surprising to him that so many people knew his name. He felt a sudden tiredness.

"I used to be," he said. "Charles William. I go by my middle name now."

Dunn studied him a moment. "You had quite a reputation."

The silence dragged out. Parker could clearly hear the ticking of a clock somewhere behind him in the room.

"Don't misunderstand me, Mr. Parker. I don't care about your past. All I care about is that you find my daughter." Dunn paused. "Or find out what happened to her."

"I will," Parker said.

*****

It was almost five o'clock when he clomped up the front steps of the Hamilton House. It was one of only two hotels in town, and he'd chosen it earlier today solely because it had been close to the point where he'd climbed down off the eastbound stage. But he was suddenly glad he had: behind the front desk was an attractive lady in a plain blue dress, bent low over an open box of what looked like bills and receipts. She looked up at him. "Afternoon. Would you like a room?"

Parker took off his hat, fished his room key from his pocket, and held it up. "Got one already. And I must say, you're an improvement over the other desk clerk."

"Careful," she said, grinning. "That's my father you're talking about."

"Ah. A family enterprise."

"That's right." She stuck out her hand. "Bitsy Hamilton. Welcome to Redemption."

"Betsy?"

"Bitsy. And don't blame Pa. My mother called me that, and it stuck."

"Will Parker." He shook her hand, then leaned over and rested his elbows on the counter. "Tell me, Miss Hamilton, where in this town can I get some supper?"

She pointed to the far side of the lobby. Tables and chairs were visible through an open doorway. "We start serving at six."

"Is your mother the cook?"

"I'm the cook."

Now both of them were smiling. He nodded, pushed off the counter, and climbed the stairs to his room.

Inside, Parker tossed his hat and coat onto the bed beside his battered suitcase, rolled up his shirtsleeves, poured a basin of water from a pitcher, and splashed it onto his face. He hadn't realized how tired he was. He looked into the mirror as he dried off and found himself thinking about Elizabeth Dunn, and the deadline he'd been given, and the strange path his life had taken to bring him to this point.

It promised to be an interesting week.

*****

Parker was the only person in the dining room that night. In fact, so far as he could tell, he was the only guest in the hotel. When he'd finished his meal and Bitsy Hamilton had come out of the kitchen to check on him, he asked her about that.

"We have only nine rooms," she said, taking a seat across the table from him. She was wearing a flowered apron over the blue dress and her hair was damp, probably from the steamy heat of the oven. "And we're never full unless a cattle drive comes through or there's an auction nearby." Amusement flickered in her eyes. "You're probably wondering how we manage to make a living, at this."

He shrugged. That was exactly what was wondering.

"We don't," she answered. "I teach during the school year, Mama takes in sewing, and Pa has a repair shop out back. But they'll never sell the hotel. Besides, we live upstairs, so this is our home." She pointed to his empty plate. "How was the steak?"

"Best I ever tasted."

Her grin returned. "I knew you were smart."

They both fell silent. Outside, an occasional horse clopped past. Dogs yapped at them, and at each other. Voices could be heard in the direction of the saloon down the street, some of them laughing. It didn't seem to matter that it was Sunday night. At some point he became aware that Bitsy Hamilton was watching him closely.

"What exactly do you do, Mr. Parker?"

He considered for a moment, then said, "I'm an investigator."

"A what?"

"I'm a detective, from a private agency. I've been hired to look into"—he paused again—"to look into a report of a missing person."

Her eyes widened. "Elizabeth Dunn?"

"You know her?"

"Not really. But everyone knows her father." She frowned. "Did he hire you?"

"You don't look pleased."

She gave a tiny shrug. "It's no surprise that you work for the colonel. So does most everybody else in this town."

"What do you mean?"

She hesitated, and lowered her voice even though they were obviously alone. "There are some things you need to know about this place, Mr. Big City Detective. Especially if you're going to be asking around, about Elizabeth."

"What kind of things?"

"Well, first off, you're lucky you're staying here instead of the Hotel Redemption. It belongs to Colonel Dunn, and so does everybody inside it. Same goes for the town's other café and the saloon and just about every business on Front Street."

"I can see that's unusual," Parker said, "but why is it bad?"

"Because they will have been told exactly what to say to any questions you ask them, that's why. And I can assure you all of them will say the Dunn girl vanished because of one person, and one only."

"Jimmy Ray Smith."

"That's right. Everybody noticed the way they'd been looking at each other. I even heard talk that he'd written a note asking her to meet him that night."

"But you don't think he was involved in the... disappearance?"

"I don't know. That's just it—nobody knows for sure. He says he didn't, and his friends say he was with them. But I promise you the colonel's convinced that Jimmy's guilty. That's probably why you're here—to find the proof." She hesitated again, and her face reddened a bit. "Whether it's true or not."

Parker, who'd been fiddling with his spoon as she talked, carefully set it down and looked at her. "Understand this, Miss Hamilton—"

"Bitsy."

He kept his voice firm. "Understand this. Colonel Dunn is my client—not my boss. I'll report only what I believe to be true."

"Whether he likes it or not?"

"That's right."

She gave him a long, solemn stare, then nodded. "I believe you."

She was about to say more when three customers strolled in and took seats at one of the tables. A Mexican waiter appeared and headed their way. Bitsy rose from her chair. "I have to go," she whispered. "But there's more you need to know."

"Can we meet later?"

She thought a moment. "No, I read to my mother in the evenings, and there's always a crowd at breakfast. I'll have the front desk in the morning, though, beginning at eleven."

"See you there," Parker said. "And thanks."

"Glad you liked your supper." She headed across the room, reknotting her apron and pausing only to nod to the newcomers. Just once, before disappearing into the kitchen, she turned, caught his eye, and smiled.

Parker found himself watching the door long after it had swung shut behind her. He indeed thanked his lucky stars that he'd picked this hotel. He'd been in town for less than a day and he already had an ally.

*****

The following morning he saw no one he knew at breakfast except last night's waiter. Apparently folks in Redemption worked long hours. Whoever was doing the cooking stayed out of sight, for obvious reasons: as Bitsy had said, the place was packed. Breakfast itself was as tasty as Parker had hoped, and afterward he found the telegraph office and sent word to Robert that he'd received a first payment from their newest client and that things were progressing.

The next two hours were spent at the Lucky Lady Saloon, nursing a midmorning beer and chatting with the handful of customers. He found out nothing new, except that two different men and the bartender assured him loudly that Colonel Dunn's daughter had been the kindest, sweetest person God ever put on this earth, and that her killer—that no-good Smith kid— deserved to be hanged from the highest tree and then laid out on the prairie for the ants and scorpions.

He also learned that some big-shot judge was due to come to town this coming Saturday, to make a speech of some kind—and that a local farmer named Eddie McPherson had been injured yesterday when he fell off the windmill he was building. When conversation lagged, Parker found himself reading the ads and notices posted on a wallboard at one end of the bar. He saw that a fine cow dog was for sale, a barn dance would be held at the home of Mr. and Mrs. Bob Adams next Saturday night, the Windham Opera House in nearby Sand Hill would reopen next weekend after being closed since March, and a man named Lester Robbins was wanted for stealing a horse. Last but not least, he verified before he left that Bitsy Hamilton had been correct on yet another detail: the Lucky Lady was owned by none other than Colonel Isaiah Dunn.

Bitsy Hamilton. Unusual name, unusual woman. For more reasons than one, Parker found himself looking forward to their meeting, and at eleven on the dot he pushed through the doors of the Hamilton House to find her standing behind the front desk. Her smile was the best thing he'd seen all day.

"If you're nice," she said, showing him a paper bag she took from behind the counter, "I'll let you share my lunch."

"No need. That breakfast you cooked up should hold me till supper." He looked around. "Where's your daddy?"

"Around back, in the shop I told you about. He has three wagon wheels to fix."

Parker pulled two of the lobby chairs close together and she came around the desk to sit down beside him. "I was wondering if you'd show up," she said.

"You told me my education wasn't complete, on local matters."

She nodded. "It's not." She wiggled a bit in her seat, settling in. "You listening?"

He wound up listening for the next twenty minutes. And she'd been right yet again: these were things he needed to know. Foremost among them was the fact that the Dunns had run this part of the county for more than fifty years, and even though the colonel was the last of the string, he was just as rich and powerful as his father and grandfather had been. And even more ruthless. Those who sided with him flourished, and those who opposed him found themselves without supplies or water or mail service or whatever else he chose to withhold. The only establishments he didn't control were the Hamiltons' hotel and the laundry at the east end of Front Street, and those were still in others' hands only because the colonel saw no great need for them.

But there were problems on the horizon.

The future thorn in the colonel's side was embodied by one man, an odd fellow who'd shown up last year with an Indian wife and two teenage kids and promptly purchased old Edwin Elwell's spread a mile or two south of town. He'd already bought up several other pieces of land Colonel Dunn had had his eye on, and was turning the former Double-E Ranch into a profitable outfit. The newcomer had also announced plans to build a second saloon in town, and possibly a new eatery. Competition was a new concept to Dunn, and battle lines had been quickly drawn.

"Who is this fly in the ointment?" Parker asked, when Bitsy finally paused for breath.

"His name's Merrill Smith. From somewhere up north, I think."

Parker felt himself blink, felt his stomach turn over. *Merrill Smith?*

"What is it?" Bitsy asked. "Do you know him?"

He swallowed and—with an effort—forced a calm expression. "What's he look like?"

"He's sort of handsome, actually. Stocky, green eyes, grayish hair. His nose is kind of funny—"

"Like it was broken once, maybe?"

"Yeah." She added, eyes narrowed: "You *do* know him."

"We never met." Parker's mind was spinning, trying to process this. *Merrill Smith was here, in Redemption?* "I know *of* him, is all."

"How?"

He hesitated. "We were in the same line of work, he and I. Long ago."

"What kind of work?"

Parker cleared his throat, searching for a way out. "We were... hired consultants. Problem solvers, you might say."

"What kind of problems?"

"It's complicated."

Thankfully, she didn't press the issue. "Does he know *you*?"

Even as he said, "I doubt it," Parker knew better. Merrill Smith had once teamed up with one of Parker's old buddies, and after a year or so wound up shooting him dead. It was said to have been a fair fight, if any fight involving someone as deadly as Smith could be called fair, but when Parker found out, he had sent word to Smith that he was coming to kill him. Smith replied that he'd be pleased to kill Parker instead, but that he was leaving next week for business in Hays City. Parker said he'd meet him there. It turned out that as each of them traveled to Hays that day Merrill Smith was ambushed by a band of thieves. (Only years later did Parker find out what had happened.) The bandits had of course picked the wrong person to try to rob, and Smith killed all four of them—but Smith's horse was shot in the melee, and the rest scattered in all directions. He was left afoot and wound up walking fifty miles with an empty canteen and a saddle slung over his shoulder, and by the time he reached civilization Parker had given up and gone home. A month later Parker's brother contacted him with the proposition to set up a business in San Francisco, and the dispute was eventually forgotten. But yes, the name Charlie Parker would be familiar to Smith. At one time they were probably the two most feared gunmen in the western half of the country.

Parker told none of this to Bitsy, who said, "Well, I'm glad you're not kin to him or anything. That could *really* get complicated."

Only half listening, Parker focused on her again. "Why?"

"Because of Jimmy Ray."

"What do you mean?"

"The prime suspect in your murder/kidnapping," she said, "is Merrill Smith's only son."

*****

Two cowpunchers wandered in shortly afterward, looking for rooms for the night, so Parker was left to his own thoughts while Bitsy resumed her job. He found himself outside again, aimlessly strolling the boardwalk that lined Front Street.

Jimmy Ray Smith was Merrill's son? It was hard to believe. Could he actually have abducted Elizabeth Dunn? If so, why? Maybe it wasn't an abduction at all; maybe they had run off together. If what Bitsy had told him was true, the son was also a half-breed, so both of them would have known

Colonel Dunn would never allow a marriage. But Jimmy Ray was apparently still here in the area. Elizabeth was most certainly not. Was she in hiding? Or was she indeed dead? Maybe her beau had killed her *because* he'd known they could never be together. Or maybe she'd broken up with him. Who knew what had really happened? Jimmy Ray did, of course, if he was guilty. But what if he was innocent? Who then would know the truth?

More importantly, how would *Parker* determine the truth?

He knew the answer to that one. There was only one way. The crime scene was two months old, the trail was cold, the victim was missing, and evidence was nonexistent. Any conclusions he could draw would be based only on questions asked of the people who knew the victim and/or the suspect.

Parker pulled Colonel Dunn's list of Elizabeth's acquaintances from his pocket. Three names: Jane Corliss, Betty Lou Ames, Isabel Thomas. Bitsy could tell him how to locate them. As for Jimmy Ray's friends, he'd have to dig a bit to find those names. But he would find them. He would also talk to Jimmy Ray, and probably—eventually—to Merrill as well. That should be an interesting meeting.

He managed to cover most of Redemption that afternoon on foot, strolling the dusty streets and leisurely watching the residents as they watched him back. He didn't accomplish a lot, except maybe to make note of the street signs and various business locations for later reference. He certainly turned up no clues that would help him in his quest. He did find that folks weren't overly friendly here, but he already knew that, and attributed it to what Bitsy had mentioned yesterday. No one knew him, therefore no one knew for sure whose side he was on, therefore no one trusted him. But that was overstating things a bit. He was quickly getting the impression that very few people in Redemption trusted *anyone*, regardless of whose side someone was on. He considered suggesting that they change the town's name to Suspicion.

There was, of course, another way of looking at the friendly/unfriendly issue. If Parker worked for the colonel, the majority of people didn't like him, period—whether they happened to also work for the colonel or not. And if Parker *didn't* work for Colonel Dunn, the majority of the townfolk probably figured there was no reason to pay attention to him at all, because he wouldn't be staying around long enough for it to matter.

After supper that night—a meal made less satisfying because of the absence of both flavor and female companionship (he was becoming fond of Bitsy, who showed up only long enough to supply him some information about his potential interviewees)—Parker climbed the steps to his room, locked the door, and sat for a while on the side of his bed, gazing into the mirror on top of the dresser. If he hadn't been in this kind of situation so often before, he would probably have questioned his reasons for being here, for doing this kind of work. Maybe he did it for the reason his brother had once suggested: it kept him out of trouble. Or at least out of more trouble.

Adrift in his thoughts, and feeling a bit sorry for himself, he undressed and scraped a chair up to the small table in the corner of his room and did something he had done almost every night for the past twenty-five years. He cleaned his gun. With great care and with fingers that could have done the job in total darkness, he stripped the revolver down, oiled it, swabbed the barrel, and wiped everything down afterward with a clean cloth. Tonight he paid the task even more attention than usual, and for good reason. The investigation had taken on a new twist, now that Merrill Smith was involved. Violence no longer seemed such a remote possibility.

If it came he intended to be ready.

*****

The next morning—Tuesday—Parker left the hotel armed with enough information to track down the people on Dunn's list. He spent all morning and part of the afternoon in the interviews with the three young women, and again learned not one fact that would help in the least. They were all still shaken by what had happened, but had seen neither Elizabeth nor Jimmy Ray on the night in question or anytime during the previous several days. They all confirmed that the two were seeing each other and had appeared to be falling in love, but they also agreed that the only possible solution was that Jimmy Ray had somehow—accidentally, perhaps, who knew?—caused her death. How else could he be here and she be gone?

That evening Parker and Bitsy again compared notes, this time over a twilight picnic in a dry wash a hundred yards behind the hotel. Bitsy had talked her father into serving as cook in the restaurant that night, which she said had secretly pleased him. What pleased Parker was that Bitsy tended to agree that Jimmy Ray might somehow be the fall guy in this situation. Yes, Elizabeth was gone, and yes, she was probably dead—but it was certainly possible that her fate had occurred at the hands of someone besides the only boy she had ever cared for, and who seemed to have cared for her as well.

Parker was beginning to think he had been overconfident when he'd sent that wire to his brother in San Francisco the day before. He appeared to be making no progress at all.

*****

On Wednesday three things happened that would change the outcome of the case. Only one could be credited to Parker's own initiative; the other two came straight out of the blue.

The first was a brainstorm that hit Parker so suddenly it made him stop his forkful of sausage halfway to his mouth. In fact its contents plopped into the runny yolk of his over-easy eggs and splattered the front of his best white shirt. He didn't care. He left the dining room without finishing his breakfast or even paying for it, and hurried up the stairs to Bitsy's family's quarters—a three-room suite. He'd been told someone else was cooking this morning so Bitsy could do other chores, and since he knew her father was downstairs and her mother slept late, he tapped on the door and hoped Bitsy was there. Seconds later she appeared.

"What was the name of the colonel's maid?" he asked her. "Do you know?"

"No. But I can find out. Why?"

"He mentioned her to me, during our meeting on Sunday. He said she'd decided to quit the week before."

"So?"

"She'd be the perfect witness if Elizabeth and Jimmy Ray ever met at the house, maybe while the colonel was away. She might've even overheard them saying something that would help. Or maybe Elizabeth confided in her. I have to talk to her."

"Wouldn't the colonel have thought of that? That she might be helpful?"

"If he has he didn't mention it to me."

"Why don't you just ask *him* her name?"

He thought about that. He could—but he didn't want to. For the first time Parker wondered if Dunn was telling him the whole truth. He also felt an excitement he'd not felt since first hearing about the case.

All of a sudden both of them heard Mrs. Hamilton calling to her daughter from the adjoining room. "I'll find the name," Bitsy assured him, and closed the door.

It was on his way back to his table in the restaurant that the second thing happened. Sitting there in the lobby was Betty Lou Ames, one of the young ladies he'd met with yesterday. She was perched on one of the lobby chairs, looking nervously back and forth between Mr. Hamilton behind the front desk and the two hands clenched in her lap. Parker saw her from the top of the stairs, and hurried to her rescue. Somehow he knew she was there to see him.

"Mr. Parker," she said, with obvious relief.

"Yes, Miss Ames. Can I help you?"

That seemed to confound her, and she again shot an uneasy glance at Mr. Hamilton.

"Let's step outside, okay?" Parker said. He took her elbow and steered her through the front doors to the hotel porch, where more chairs awaited. He sat and guided her into the one beside him. "What's the matter?"

Betty Lou Ames swallowed and said, "I don't know if this means anything..."

He stayed quiet, urging her on with a nod.

"When you talked with me yesterday, I couldn't help seeing the names on the list you had in your hand. You know, the ones you said were friends. Me and Jane and Isabel."

"Yes? What about it?"

"Well—it wasn't right, Mr. Parker. The three of us liked Elizabeth and everything, she's a nice girl, but... we weren't friends of hers. Not close friends."

She fell silent, apparently searching for words. Parker felt himself losing patience. "What are you saying, Miss Ames?"

"I'm saying the name that should've been on your list *wasn't*. Her only real friend was Gabriela Sanchez. From... you know." She turned and stared east, toward the Mexican section of town.

"Gabriela Sanchez?"

She nodded. "The street just past the livery stable. Second house on the left."

Parker turned also, following her gaze. Then he looked again at Betty Lou, who seemed more confused than ever.

"She's the one you should talk to," she said.

"I will. Thank you." He repeated it in his mind: *Sanchez, next street past the stable, second house on the left.* He vaguely remembered the area from his stroll the previous afternoon.

Betty Lou was still staring at him.

"Was there something else?"

She pointed and wrinkled her nose. "There's a spot on your shirt," she said.

*****

He watched the Ames girl flitter away, then turned and went back inside the hotel. His hat was still lying on his breakfast table, his coat draped over the chairback where he'd left it. He picked up both of them, left a dollar beside his plate, and went back through the lobby, on his way to the front door. And then the third thing happened.

The look on Mr. Hamilton's face stopped him in his tracks.

"What is it?" Parker asked.

Hamilton said, frowning, "There's someone waiting in your room, Mr. Parker. He came in through the restaurant a minute ago, asked for your room key, and went up to wait for you."

Parker blinked. "You gave someone my room key?"

"He said you'd understand. He also asked me not to tell you who he is."

Parker stood there staring. At first he wasn't sure what he was seeing in Hamilton's face. Then he understood. It was fear. The man was afraid.

Without another word, Parker backed away, laid his coat and hat on a chair, and eased his way up the stairs. At the top he stood there a minute, letting his breathing even out, letting his heart slow down. Carefully he drew his revolver and tiptoed down the hallway to his door. Once there, he rested his left hand on the knob, turned it, counted silently to three—

And threw open the door.

Sitting there in the room's only chair, his legs crossed and his hat balanced on the one knee, was a man with a broad face and a shock of steel-colored hair.

For a moment neither of them spoke. Parker had told Bitsy the truth: he'd never laid eyes on his old enemy. But the description matched.

"Merrill Smith," Parker said.

"Hello, Charlie."

Parker entered the room, shut the door behind him, and holstered his pistol. "Remember Hays City?" he said. "I waited two days for you."

"You're lucky I got sidetracked," Smith said. Then he sighed. "Long time ago."

Without looking away from his visitor, Parker moved to the bed and sat down on the edge. Less than four feet separated them. A long silence passed.

"What do you want, Merrill?" he asked.

Merrill Smith tilted his head and looked Parker up and down. "It's funny, isn't it? I figured you'd be taller."

"What do you want?"

More silence. Then: "I want you to go home, Charlie Parker. That's what I want. I want you leave me and my boy alone."

"I don't know what you've heard," Parker said, "but I'm not after your boy. All I'm trying to do is find out is what happened."

"Somebody kidnapped that girl, that's what happened. But not Jimmy Ray." Smith took his hat off his knee, uncrossed his legs, and leaned forward. "You hear what I'm telling you? My son's innocent."

"I hope he is, Merrill. And if he is he's got nothing to fear."

"He's got everything to fear! You don't know this town. All Isaiah Dunn needs to put Jimmy away is to get a so-called out-of-town expert like you to bless the lies he's already telling everybody. Then he can take this to whatever law he can find and get Jimmy convicted. Get him hanged. Don't you see that?"

"He could've already done that, with your sheriff."

Smith snorted. "Our sheriff? He's in Dunn's pocket, that's true, but he can't handle this kind of thing. He's also scared of me. What Dunn wants is something solid, and foolproof."

"Wait a minute, here. You're saying the colonel would do all this to get back at *you*? All this because of a power struggle?"

"Yes! He'd do that and more. What do you know about me, us, Dunn, this town? Nothing, that's what." Smith paused, breathing hard. "Listen: Dunn's invited an old friend to visit, this Saturday. He already has a room reserved at Dunn's hotel. The old friend's a high-powered judge, from St. Louis. You following this?"

"I'm listening. I heard something about it yesterday."

"Well, I'll bet you ten to one Dunn told you to wind up this... witch hunt of yours... by this Friday. Am I right?"

Parker blinked. *How could Smith know that?*

Smith just nodded. "I figured he did. You know why? I think he wants to turn whatever evidence you can find over to this famous judge, this old buddy of his, and put together a trial that'll be over and done before Dobbin can twitch her ears and whinny. My son'll wind up either dead or in prison by the end of the month. Now do you understand?"

Parker shook his head, thinking. Something about that didn't make sense. Besides...

"You're assuming that what I find will—"

"Enough," Smith said. "Enough talk. I'm no fool, Parker. He's paying you to find what he wants found, and I won't allow it, you understand? I won't."

For a moment they just sat there and looked at each other.

"I got a job to do, Merrill. That's what *you* better understand. I got no fight with you anymore."

Smith raised a finger and pointed. "That's where you're wrong. Hear this. If you keep this up—if you stay here snooping around—I'll kill you."

"Is that so."

"You been warned. I'll kill you."

"How do you plan to do that, Merrill?"

"Just like old times, that's how. You got one more day. Twenty-four hours." Smith fumbled in his vest and pulled out a pocketwatch. "It's a quarter to nine. If you're still here at nine tomorrow morning, you meet me out there in the street."

Palmer stared at him. "I'm staying."

Smith rose suddenly, marched to the door, and wrenched it open. "One more day," he said.

And left.

*****

Parker didn't. He sat there on his bed in the hotel for at least half an hour, thinking about what he'd just learned. He wasn't overly worried about Merrill Smith's threat; he figured he could talk Smith out of a fight, if it came to that. What bothered him most was what Smith had said about the judge. And what Colonel Dunn had not said.

But something else was wrong, too. Parker simply could not believe that Dunn would go these lengths, to get back at his enemy by convicting the enemy's son. Personal pain would result, yes, but such a thing would make the father even more of an enemy, and from what Parker was learning about the colonel and his need for power, that wouldn't be the correct approach. And something was still wrong about the kidnapping itself—if that's what it was.

That was what he would concentrate on. He still had a job to do, and he felt as if he was finally making some headway.

He stood up, rubbed his face hard enough to make his cheeks tingle, and headed downstairs to the lobby. Both Bitsy and her father were there, behind the counter, but Hamilton—after an apologetic glance at Parker—excused himself and disappeared through the door to the restaurant. As Parker retrieved his coat and hat for what seemed the tenth time that day, she gave him a guarded look. "Pa said to tell you he's sorry about what happened," she said. "Mr. Smith can be a little intimidating."

So can I, Parker thought. He wondered what Mr. Hamilton would think of the conversation that had just taken place in the room upstairs.

"No problem," Parker said. "It was time we finally met each other."

Bitsy looked as if she was about to say more on the matter, then changed her mind. She took a slip of paper from her dress pocket and handed it to him. On it was printed the name JUANITA DELGADO. "That's the colonel's maid. Carlos, our waiter, says she's been staying with her niece since Dunn fired her."

"He fired her? I heard it was her decision."

"Does it matter?"

"It might. Did Carlos give you the niece's name?"

"Maria Vega. She worked for us awhile, years ago. Tell her I sent you." Bitsy leaned closer and lowered her voice. "Carlos wasn't too thrilled to be talking to me about this. Apparently the aunt is staying there in secret."

"Interesting. You know where Maria lives?"

"I drew you a map."

*****

It took five minutes to walk to the home of Gabriela Sanchez, the friend of Elizabeth's that Betty Sue Ames had told him about. No one answered the door, and as Parker stepped down off the narrow porch he spotted someone hoeing weeds in a vegetable garden behind the house. It turned out to be Gabriela. It also turned out that she was able to tell him only one thing of interest, but it was significant: Jimmy Ray Smith had used her as the messenger to deliver his note to Elizabeth on the morning before the night she went missing.

"Do you know exactly what the note said?" Parker asked her.

Gabriela started to answer, then paused. "Jimmy told me to read it, so—well, so if I couldn't actually give Lizzie the note, I could tell her instead. You know, because of the colonel."

"He didn't like it that she was interested in Jimmy Ray, did he?"

"I'm not sure he knew. But he wouldn't if he did."

"What did the note say, Gabriela?"

"Something like 'Meet me at the pond at nine o'clock.'"

"The pond?"

"It's just west of the Dunns' house, past their property line. Lizzie said the colonel fishes there sometimes."

Parker nodded, thinking. "How'd you get there, with the note?"

"To their house? I borrowed my brother's horse."

"Did you hand the note directly to Elizabeth?"

"No, I had to knock on the front door, and when Senora Juanita—she's the housekeeper—when she answered the door the colonel was standing right there behind her. I just gave it to Juanita to give to Lizzie, and left."

"You didn't want to deliver the message yourself?"

She shrugged. "The colonel doesn't like for me to come inside."

"Why not?"

Gabriela Sanchez gave him a look far beyond her years. "Welcome to Redemption, Mr. Parker."

Parker just nodded, embarrassed. "One more thing," he said. "I was told Juanita no longer worked there, at the time."

She shook her head. "You were told wrong. She's the one I handed the note to."

That gave Parker something to think about on the way to Juanita Delgado's niece's place, which was one street and five houses away. Trudging down the dirt road, he doubted a white man had ever spent this much time on the Mexican side of Redemption.

The young lady who answered his knock introduced herself as Maria Vega, and was holding a needle and thread and a handful of checkered fabric. Parker remembered what both Bitsy and Colonel Dunn had told him, about ladies around here and their sewing. He figured there was probably a seamstress in almost every house.

"Miss Vega, my name's Parker. I'd like to ask your aunt Juanita some questions."

Her eyes widened, but then she seemed to recover. "I know who you are," she said in a meek voice.

Quickly Parker said, "Don't worry. Bitsy Hamilton sent me. I swear I won't tell anyone your aunt's here."

They stood there for a long moment. Finally Maria blew out a nervous sigh, invited him in, and vanished into the rear of the house. He could hear small children playing in one of the back rooms. Two minutes later Maria returned with an elderly lady.

"Aunt Juanita, this is Mr. Parker," Maria said. "He's a friend of Miss Hamilton's."

"How do you do," Juanita said. Her words were careful and precise.

Parker smiled and exhaled with relief. He'd been afraid she couldn't speak English.

The three of them sat together in what appeared to be the living area. It was small but neat, with vases of flowers on every flat surface. As if to balance things out, the ugliest cat Parker had ever seen glared back at him from a windowsill.

Parker cleared his throat. "Juanita—may I call you that?—I have only a few questions, about your employer, Colonel Dunn."

"My former employer," the old woman said.

"Yes, ma'am. Matter of fact that's one of my questions. When exactly did you stop working there?"

"The day after Miss Elizabeth went missing," she said.

"I was told it was the week *before*."

She studied his face. "Did Colonel Dunn tell you that?"

"Yes, ma'am, he did."

She smiled sadly. "Let me tell you something. I did not 'stop working there.' I was dismissed. I worked there for nineteen years. I took care of Miss Elizabeth as a baby, and her mother taught me English. And then I was told to leave, and not just to leave his home—he told me to leave Redemption." She raised her chin. "That part I refuse to do."

The room went quiet. The old woman wiped her eyes with an angry swipe of her hand.

"But why?" Parker asked. "Why would he fire you?"

"Because of what happened with Miss Elizabeth," she said.

He blinked. "I beg your pardon?"

Juanita glanced at Maria and must have noticed her expression, because she gave her niece a comforting nod. "Do not worry, child. I have been waiting to tell somebody this." She turned back to Parker and said, "I think I understand most of what happened that night. If I tell you... will you make sure nothing bad happens to my niece? That is my only concern."

Parker felt his regard for the colonel go down another notch. He looked Juanita in the eye. "I can't promise I won't use the information you give me," he said, "but I promise no one will ever know who provided it. Nothing bad will happen to either of you."

The old woman seemed to consider that. Finally she nodded and settled deeper into the chair, her hands folded tightly in her lap. After a long breath she said, "The colonel has been telling people he heard a shot, right? And that he then grabbed his gun and went out to see what was going on."

"That's right," Parker said.

"Well, that is a lie. I was there that night, in my little room behind the house. I heard the shot too. And it happened fifteen minutes *after* the colonel left the house with his gun."

Parker stared at her, stunned. "Are you certain?"

"Yes. I am hard of hearing, but not as much as he thinks I am. and since I go to bed early and did not come out to investigate or light my candles or say anything about it later I think he thought I did not hear it. But I did. First, I heard him leave the house—he always lets the back screen door slam shut—and I watched out my window while he stopped to pick up some stones and then crept away with that buffalo gun of his, and a little later I heard the gunshot, and later still I saw him sneak back in." She paused, remembering. "He has a big, ugly clock on one wall in the kitchen, that I can see from my window. He left at fifteen minutes to nine and came back around nine-thirty."

"He picked up stones?"

"Two or three big white ones, out of Mrs. Dunn's back flowerbed."

Parker was frowning now. "But—I don't understand. If he didn't know you saw him... why would he consider you a threat to his story?"

"Because of the note," she said.

"The one Jimmy Ray sent to Elizabeth?"

"That is right. The note little Gabriela Sanchez rode out there with, that morning. I went to the door and she handed it to me to give to Miss Elizabeth, but the colonel saw us. He did not stop me from delivering it upstairs, because he did not yet know what it said. I took it to Miss Elizabeth and she opened it and read it right then, and gave me a smile as bright as that morning's sun. She even showed me the note, let me read it, before she tucked it into her dresser drawer."

Parker considered that. "When *did* he know what it said?"

"I am not sure. Sometime later that day."

"Did you see him with the note?"

"No."

"Then how can you be sure he read it?"

She studied him a moment, then opened her folded hands and handed him a piece of lined paper. On it were the clumsily printed words MEET ME TONIGHT, 9 O'CLOCK, AT THE POND. J. R. S.

Parker stared at it. "Jimmy Ray Smith."

"That is right."

"Where did you find this? In Elizabeth's dresser drawer?"

She smiled. "I found it in Colonel Dunn's desk. The afternoon before the night Elizabeth disappeared."

Parker swallowed, thinking that over. "So somehow he took it from her room, that day. And when he found it missing the next morning from his desk—"

"He fired me. He knew I had taken it because no one else is allowed in his office. Not even Miss Elizabeth." She paused. "But he did not fire me because I took it—do you understand that?"

"I understand," Parker said, "It was the fact that he knew that *you* knew he'd already read the note before that night. That he had known beforehand that the two of them were supposed to meet, and when, and where."

"Yes," she said. "And that night, at fifteen minutes before the time they would meet, he left the house to go to the pond. To kill Jimmy Ray Smith."

The room fell silent. Parker thought he could actually hear everyone breathing.

Finally he said what all of them were thinking: "But Jimmy Ray's alive."

Juanita Delgado nodded slowly. "That is the part I do not understand."

*****

Just after noon, during a lull at the hotel—lulls occurred ninety percent of the time, according to Bitsy—she and Parker sat together in the two rockers on the porch, watching the sparse traffic of horses and wagons in the dusty street.

"So here's what you know so far, that you didn't know before," she said, holding up her fist and raising a finger as she spoke. "First, the colonel didn't tell you about his maid, except to lie about when he fired her."

"Correct. He also implied that she decided to leave on her own."

"Second"—another finger—"he didn't list Gabriela Sanchez as one of Elizabeth's acquaintances."

"Possibly because she was Mexican," Parker said, "and—to him—wasn't worth mentioning. Probably, though, to keep me from finding out about her delivering the note, and thus involving Juanita."

"Third, he lied to you about the time of the shooting, and about when he found out about the planned tryst—"

"Tryst?" he said, smiling.

"—between his daughter and Jimmy Ray Smith."

"Right."

"Fourth, the note specified the time and place where they were supposed to meet."

"Which," he said, "might or might not be important."

"It's important if the colonel really did intend to go to the pond and kill Jimmy Ray."

Parker shrugged. "If he went there to kill Jimmy Ray and Jimmy Ray was there, Jimmy Ray would be dead."

"Maybe he wasn't there."

"Are you kidding? He's the one who wrote the note."

"Two of his friends apparently say he was out of town, with them."

"I'll find out more about that late this afternoon," Parker said. "Maria Vega told me their names and where to find them."

"Oh, I almost forgot." She spread all her fingers. "Fifth and last, Merrill Smith has promised to shoot you dead tomorrow morning. Did I leave anything out?"

"I think that covers it. You know, I still haven't met your sheriff."

"No loss," she said. "He's an idiot. You don't need him, and if he wanted to meet you he would have already."

They sat there and rocked awhile. The afternoon sun wasn't as hot as usual, and a pleasant breeze was stirring. A little brown bird was hopping around underneath the empty hitching rails, probably looking in vain for a worm. *I know how you feel,* Parker thought.

"Where's your horse?" Bitsy asked.

"Since yesterday I've just been leaving him at the livery stable unless I need him. Been doing more walking than riding."

"That's because I've been doing a good job of pinpointing your interviewees."

He grinned. "For this case, that's a better term than 'witnesses.' Nobody's witnessed anything."

After a pause, she said, "You realize you probably won't get a chance to talk with Jimmy Ray."

"Yes. I'm sure Merrill wouldn't allow that."

Both of them stayed quiet awhile, enjoying the day. Finally she said, her voice lower than usual, "Merrill Smith was a gunfighter, years ago. Wasn't he."

"Yes."

"Like you."

Parker let several seconds go by. "Yes."

He was facing the street, watching a buckboard rumble past, but he could feel her staring at him. He could hear her rocking.

"Tell me honestly, Will. Is there any chance, if you two do fight tomorrow morning... is there any chance he'd win?"

He turned slowly and looked her straight in the eye. "No."

*****

At five o'clock Parker strolled down the street to the dry-goods store, where— as Maria had predicted—Merrill Smith's ranch hands were gathering supplies. Smith and Jimmy Ray were usually on hand for this, she'd told him. Not today, though. Parker knew why.

But he wasn't looking for the Smiths anyway. He was looking for Boone Rogers and Sonny Farris. He picked them out easily from descriptions Maria had given him, and from the fact that she'd said the two of them were always together.

Parker waited until they were apart from the others, sitting on barrels in the alley beside the store and rolling smokes.

"Boone and Sonny, right?"

They looked up at him as if they'd been caught stealing candy. "Who are you?"

"My name's Parker," he said. "Has Mr. Smith told you anything about me?"

"Mr. Smith don't tell us nothin'," the one called Sonny said.

Parker pulled up a barrel and sat facing them. "Well, I'm trying to figure out what happened with Jimmy Ray that night the colonel's daughter disappeared."

That was enough to scare them both. They bent over with their elbows on their knees and puffed furiously on their smokes, but—to their credit—stayed put.

"I understand he was with you two that night," Parker said. "Where'd you go?"

"We told the sheriff that," Sonny murmured. "The three of us went to that showplace in Sand Hill, to see a..." He looked at his friend for help.

"A play," Boone said.

Parker frowned. "A play?"

"Like when people get up on a stage and sing and talk to each other," Boone added.

Parker thought about that for a moment. "Sand Hill," he said. "That's a long ride."

"We got good horses."

"And that sounds like a funny place for three teenagers, on a weeknight."

"Our folks think that's better'n sneaking into the back door of the saloon," Sonny said, with a snorting laugh. Boone giggled.

Parker looked hard at the two boys. Their smiles vanished. "Let me tell you fellows something," Parker said, "I spent a long time, years ago, talking to people about crimes. And one of the things I found out was that most folks, especially young folks, seem to think a lie is okay as long as they believe it's for the right reasons. You see what I'm saying?"

Both boys just stared at him. Their eyes had gone wide. Ashes fell unnoticed onto their shirtfronts.

"I saw a notice in the saloon the other day that said the Sand Hill opera hall has been closed since spring." He paused, letting that sink in. "Want to tell me where you really were?"

They both blinked. It had gone very quiet in the alley.

Finally Boone seemed to recover. He took his smoke from his mouth with trembling fingers. "Look, Mister. You gotta understand something, here. Jimmy Ray didn't do whatever they say he done. He loved that girl."

"That's not what I asked," Parker said. "Where were you two, that night?"

"We was courtin' some Mexican gals, south of town."

"And Jimmy Ray wasn't with you, was he."

"No sir."

"He went to meet Elizabeth?"

"Yessir."

Parker nodded. "Did Jimmy Ray come up with this Sand Hill story?"

"Yessir."

"That wasn't very smart, you know." They nodded together, as if pulled by the same string. Both looked physically ill.

"Did Jimmy tell either of you what really did happen that night?"

Boone swallowed. "He said nothing happened. He said his horse threw a shoe, and that he got to the pond—the place they were supposed to meet—half an hour late. He said he waited there a while but Elizabeth never came."

Parker kept eye contact for almost a full minute, then relaxed. He believed them. And if what Jimmy Ray had told them was true, that thrown horseshoe had probably saved his life.

"You going to tell Mr. Smith about this?" Sonny asked.

"No." Parker made a throwaway gesture with one hand and said, "You boys get back inside. Best you not be seen talking to me."

They apparently agreed with that. Ten seconds later Parker was sitting alone in the alley, staring down at the ground between his boots. He thought he knew, now, what had happened that night, or at least most of it. But there was still the underlying mystery. If the colonel was behind all this, why in God's name had he hired Charles William Parker, all the way from San Francisco, to come snoop around into it? On that score, Parker only knew he didn't buy Merrill Smith's reasoning, about the plan to have Parker accuse Jimmy Ray and have the judge come here to ramrod it through. That made no sense at all.

Parker shook his head.

Who was it who'd said he was a good detective? Maybe he should still be eating dust on a trail drive.

*****

The next morning he was present at his usual table in the restaurant, chowing down on bacon and eggs, when the kitchen door swung open and Bitsy Hamilton stomped out in her apron and plopped down in the chair across from him. Her face was red, but he doubted it was from the heat of the stove.

When she said nothing, he asked her, "You gonna let these other customers go hungry?"

"Where were you last night?"

He swallowed what he had in his mouth and put down his fork. "I met with Jimmy Ray's two buddies, then I talked Mr. Wallace down at the telegraph office into staying late so I could send a wire to update my brother in California."

"Did that take all night?"

"No, but it took till seven o'clock. You told me you begin tending to your mother around that time every night."

She nodded. He could see that she was still upset.

A little more calmly she said, "Were you going to say anything to me at all, before..."

"Before what?"

"You know." She pointed to the clock on the wall beside the windows. It was half past eight.

"I'll see you in a couple hours," he said. He reached across the table and—in spite of the gazes of the other diners—took both her hands in his. "Maybe you can help me put all this information together."

"I'm not talking about your stupid *case*," she whispered. "It's Thursday, and it's almost nine. What if he—Smith—what if he kills you?"

Parker couldn't help grinning. "I told you, I won't get killed." And then his smile faded. If he were smarter, if he could manage to work out these last few details, maybe *nobody* would have to get killed. But he wasn't quite there yet.

"I'll see you later," he said. "I promise. Go fix these folks some grub."

*****

After breakfast he checked the clock again. Ten minutes to nine. He put on

31

his coat and hat, left the restaurant, and walked down the street to the Lucky Lady. He stood there at the batwing doors a moment, one arm propped on each. Besides the bartender, there were three people in the saloon: two cowboys Parker didn't know, and Merrill Smith. Smith sat at a table alone, sipping a whiskey. The two cowpokes scraped back their chairs and hurried out the side door. It was always the same, Parker thought. Folks just seemed to know, somehow, when something was brewing between people like him and Smith.

Parker pushed through the swinging doors, crossed the room to Smith's table, and sat down. The bartender raised an eyebrow to him, but Parker shook his head. Merrill looked at him and said, "You ready?"

Parker studied his face. "I'm surprised to see you drinking in Dunn's saloon."

"No place else in town to drink." He pulled out his pocketwatch and checked it. "I asked if you're ready."

"I guess."

"You *guess*?"

Parker shrugged. "It's unnecessary. We don't have to do this, you and me."

"Yes we do. I asked you to let it alone, and you didn't." Smith drained his glass and pushed back from the table. "And yesterday, you were seen talking to my men."

"Two of them. Your son's friends."

"So you're convinced, now? Is that it?"

Parker sighed. *If you only knew*, he thought. The truth was, despite all the facts to the contrary, Parker was fairly sure at this point, in his gut, that Jimmy Ray Smith had been no more than a minor and unknowing player in the disappearance of Elizabeth Dunn. But telling that to Merrill would do no good. There was no proof, either way. Of anything.

"Think what you want," Parker said. Suddenly he was frustrated with the whole business, and besides, this was the man who'd killed his partner years ago. He stood up and walked to the door, and he could hear Smith rise from the table and follow him. Somewhere, in one of the stores that lined the boardwalk, he heard a clock chime the hour.

*****

He strode to the middle of the street, eyes straight ahead, moving neither slow nor fast. Then he turned and waited. Merrill Smith did the same, positioning himself such that fifteen feet or so separated them. The sun was high enough not to be a problem, and no one else was traveling in the street. Whether that was by chance or whether the townspeople had the same sixth sense the cowboys in the saloon had, he didn't know. The boardwalks on each side, though, were thick with spectators. Customers, shopkeepers, passersby, the bartender, the staff of the other hotel, even a man with a bright sheriff's star stood there watching. Beside him were two men with deputy's badges. Parker didn't see Bitsy or her father in the crowd, though, and for that he was grateful.

Merrill Smith stood relaxed and ready, his coat tucked back on the right and his hand poised six inches from the handle of his pistol. Parker shrugged out of his own coat, dropped it to the ground beside him, and turned so they were facing each other. How many times, and in how many towns, had he done this?

He drew in a lungful of air and let it out. His conscience was clear. He didn't want this fight and had said so, but he'd been given no choice. He had cleaned his revolver last night and checked his ammunition and slept sound as a baby, and he was ready. Merrill Smith was about to die; he just didn't know it yet.

As always in situations like this, Parker's senses were superalert. He heard the buzz of a fly, the stirring of the wind in the trees beside the post office, the cry of a bird somewhere on the prairie nearby. The blood was singing in his veins. He was Charlie Parker again.

And then he thought of something.

The sheriff. He hadn't set eyes on the sheriff in four days, and now here the man was, along with his deputies and what looked like every shopowner and town employee.

They were all here. Standing here, watching.

Witnesses.

And just like that, as sudden as a slap in the face, he understood.

Parker raised both his hands and held them palm-out to Smith. "Stop," he said.

Merrill Smith blinked. His open hand hovered an inch above his pistol, his body drawn tight as a bowstring. "What?"

Now Parker was walking forward, hands still out. He kept moving forward until he and Smith were standing a foot apart.

"We have to talk," Parker said. "I've figured it out."

"You've *what*?"

"I know what happened."

*****

Fifteen minutes later the two of them were seated at an empty table in the exact center of the empty restaurant of the Hamilton Hotel. All the doors were shut—they had no locks—and Bitsy had placed a CLOSED sign outside each one. Parker had assured her father that this meeting would be finished long before the lunch crowd was due.

He had also told Merrill Smith part of what he had worked out, in those seconds when they faced each other in the street. Not all of it, though. Some of it he held back. Some of it he wanted to say in the presence of Colonel Isaiah Dunn.

"What if he doesn't show up?" Smith asked.

"He'll show up," Parker said. "Bitsy told me all five of his ranch hands were here, in the crowd, and when she pointed them out a few minutes ago I gave them the message myself, to take back to him."

"The invitation," Smith said.

"Right. The invitation to join me here, to discuss my, ah, findings. Not to mention my employment." Parker paused, keeping an eye on the windows to the street. "He'll come."

"But what if he doesn't?"

"Then we'll go get him."

"You said he has five men. Could that be worrisome?"

"Not for me. Five too many for you?"

Smith smiled grimly. "It'd be a shame not to kill *any*body today." Then he seemed to have a thought. "I take it you didn't mention my name or my presence here, in your message to Dunn."

"I thought you might want that to be a surprise."

Smith's grin widened. "I think I would."

Within minutes Parker saw horses galloping past the windows, and a moment later heard footsteps in the lobby. Then the door opened, and Bitsy stuck her head in. She looked out of breath, but happy. "Gentlemen," she said, "Colonel Dunn has arrived."

She stepped aside to let the colonel storm into the room. His eyes were intense, his face even pinker than usual. His expression hardened further when he saw Merrill Smith sitting there. "What's the meaning of this?" he asked Parker. "What's going on?"

"Confession time," Parker said. He pointed to a third chair at their table. "Take a seat."

Dunn stood there a moment, seething, then sat.

Parker glanced once at Smith before focusing on the colonel. "Here's what's going to happen. I'm going to tell you—tell you both, actually—what I think happened on that night of June sixth. Colonel, you will not interrupt and you will not leave. When I'm done you can say whatever you want to say. Do you understand?"

Dunn looked as if he might explode. "Who are you to tell me—"

"If you do interrupt, I will stand up and walk over there and knock your teeth down your throat. If you try to leave, Merrill here will shoot you once and I might shoot you again, just so I won't be left out. That's what's going to happen. Now, do you understand?"

Dunn sat there trembling with rage, but Parker was pleased to notice that he'd also turned a bit pale.

Parker took a breath, let it out, and said, "I have information to the effect that on the day in question, you found, in your daughter's possession, a note from Jimmy Ray Smith to her, asking her to meet him at nine that evening, at the pond in the hills not far from your house. Knowing that, I think you waited until she was upstairs in her room that night and quietly locked her bedroom door so she could not leave the house to—presumably—use her telescope as she had been doing for the past week. Then, at around a quarter to nine, you took your buffalo rifle and left the house and walked to the pond, with the intention of stopping this relationship for good. You planned to shoot Jimmy Ray Smith and dump his body into the pond."

Parker paused with his eyes locked on Dunn, who glared back at him. Though neither man looked at Merrill Smith, Parker could imagine what

Smith was thinking and feeling, at the moment. He hoped Smith wouldn't pull his gun right now, but wouldn't be too surprised if he did.

"I believe you then lay in ambush near the pond, waiting for Jimmy Ray to get there. There wasn't much light that night—just a fingernail moon, I'm told—but at exactly nine o'clock you saw and heard someone arrive in the gloom, saw a shape walk to the pond and stand there, waiting. Very calmly you shot that person dead, then walked over to dispose of the body. But it wasn't Jimmy Ray at all. It was Elizabeth."

Another pause. Now Dunn's face was contorted, though whether from anger or sadness it was hard to tell.

"This is the only point where I almost feel sorry for you, Colonel. Because I think you were petrified with grief and amazement at what you'd just done. But within minutes—maybe seconds—you realized what you had to do. After all, how could you explain what had just happened? You weren't out hunting—not with a buffalo gun, in the middle of the night in the middle of nowhere. The pond was almost half a mile from your house. As horrible as this was, you had to try to cover it up. And that's what you did. You weighted your daughter's pockets with stones you'd picked up for that purpose in your back yard and threw her body into the pond—just as you would have done with Jimmy's Ray's body if things had gone as planned."

This time Parker did turn to look at Merrill Smith. He was staring down at the tablecloth with fierce intensity. Colonel Dunn's face had gone blank.

"Then I think you probably waited a few minutes more for Jimmy Ray, and then you finally went back to the house, unlocked the door to Elizabeth's room, and left again, this time on horseback and this time going eventually to town to round up your men and the sheriff and his deputies, for what you knew would be a fake search for your daughter. Luckily for Jimmy Ray, who had arrived late at the pond, you never saw him and he never saw you. As for the shot that had killed Elizabeth, you decided to tell everyone you had heard a gunshot at nine o'clock because you figured your neighbor might have heard it also—which she had—and, since you didn't think there were any witnesses who would disprove it, you told everybody you'd left the house *after* the shot was heard. And you even said it sounded like a *pistol*, in case anyone should ever start thinking in terms of your fifty-caliber cannon.

"You had already, at some time or other, hidden Jimmy's note in your desk drawer, and when you found it missing the following morning you fired your maid because she now knew that *you* had already known where those two kids would be, the night before. And to be extra safe, you told her not only to leave your house but to leave Redemption, and never return. You thought you were covering all your tracks, but actually you were beginning to make big mistakes.

"And then you took everything a step further. As soon as you were sure you wouldn't be caught—after all, no one had seen you and no one would find Elizabeth's body—it occurred to you to use this terrible accident as a way to get what you so badly wanted, businesswise. You would push suspicion onto Jimmy Ray and use it to discredit Merrill. But the more you thought about it, that turned out not to be as practical as it sounded. You were also making one of your enemies an even more bitter enemy, and wouldn't realize any monetary gain from it.

"But then you saw the ad in the newspaper your traveling friend gave you, and you had either heard of me or you did some checking and learned about my history, and it all came together. You invited an old judge friend to visit town and then wired me to come as well, to perform a thorough and supportable "outside investigation" of the incident. Then you told me to finish up the day before the judge arrived. Why? I admit that confused me. Merrill figured it was so you could turn my findings over to the judge and get a quick trial and conviction of his son, but that wasn't it at all. The truth didn't hit me until today, as Merrill and I stood in the street getting ready to shoot it out. And I saw all those people standing there."

Parker paused for a beat, his gaze fixed on Isaiah Dunn.

"They were waiting for that fight, weren't they, Colonel. You'd told them to be ready, and watch for it sometime today or tomorrow. Because that gunfight was exactly what you'd planned for, all along."

"What?" Smith blurted. Parker, his eyes on Dunn, didn't reply—he just held up a hand to silence Smith, then went on.

"A showdown between us was just what you'd wanted. Because it was a win/win situation for you. If I killed Merrill, your problems were over. He was out of the picture. If both of us killed each other, your problems would still be over, because Merrill would be dead. And if *he* killed *me*, you'd get a dozen witnesses in the crowd to testify that he drew first and didn't give me a chance, or tricked me, or whatever they'd need to say. Because almost every spectator today *was one of your people*—the storeowners, your cowboys, and others too, especially the sheriff and his two deputies. That didn't dawn on me until we were out there and almost ready to draw. That was the real reason you wanted the judge to be here soon afterward. If Merrill killed me, your backers would swear to the judge that it was murder, not a fair fight, and justice would be swift, and Merrill would be in prison or hanged, and out of your hair. *You would win either way.*"

Merrill Smith spoke up then. "Wait a minute, Parker. There's something I don't understand, here. If the judge was coming here to nail me in case I killed you, and not to prosecute Jimmy Ray—why did Dunn even bother to give you a deadline on completing everything and reporting to him?"

"To make me press hard enough to make you threaten me. Everything depended on you being so worried about my implicating Jimmy that you'd be forced to do whatever it took to stop me. And when people like you and me are involved—well, he knew our past, and knew neither of us would back down."

In the silence that followed, Smith kept his eyes locked on Dunn. To Parker he said, "Can you give me any reason I shouldn't shoot him, right now?"

"Yes. You'll go to jail if you do."

He glanced at Parker. "You'd turn me in?"

Parker thought it over, and nodded. "Yes."

The moment passed. Parker turned his attention to the colonel, whose expression still wavered between rage and fear.

"Now, Colonel, you may speak. You care to deny any of this?"

Dunn leaned forward across the table, a blue vein pulsing in his forehead. "I deny all of it. May I remind you, you have no *proof*." He waved a hand. "Do you really believe any of this would stand up in court?"

"It won't have to," Parker said.

"What?"

"I have a proposal for you, Colonel. If you do what I ask, I'll never mention any of this outside of this room. It'll end here."

Dunn studied him a moment, then looked at Merrill Smith, then back again. Carefully he said, "What kind of proposal?"

"I suggest you put half of your business and property holdings up for sale, at a fair price, with a quarter of them—"

"What?!"

"—with a quarter of them available first to Merrill Smith. This town could use a little competition."

"That's *ridiculous*—"

"I also propose that you pay Juanita Delgado the equivalent of ten years' salary, in a lump sum. All this must be done within the next four days."

"I will not!"

"Correction: you will pay Juanita Delgado the equivalent of twenty years' salary."

Breathing hard and scowling, Dunn said, "Or what?"

This time it was Parker who leaned forward over the table. "Or I will drag that pond for the body of your daughter. It's not on your property, and I've already spoken with the owner—as you know, Mrs. Fairley might be a neighbor but she isn't your biggest fan. I will drag the pond, and if the body's not there you have nothing to worry about. But if it is there"—he paused—"I swear I'll see that you go to prison."

"How? There was no murder—"

"I realize it was technically an accident, but I also know you shot her while trying to kill someone else and as the result of a premeditated *plan* to kill someone else. And weighted her body and sank it to protect yourself. Whatever they choose to call it—manslaughter, negligent homicide, attempted murder, or a combination of those—you'll be put away. There's not a jury in the world that wouldn't convict you."

Isaiah Dunn's anger seemed to have seeped away. He sat there gulping like a landed trout. Then he blinked. "You've forgotten something," he murmured. "Even if there's a body there, she could've been shot and put there by anyone—"

"No. There aren't many buffalo guns around here, and what a fifty-caliber bullet does to someone would be evident even after two months in pond water. And the stones in the body's pockets will match those in your wife's flowerbed. You'd be the only suspect."

Parker watched the colonel's shoulders slump, his face sag. The silence stretched out.

"Do you agree to what I've proposed?"

Weakly Dunn raised his eyes. Hate still simmered there, but not defiance. He knew it was over. He was beaten.

"Yes," he said.

"You have until Monday." Parker wished he had a gavel.

"One more thing," Merrill Smith said. Both the others turned to look at him.

"I assume you still owe a fee to Mr. Parker here," Smith said. "And you can include a bonus. After all, he found your daughter—"

"He did not find—"

"He found her," Smith said, "and found out what happened to her." He pointed and said, "Pay him."

Colonel Dunn rose from his chair like a man who'd aged twenty years in twenty minutes. He looked once more at Parker and once at Smith. Then he took out his wallet, counted out a stack of bills, tossed them to Parker, and staggered out the door.

After a minute of so of silence Smith turned to Parker and said, "Would you really turn me in if I'd shot him?"

"Yes." Parker waited a beat and asked, "Would you really have shot him?"

Smith sighed. "No."

"Then I guess both of us have changed."

Parker stood, and Smith followed suit. Smith looked tired.

"Will he do what you told him to?" he asked.

"I gave him four days. I'll stay until then, to make sure."

"What if he sends his men for you tonight, or tomorrow?"

Parker grinned. "I hope he does." Then he shook his head. "But he won't. It's too late now—even if he killed me, you know the truth too, and so does Bitsy."

"Bitsy." Smith smiled also, and glanced toward the now-open door to the hotel lobby. "What exactly are you going to do about her?"

"I'm not sure."

Smith chuckled. "Then you're even dumber than I thought."

He turned then, and walked through the door to the lobby. Parker followed.

Bitsy was there, waiting for him.

*****

They were sitting together, the two of them, on the hotel porch. Parker had become fond of one particular rocker, and was leaned back in it now with his boots propped on the porch rail. Four days had passed. It was Tuesday afternoon and sunny, but clouds were gathering in the west. The town needed the rain.

"I heard the Teasley brothers bought the café," Bitsy said. "The bath house too."

Parker nodded. "Good."

"And Merrill got the saloon."

"Long as he doesn't change the name." He tipped his hat back. "What did Juanita think about getting her back wages?" The lump-sum payment had been hand-delivered to Juanita Delgado by one of the colonel's cowboys, three days ago.

"She told me it was more money than she'd ever seen in her life."

"Good," he said again.

"And Pa talked to her niece about coming back to work at the hotel. She starts tomorrow."

"Maria? Think she'll be as good a cook as you are?"

"What do *you* think?"

Both of them grinned. Bitsy brushed a strand of hair from her eyes and looked up and down the street.

"It's going to be a booming town soon," Parker said.

"Big enough for a detective agency?"

He smiled. "I don't think so." He shifted in the chair, enjoying the breeze ahead of the coming storm. "Not even big enough for both Merrill and me. I think I make him nervous."

"Just as well you're leaving, then. You two have already tried twice to kill each other. It's best not to tempt Fate."

He was opening his mouth to reply when the westbound stage pulled into view. It rattled up the street pulling a tail of white dust behind it, and stopped thirty feet away. The coach was empty. The four horses wheezed and tossed their heads while the shotgun rider climbed down and stomped into the stage office across the street.

Parker turned to Bitsy and said, "Time to go."

"I know." Her face had gone solemn.

Her gave her a quick kiss, then rose from the chair, picked up the two bags at this feet, and stepped down off the porch. She watched him a moment, then went back into the hotel.

Parker glanced down the street at the saloon and saw Merrill Smith standing out front. Merrill held up a hand in salute. Parker nodded.

He arrived at the stage and tossed the bags up to the driver, who'd climbed behind his seat and onto the top of the coach. Then Parker turned and looked back at the hotel. Just ten days here, he thought. Not long, but enough to change my life.

Bitsy appeared then, giving her mother and father a final hug, and hurried into the street with the last of their bags. She stopped when she reached Parker and looked up at him. "Tell me we're doing the right thing," she said.

He took her in his arms and kissed her forehead. "You bet we are."

He handed her up through the door, and was about to follow her when the driver leaned over the top of the coach and said, "I know you. Ain't you Charlie Parker?"

Bitsy stuck her head out again and looked up. "He's William. They just look alike."

Grinning, Parker hauled himself inside. They sat arm-in-arm on the dusty seat, looking out at the town where they'd found each other. After a moment the coach lurched and they were off, Bitsy waving a last goodbye to her parents.

"I have a question," she said, cuddled into his side. "Why exactly did you come here?"

"You know why. I was hired to do a job."

"There were other jobs closer by. Why all the way out here? For that matter, why did Merrill Smith come here?"

"I have a feeling you're going to tell me."

Her eyes twinkling, she said, "To find redemption."

"Redemption?"

She grinned. "Good a reason as any."

They were out of town now and headed into the wind, into the sun-tinted cloudbank, happy and free and lulled by the rattle of traces and the rhythm of hoofbeats in the dirt. Headed for a new life.

Parker closed his eyes and smiled.

Rebel Seed

—Joe Flint Book One—

Alexander Frew

Chapter One

William Shaw watched the cattle drive from the back of his favourite horse, Shawnee, a big grey who stood there patiently while the rest of the world around them seemed to go mad. The cattle were crossing the Cimarron River, part of the Chisholm Trail, for getting the cattle to market from San Antonio through to the Red River Station railhead. William felt justified in staying where he was for the moment. He'd been with the herd since they set off from the foot of the hill country out there in Texas. He was aching all over from taking part in the drive to get the cattle here to the river. He was sixty years old, was the owner of a large number of the steers, and the boss of the men who were currently plying their trade along the banks of the river.

He was taking a breather because, with the best will in the world, he could no longer keep up with men a third of his age. No one could have said that he was unwilling to work, and it was common knowledge he always did more than his fair share. He had never allowed any favouritism regarding his presence, and indeed many of the men who had been brought in just for this cattle drive, didn't even know who he was.

The thought crossed his mind that he should never have come here in the first place. He pictured Old John Henderson, the other owner with whom he had agreed to share the drive. Old John would be out in *Eagle Cross* in the comfort of his family. Like the Shaws, he had a son and a daughter, but his son Rawley, at seventeen, was the same age as the Shaw's headstrong daughter Catriona, while the youngest Henderson, Jo-Ann, was barely ten.

At the thought of his own family William screwed up his eyes, grateful for the bellowing cattle since they helped distract him from thinking of his wife, Elizabeth. He'd always liked strong women, but sometimes a forceful woman could be rather a cross to bear.

After his first wife, Mary, died in childbirth, William had taken to the business for a period of ten years or so, riding out until he was just over forty, then he'd met Elizabeth at one of the county 'socials'. This was an event where the local ranchers and their hands would get together in the big barn at *Eagle Cross* (the Henderson's were pretty gregarious) to eat, drink and dance to fiddle and squeeze box music.

Elizabeth was set to meet a farmer, a life where a woman could settle down, have babies and help with the crops, a hard life. But the first time she met William she set her cap at him. He didn't want to be at the dance, but he had been doing some business with John Henderson and had felt obliged to stay for the evening festivities. William, in his early forties, was still a big, handsome man and still had a way with the ladies. He was also a landowner and cattle merchant of some repute, so it was no wonder that the girl had been attracted to him. And it wasn't long before they were married.

Then, twenty years later – at the start of the previous month – she'd faced him across the kitchen table as he'd announced that he was going on the summer cattle drive. In the intervening years, after giving birth to their two children, Gilbert and Catriona, she'd become a formidable force in his life. In between raising their children she'd helped him build up the business, and he considered her a partner, as well as wife.

"You want to do *what*?" The coffee pot bounced back onto the table.

"I want to go on one last cattle drive."

"Why?"

William found it difficult to answer her. In his eyes she had never lost her beauty. Almost as slim as the day they wed, her hair was still long, brown and glossy. And she still had a formidable personality. He was a man who could order any ranch hand to do what he wanted, yet he became almost a shy child in the presence of his wife's anger.

"It's something I need to do," he told her.

"Why?"

He was not a man who found it easy to articulate his feelings. He could have said his desire for the drive was because he was a businessman. The ranch, *High Wynd*, had been started by his grandfather, a Scot, from

Edinburgh.

He could have said he had started working on the trail when he was fourteen, pushed out there by his father along with his now dead older brother, Matt. That was one reason.

He could have told her he was getting old. Sixty was quite elderly out here in the hill country, and that in two or three years he would be unfit to ever go on another drive.

Most of all, before he died he just wanted to recapture part of his youth, remember what it was like, so that when his time came he would be a whole man again, and not some pen pusher who made deals and slept easy in his big bed while young men risked their lives for him.

In the event he said none of those things. He just made a face of thunder and lowered his head.

"You wouldn't understand." He said.

"And what if you get yourself killed?" she got up and started to the clear the table briskly.

"Then you'll get everything," he told her.

She stopped clearing up and stared at him.

"I don't want this place without you."

It was that moment he finally understood his wife really had married him for love, and inside he thanked her for it, as he knew her fears were far from unfounded. The trail was not an easy place to be for anyone. Besides the obvious risks, one night of being soaked to the skin could leave him open to a cold, 'flu or ague, far from home comforts and medical expertise. He decided to ignore that side altogether.

"It ain't like the early days," he told her. "The Indians are almost all gone now. Matter of fact, some of the beef goes to their reservations as part of the deal they made with the government. No hostiles out there now. Well, not many. This is just something I have to do."

She was still pretty sore at him, he guessed as he sat there, and no amount of persuasion on her part could make him back down.

The day he rode off from *High Wynd* with McQuade, the trail foreman, she hadn't even come to the door. He'd seen her standing at the front window but she'd not waved goodbye at his departure.

He'd been hoping to take his son Gilbert with him, but the boy had declined with a vehemence that bordered on anger, but not quite. Gilbert was a timid young man. Although he had passed his twenty-first birthday, he'd not yet learned to ride properly. He was engaged to a girl he'd met out east when on a grand tour of the States. The family had yet to met her.

These thoughts were on William's mind as he watched the remainder of the cattle flounder their way across the shallow part of the river. Only one or two had found themselves stuck this year, so it was with wonder that he had seen thirty hundred long-horns stream past in a seemingly endless white and brown ribbon. The supply wagons and the mules would follow to join the cattle and the cowboys on the far bank.

When he wasn't thinking about his wife, one young man in particular had caught William's eye.

As always, when most of the steers had crossed the shallows without too much bother, a bunch of stragglers were left behind who were either too stupid or too stubborn to do as they were told. A young man was riding down the stragglers and urging them across the water. He had the nut-brown colour of someone who worked a great deal in the sun without a Stetson hat, although given the heat of the day he was wearing one right now. As the strays kicked up dust he pulled up the red bandana he wore around his neck and covered his face, his eyes dark and intense as he went about his task.

He fell to it with a will, seeming to be in about three places at one, his whip-thin body in his dark clothes tireless as he pushed the steers forward, sometimes using his lariat to get them by the horns and jerk them forward.

William could spot a natural horseman when he saw one, and he watched the young man in silent admiration as McQuade came riding up to his side

"He's doing a great job that boy," said William. "What a horseman."

"Yep, that one was in the saddle from almost the day he was born."

"You know that?"

"That's the way Indians raise 'em."

"He's an Indian? Doesn't look it."

"Raised on the plains by the Comanche. His parents, we think, was farmers. They had their smallholding burned to the ground, and injuns took the kid. They do that. Raised him as their own."

"When did they get him back?"

"The cavalry raided their camp when they was pressin' 'em to a reservation. The boy was there, 'bout ten years old, near as they could judge. Wild as a grizzly. They called him Joe Flint."

"Because he was hard to find?"

"No, because he had an axe made of flint lashed to a wooden handle. Wounded three troopers before he was brought back to civilisation. Dang nearly killed one of 'em."

"You know, I was thinking of taking him back with me once the drive is over, getting him to teach Gibby to ride. You put me off a bit, sounds a bit too wild for my taste."

"That's the bit. He ain't wild at all. Unlike some of the men, he never answers back, does more than his share of the work and never complains no matter what the weather. He don't even take hard liquor far as I can tell. Some of them boys is liquored the minute we settle down for the night."

There was an unspoken addition to the comment.

William looked over at McQuade. "But?"

"He ain't popular with the men. A loner, keeps to himself, never joins in the campfire yarning. Goes off by himself. Doesn't even mind standing shotgun over the herd at night."

"Well, it was an idea," said William. "Gibby should know how to ride, even though he's resisted the idea for years and this boy's a natural. Pity he's so lackin'. Ah well, it was a good thought."

McQuade said nothing but William knew he was thinking that if Gilbert didn't want to ride then there was no point. But William? He was getting on in years and he wanted his son to command the men who would be working for him when William was gone. If Gilbert couldn't ride he would lose their respect, because in Texas that meant a lot. It could even end the business.

Out of the corner of his eye William saw one of the big steers, last of the stragglers, suddenly decided to make a break for freedom along the bank of the river. Alerted, Flint came riding hard behind him, but not before the steer thundered straight for Shawnee. Angrily sweeping his wide horns from side to side in a motion that could, if low enough, disembowel a horse, the steer continued to charge. Shawnee knew danger, gave a snort of alarm and reared up, almost unseating William. Luckily he was an experienced old hand and managed to stay in the saddle. But the horse turned, making a panic-stricken dash away from the beast.

With Shawnee in flight mode, William knew that he had to give his horse its head, but the problem was the approaching river. The banks were far from straight and the ground was treacherous. They were heading away from the shallows, so if Shawnee hit mud he could well fall into deep water along with his rider. Shawnee could swim as well as most horses, but William was far from certain he would survive if swept away by a fast-moving current. He saw an image of his angry wife with her hands on her hips and the phrase *I told you so* on her delicious lips.

He was only dimly aware of a darkly clad figure at his side and a sinewy arm seizing the reins and jerking the head of the horse to one side to make him gallop over the plain away from the dangerous, open water. When Shawnee saw that another steed was beside him going at the same pace, but slowing, his panic lessened. A few seconds later he slowed down too, and came to a panting halt. Then he lowered his head and began to crop the grass as if nothing had happened. The steer halted then ambled back to his cows.

"Thankyou. That was some nice handling," William said.

"Most people would've been thrown and trampled by now. You did good." His accent was a little strange, as if English was a second language.

With most people William would have suspected them of flattery. His younger self would have seen the mood of the steer and he would have handled it himself. His riding ability had been allied to the restraining hand of this young man. Joe Flint pulled up his bandana and whispered something to his horse, a large bay. The horse gave a snicker as if agreeing with him, turning away.

"Wait," said William. "You took me away from the river. If this son of a bitch had taken me any further we'd have been in the water. I could've drowned."

"No bother mister," said the youth. "But there's a bunch of them mavericks still to round up, it's early evening and I aim to eat tonight. If I don't get on, McQuade'll give me a hard time, and he'll be right."

"Flint, isn't it? Is that what they call you?"

"Sure, Flint. Sometimes Joe. No-one knows my real name anyways." He was eager to be off, as if saving the life of another man was all in a day's work.

"Look, Flint, I was going to ask you for a favour. I guess this has brought us closer. I've already been discussing you with McQuade."

"Why? What have I done wrong?" Flint's face suddenly became guarded. He had fine, even features, and strong white teeth. As he moved his Stetson and wiped some beads of perspiration from his brow with the back of his hand, William saw that his hair was very dark and coarse, an almost straw-like texture. His eyes were most remarkable of all, deep and dark. He might be a young man, but his eyes were of someone a thousand years old. He was not alarmed, just wary, like a desert fox waiting for an enemy to strike.

William did his best to smile. "Don't worry, you haven't done anything wrong before you rescued me, just the opposite. You work like a demon, son. I can use a man like you at the ranch."

"What ranch?"

"High Wynd. Now don't be alarmed, I'm Billy Shaw, I'm the owner of most of these here cattle. Mr Henderson might argue that point, but we'll soon see when we get them to the stockyards and get a decent count."

"Nice to meet you mister." Flint did not seem particularly impressed. William could understand this. McQuade was the day-to-day powerful boss, knew the ropes and got things done.

"Now I have a proposition for you. I have a boy who's always been leery about dealing with horseflesh. That can be a serious handicap in our business. So I want to give you a job."

The young man considered the matter for a short while, head tilted to one side like a bird.

"No thanks mister. Got to go." He gave a short yell to spur his mount and left behind a frankly astonished man.

William Shaw was not a man used to being refused, and even though the youth was gone, the matter was far from over.

Chapter Two

Old John Henderson sat looking at his family in the kitchen of his rambling ranch. The main house had been built on the Texan plains in the old colonial style, boasting influences from both the old country and the Spanish settlers.

It was two stories high and built in a mixture of wood, solid brick and adobe with a few flourishes such as the fancy iron gates that could be chain sealed in a moment.

This had been a necessity in the days when the plains Indians would still attack settlers.

Old John was not really old at all. He was a big man in his fifties who had allowed his white hair and beard to grow Biblical-prophet style so that they overflowed both the back and front of his red shirt and concealed the braces that held up his trousers. This, coupled with his size, his flashing eyes and booming voice made him a compelling figure.

Across from him sat his one and only son, Rawley. The name was a corruption of Raleigh, a hero from the old country who had been to the Americas frequently. Rawley could not have contrasted more with his father. He was still only seventeen years old, slim, and dressed in clothes that had never seen a day's labour. Working and settling down was what they were going to discuss today.

Jo-Ann, his daughter was also present. A small girl of ten, hair in bunches, who wore a cotton dress, but she was no more part of the discussion than Rebecca, her mother.

"Rawley, you've hardly touched your food," boomed the older man.

"Gluttony is its own punishment papa. Besides, I should not like to end up looking like that pig, Gibby."

"You are wise in your years. You know why I would speak to you?"

"No, I do not."

"You have been a frequent visitor to High Wynd lately."

"I find the countryside there's much greener, more pleasant than these dusty plains. It's a place to enjoy riding and shooting."

"Is there is another reason why you enjoy the place?"

"Don't torment the boy," said Rebecca.

"There is company at High Wynd from which he does not shrink," boomed Old John.

"At times Gibby can be agreeable," said Rawley. "We have taken to having a beer together of the Mexican variety. He has a coarseness about him that repels some, but he has been well-travelled and has many tales to tell."

"You display an evasiveness in your speech that may please some of those you call your friends, but you know full well of whom I speak."

"Catriona is a mere slip of a girl."

"She's the same age as you!"

"That is true, but as you well know father, someone can display a number of years without being that way inside their own head, but be far younger in their thought and behaviour."

"What do you think of her son?"

"She is fine." His mother caught the slight hesitation in his speech.

"Your mother was not much older than you when we married," said old John. "If a man marries young it can be to his betterment, not his detriment..." He paused "She is a fine-looking young woman, isn't she?"

"Father, what are you trying to say?"

"Only that if a young woman like Catriona is launched into what little society we have out here, she will be quickly snatched up by some clod-hopping farmer or older man in search of a young wife."

Rawley was silent for such a long time that his father was due to burst into one of his trademark roars of thunder.

"The idea is not displeasing to me, to tell the truth."

"Splendid, then, don't leave the question for too long, and do not leave her in doubt about your feelings."

"All right father." Now that he had the tacit approval of that parent he seemed fixed as only a young person can be. He would ride out that very day.

Rebecca watched her son go after he gave her an affectionate kiss, then turned her attentions back to her husband.

"John, I want to know what this is all about."

"Nothing. Just helping two young people along."

"Why encourage him in what he was already thinking?"

"A pot may boil sooner if the coals are stirred to make a fiercer heat. That girl may one day inherit a spread of land worth more than ours. It is a consideration."

"But she has a brother, who will be married soon, who will inherit first."

"Aye, there is that. But Gibby is like his father, subject to violent changes of mood and behaviour. Would you believe that old fool is out there on the summer drive right now? Gilbert was never a strong lad, and I do not see him making old bones."

He did not add that there were ways and means to make sure that this would be the case. A quarrel between two men could soon be manufactured and settled with the use of firearms. John knew that Gilbert liked to play poker and faro in town, also that he was quick to rise to the bait. He gathered information like that all the time. Once Gibby was gone, should his son marry, then Old John would get everything. His wife stared at him, wondering what plans were on her husband's restless mind. He hoped she would never know.

At least for now.

*****

When William approached the road leading up to High Wynd, he turned to the dark youth beside him.

"Wait here for five minutes, then come to the front door." The youth gave a brief nod of agreement.

William strode into the main house and called for his family to join him. Catriona was the last to arrive, but it was she who gave him the warmest hug, although she had to compete in this with her mother. Gilbert stood across from them in the large hallway. He greeted his father awkwardly, yet with some warmth.

"Look at you," said Elizabeth. "You've lost so much weight you look gaunt. I hope you ate well."

"On the drive itself, not so much," he told her. "When we went into a town along the way, then I had good meals." His wife was glad to see him again as were his two children. It was one of the happiest moments of his life, soon to be ruined by what was to come, and not just in the next few minutes either.

"Look at your hair and beard," scolded Elizabeth.

"Yes, you're turning into Old John Henderson," teased Catriona.

"I don't have his lungs," protested William.

"Have you brought us back presents?" demanded the insistent young lady.

"Yes, I—" but at that second he was interrupted by a knock at the door which he had so carefully closed.

"Gibby, remember how I said that the finest thing a man can do is learn to ride well? This is your present. Soon you will command the respect of every man I employ."

He turned and opened the big pine front door with a dramatic flourish. On the doorstep stood the dark, dusty figure of Joe Flint. It was easy to see the reaction of his two children because they made no attempt to hide their feelings.

"What the hell is this?" asked Gilbert. "Do you think you can tell me what to do, and take lessons from *that*? Why did I bother even thinking you would have thought of me?" He strode off to his own room.

"Come in," said Catriona pleasantly enough. The youth hesitated then stepped over the threshold and into the large hall. The girl waited until he was passing her, put out a shapely leg and tripped him up. The young cowboy sprawled wordlessly to the stone floor. "How dare you think you can just walk in here," screeched the girl.

Her father snatched her up and would have punished her there but her mother intervened.

"You," she said to her daughter. "Either go away with Neela, or go upstairs and think of the disrespect you have just shown to a guest in our house."

Giving one of her darkest scowls, and she was good at those, the girl fled from the room shouting for Neela, the orphan Indian girl who had been her childhood companion, and to whom she always turned in times of need.

"What must you think of us?" Elizabeth went over to the young man, but he helped himself up and was already dusting off his trail-worn clothes.

"What I think doesn't matter," said the young man, "I came here because I was offered a job, and I'll do it if I'm given a chance."

"Look, go into the kitchen, cook will get you some food," said William, showing him the way. When the door had closed behind the new arrival it was time for him to face his wife.

"Willie, you are a wonderful man, but you can be so stupid sometimes."

"I just wanted to help Gibby," said William.

"Where did that young man come from?"

William related to his wife the part about seeing how well Flint could ride – though he tactfully missed out the part about the runaway horse.

"The sad fact is," he concluded, "is that Flint didn't want to come here in the first place. I persuaded him to come here by saying he could sleep in one of the barns and eat on his own if that was what he wanted. Just so long as he would stay here long enough to teach our boy."

"You were trying to do something good for him," said his wife, referring to her son. "I'll speak to him. As for Catriona, she's never taken against anyone so much in all her days. If he stays, best we keep those two apart."

*****

The next day, at eleven, Gilbert turned out in his riding gear, new canvas trousers, chaps, cloth waistcoat, and even wore boots made of fine soft leather. These were handcrafted and made with the hide from his own father's cattle.

The riding lesson was to be in the corral around the back of the bunk house and stables. This was a huge grassy area surrounded by a gravel path, with stables at the back that also acted as a paddock for their horses. Flint was already there when Gilbert arrived, holding the reins of a placid brown mare that stood patiently as he came towards them.

Flint had changed into fresh clothing and he was polite and courteous but very reserved. Anyone else might have walked away at his or her treatment from the two siblings, but he had a secret that he kept from everyone he knew, especially McQude. His secret was simple enough, he did not like riding the cattle trails. The work was long, hot and wearisome. The other riders were a fine bunch of men and he had nothing against them personally, but they were always trying to get him to join in their poker games, or sing around the campfire, or go whoring and drinking whenever they pulled into town. In some ways he didn't know what he wanted, but he was certain it wasn't that. He was not afraid of hard work, but the trail had a way of eating men up and he did not want that to be his life.

What Billy Shaw had given him was an opportunity. From here he could gain experience, respect even, and move on to other fields of endeavour.

As for the hatred of Billy's daughter, Catriona, that was something he had decided to bear with the stoicism he had learned from Running Elk, the Indian he had known as father for all those years. Small injustices could be borne well if they enabled you to win the battle.

Surprisingly, after all that his father had implied about his ineptness, Gilbert turned out to be an extremely apt pupil. He obeyed the instructions he was given so that within the hour he was riding around the corral as if he had never been frightened of a horse in his life.

He didn't hide his dislike of the new teacher and hardly spoke to Flint other than curt acknowledgements the whole time.

They might have warmed more to each other if they had been left alone, but Catriona turned up with another young man in tow who was dressed in a light suit and hat, looking as if he was going to a gentleman's club in some big city, rather than spending an afternoon on a ranch.

"So this is the injun?" said Rawley. "He rides all right," he said rather patronisingly as someone who was not too bad at the activity himself, "but who's that sack of potatoes over there?"

Not surprisingly this was not what Gilbert wanted to hear. He jerked at the reins, stopping the mare in her tracks, then got off her back rather clumsily, falling to the ground and landing on his back. This was the cause of much merriment to Catriona and Rawley – and even Flint could not hide a hastily smothered laugh.

"Go to hell," said Gilbert marching back to the main house. The young man had never ridden well enough for his father, and had been so anxious to try and please the old man he'd agreed to take lessons, even though he hated horses. Now he was being mocked for trying.

Flint didn't know what to do concerning the girl and her companion, so he decided to do what was in his nature and tended after the horses. Privately he thought Gilbert was acting rather like a spoiled child. He nodded to Catriona and her companion then began to lead his own horse and Gilbert's to the stables

"So, injun, you can ride?" asked Rawley. "Why don't you come out with us one day and show us your skills?" Lately he and Catriona had been spending a lot of time in the countryside around the ranch, enjoying leisurely days amid the greenery, with Neela as their chaperone.

"That isn't part of my job," said Flint. "Who are you anyway?"

"He's Rawley Henderson, and we are engaged," said Catriona, a flush coming to her cheeks.

In reply, Flint said, "I always thought it was custom for the men to speak for themselves, instead of letting their women do it for them."

For a moment it looked as if Rawley was going to pull Flint from his saddle, but he recovered himself, speaking as if he bore no resentment.

"Yes, we'll ask Mistah Shaw to get you out there into the country with us. Then we'll see what you can really do."

"Sounds like a challenge," said Catriona staring at him and tossing her head, and Flint saw that she had very green eyes.

"That's fine with me" said Flint, then departed.

Chapter Three

True to his word, Flint had bedded down in one of the barns. He never felt more at peace than when he was looking out of the hayloft window at the gathering dusk – though to be sociable, he always ate with the rest of the farmhands.

Teaching Gilbert to ride was a thankless task. The son of the house had decided that this was not for him and he was only going through the motions and that was all

After a week or so, William came to the daily lesson and lamented his son's lack of progress, hinting that if things did not improve Flint would soon be out of a job.

"A warnin'," said Old Jacob, who worked beside Flint and who was the stable master. Despite his time in the US, he'd never managed to lose his Celtic accent. "Ah've been wi' this family forty year. Gibby will ne'er learn because he disnae want to. As fur that wee Catriona, keep awa' frae her."

"Well that's bad news," said Flint' "we're going out for a trail ride today.'

He had managed to get out of doing this before. William, besides using Flint as a trainer, had a fondness for the young man, and often took him away from his duties to sit him down with a beer and talk about the cattle drives of the past. Really, he just wanted someone who understood what it was like, with Flint making a good ear.

Flint didn't mind working in the stables, or being with William, and it gave him a chance to keep away from the girl. But she had finally gone to her father and suggested that if Flint was such a good horseman he should accompany her and Rawley on a trail ride of a few miles. Her father, to whom she could do no wrong most of the time, readily agreed.

Mounted on a piebald stallion, Flint led the horses to the ranch gate, where he found the other two were already waiting along with Neela. They all mounted and headed off into the verdant countryside at a fairly gentle pace.

But it wasn't long before Flint noticed that from time to time Catriona exchanged sly looks with Rawley, who was being very constrained and polite for a change – yet sometimes they gave wide grins to each other as people who shared a private joke. Flint gave them the benefit of the doubt and was content to ride beside Neela. She was copper-skinned and dark-haired like most of her people, with serenity about her he much admired. It was the tail end of summer and the rivers and creeks were low, the ways were often rocky and steep, but they followed a trail downwards until they found themselves is a long, low valley shrouded by greenery from above.

"This is Paradise Vale," said Catriona. "We often come down here because the way is clear and it allows us the chance to give our horses their head. Not too much, because they have a steep climb on the way back."

"So we were thinking," said Rawley, "you seem to know your way around that stallion of yours, I have a fine quarter-horse, why don't we go for a little point-to-point ride?"

"I don't think that's such a good idea," said Flint.

"The master would not like it," put in Neela.

"There would be a wager," said Rawley, "your horse would come to me if I win, and vice versa."

"No," said Flint. "He's not mine to wager with."

They rode on in silence for few seconds then Rawley made a sound like a chicken. Flint reddened to the roots of his coarse hair. He knew he should not rise to the bait but he spurred his horse beside Rawley's.

"Okay, I'll do it."

Catriona rode away from them to the end of the valley. She had with her a light-coloured wrap to put around her shoulders if the weather changed. When she was far off on the horizon she used this as a signal to the riders and they were off.

It was obvious from the outset that Rawley was a superb rider. Spurring his mount on, he was soon ahead by a couple of lengths.

But Flint understood the power of holding back his piebald stallion. Well-bred horses could turn an impressive burst of speed, but they lacked stamina over a longer distance. Soon the gap between them narrowed to one length, and the pair were nearly at the head of the valley. Flint leaned forward, about to whisper the necessary words that would spur his on, when there was a disaster. They came to a ridge in the uneven ground of the valley. To avoid this, Flint drew his horse to one side, falling behind by three lengths, while Rawley – who had been expecting the flaw – had indeed counted on it, and had his horse perform a minor jump that took him completely clear. It looked as if Rawley was going to win.

What he didn't count on was Flint's attitude to life.

He kicked the sides of his mount, since he was not wearing spurs, and his horse shot forward like a black and white thunderbolt. Rawley, who had made the mistake of relaxing a little, so used was he to winning, found the gap on his left breached by a snorting, pounding fiend that carried a hatless devil on its back. They were within feet of Catriona, who was shocked to find a different face draw up in front of her in a cloud of dust and nostril steam. She drew back in fright at Flint's close proximity. Without his wide-brimmed hat he looked wilder than ever, but she found that something inside her could not make her dislike him for what he had done.

Rawley came to a more leisurely halt. He was a gambler by nature and did not look at all disconcerted by his defeat.

"Congratulations," he said, "well ridden, I didn't think you had it in you. I suppose you'll allow me to finish this day's activities before I hand you your prize?"

Flint merely nodded. Serenity seemed to have come over him now that he had won and he did not seem in a hurry to return to the ranch.

Neela joined them and they allowed the horses to crop grass and drink greedily from a nearby creek, before moving off again.

They were now starting to come towards the plains where Shaw kept his cattle. In the distance they could see a small outstation from which the men worked. It consisted of a water tower and wind pump, bunkhouses, barns, a corral, and a cookhouse. To their left lay a line of hills and imposing rocky outcrops. Bright shades of red reflected the composition of the sandstone, heavy with iron oxides.

Rawley and Catriona continued to ride ahead of the other two. They were once again whispering and laughing with each other. Finally, when they had gone for a mile or so more they came to a singular, rocky outcrop that stood on its own near the cliff face.

"Spire Rock," said Rawley, pointing out -the obvious name as Flint and Neela halted beside Catriona. He looked directly at Flint. "How would you like to take on another wager?"

"No," said Flint simply.

"If you win, I'll give you a hundred dollars. But if you lose, I get back my horse and yours as well."

"Do not do this," said Neela sharply.

Flint didn't ponder the question too deeply. With a hundred dollars he could go into town and start his own business and get away from all this. "All right, what do we have to do?"

"Climb," said Rawley. "The one who reaches highest wins."

He pulled off his shirt revealing a surprisingly broad chest, but kept on his hat. In lieu of hat, Flint wrapped his bandana around his head and stripped to the waist as well. He was skinny but wiry and there was something about him that promised a broader, tougher man as he aged. Catriona gave them the signal and they began to climb.

"Flint doesn't know it," Rawley had told Catriona on the way there, "but I've climbed the spire before, many times."

The two men were about halfway up the spire when it became clear that Flint was the lighter and more agile of the two. Then Rawley came to a complete halt. He suddenly let out a cry of despair.

"Help me, I'm stuck."

Flint ignored him and kept climbing, but Catriona looked up with a piteous expression. "Please help him," she shouted. Flint could not ignore a direct plea from the daughter of the ranch. He worked his way around the rocky surface with impressive agility and came to where Rawley still clung. He held on with one hand and helped with the other. Rawley pushed into a better position then laughed in Flint's face.

"Now I win." He kicked himself up and Flint received a flurry of dust and pebbles on his upturned face. He spluttered and shook his head, dislodging his other hand, and seconds later he was falling to the ground from a height of at least thirty feet.

Luckily there was a large amount of foliage below the rock, which broke his fall, yet even so, when the others got to him he was so bruised and bloodied that they feared he was already dead.

That day took on the proportions of a nightmare. They managed to get Flint back to the outstation, wrapped in a blanket and carried by his own horse. Thankfully the cook, Jesse Coggins, a crabbit man of the first order, was also an experienced field medic. He had diagnosed the young man as having several broken ribs, a badly twisted knee and ankle, concussion and multiple contusions – and had used a small amount of morphine to keep Flint sedated while he did the best he could with limited resources.

After a few days William Shaw sent a wagon down to fetch him and Flint, still heavily sedated, was brought back to the main ranch.

As a penance for her behaviour, Catriona, along with Neela, were given the task of nursing the young man back to health, while Rawley was banished altogether for the time being. They had to change his bandages and nurse his wounds. Although unconscious, he spoke often in a low voice in a language that even Neela did not understand.

Eventually, on the fourth day, he awakened.

"Who won?" he asked Catriona.

"We called it a draw," she said.

*****

At first Catriona resented looking after Flint. After all she was a daughter of the local gentry. Who was he to be looked after by someone like her? But she was also aware of her father's anger, and knew that he was quite capable of curtailing her social activities and making her unavailable to her friends, something she did not want to happen.

As time went on the penance began to seem less so. William would often drop in and talk to the uncomplaining patient and the two would yarn about the cattle drives. She found their stories highly entertaining and they made her understand why her father was the kind of man he was.

In the intervening days between the fall and Flint's return to *High Wynd*, Gilbert left to pursue his travels again. He had first departed when he was just nineteen, eager to learn about the ways of business out East. 1836 had seen things shift from Philadelphia, over to New York, where the financial markets helped to bolster the work of ranches out in Texas. He knew that business was moving towards banking and commerce, and that was the side he was more interested in rather than the day-to-day workings of a ranch. While out there before, he'd met the young lady with whom he had been corresponding for the past year. She was not rich, but she came from a good family, and he'd promised his parents that he would bring her home with him.

Then came the time to help Flint start walking again.

Such was his determination that within a fortnight he was walking around the room by himself, and in another week he was striding about the grounds with the two young women, his step barely faltering as they watched his steady progress.

When he insisted on getting back in the saddle they were initially reluctant to let him do so, but being on Shadow seemed to revive his spirits, and there was soon nothing but the odd grimace of pain to show that he had been in the accident at all.

Strangely, although they spoke little on these walks, with Catriona providing much of the chatter, she found herself growing closer to him. To the point when he'd expressed a desire to walk unattended she had felt a desire to go with him, although he insisted on being alone.

With her brother now gone, and seeing little of Rawley, the next time Flint travelled outwards she had insisted on going with him, with Neela as their chaperone.

That had been when Flint had come to realise that the time of peace and mending was soon to end.

Chapter Four

Rawley arrived at *High Wynd* after three months had passed since the incident. He had ridden for miles and was hot and dusty. Elizabeth invited him in and gave him a cool drink in the formal front parlour.

"I expect you've come to see that girl of mine." she said with a warm smile. "I'll just get her for you."

"Thank you kindly ma'am," said Rawley in his rich southern voice. But when she returned she had a frown on her usually clear brow.

"I am afraid Catriona is out for the day, trail-riding with our horse-instructor, Flint. She has been trying to improve her horsemanship lately."

"Ah see, and does this household allow a young lady to travel out unescorted with a male servant?"

Elizabeth flushed at this, and for the first time her tone sharpened.

"Flint is not what you would call a servant, he is more part of the household now. He is more like...well William is very attached to him. In fact we..." She stopped as if a little confused. "There was a gap when Gilbert left. Neela is with them." She said this with a tone of finality.

"And Gilbert, he is due back to see you?"

"Yes, he is bringing Isabella, his new love, with him."

"Well, thank you for your hospitality ma'am, that was refreshing," Rawley handed the glass back to his host. "Please give my regards to Miss Catriona, and tell her I called. Perhaps if I come over in two days she might be here to see an old friend?"

"I'll let her know Rawley. But why not wait first? They may be back soon."

"It is early enough to get back before the midday sun, but thank you for the thought." Soon he was riding off.

His pretended nonchalance was a pose. He didn't like Catriona seeing this glorified servant boy. He was supposed to be engaged by now – his father was certainly pushing for the union – so how was he going to react when he found the engagement had stalled?

It was time to put this Flint in his place.

*****

Flint and Catriona were out on the trail together, with Neela keeping a discreet distance from them.

It wasn't only the season had turned warmer. It was springtime, and Flint now felt as much a part of the Shaw family as Gilbert had ever been. Catriona had always been the fiery, demanding one of the pair, with no love lost between the two siblings. But William and Elizabeth had accepted Flint into their family, adopting him in all but legal paperwork.

Soon the three of them came to Paradise Valley where Flint had raced against Rawley on the day he had sustained his injuries. She had become closer to Flint since that time and he had grown to be a part of her life. Even so, they knew they couldn't spend too much time together without tongues wagging in a not entirely pleasant way.

Catriona leaned in her saddle towards Flint. "I have a secret to show you. You, Rawley, and Neela are the only ones who know."

They tethered the horses, and Catriona led him to a group of cottonwood bushes that grew against the side of the valley. Catriona parted these and revealed a large cave entrance, seemingly invisible from view.

Flint said nothing as they went into the semi-darkness, but Catriona bent down, pulling up her skirts a little as she did so and scooped a handful of what seemed like rough stones about the size of her fingernails.

"I call this the crystal cave," she said. "We found it when we were children. I often come here." Once outside she washed the stones in a nearby rock pool and their colour - white, but with a strange yellow glow inside - began to emerge.

"Look," she held up a rawhide wristband. He had seen these before; the Indians often wore them as decoration. "Neela showed me how to make this. I made it just for you." Catriona was suddenly a little bashful. Deftly she inserted the quartz crystals into little hollows scooped from the rawhide. "Hold out your right wrist." She tied it round then inspected it with her head on one side like a bird. "That's my token of friendship present to you. Promise me you'll wear it always."

"I promise," said Flint.

Flint opened the neck of his blue shirt and undid the string around his neck. He held it out to her, an oval amulet made from black obsidian as hard as his name, dangled from the string.

"Take this," he said, smiling faintly as if a little unsure of her acceptance. "Made from stone that fell from the sky, real good luck."

Catriona was about to refuse, but she saw Neela, who was sitting on the grass behind him, purse her lips and shake her head. This was the Indian way, a gift for a gift in token of friendship, with a refusal taken as a cause for offence.

"Thank you," she said, pulling her long, dark hair aside, "Tie it on please, I fumble so." He did so with slim, sure fingers, her fair neck tingling when they brushed against her skin. Soon they were back home, with a secret bond between them.

*****

Not long afterwards Gilbert arrived back at *High Wynd* with what his family thought was his bride-to-be. He got out of the carriage first. He was wearing a well-tailored suit but it was cut in an ostentatious way. It had wide lapels that no Texan would have looked at, and his large knotted tie was a garish red and blue. Even his usually messy hair had been cut. He smiled as the family greeted him, although frowned with puzzlement for a second when his eyes lighted on Flint. He went round to the other side of the covered carriage and helped his beloved down the step.

"This is Isabella," he announced. The young lady wore a cream travelling ensemble – jacket, blouse and close ankle length skirt. Her hair was long and black and cascaded down her shoulders, topped with a sun hat that was held in place with an ornate enamelled hat pin.

"Hello everyone," said Isabella. "I've heard so much about you." She looked directly at Flint. "But I don't think Gilbert has ever mentioned you."

Gilbert leaned close to her. "Ignore him, he's a glorified servant."

Elizabeth came forward and kissed Isabella on the cheek.

"We're so glad to finally meet you. All we've ever seen are the photographs you sent, and those do not do you justice."

Catriona and Flint said nothing. They were still trying to take in the new arrivals, but William gave one of his booming laughs and shook Gilbert by the hand while clapping him on the shoulder.

"You've chosen a beauty son. This will be a fine marriage."

"I have an announcement to make," Gilbert stepped back, his hand at the waist of his beloved. "There is no more of an engagement between us. We are already married."

"What? It can't be, surely?" asked his mother.

"But it is the truth," Isabella answered for them both, proudly showing off her golden wedding band and the diamond set therein.

"You see," said Gilbert, "her family did not want to see me disappearing out West with her with just an engagement between us. I thought it would be a nice surprise for you all."

William looked as if he was about to swell up and burst, then he looked at his wife, who shook her head. Catriona merely shrugged, bored with the whole thing because none of the attention was on her, while Flint was completely indifferent to Gilbert's domestic arrangements, although he did notice the new bride looking at him a little too intently.

"Just like all the Shaws," said William with a loud guffaw. He clapped his son on the shoulder again. "Impulsive. However, this is an event that will not go unnoticed by this family."

Seeing a way of breaking her boredom, Catriona seized Isabella's hand. "Come inside, you must be tired from your long trip. And we have such a lot to talk about." Her voice echoed as she led the new bride into the main house.

"You," said Gilbert to Flint, "just keep away. This is my time to show my wife her new home."

"Welcome," said Flint. He went away to his hayloft. He had nothing to say to them anyway.

*****

Soon the Shaw family held a ball in honour of the newly married couple. They had no room at *High Wynd* to hold the event, but this was no problem, because their old friends, the Henderson's. Not only did they have plenty of space in one of their larger outbuildings, it was regularly adapted to host this kind of event, so they could easily invite neighbours from miles around to the celebration.

Everyone was invited who had any kind of standing in the district and the guest list was soon over the two hundred mark. Those ladies who liked a marriage were not disappointed, and to accommodate, Gilbert speedily agreed to renew his vows with Isabella in the biggest church in the area. It was a simple ceremony, conducted by Tom Harper, the minister, who would also attend the ball. Gilbert had been quite happy to compromise with his mother over this event because he knew it would make her happy, although it did not stop his father getting drunk and murmuring that the boy was not getting a real marriage.

The ball itself turned out to be a splendid affair, which was why Flint had not wanted to attend.

"They don't want me there," he told Catriona. "Besides, I have only my work clothes. I don't have a fancy suit to match your brother."

"My brother looks like some seed salesman in that get-up," she said. "Get Jackson the town tailor to run up something for you. My family has an account there. Just give him a visit."

Flint went to see the tailor, against his own wishes. He had never been one for wasting his money on unnecessary clothes or comforts, but he wasn't averse to taking her present.

By the time it was finished, Flint had a new dark blue shirt, a black waistcoat with silver stitching, black trousers and a pair of high polished black leather boots with hand-made swirls on them. He offset this with a dark tan hat.

From there he went to the hardware store to buy a revolver. It wasn't the first gun he had ever owned, because out on the trail you needed protection from wild bulls, predators such as bobcats, bears, and even other men. But it was new. He also bought a new knife, since the old one that had become worn with use.

As he had no partner Flint went to the ball with his hosts Elizabeth and William. Coloured lanterns already lit the barn when they arrived, while music could be heard from within. The happy couple greeted the guests as they arrived with only a minor hiccup when Gilbert chose not to shake hands with Flint. Over the last few months Flint had become used to the pleasures of alcohol, for William was a drinker of large capacity and liked to imbibe while they were yarning. Flint headed for the bar ordered a beer, determined to stay there all night if he was allowed to. Catriona tried to get to him but it was soon plain that he was an object of interest for many of the young ladies present, and he soon had a group of four around him all angling for a dance. It took him some time to shake them off without causing offence, but by then Catriona was gone.

He decided to watch the square dancing, while getting away from the crowd. By this time he was standing at the entrance, finishing his beer, when he saw Rawley and Gilbert make their way towards him through the smoke of the spectators, the one tall and slim, the other shorter and thickset.

"Hello son," said Gilbert. He and Rawley suddenly grabbed Flint by the elbows and hustled him out into the night air where Flint was illuminated by the light from inside that made shadows of the other two as it shone behind them.

"What do you want?" Flint stood back from them, rubbing his elbows.

"I've seen how you look at Catriona," said Rawley. "Let's just make it plain, boy, she's my gal. You keep away from her in future, you hear?"

"Shouldn't that be up to her?"

"You keep away from my parents too," said Gilbert. "I don't know what mumbo-jumbo spell you've put them under, but they're treating you far too well for some jumped up trail rider. Butt out."

"I'll give it a thought," said Flint. He was treading fairly carefully because this was supposed to be a night of celebration and it wouldn't look good if someone ended up injured or even dead, especially if that someone was one of the young men of two respected families.

"I reckon we should treat this Indian boy to a lesson in manners," said Rawley. "Hold him Gibby." Gilbert stepped behind Flint, pinning the young man's arms to his side. While he did this, Rawley rolled up the sleeves of his silk shirt, not wanting to get blood on them. Quickly done, he lashed out at Flint's tanned features.

What neither of them knew was that Flint had been fighting since he was a child. He did not panic and struggle in this kind of situation, which would just have tightened the bear-like grip of Gilbert, instead he calmly took stock of the situation, realised that his legs were still free, lifted his foot and raked Gilbert's shinbone with the heel of his new boot. Gilbert gave a cry of agony that doubled when Flint deftly ducked Rawley's punch, spun around and kicked Gilbert on the other shin. That was the moment when Gilbert lost all interest and retreated from the fight.

Flint turned to face Rawley, who now rushed at him, and stepped aside, allowing the taller man to rush past, and then put out a foot to trip him up. Carried forward by his own weight Rawley sprawled upon the newly scythed grass in front of the barn.

"Reckon that's us about even," Flint said without rancour, stepping back inside the building, only to find that he was confronted by Catriona. Her face was contorted in fury, and for a moment he thought she had misconstrued the situation, believing Flint had attacked her brother and friend. But she was looking straight past him at the other two. As he went in, she silently went out. For a moment he thought of going with her, but he already knew the volatile girl well enough to sense that his presence was not needed. Besides, he needed another beer. Hard work makes you thirsty.

*****

Old father Henderson had seen his son going outside with Gilbert and the upstart, so when he saw Flint strolling back in without the other two, he decided to investigate. What he discovered was Catriona standing, berating the two rather shame-faced young men.

"What do you think you're doing? He is a guest in our house, Gilbert. You do not abuse hospitality because of your imagined slights. As for you, Rawley, if you think I can have a future with you after what I've seen, you can go to hell! Our engagement is off!" The girl slid the ring off her finger, then threw it in his face before marching back to the dance.

Numbly her now-ex fiancée' picked up the ring.

"That was some show," boomed Henderson, coming forward. "You two young nuts deserved that. Picking a fight on this, of all nights, thought that young tough would be easy."

"I'm going to string him from the nearest oak," said Rawley, breathing hard, his teeth bared.

"And I'll pull on his legs for you," agreed Gilbert, who had just finished massaging his painful shins.

"You'll get him," said the old man. "Just do it at the right time. And you, Rawley, you make sure you make it up with that girl. She's worth having."

He didn't labour the point, not with Gilbert there, but Rawley saw what his father was getting at. Once Flint was gone and the engagement was back on, Gilbert's demise would follow not that long after. Rawley calmed down and they went back inside, joining in the celebrations as if nothing had happened.

Chapter Five

Catriona did indeed get over her fury, and eventually resumed her engagement with Rawley. Meanwhile Gilbert and Isabella quickly took up residence in a new house that William had commissioned as a wedding present to the young couple. Not only was he kept occupied looking after his bride, but there was also the administration of the ranch. So it wasn't long that he found himself spending a great deal of time on the price of cattle feed, fence posts and wages. This, and a thousand other tasks that occupied him pushed thoughts of revenge against Flint to the back of his mind. He still disliked the way Flint had managed to worm his way into William's affections in a short time. Gilbert, who had wanted nothing more in life than to please his father, found he couldn't forgive the upstart Flint for being in a place that he, Gilbert, could never reach. One day Flint would find this out to his cost.

In the meantime Rawley regained some of his old position in Catriona's life. He was, after all, light-hearted and fun-loving, being a man who had an entirely different outlook on life from Flint, who liked his own company and rarely smiled.

Rawley too, was adept at hiding his true feelings as he escorted Catriona to dances or into town, sometimes going for country rides with her, while pretending that he did not mind her frequent trips with Flint. He knew there was some kind of bond between them. Yet he was quite ready to wait until he and Catriona were married before attempting to break that bond.

Besides, it was fiendishly difficult to try and trap Flint. Rawley didn't want anyone else to know of his plans so worked alone when contemplating the removal – ideally permanently – of someone who he saw as his rival. The plan was simple enough, to get Flint in some lonely spot and throw him off a cliff or start an avalanche atop him, or startle his horse and get it to throw him - anything that would look like a natural accident. But the instincts of the Indians seemed to have passed into him and Flint avoided the many traps laid down for him, changing routes frequently and being unpredictable. This too was the Indian way.

Then disaster befell the Shaw family at the turn of the season. It could be cold in the hill country, with snow falling fast and thick. Just after that Christmas, Elizabeth fell ill with a fever she caught when making her way to see a neighbour. The horse pulling her carriage had thrown a shoe and caught a stone, making it lame. It was too valuable, and against Elizabeth's nature to leave the horse stranded in the snow, so she decided to walk home with it, and send someone back for the carriage.

Elizabeth was not a well-built woman, and within a week she had fallen victim to fever and Influenza.

Flint and Catriona were both at her side. Flint had never really known his own parents and he had transferred any devotion he had over to William and Elizabeth. He looked after her with patience and a growing concern – stoically accepting the inevitable outcome.

They were all with her on the morning she died, William gazing into the fading eyes of the woman who had given him the greatest happiness he had known.

From the day of her death, through to the funeral and afterwards, William was a broken man. Up in hill country, beyond 60 years of age was considered old, and although he had been energetic and motivated up until that time, he soon started to slow down. Even when the spring came and brought the relative warmth of the thaw he still did not stir from the building. Instead he spent most of his time beside the fire.

Flint found himself elevated to the position of go-between for his employer. He would visit the foremen, spend some time with them, then come back and report to William what had happened. William would sit beside the built-up log fire, his chin resting on a silver-topped cane he used to get about now, nodding sagely at the news he was given and issuing various work orders.

In a sense it was good for him to do business this way, for he was able to sit and consider his business dealings and transmit his desires to Flint.

At night he still liked Flint to sit with him and talk about the old times on the Chisholm Trail. Only now he would often pause, losing the thread of what he was saying.

Catriona was dutiful in seeing her father. He was always bright at those times and grateful to see his 'mountain rose' as he liked to call her, careful to conceal any of his ills from her, not wishing to burden her with his fears for the future.

Perhaps a little surprisingly she did not appear to be particularly affected by her mother's death. She was at that age when youth springs back quickly from every setback. She mourned, then resumed her life.

She was also quick to notice the absence of Flint. Her father kept him so busy that they didn't see each other half as much as before. This, too, flung her into the company of her fiancée. She understood Flint had to earn his living, even though her father looked on him with favour. At other times, when he was with her father for company, she did not want to interrupt them.

Flint was with William the night the old man went into a particularly long ramble about his past. Then William, after one particularly loud statement about his life on the trail, gave a gasp and sank his chin on the silver head of his cane. There was a knock at the door, and Catriona came in.

"I was just going to bed," she said, "when I heard some shouting. What's wrong?"

"Your father isn't well," said Flint, "Help me get him to bed. His mind, I'm sorry to say, isn't what it used to be."

They both stood beside the old man.

"We've come to take you to your bed," said Catriona.

"My mountain rose," said William faintly. "You look after her Flint. Promise me?"

"I'll always look out for her," said Flint, with a faint smile to please the old man. His smile faded when William called out, "Elizabeth!" then gave a gasp that ended in a rattling noise that came from his throat.

With his chin still resting on hands that grasped his stick, William died.

*****

After the funeral, which was attended by so many mourners they could not all fit into the church, Flint took stock of the situation. Mentally he had a foreboding of what was going to happen to him within the Shaw family. He could ride out and away any time he wanted. The trouble was, he did not want to leave Catriona to the non-tender mercies of her older brother. When Gilbert attended the funeral with his wife, he'd glared at Flint the whole time. Rawley, there the other Hendersons, ignored the young man completely, even though they all sat on the front pew.

Then there was the question of property rights. It was Catriona who broached the subject with Flint after the funeral. They were back at High Wynd and everyone had finally left. It was a beautiful spring day, an auger of the summer to come, as they rode out together on one of the byways leading from the main house. Rain clouds were visible on the horizon.

"Flint, shortly after mother died, my father drew up a new will."

"Did he?" Flint seemed deeply uninterested in the subject.

"Yes, and the reason I'm telling you this is because I found out accidentally - when I found a draft on his desk - that you are one of the beneficiaries."

"That was good of him," said Flint, "but I would rather have your father here than a few dollars from his estate."

"It is more than that, Flint. He divided the estate between the three of us, you, me and Gilbert. You are now a rancher."

He should have been filled with joy at her words. He had come from being a penniless orphan to being a propertied landowner. Somehow, though, there was no pleasure at the thought now that he had lost two of the most important people he had ever known. The black clouds that had once been in the distance-roiled overhead, releasing a torrent of rain and forcing them to turn back, so that they were sodden by the time they reached *High Wynd* again. It seemed an auger of what was to come.

*****

Gilbert soon came to the ranch without his new wife, but driving a cart laden with many of their worldly goods. He also had with him a group of ranch hands, all of who were armed. It was about three days after his father had died. Catriona was the first to face up to him. "What's going on?"

"We're moving in. Not right now of course, but we're making a start."

She sounded confused. "You have your own place."

"But this one's better. Don't be selfish sissy, there's plenty of room for us all."

"What about my father's will?"

"Yes, what about it?" Flint appeared from the dining room doorway.

Gilbert bristled at the sight of his enemy. "The will? It hasn't even been read out yet."

"Why not?" asked Flint.

"At this precise moment, as executor of the estate and the eldest sibling, I am doing what is necessary.".

"Then why the secrecy?" asked Flint.

"Catriona, it is time to tell you the truth," said Gilbert, Deliberately ignoring Flint. "Father clearly made his last will and testament when he was of unsound mind. Right now the will is with Hailcheck and Devinchy, my lawyers in town. As executor of the estate I have the power to act in the best interests of those involved. The estate should have been mine with provision for your upkeep. As for this - intruder - he deserves no more consideration than a pet dog or what he really is, a snake who wormed his way into my father's affections, poisoning him with the slow drip of his lies, turning my father against me. I'll die before he gets a thing."

Catriona's face whitened with fury and her mouth was a grim line. They say that when beautiful women are angry this adds an edge to their looks, but this proved that to be a lie. Catriona was angry and her features were ugly.

"You know our father gave us all what we deserved. It's not even as if he favoured us above you. You were going to get your share. Now you're trying to take it all away from us."

"I take nothing away. You can both live here as long as you want - although Flint will have to give up his room within the main house. You are my sister; so you can carry on as before. You, Flint, are good at your job. Nothing will change, but I will have what is rightfully mine."

At that moment the whole outcome turned on Catriona. The men Gilbert had brought with him were alert now, hands on their guns. They were all good men, and they knew Flint from his work, but not one of them would hesitate to gun him down if he made a wrong move. Catriona turned to Flint. He did not look at her directly, but she knew that on her word he would attack Gilbert with his bare hands, such was his loyalty to her and the late departed Shaws. She also knew that Flint could have snapped her brother's neck like a twig before the gunmen had shot him to death. Then she would have a victory of sorts – but the estate would be hers at a terrible cost.

"Leave this," she said to Flint, "Let him have his day."

"If that's really what you want," said Flint. She nodded. Such was the bond between them that he knew to take the issue no further. Walking around Gilbert, Flint left the house, taking his time to walk across the yard as if he had not a care in the world. With eight pairs of eyes following his progress, he mounted and slowly rode off.

*****

Gilbert and Isabella soon moved into the main house, bringing with them all the decorations and gee-gaws his wife thought necessary for life. Catriona, quite naturally, talked the matter over with Flint. He thought that most lawyers used a language people did not understand in order to bilk a man out of his fair rights, but she knew as well as he did that Gilbert, as the son of the house and executor to boot had the force of the law on his side. As expected, the will was taken to court and the judge, who sat on the bench part time in a place where most disputes were settled by the fist, gun and boot, ruled that William Shaw was of unsound mind when he made his will and that the entire estate should go to Gilbert Shaw.

The judge was Old John Henderson.

*****

Next, Rawley decided it was time to visit his old friend Gilbert. They still drank together, with Rawley drinking less so he could get Gilbert drunk and influence him. Behind his supposed good-natured façade Rawley hid his fury that Flint was still seeing his fiancée, but it was an issue he was not going to put up with for long.

"Gibby, that fellow, Flint, why do you keep him around?"

"I have a lot of reasons," said Gilbert. "After all, what do you do with a dangerous dog that might be useful to you? Do you let the thing roam around where it might bite out at random, or do you chain it up in your yard where you can keep an eye on it?"

"Neither," said Rawley, "you shoot the mutt and make everyone's life easier. You should get rid of this Flint as soon as you can."

"Why?"

"He's trouble."

"The Indian is useful to me," said Gilbert. "He works hard, is loyal to my sister and he is mine to do with as I please." Gilbert's features took on a particularly stubborn look. Inwardly Rawley sighed; he knew that look of old. When Gilbert was in that mood he could not be shifted. He was a lot more like his father than he thought.

"All right, Gilbert, you want your servant because he reminds you of the old days. Fair enough, but you must agree it is far from right that he sees your sister, my fiancée, on such a regular basis. Catriona is young, she is foolish, and she does not see yet that these things matter. Tongues are already wagging. If I approach her on this matter she might well end our engagement again, this time for good, and you will lose an alliance that will be useful to you. If you end the relationship what are you going to lose? She has already taken you to court once, and lost. She is not going to heap any greater hatred on you than she already has."

"That is true."

That is why the next time Flint was going to go out on the trail with Catriona, he found Gilbert waiting for him at the gate.

"Time for you to go your own way," said Gilbert.

"What?"

"My sister has been informed she can't go with you anymore. She is a woman who is shortly to be married. She cannot be seen with the likes of you."

"The likes of me?" Flint was very still, his face betraying not the slightest sign of emotion. He was not a man who cared about property, indeed his third of the estate had been just words to him, so that when it was removed by the trickery of lawyers he didn't care, because the concept of owning things meant little to him.

But this was different.

Gilbert carried on. "Catriona is young. She is to be married it's not seemly for her to go about with you. When she lives in Eagle Cross she won't be seeing you anyway. You've not done anything wrong in your friendship, Neela is close to her and has assured me of that, but this has to end. You can still see Catriona, but not like this."

He didn't think it necessary to tell Flint about the fight he'd already had with Catriona, who had refused to accept that she couldn't continue with her friendship as before.

Flint thought about the matter. Catriona was engaged to Rawley, who would marry her in due course. Yet Flint had a bond with her that could never be broken. He was more than a friend, and they both knew that if she said the word, he would run away with her. But that was not her choice to make. Although he hated Rawley, and Gilbert too, she had made the decision to stay here. If he could be close to her, that was enough until times changed. He was a fatalist, knowing that his time would come.

"Very well," he said, "I agree."

*****

Catriona had indeed been furious at her brother's intervention. She didn't see why she should not see Flint whenever she wanted. She didn't want to lose Rawley, and her social position meant a great deal to her, so she was stuck between two extremes. So, for a while, she concentrated on Rawley, avoiding Flint altogether, which gave them both space to adjust to the situation. It was a space soon to be filled.

Isabella quickly realised that Gilbert was a boor. Where she had pictured her life as being amongst Western gentry, she very quickly found that her new husband was not what he seemed. He regarded his wife largely as an extension of his property. He would pick her up, then put her down as soon as he grew tired of her, or needed to concentrate his attention on the ranch and business.

With neglect comes boredom, and to alleviate this she would spend some time with her sister-in-law. Before the ban on Catriona and Flint riding out together, she had been on the trail with Flint. She discovered a fascination with the young man that would not go away. In fact, her mind became filled with him, and when Gilbert was not at home she would find excuses to seek him out and talk to him in the yard, or ask him in for food or found a thousand other ways to interact with him.

But Flint was not flattered by these attentions. He didn't fear Gilbert, but he didn't want to rouse the man's anger in case he was sent away and could no longer be near Catriona. He was polite with Gilbert's wife and always treated her with respect. He was not to know that his standoffish attitude had made him an object of even greater desire, mostly because he did not really understand women.

When Isabella found that Flint slept in a hayloft she was fascinated.

"Why do you not have your own room in the house?" she asked him.

"It suits me better ma'am," he told her. "I never led the easy indoor life."

The first summer after William's death, Gilbert was often away on business, although she suspected his business was more to do with staying in town drinking and playing cards than with stock management. It was a warm night and dusk had fallen over the ranch like a velvet blanket. In her lonely bed, Isabella found her thoughts turning to the young man in the hayloft not two hundred yards away. She could not sleep, so she got up and went for a walk. It was a beautiful night, with a full moon shining over the ranch illuminating the barns and bunkhouses nearby.

The balmy night air felt good on her skin and she wore only a thin cotton nightdress. For a moment she turned and looked back at the main house. Was there a faint smudge that could have been a face at one of the windows? Then the smudge disappeared and she continued her journey. If she had met a single human being her mood would've been broken and she would have scuttled home.

The next thing she knew she was climbing the ladder to the hayloft. Flint had cleared a sizeable area behind the bales of hay. He had a few simple accoutrements to aid his life there - a low wooden stool, a chair, a store of various foods, water, and a bag for his clothing and his bedroll. These were all the home comforts he needed.

The loft had twin wooden shutters that opened to reveal an upper door. This was where the bales were thrown out to the carter when hay was needed for the animals, but could be secured from inside in stormy or cold weather. Isabella climbed the ladder. Then her head and shoulders emerged through the big trap to see that Flint was sitting with his back to her looking out at the big full moon. Beside him was a bottle of whiskey from which he had been drinking. He was so still and dark that for a moment fear gripped her heart, then she was standing behind him. Flint threw his body off the stool, out of the moonlit pool of light and emerged from the darkness holding his Colt .44.

"Who the hell is it?" he asked.

"Only me," Isabella emerged from the shadow at the loft entrance into the moonlight. Recognising her now, Flint holstered his gun.

"Mrs Shaw, what do you want?"

"I'm called Isabella. I'm just...I don't know. It seemed like a good evening for a stroll."

"Dressed as you are? You'll catch your death. You'd best get home ma'am."

"I don't have a home, not really. I'm just a possession. What do you think of me, Flint?"

"You're a fine looking woman." Flint was a man who did not drink much, but one of the other hands had given him a bottle of sipping whiskey as a reward for helping him with a difficult task, and Flint had been sitting in the moonlight contemplating his next action. The first was to get Catriona to leave with him. The alternative was to slit Gilbert's throat, also worth considering, and the third was just to leave for good. The last seemed the best idea. A stake in the property and lifelong attention of Catriona would have made him stay, but since he had neither of those and was contemplating the demise of his employer, it didn't seem wise to stick around much longer.

That was why, when Isabella appeared, he spoke to her briefly before finding her in his arms. His mind partly befuddled by whiskey he experienced that element of human intimacy he had never experienced before, and ended up introducing her to a fact he had long known that bales of hay make a surprisingly comfortable bed.

Chapter Six

Matthew Jacob was a servant of the Shaw family. He was loyal to the Shaws, even though, in his opinion, young Gilbert was not a patch on his father. As for that Rawley Henderson? Matthew Jacob felt that he should shed his clothes and wriggle along the ground on his belly like the Sidewinder he was. Should there be a showdown between either Gilbert, Flint, or Rawley, one or other would hit the dust and the house would go to Catriona. And there was no way he wanted Rawley to be the new master. So when he saw Isabella Shaw walking across the yard that morning, Matthew decided it was time for him to take action.

"Mister Gilbert, sir. You have been away a few days at a time this summer," he said as he served breakfast in the dining room. He could speak easily because the mistress liked to lie abed until noon.

"This is true Jacob," said Gilbert heartily. He had been brought up with the old servant and was fond of him rather as you might be fond of an old, arthritic dog. "Business is business. I have been negotiating deals that should net us more money by reducing the amount of time our cattle are housed in stockyards. Do you know those thieves charge more per steer than it costs a man to bed down in a cheap guesthouse for a night?"

"Aye sir, there are all kinds of thieves and cheats oot there." Matthew eyed his boss warily. "I think you should know that the missus is not taking yer absences well, sir."

Gilbert put down his knife and fork. "How do you deduce that?"

"She's spending a lot o' time wi' that Flint. He's not good for her."

"Then I'll just have to increase his workload." At the mention of Flint, Gilbert had stiffened. in his seat.

"Nae use, she'll still pursue him."

"Then I'll have a word with her."

"Why no' make the whole thing easier and get rid o' him altogether?"

They both knew the answer to that one. Gilbert liked to keep Flint around to remind everyone of how dominant he was, to keep in servitude one who was superior to him in every way. But this was different; he couldn't have the community know that his wife was making a fool of herself with a servant. Picking up his knife and fork again he sliced his bacon and ate it thoughtfully.

Moments later, as Matthew refilled Gilbert's cup with coffee, Gilbert said, "Matthew, you're a wise man. Like you say, it's time for a change."

*****

Flint took the news from Matthew with his usual lack of expression. He wasn't being dismissed, but Gilbert was sending him out to head up the main outstation. He was going to be away from both Gilbert and Catriona. It had become clear over the intervening weeks that Catriona had lost all interest in him.

And in the back of his mind was also the thought of what had happened with Isabella just a few days before. They had met once since that time and she'd looked at him with a boldness in her eyes that he had walked away before he revealed too much. He had enjoyed that night more than he could have expressed in words. He was young, healthy and he responded to the sensual touch of a woman as well as any other man. In a way, being told to leave was a relief. It would take him away from a situation that could only end badly.

He packed up his possessions into two saddlebags, then rode out of *High Wynd* without a backward glance.

*****

Catriona found that life with Rawley was good, but sometimes she tired of his shallowness and often felt the urge to spend some time again with Flint. She knew she had neglected him, but she was young, pretty and had many invitations to social gatherings in both the town and country. When those obligations were met, though, she had an empty feeling inside her, and often when she was at a gathering with Rawley she would find her mind wandering to thoughts of what she and Flint had done in the past.

And in truth, Rawley was becoming a little tired of her. He had other women he wanted to see, although he was careful to keep her from those circles, and he had to constantly keep himself from making slights against Flint. He could say what he wanted when they were married and Gilbert was gone, because by that time he would have dealt with the upstart. But it was always tiring having to keep up your guard like that over a long period of time. So when Catriona indicated she wanted time to herself he was quite happy to let her go.

Catriona rode her bay mare into *High Wynd* with a strange feeling of uplift in her heart. Even though the old place looked somewhat grim compared to the brightly painted adobe and wooden frames of *Eagle Cross*, it was her home and she loved the place like no other. The feeling was also because she was about to see Flint again after nearly a month. She would beg his forgiveness, first of all for her unwarranted neglect, then she would explain that she had certain social responsibilities.

She tied her horse to hitching-post, but instead of going straight to the house, she went over to the barn and climbed up to the hayloft.

But there was no sign of Flint. She'd been used to visiting him here, but now there was nothing, not even a sign that he was out and working. He would have left his bedroll, at least. Bewildered, she climbed back down.

The yard was busy with men going about their duties, but their wives lived elsewhere. Only Matthew Jacob was there in the main house to greet her, which he did with genuine warmth. She hugged the old man with an air of bewilderment.

"What ails thee lass?"

"I went to Flint's place, but he wasn't there. I know he works, but there's no sign of him at all."

"Aye, he's not been here these past few weeks. He's gone."

"Gone? What do you mean?" The girl gazed at him in confusion.

"What does gone mean young 'un? He's not here, that's all."

"Has he left for the trail?"

"Nay, though that'll happen soon. He no longer lives here at *High Wynd*, but down on the plains. He's a cattle man again."

When Gilbert came back that night Catriona was by her brother, but not so enthusiastically by Isabella. The girl knew better than to broach the subject of Flint with Gilbert the minute he walked through the door. She waited until they had dined that night even though impatience gnawed away at her insides.

"Gibby, I'm glad to be back. It's good to see everyone again, even old Matthew. But one old friend seems to be missing."

"Is that so?" Gilbert was carefully selecting a cigar from a carved black-and silver box.

"So, I was wondering, why isn't he here?" As she finished she heard a gasp from the other side of the table. Isabella, who had just finished eating, scrubbed furiously at her mouth with a napkin, threw it down and stalked out of the room.

"There is your answer," said Gilbert, puffing calmly on his cigar. "If he comes near this house again I will personally shoot him like the dog he is."

"You bastard! I thought things had changed between us and that you could be a real brother to me! That I could live with you like this! But I see now I was wrong. You're the evil one!" Catriona was so choked up with fury that the words would no longer come. If she stayed she would have to commit an act of violence, so she stormed out of the room and ran to her own, throwing herself on the bed and sobbing violently. It was minutes later that she became aware of a figure at the doorway. Still angry, she sat up, ready to remonstrate with Gilbert for following her. But the one who stood there was Isabella, who seemed suddenly frail.

"I can tell you where he is," she said.

*****

Flint found that his return to life in the bunkhouse was not as bad as he'd feared. True, he'd lost much of the privacy he'd enjoyed at *High Wynd,* and that was indeed a sore loss because he was very much his own man. But communal life was no longer as hard for him as before. He wondered why this might be the case. Since he looked so young the men still ragged and teased him like before. In the old days he had always done his best to avoid them, but now he answered them back, even enjoying the wordplay, finding that they warmed to him because of this, calling him names like 'sassy'. He even took part in their card games and such, though he was careful not to show his dexterity and quickness of mind when it came to Poker. In this way, along with his hard work, he became quite popular.

In his own mind he knew he had one person to thank for the transformation, and that person was Catriona. He had spent so much time with her and Neela, enjoying their chatter, especially when he was healing from his accident, that those he was mixing with now seemed, in comparison, quite quiet and withdrawn. Most of their time was spent at work, so he was now easily able to cope with the times when he was thrown into their company.

He was also, to his delight, able to make his re-acquaintance with his old foreman, McQuade, who scratched his greying head at the seeming change in the once reticent Flint.

"Boy, you're too much of a social animal. I got to work you hard." Though the foreman had a soft spot for Flint, he was careful not to show.

At times, when it was Flint's turn to guard the herd at night - being a rider was a twenty-four hour job because you had to look out for strays and rustlers even when the herd was bedded down - Flint would let his mind wander back to Catriona. He missed her with an ache that was more than physical, and there was a yearning in him for her company. He'd been told that she had since returned to *High Wynd*, and in his own mind he knew that he would go and see her, even at the risk of infuriating Gilbert. If she spurned him or told him to leave, he would go, but at least he would be with her for that time.

*****

It was with this thought in mind that he saw a dark figure riding towards him. He was immediately wary as rustlers were fairly common. Not just Indians, but poor whites who would hive off a few strays from the edge of the herd, then either sell them or slaughter them for food. Not only did he have a hogleg at his side, his foreman, McQuade, had supplied him with a Winchester.

"Halt right there mister," he said.

"Typical," said a familiar feminine voice as the rider came closer. "Your eyesight never was that good."

Astonished, he saw the rider pull back her hood to reveal the long, flowing hair of the very woman of whom he had been thinking.

"Catriona! What are you doing here?"

"Leaving."

"What do you mean?"

"Exactly what I say. I'm leaving and taking you with me. I've had enough of my brother telling me what to do. As for Rawley, if he wants to keep seeing me he can do so on my terms, not his."

Flint felt a rush of excitement. He had a bolder nature than some might've thought, mistaking his quiet ways for shyness and caution. It was why he'd elected to stay at *High Wynd* for so long. Now that she was here he elected to throw all caution to the wind. Whatever she wanted to do, he would go along with her.

"I have to change watch in about half an hour," he said. "Do you think you can wait until then? It won't take long to get my gear together after that."

The girl had wanted to ride off right away, but she could see the sense in what he was saying. He managed to hide her in a dip of the land near the bunkhouse, and came back to see her when another man went on watch. A few minutes later, instead of bunking down with the rest of the men, he had changed horses and was riding out with her.

It was still dark, just after midnight and with no moon, but they could hear the sound of hoof beats in the distance and men calling to each other. Flint could not see much of Catriona's face, but he could sense a change in her mood.

"I think they've got wind of what we're doing," he said. "Did you tell anyone what you were going to do?"

"No-one," she said, except –"

"Who?"

"It doesn't matter, let's get out of here."

Given their riding abilities it was no great stretch for them to go back up into the hills and evade those who were looking for them. The land around the plains had plenty of gullies and drifts where they could hide.

The trouble with being in a gap in the hills was that although it provided a good hiding place, there was no shelter for them whatsoever. The weather was just as likely to break as it had before, and when the rain came in Texas it was not like rain anywhere else. So it was no surprise that as they headed towards town, the storm finally broke. Whipped by strong gusts of wind the heavy rain soon soaked the pair of them to the skin. Flint had his slicker in his saddlebag, but the weather turned so suddenly he had no time to stop and put it on. Lightning forked across the sky in front of their frightened horses, followed by the heavy rumbling of thunder overhead.

Following the edge of a flash flood river upstream, the two of them eventually made it to Caulder's Rock, an outcrop that gave them shelter until the storm had passed on, moving towards the outstation.

*****

So far they had not discussed where they were going, but Flint had money in town, in the bank. His plan was for them to go into town – some ten miles away – stay until morning and then ride out, refreshed. They could discuss where they were going to go after he'd drawn out his money.

Flint had to take a step he would have avoided if he could. He veered off the trail.

"Where are we going?" yelled the girl.

"To the nearest place of safety," he said. She followed him without question, soothing her horse as she did so. The mare had never been so far from home in this kind of weather before, and Catriona could feel the horse trembling violently from shock and cold. Flint's horse was a lot sturdier, having experienced a great deal more, but even the stallion's wide eyes told of his terror.

As they rode on a building appeared in the near distance. It was an old barn. The main doors were closed against the weather, but luckily there was a smaller access door incorporated into one of them for easy access. Without hesitation Flint dismounted, kicked it open then slid back the huge wooden restraint that held the main doors in place. Sodden, sombre, but quietly triumphant, he led the two horses inside. This was one of the Henderson's buildings, the same barn in which they had celebrated the return of Gilbert with his new wife. Now it was a dark, cavernous shelter. Such a place would have oil lamps as a matter of course. Flint carried some lucifers with him wrapped in oilskin and embedded in wax. He retrieved one, struck it and lit the lamp hanging from a hook fixed into one of the frame timbers, closing the main doors and sliding the wooden beam back in place.

Now warm and dry, the horses settled and soon began to dry off, as did the couple. Flint wrapped a spare blanket from his saddlebag around Catriona, and sat opposite her on a bale of hay.

"We'll stay here until first light, then head into town," he promised her.

His promise was to be short-lived.

There was a bang at the smaller door, then Rawley marched in, his lean frame covered in a black oilskin which he threw off as he entered.

"I thought so," he said with his characteristic grin. "When they told me you were out together I just knew you'd have to shelter somewhere, and this seemed the most likely place. The other riders took shelter at our ranch."

Although he would not have done this in an ordinary situation, ready to give another man a chance, Flint drew his gun from its holster, aimed it straight at Rawley, and pulled the trigger.

Nothing happened except for the loud snap of the hammer spring breaking, effectively neutralising the firing mechanism. Flint did not hesitate; he threw his gun at the tall figure, and then lunged forward to throw him off his feet. Rawley, who had just drawn his own gun, was caught off guard, the weapon torn from his grasp and kicked away into the shadows.

Catriona could do nothing but watch as the two of them began slugging it out in the middle of the barn. Rawley was the taller and heavier of the two, his wide grin showing that he expected this to be over in seconds to his advantage. He had forgotten his experience that evening outside this very building. Flint was smaller and quicker by a fraction of a second. He ducked under the assault from Rawley's fists and pounded his opponent in the midriff. Rawley gasped for breath, but a wild swing made contact with the side of Flint's head. Flint went down. No time for a fair fight, Rawley kicked out with his boot, aiming for Flint's head, but the other man was no longer there, rolling over on the dusty ground, a bony hand snaking out and pulling his opponent down to join him. Flint punched Rawley on the nose, knowing that this would take all the fire out of his enemy. He jumped atop Rawley, pinning the dazed fighter down, then grasped Rawley's hair and began to pound his opponent's head off the ground.

Catriona was on her feet by now.

"Stop, stop it now!" she did not want Flint to be tried for murder, which he surely would be if this continued. Flint got to his feet, wiped some blood off his face and staggered a little to one side.

"Find some rope and we'll tie him up," he said, then realised that Catriona was gazing behind him with wide-eyed horror.

"No you won't son," said a voice from the doorway. Flint turned to find a colt levelled at him, held by one of the grim-faced riders sent out by Gilbert. "You're comin' with us, back to High Wynd."

Chapter Seven

Catriona had never really contemplated what she was going to do after she ran away with Flint.

Were they going to start a new life together in a different state? What would she turn her hand to in order to help support them? He was a trail rider and she was a woman who had never worked a day in her life. Maybe she could have found a job in a bank as a clerk, or worked for one of the cattle merchants? She would've had to change her name so that her brother couldn't track her down.

In the cold light of day, and for several days afterwards when she was kept a virtual prisoner by Old John Henderson, this prospect seemed far from appealing.

Once more she had been the victim of her own impetuous nature.

She'd refused to go back to *High Wynd* and be with her brother. She felt she couldn't sit in the same room as a man who had barely bothered with his parents when they were alive, and who now ruled his domain as a tyrant.

As for Flint, she had been plain enough in her discussions about his fate with Rawley.

"If you try to have him hanged for attempted murder I'll appear as a witness for the defence, telling them how you attacked him first without even giving him a chance. I'll also tell them how I was the one who asked him to go away with me, that he didn't kidnap me. I'll also tell them how easily you were beaten."

Not surprisingly the last sentence was the one that swayed Rawley. Originally he'd been all for hanging Flint and having the thing done with. The trouble was this devilish attachment that the girl had for him. Should she stay at *Eagle Cross* it would be easy to wear her down and he had plans to ask her for a festive marriage at Christmas. But if he took care of Flint, she would find out, because Flint was popular amongst the men now. And if she found out then she would never talk to Rawley or his family again. He had to placate her despite the wounding of his soul.

"Very well," he said, "I'll put his case to your brother and ask him to retain this miscreant in his service." There was an unpleasant glint in his eye as he said this. But Catriona took it to be the natural chagrin of one who had been soundly beaten by a man who he considered to be his inferior.

"I mean it," she told him. "I'll make sure you rue the day if Flint is harmed by your hand."

*****

The trial was quickly held in the town court. Old John, forewarned by his son, proclaimed that Flint had been foolish enough to become swayed by the whim of a young woman. But such a thing could happen to any man, and so decreed that Flint was to return to the service of Gilbert Shaw – his punishment being two years of indenture without pay.

Flint had, given the family ties, expected far worse, but decided that when he was out on the plain it wouldn't be difficult for him to escape and start a new life. He knew now that Catriona would never really be his; their lives were just too far apart. In his prison cell, pending release to Gilbert Shaw, he decided that at the right time he would leave and never come back. He would miss the girl, that was for sure, but for a long time she'd been the only reason he had stayed.

As Flint walked out of the courthouse, McQuade came up to him.

"Son, I've been tasked look after you, and if not me then making sure you have someone with you. It's not going to be easy for any of us, but to be honest you're one of ma best workers."

Expecting to go back to the plains Flint began to follow McQuade to the livery, but two riders from *High Wynd* stopped him. The foreman looked back with a grim expression on his face, but there was nothing he could do.

"You're coming with us to see Mr Shaw." They bundled him into a cart and took him back to the ranch, not saying a word to him on the way. Soon after his arrival he was taken into the presence of Gilbert who remained expressionless as Flint was brought to the main house, then led through to what had once been William Shaw's office.

Memories of William were replaced by the image of Gilbert.

"So it's my old friend. Hope your stay in prison was bad. Mind, it's not too harsh a judgement considering what you tried to do. Kidnap and attempted murder? You should be swinging high right now, the crows eating out your eyes."

Gilbert stood up from his desk and walked casually across the room to a high wooden cabinet made from red cherry wood.

"You know my father tried to teach me all sorts of skills when I was young. Never did take to riding horses, mainly because I find them disgusting animals, but he did teach me one little skill you cattlemen sometimes use."

He reached into the cupboard and pulled out an 8ft long, bullwhip made of woven leather, the handle covered in snakeskin.

"He gave me this when I was fourteen to use when I was out training with the cowboys. Never did get to use it for that purpose, but took to it just the same. Used to practice in that very corral where you failed to teach me." He gave a sideways flick of the head. "Take him outside."

But Flint didn't go to his fate easily. He pulled away from the two men and began to run out of the door, but was slugged on the back of the head by the butt of a gun and fell to his knees, half-conscious. The two men half walked half carried him outside, over to a newly planted wooden post in the middle of the corral.

Groggy, still only half-awake from the blow, Flint was tied to the post with a length of rope, while another was tied around his waist to support his body.

Gilbert grabbed hold of the man's shirt and ripped it in half, baring Flint's back to the sun. Gilbert stepped away and cracked the whip a few times, gauging the distance, then he began the private punishment that no court would have given at that time. His blows were slow and landed where they would, breaking open the skin and deliberately inflicting wounds that would leave scars for the rest of Flint's life.

During it all Flint didn't shout or cry out once, although he did make grunts of pain as the blows landed until, inevitably, he sagged, unconscious against the wooden post. Gilbert flung the bloodied whip aside with a gesture of contempt.

"Take that away," he said, "and make sure he survives."

*****

The journey back to the outstation was not one that Flint remembered. He was vaguely aware of being transported when he felt the movement of the cart beneath his body as he lay on old blankets used to cushion his body. These were hardened riders, but they were sickened by what Gilbert had done to one of their own.

Luckily when they finally arrived, Coggins was available to help patch him up. The cook-cum-medic knew how to sew, stitching the major wounds together, covering the injuries in an ointment which contained God-knew what and had the Sulphurous smell of the devil about it, before wrapping several bandages around his body. During this process Flint kept slipping in and out of consciousness.

"Hell of a punishment for just running off with someone," muttered Coggins as he gave Flint a shot of morphine to help with the pain.

Flint was put in a bunk in the cook's own private quarters where he lay in a feverish state for three days. In all of that time he took only water, poured down his throat by the cook, losing most of it in the form of the sweat that poured off his body night and day.

On the fourth day Coggins was setting to in his kitchen to make a meal for the evening watch when Flint came through the door whiter than the bunk sheet wrapped around his body.

"Anything to eat? I'm starving – thirsty too."

"Sure thing," said the old man, accepting the miracle for what it was. One more meal was nothing to him. "Boy," he added, "First you break half your limbs and put me to all that bother of bracin' bones, now you have me sewin' like an old maid. You're nothin' if not a glutton for punishment."

That same night Flint went back to the bunkhouse and picked up his place on the shift system. The other men were a little awkward with him at first, because the news of what had happened had been relayed to them via various sources. But Flint acted as if nothing had happened. He gave the occasional grimace of pain, but let it pass without remark. One or two of the men attempted to sympathise with him to see what he would say about Gilbert, but he saw this for what it was and brushed off their attentions with a few light remarks.

He thought only of Catriona, wondering if she ever gave him any consideration, not knowing that she had probably saved him from being hanged.

Soon he was back on his horse, although the first time he went out, the healing wounds put him in so much pain that he had to dismount several times.

*****

In the meantime, at *High Wynd*, Isabella had some good news for her husband. They were having breakfast a week after Gilbert had sent Flint back to the plains.

"Husband, I have been sick in the mornings this last fortnight and this is the first day I have been able to face food."

"Then take some patent cure."

"Don't you don't understand? I am with your child."

Gilbert thought the matter over. He knew full well that Isabella had been involved with Flint, and the child might very well be his. She had obviously steeled herself to tell him the news, knowing he might react badly, but not knowing what else she could do.

Gilbert looked at his wife for a long time, his face stony, then he gave a delighted smile.

"I hope we're going to have a boy."

In his own mind he had chosen to believe that the child was his. After all, who was to say it wasn't? Later that morning Gilbert went off on business leaving behind a woman who was extremely relieved by his reaction.

When Isabella found out that her husband had been responsible for having Flint whipped until he was nearly dead, she was moved to tears. In her condition tears came easily anyway, but she felt driven to see Flint, despite the fact that she might very well put her new status with Gilbert in danger.

So it wasn't long before she was travelling to see her friends at *Eagle Cross* to tell them the good news that she was with child. She took with her Neela, and they used a light carriage. Two hands from the ranch rode guard with them, and they would be passing the outstation on the plains. Isabella waited until they were nearly there, and pleaded with her companion to stop.

"What is it ma'am?" asked Neela. Unlike Catriona, with whom she had grown up, Neela had to address the mistress of the ranch respectfully. Neela did not like Isabella, whom she regarded as selfish and capricious. This was a strange judgement for one who had grown up with Catriona, but the latter had a generosity of heart that cancelled out many of her other faults.

"I do not feel at all well, let us stop here for a while."

"It is not a place for you ma'am. Besides, I have here water and a herbal remedy that will help your symptoms."

"I do not want your plants! Just do as I ask!"

Neela did not argue, but rode into the encampment with her. This was a more like a small village than anything else, with a large bunkhouse, cookhouse, furrier's shed, a smithy, stables, storehouses and even tents where some of the men lived on their own. Isabella stepped off the carriage, assisted by her servant. Dressed as she was in finery, her skirts trailing on the earth, she looked around.

McQuade, came over to greet the unexpected visitors.

"How can I help you two ladies?" he asked.

"My mistress is not feeling well. This is Isabella, wife of Mr Shaw," said Neela.

"We've met," said Isabella, eyeing the big overseer.

"She's not feeling well and needs to lie down awhile," said Neela, "for she is with child."

"Why, that's a cause for celebration," said McQuade. "Well, it's not much, but you're mighty welcome to stay in my cabin 'til you feel better."

They went to his quarters where he hastily threw a clean sheet on the bed in the corner of his cabin, and Isabella elegantly sat.

"Thank you, that feels much better. I will wait here awhile."

"Is there anything I can get you to eat or drink?"

"No, thank you."

"Well, I'll be on ma way. And thank you for the good news ma'am." He turned towards the door.

"Wait, there is one thing. We used to have a young man work at High Wynd. His name was Joe Flint or something like that. Could you seek him out and bring him to me awhile?"

There was a silence more pregnant than she was. McQuade was far from stupid. He immediately knew what was going on. He also knew that this woman, whether she knew it or not, was putting Flint in mortal danger

"No, I'm afraid I can't do that."

"Why not? I am the wife of your employer, I can see who I want."

"Yes you can, but you'll have to wait two months for the privilege."

"What do you mean?"

"We've had a big exchange of steers with a ranch over in Randall County. They need some bulls for breeding, and I gave Flint the job of riding them over. Now, if you'll excuse me, I have work to do." McQuade was telling the truth in many respects, they had indeed sent cattle to The Lazy J, but with a different overseer. Isabella could not very well check with her husband to see if he had been telling the truth. His conscience was clear.

Inside the cabin Isabella got to her feet.

"Shouldn't you be resting?" asked Neela.

"I feel much better. Let's go." They walked to the carriage, aware now of the stares of those around them, the few women openly admiring her clothes. The escort, who had been waiting patiently, followed behind as the carriage rattled out over the ruts in the trail, and headed for *Eagle Cross*. Isabella lay back in her seat, tears in her eyes. He had moved on. She would never come here again.

Later on that evening Flint came in from a twelve-hour shift. McQuade accosted him as he came in through the gate and took him to a place where they could talk in private.

"Listen, that woman was here to see you."

"Catriona? But her brother – " Flint was aware of a sudden uplift in his mood despite his weariness.

McQuade shook his head. "No, Isabella, your boss's wife. Avoid that woman if you ever see her. She's trouble for you. She made some excuse about feeling sick so she could rest here. She's expecting. Have nothing to do with her."

Flint didn't have to be told more. He knew why she had come to see him, and he also knew that by lying so convincingly McQuade had literally saved his hide. If Gilbert knew that she was still trying to see him, then Gilbert would see to it that she never saw him again, because he would be lying in his grave.

Better he kept to this life. One day he would be free and that was all that mattered.

Chapter Eight

Rawley met with his father one fine morning to discuss Catriona.

"That girl! Despite all I try to do, she will not agree to a wedding date. Can I send her home?"

"I think you're right to say this," Old John sat with his hands together across his midriff, twiddling his thumbs together. "I sense that although she likes you, she'll more likely set a date if she was flung back into the company of her brother."

"He is an oaf of the first order," admitted Rawley. "But I do like the way he handled that Flint."

"Very well, I'll see she returns to her family. Besides, she has an interest in that Isabella now that her term comes close."

So it was that Catriona came back to *High Wynd*. Despite the fact that she was still far from comfortable with her brother, he was the only surviving blood relation she had. Besides she missed her horses, Neela and even Matthew Jacob. The old servant was there to greet her as she arrived, along with her brother and Neela.

Gilbert was smiling widely as he stepped forward.

"Welcome back little sis. That is the way it should be. You left as a young girl and now you are a fine woman." She was aware that he was right. Her former hosts were a family who knew many wealthy people. Rawley was outgoing and often took her on trips to some of the big cities where she had acquired some of the current fashions. The servants and even her brother were dressed in plain, homely clothes.

The one person she wanted to see was not there, but she knew better than to ask her brother where he was.

"Where's Isabella?"

"Oh, she's resting," said Gilbert. "She does a lot of that now that her time draws near. Come in and tell me the secrets of Old John and the tricks he's trying to pull on me."

The truth was, her brother was making an effort to be good company, and later after a good meal with him and Isabella, she felt herself mellowing towards him. Perhaps he was not such a bad person after all. She knew that he had sent Flint away, but perhaps that was understandable.

Gilbert retired to his study with a good cigar and a bottle of brandy. His inclination towards the bottle was now more pronounced than ever, and he readily abandoned his sister to Isabella.

At first Catriona attempted to converse with her regarding the child she was expecting.

"It's a boy," said Isabella.

"How can you know that?"

"I know many things," said the dark-haired girl enigmatically.

"Perhaps I should go out with Neela, leaving you in the peace you obviously want." She had meant to say the words lightly, but they seemed to have a sarcastic edge she did not want to give them.

"No, stay here. I want some intelligent company," said Isabella. In a way it was peaceful, but to Catriona it was a slow process of torture. She was a young woman who could barely keep still, who always needed to be busy. In the event she was glad she had decided to stay.

"You're thinking about him, aren't you?" Isabella asked.

"Who?"

"He was here and now he's gone." She ignored the query. "I thought I could see him. Get him to do - something - but that wasn't to be."

"I thought you could have had him here at the ranch," said Catriona, dropping all pretence. "I half expected him to be here beside Neela and Matthew."

Isabella seemed surprised. "You do not know about the trial?"

"Trial? What for?"

"The original charges were kidnap and attempted murder, but someone pointed out there was no kidnap, and you had Rawley drop the charge of attempted murder."

"Wait, you said there was a trial."

"In town, yes."

"But Rawley promised me he would drop the charges."

"Flint assaulted the son of a cattle baron, do you really think they were going to let him off with a pat on the head?"

"What was his sentence?"

"Not too bad really. Two years of indentured service without pay, to your brother."

"That's terrible!" Catriona was more aware of the injustice of this than Isabella, who had no idea that Flint was supposed to inherit a third of the ranch. He was now a slave to the man who had robbed him of his inheritance.

"You should know that your brother decided it was time to teach Flint a personal lesson."

"What do you mean?"

"A bullwhip's a terrible thing. Leaves scars, I expect..." Suddenly Isabella dissolved into tears, running from the room as fast as her condition would allow.

Catriona sat in the pool of light from the oillamp for a moment, but instead of following Isabella to her room she went to the servants quarters where she disturbed her old friend.

"Neela, what is this I hear about Flint?"

The Indian girl looked at her warily. "He has been sent away. That is all you need to know."

"Did my brother brutalise him?" Catriona was silent for a long time as she scanned the features of her former companion. "That bastard! Just when I was going to trust him again. I'm never going to talk to him or Rawley again."

Neela spoke up. "To be fair, this isn't Rawley's fault."

"What do you mean?"

"If you had gone your own way, you would have left Texas with Flint. Rawley was engaged to you, to him it looked like you were being abducted. Flint pointed a gun at him and pull the trigger. I think Rawley was very forgiving, in the circumstances. You were the hand that held him back."

Catriona had to admit that Neela spoke wisely, that the trial would have been much worse if the original charges had gone ahead.

"But why did my brother beat Flint? How bad was it?"

"He went to the outstation. They say he hovered between life and death for a long time."

"And all the time I was attending socials and concerts, enjoying myself while he was lying there." Her voice faded away. "I am a bad person."

"No you're not, you just didn't know."

"I must go, I must go to him right now."

"No, not now. It's too late and there's no moon tonight. It would be better if you visited him during the day."

Catriona started to leave. "You're right. But I will say this; I'm going to remain here at High Wynd until the situation with Flint is resolved once and for all."

Back in her bed her mind was full of dark thoughts that got darker as the night wore on and sleep escaped her troubled mind.

Chapter Nine

Neela was as good as her word. Even though she had been with Isabella months before, when the women had visited the camp, she had not believed a single word McQuade had said.

"He told Isabella that Flint was on the trail, taking steers to Randall County.

"Why couldn't that have happened?"

"Because Flint was still recovering from the whipping your brother gave him, and he wouldn't have had the strength to go out on the trail for months afterwards. McQuade might be a hard man, but he's not stupid."

"Then why didn't Isabella try and see him again?"

"She didn't have the opportunity. Now she can't do so, not without risking the child."

Neela had already prepared two horses ready to take them to the outstation, and Catriona left a note for her brother to let him know that they had gone out for an early ride. Gilbert knew she liked the countryside so this would allay his suspicions.

"I think Flint has recovered from his wounds," said Neela, "but you may find him a very different person."

"I don't care, I have to see him. As far as I'm concerned nothing has changed. If only I'd known."

"What could you have done?" Neela was forever philosophical.

The weather was overcast as they made their way to the plains, though Neela didn't think there was bad weather on the way.

"If he's out working I'll be able to tell," said Neela. "I know his horse, and I'll be able to tell how old the tracks are."

Soon Neela was looking at the ground with an expert eye. Catriona, who was not inexperienced either, noted that the herd had been moved to an area with fresh grass, to the south of the camp. By this time they had ridden nearly twenty miles. The cattle would not be much further on. To keep the stock fat for market the riders tended not to run them too much in one-day.

Eventually they came to the edge of the herd. It was near midday and some of the bulls were a little restless, patrolling around the edge of the herd and taking care of their perceived territory. They had also been feeding on fresh grass, which gave them increased energy. One bull took the new arrivals to be a danger. He was heavier than the two horses and riders combined, but took exception to them, snorting, and pawing at the ground.

The women had come upon him unexpectedly, riding over a bluff that had temporarily hidden the herd from view.

"I don't think that particular bull is happy," remarked Neela.

"I think we should get the hell out of here," said Catriona.

Usually she had good control of her horse, only this time she wasn't on her usual mare but a skittish thoroughbred. Instead of rearing up and fleeing, the mare turned in a circle, reared and fell over. Quickly she scrambled to her feet leaving her rider on the ground. Fortunately Catriona was unharmed but the fall had left her shaken. Dazed, she managed to stand, but was still the bull's target.

Then a loud whistle, and a shout of, "Hey, el torro!" A figure in dusty clothes, lariat in hand, rode his quarter-horse close to the animal. The bull responded with a sweep of his horns, still intent on attacking Catriona, and did not even feel the rope drop around its neck. The rider looped rope around his saddle's pommel, then turned his horse sideways so that the bull jerked to an abrupt halt, falling to his knees in the process. The bull got to his feet snorting with new-found anger, turned his massive head and went after the fresh enemy.

The rider led the bull on, feeling the pace slow as the bull became tired, finally letting him back into the herd where he could focus on his cows.

Catriona staggered to the other side of the bluff where her horse, now recovered, was quietly cropping some grass. The rider came back to see them, a red bandana around his nose and mouth.

His opening question was curt. "What the hell do you think you're doing, riding straight at the herd like that?"

"It's us," said Catriona, pulling off her hat.

Flint pulled down his bandana. Besides his leather jacket he wore long, sheepskin chaps and high boots. "You could have got yourselves killed,"

"Yes, but – "

He cut her off. "I thought you, of all people, would have known better! Unless you wanted to play the role of damsel in distress?! Hope that someone would come along and save you, is that it? A little diversion to alleviate your boredom?!"

There was the sound of hooves behind him as his Jason, Flint's watch partner, rode up behind him.

"Everything okay here? I saw you turn the bull back to the herd and wanted to make sure…"

He recognised Catriona, and behind her was Neela. He nodded politely. "Ma'm."

Burning with resentment Catriona said, "You can escort us to the outstation." She looked pointedly at Flint. "And you can go to Hell for all I care!"

What she didn't know was that when Flint's head settled on his pillow that night, his thoughts were of how he had spoken to her, knowing full well that he had done so only for her own protection.

Chapter Ten

McQuade was a cattle man through and through, but he was also a shrewd observer of human nature. This was the reason he'd sent for Flint as soon as the latter came back from his shift.

They met in McQuade's makeshift office – nothing more than a glorified shack – but good enough for his purposes. McQuade sat behind a desk laden with papers and Flint picked one of these up as he strolled in, studying it with great interest.

"Invoice for a couple of thousand from one of the cattle stations. They sure are hustling you for the price of keeping your herds safe."

McQuade was a little thrown off by the young man's easy assurance.

"Wait, where the hell did you learn your letters?"

"I was put with a missionary, a minister from the Lutheran church when they took me from my people. Pastor Williamson made sure I had a good schooling before I left to go on the trail when I was fifteen. Had a handy touch with a rod too, beat my letters and numbers into me with God's kindness, and a switch."

"Wish I'd known that sooner," said McQuade. "Hell, got a lot of good boys in the camp but most of them has to make their mark or at best learned to sign their name. I hate this blamed paper work. Anyways, there's a reason you're here. Heard you've been consortin' with the kind of people you ought to avoid."

"You could say that."

"Are you stupid? You could end up back in the hoosegow and I could be lookin' for a new rider just when the season's gettin' busy."

The young man flushed. He resented being spoken to as if he was an idiot, even though he knew the older man had his interests at heart.

"You can take that back McQuade, I ain't stupid. The situation was imposed on me."

"Maybe I should knock some sense into that brain of yours." McQuade stood and came around to the front of his desk.

Flint held his ground. "You could try."

By this time McQuade's good sense evaporated as his temper boiled over and he hit out at the younger man, landing a good-sized blow on the side of his face.

Flint had put up with a great deal. He had been a free man with a space of his own, he had been treated as a son of the Shaw family. What's more he once had money in his pocket and friendships that he valued, albeit with the daughter of the ranch. Now all that had been taken from him and he was being punished because he'd shown some sense and given that very person some good advice.

In the past he might have accepted the blow for what it was, a show of dominance by the older man. Instead he pulled back and stared in the face of his overseer and McQuade felt uneasy by Flint's fathomless eyes and the set expression on his tanned face.

"Looks like you've decided to go down the insolent route," said McQuade, attempting to land another blow. Instead his fist met with empty air. They were in the middle of the building by now, with a reasonable amount of floor space between them. Flint had just finished a twelve-hour shift, but he found that the adrenalin in his blood had given his a rush of energy just when it was needed most. He knew he was puny compared with his foreman, who was eighty pounds heavier and about six inches taller. What McQuade did not have was the ability to move out of the way at a speed that seemed almost supernatural. The foreman hit out again, lumbering around to meet his target, but Flint ducked under his arms and landed a flurry of blows on McQuade's stomach with his clenched fists before pulling away again.

McQuade roared, turning on his heel towards Flint, who had gone to his side. As the older man spun, Flint put out a leg to catch him off guard and McQuade sprawled face down on the dusty floor. The older man gave a growl and began to push up with his hands, but Flint kicked his right hand away from under him then hit him hard on the back of the neck with both hands clasped together in a hammer blow. McQuade gave a loud groan and lay still for a few minutes.

When McQuade finally came to, Flint was there to help him to his feet. The older man sat down groggily behind his desk.

"Hell of a thing, when did you learn to fight like that?"

"I was brought up by people who knew how to use the strength of their opponents against them,"

McQuade still rubbed the back of his neck. "You sure knew how to do that."

Flint went over and leaned against the doorframe. "Now, if you let me finish, I'll explain what happened."

He told McQuade about Catriona and Neela coming up on the blind side of the herd, and about how he had roped a bull away from attacking them, before arguing with Cartiona, and Jason bringing them to the outstation site.

"So I won't be leaving here until my sentence is done," he ended. McQuade looked down at his desk for a long time. When he looked back up there was darkness in his eyes.

"I suppose you're thinkin' of doing some boasting on Saturday night about how you bust the chops of a bigger man?"

"Not me," said Flint.

"Why not?" McQuade looked at him in surprise. "You've had everything taken from you. You could get free drinks for a month on a tale like that. Especially if you embellished the story. I know I would."

"It is not my way. I want to do my time here, earn some money again. Maybe think about leaving, but that's in the future."

McQuade looked at the pile of documents on his desk. Inwardly he groaned. He was good at his job, but he hated paperwork.

"Say I was to bring you in here, reckon you could deal with this kind of dross?"

"You show me what to do, I guess so."

"Tell you what," The big man lumbered to his feet. "You help me sort this out, and I'll get you some extra money, liquor and maybe sort you out with one of the local girls. I'll give you a month at it to see how you are, and the rest of what happened stays between us." He stuck out a meaty hand. "Deal?"

"Deal," said Flint, shaking it. He still missed Catriona, but his day had suddenly become a lot better.

*****

He had been quick enough in the saddle, but he was surprised when he discovered he also had a gift for paperwork. His eyesight was keen, he was good at numbers - better than his trainer in fact - and his handwriting was neat and legible. What he did not know was that McQuade had been testing him. The older man had once worked for William Shaw, as far as he was concerned Flint was a far better potential son than Gilbert had ever been. The only thing that had worried him was the fact that Flint appeared to be taking his situation lying down. Now McQuade knew that the young man was made of harder stuff and was doing what had to be done until he could get away from this job for good.

Flint worked just as tirelessly for his boss inside as he had outside. He learned quickly about all the regulations involving the transfer of cattle from one state to another. Orders that had been imposed on him when he was a trail rider now made some kind of sense. He learned that Kansas did not like Texan cattle coming through their country because the local cows were not immune to the diseases carried by the ticks from those outside their borders. Cattle could also carry yellow fever. This was why the trips to the railheads sometimes took so long and involved crossing so many rivers.

Flint was assigned space in part of the tack cabin. Items of all kinds lay heaped up in the corners, including saddles, ropes and other spare equipment, while there was a large walk-in cupboard that contained junk that had accumulated over the years. McQuade had always meant to get round to this, because it would've provided storage space for all the documents that McQuade had never found the time to check and file away.

After several weeks, when Flint was finally on his own, he decided he would tackle the task of totally reorganising the cabin office. Once that had been completed, he could use the shelving within the cupboard for the documents.

He'd settled down to start tackling the piles of paperwork when he heard two familiar voices at the step. They belonged to Rawley Henderson and Old John, the last two people with whom he wanted to communicate.

Their presence in the camp was no surprise because they often combined herds with *High Wynd* during one of the two cattle driving seasons. Flint had always been away for work and had managed to avoid them so far, but at this second he could not trust what he might say to them.

It was not that he hated Rawley, he regarded the other man the same way you might look on a deadly rattlesnake. You never knew when it might strike and use its venom.

Old John was not someone he was much acquainted with, except for his trial, with the old man as the presiding judge. But Catriona had always spoken well of him.

From behind the cabin door he heard John shout: "McQuade! Where are you, you old dog?"

Flint hastily pulled the cupboard doors towards him from the inside. To his mind this wasn't cowardice but strategy. He would simply wait until the pair left.

"No-one here," said Rawley. Flint could hear the door open and the scratch of their boots as they trod across the floor.

"Place is getting ever more crowded," said Old John. To Flint's disappointment he heard a groan as the old man deposited his ample frame on the chair behind the desk. It looked as though they were going to wait for a while, and Flint knew he couldn't crouch in the darkness forever. Seconds later he was glad that they had waited.

"So you've managed to persuade that girl to have her fancy ball?"

"Catriona loves parties," said Rawley. "It's one of the things we have in common."

"Being married, that's the thing. Any sign of that happening yet?"

"Your suggestion that she should go back to her brother was just about the best thing that could've happened. She's ready to agree to a spring wedding.

We'll make the announcement at the dance tomorrow night."

"She's told you this direct to your face?"

"Yep. I was up seeing her a month or so ago. She seemed in a low mood at the time and agreed with me. Her brother has sapped some of her spirit, I think."

The previous month was when she had visited Flint only to be rejected. No wonder her spirits were low.

"Well thank the Lord this is nearly finished. We've waited a long time to get the girl into our family."

"Father, don't talk about the woman I love in that way," Rawley's words should have been a warning, but they were spoken in a light, amused manner that made the hairs rise in the back of Flint's neck.

"She may be that, but she's a lot more son. The prize is worth the taking. Once the ring's on her finger you'll own everything she owns."

"Which is nothing."

"Well we all know that's going to change pretty quickly. Won't be too much of an effort to take out Gibby when he's in town playin' cards and whoring. It just takes us to set up one disagreement, he gets a bullet through the heart an' the ranch is yours."

"What about his wife? Surely she'll inherit."

"For as long as she survives."

"You know I'm genuinely fond of Catriona?"

"All the better for you both when you become the patron of High Wynd."

Flint felt nothing but anger at the disclosure. He wanted to burst out and throttle them both. Then he heard heavy footsteps enter the cabin.

"Mister Henderson, Rawley. How you doin'?" McQuade sounded surprised to see the two men.

Old John tried to get out of the chair, but decided to sit back and maintain his dignity. "Just came to discuss the team you're sendin' out and the money arrangements."

"Sure thing. Did you meet anybody in here?"

"No, should we have?"

"Place is a mess," said Rawley.

"He must've been clearing it out," said McQuade to himself.

"Who?"

"Doesn't matter."

Flint detected a note of relief in McQuade's voice. He probably thought that Flint had somehow learned they were arriving, and had made himself scarce.

McQuade changed the subject. "I guess you're here to take a look at the cattle? They're all fine and dandy. Why don't you two come on out and see for yourselves?"

McQuade had taken care not to tell the two Hendersons about the promotion of Flint to his second-in-command. He had a shrewd feeling they might well communicate the matter to Gilbert, sending Flint back to herding.

Flint kept well out of the way until he observed the pair riding off. His first impulse was to leave right away and warn Catriona, but he had a feeling that she might well be making the arrangements for the ball out at the Henderson's.

If he took his horse and followed in the two women's tracks he would be placing them in a dangerous situation. Yet if he went to Gilbert there was a chance that Flint would be restrained or even killed for his insolence.

He had to get them in a position where he could warn Catriona about what they were going to do to her. He returned to the cabin only to be met by McQuade.

"Where the hell have you been?"

"Keeping away from those who might not approve of your new accountant out here."

"All right." McQuade said nothing more, a sure sign of approval. "Just make sure you get those lading bills done tonight."

"Sure will," Flint set to work, but in his mind a plan slowly took shape. What he was going to do was audacious, but if it worked would make sure that *High Wynd* was safe from the clutches of Old John and his avaricious son.

Chapter Eleven

Flint made careful preparations for his trip. He made sure that he was well shaved, thoroughly washed and dressed. He'd managed to get a white linen shirt, black string tie, dark waistcoat and good black trousers from a travelling salesman doing the Country circuit.

There was also a gun holstered at his hip, a single action Colt .44. He'd found the old Civil War piece stowed away in the office. As he strapped it on he knew that he was about to break every stricture placed on him. If he could save Catriona then the sacrifice would be worthwhile.

As he went to the livery to fetch his horse he realised he was also betraying a trust. That couldn't be helped. He was dealing with something far greater than the unjust sentence meted out to him by Old John.

*****

Dusk had already fallen when he arrived at the *Eagle Cross* ranch where most of the invited guests were already at the dance. The place was lit by a hundred lanterns, with the sound of laughter and music from within. He tied his horse outside to a hitching post then boldly stepped into the barn.

He didn't feel all that bold inside, but his success depended on looking supremely confident. Most there didn't know who he was, although one or two young ladies regarded him with interest. Looking around he found Gilbert standing at the bar. He was surrounded by a group of those who wanted to keep in with a rich and powerful man.

"Evening Mr Shaw," said Flint, tipping his hat. "How goes it?"

For a second a look of confusion spread across Gilbert's face. This was the very man he had whipped only a few months before, yet the intruder had the audacity to come here on this night of all nights.

"I need to talk," said Flint, "right now. It's to do with your sister."

"Speak to me here," said Gilbert

"You'll want to know this in private, believe me. Come outside."

"How do I know you won't shoot me?"

"After what you did nothing would give me greater pleasure." Flint slid the .44 out of its holster and put it on the bar. "There, now will you talk?"

Gilbert was tempted to tell the young man to go to hell, but he was also filled with curiosity about why someone in his position would risk everything for this kind of confrontation. Flint had already noted that Catriona, Rawley and Old John were making a fashionably late appearance at their own ball, so he didn't have much time.

"Okay, let's talk." They went out into the night air, with two of Gilbert's men following close at hand.

"I have no liking of you," said Flint in a low voice. "That's a given. But I feel bound to tell you, I've heard that you're going to die, and quite soon."

"Die? What are you talking about you idiot?"

"Listen, I don't have much time. I know what plans Old John has for you. I heard him talk about them to that fop of a son of his. The bottom line is, Old John wants you dead. If you're dead, in law, your sister will inherit the ranch, but everything she inherits belongs to her husband."

Gilbert looked doubtful. "These are the ravings of a sick mind. I have a wife, and there is a child on the way. For some reason she's convinced it will be a boy. They will inherit everything should I pass away."

"Do you think a woman and a small child will get in their way? Isabella will have an 'accident' that kills her and the baby. I can guarantee that as sure as the Lone Star is on the state flag."

"Why should I believe you? What if you came here just to cause trouble?"

"Perhaps I did, but I'm not thinking of you. I'm here because of Catriona and Isabella, and you know why."

Doubt was replaced by thoughtfulness. "Go back in there, get your useless gun and go."

"But their plans for you – "

"Get your weapon and go." Gilbert's voice was a low determined growl, which made Flint decide that enough had been said. He went back to the bar, took his weapon, and began to walk out of the barn.

But Fate, being what it is, he saw approaching the very people he'd had been discussing.

Catriona, looking very pretty, walked in accompanied by Rawley. Old John, accompanied by his diminutive wife, followed them.

Flint was immediately worried that Gilbert would accost them there and then, causing Catriona to be hurt in some way, but Gilbert held back. It was common knowledge that Gilbert was a man who held his grudges within, and it seemed this was another he had decided to hold until the time was right.

The minute Catriona saw Flint her face lit up and she gave a cry of recognition, soon turning to confusion. Flint played it calm and tipped his hat to her.

Rawley scowled, a look of thunder on his face as he stepped forward. "What the hell are you doing here?"

While he was speaking Old John turned and had a quiet word with the men who were there, barring the entrance to the improvised dance hall.

"Just thought I would come and congratulate you and Catriona on your impending wedding." Flint tipped his hat again to Catriona. "Congratulations ma'am."

"Oh Flint, you shouldn't have come here." But she smiled nonetheless.

"Take him away," said Rawley, nodding to his men.

Henderson's men surrounded him now. With over a hundred guests at the ball, some of them prominent citizens, it was too risky for them to shoot, but he knew he would be pinned down by sheer force of numbers.

Flint was used to dealing with herds. He sometimes had to weave on foot between their dancing legs where one fall would mean a crushing end. He decided to treat the human throng rather like his cattle. He would use them to confuse each other. He bent down, ducking beneath the encircling arms, and dived into the crowd between the legs of the spectators. From being a clear target he was now surrounded by other people. Moreover they too were confused, turning to see who was in their midst. He took advantage of that confusion by weaving amongst them again, but this time in a different direction. This had changed the game once more, as the Henderson hands had to shoulder their way through the people present to get to him.

He was now approaching the back of the barn where he saw that the ladder for the loft was still fixed to the ground beside spare barrels of beer and bales of hay used for those who couldn't find a seat. He was thankful, because it would be his only means of escape. However as a diversion he dived once more, but in the opposite direction to the one he wanted to take.

To add to the confusion, someone shouted 'There he is!' He waited for the men to go in that direction, then moved forward rapidly and began to climb the ladder.

He was almost at the top when he heard someone call out: "Stop or I'll shoot!"

Flint risked a glance back and saw that Rawley had pulled a chrome Remington derringer from his jacket pocket and was aiming it at him. Rawley tried to line up the weapon with his target, then fired off a shot. Flint had already turned his back, scrabbling to get through the hole into the loft, heard the roar of the weapon and saw in his mind his own body falling to the ground below.

But it didn't happen. At the last second Catriona gave a moan of distress and fell against Rawley, giving his arm a forceful push that set him completely off target, before fainting clean away at his feet. Flint felt the bullet whistle past his head, lodging in the wood above. One very close call.

A quick, cautious glance back through the loft hatch, and Flint saw that Rawley was helping Catriona to her feet.

Flint crouched in the relative darkness of the loft, giving his eyes a few seconds to adjust to the light coming up through the floorboards. It was enough for him to see where the loft loading doors were located, and that they were securely shut.

He dragged out the wooden beam that held them shut, pushed them open, and was pleased to see the block and tackle still in place, with a long length of rope for lowering the feed to the hay cart. He pulled this over, clasped the rope with both hands, and made a rapid descent to the ground.

Half a minute later Flint found his horse still tied to the rail, unhitched it, and was away just as two of Henderson's men came out and mounted their horses.

But Flint was used to riding at night. He kept low in his saddle and let his horse take off, and with his head start he was soon swallowed up by the night.

The other two were good at their job, and one of them drew his gun and tried to hit the shadowy horse and rider. In daylight it would have been a hard shot, in the semi-darkness without the light from the barn, it was almost impossible. Flint to felt the shot go over his head, and realised it could have hit and killed him by chance. Still it wasn't long before the two pursuers fell back, and Flint had a chance to slow and take some control of his horse again.

For a while, as Flint rode with no particular destination, the question kept going through his mind. It was simple enough.

What was he going to do now?

It was impossible for him to go back to his old job because he was now a wanted man. He could only hope that Gilbert had heeded his warnings and that the owner of *High Wynd* would look after himself.

Those thoughts struck a chord in him. He knew the area around that ranch perhaps better than anyone except Catriona. He could easily hide in the hills there and sleep in outlying buildings, hunting for his own food.

Flint urged his horse in the right direction. There was plenty of horse feed between here and the hills, and once he was a few more safer miles away he could rest.

Yet he had to return and fetch the necessities of life. That would be a risky business. If he was caught he'd be imprisoned, since both Gilbert's and Henderson's men would not want to risk the wrath of their respective bosses.

His one regret was that he had not said goodbye to Catriona. This was made all the more painful by the fact that she had almost certainly saved his life when he was on that ladder.

*****

Back at the barn, Old John remained as seemingly affable as ever and in charge of the proceedings.

"Well folks, that was a mighty fine display we had here tonight, but let's not forget what this evening is really all about. Let's eat, drink and dance!" This homily drew forth laughter and applause and the crowd were more than happy to comply – though the attack was the chief source of conversation.

"Don't worry," said Old John, putting a friendly arm around Giblet's shoulder. "We'll soon find the devil and have him put on trial. Either that or we'll just shoot him down."

"No," said Gilbert, "you won't."

"What?"

"You'll leave him alone."

"Rawley, come here." Old John called over his son. "How is your fiancée?"

"Catriona's fine. She's with a bunch of ladies over in the corner, all talking about how handsome the intruder was."

"Gilbert wants a word with you."

"I merely said, don't bother hunting Flint."

"What? It's obvious he came here to cause trouble for the sake of it. He needs to die."

"You harm Flint in any way and you'll never marry Catriona," said Gilbert. "She'll never forgive you."

The calculation showed for a second in Rawley's eyes.

"I never thought of that," he admitted. "Very well, I'll assure her that he will not be harmed, but privately we know, all sorts of accidents can happen to a person that can never be shown to be our fault, eh Gibby?"

"That's so," said Gilbert, he was a little drunk, but not as much as might have been thought. His willingness to let the marriage go ahead to a man who had, according to Flint, expressed a desire to have him killed, might have seemed stupid, even suicidal on his part. But forewarned is forearmed – and from what he'd seen, there was little doubt that what Flint had told him was true.

Now that he knew he was some kind of target Gilbert had decided that he would be very careful indeed. When his child was born he would confine his drinking to the ranch and become a model husband.

And it was a double-edged sword. When Rawley married Catriona, should *her* husband die unexpectedly, ideally just after Old John had passed, then Gilbert would inherit *Eagle Cross*. Now that truly was a prize well worth having.

As for Flint, Gilbert felt an emotion towards him he never thought he would have. He was grateful for what the young man had done. Let him have his limited freedom. He did not matter anymore.

Chapter Twelve

In the depths of *High Wynd* could be heard the sound of a child crying. A female voice tried to soothe the child but he could not be placated and sobbed his heart out. The soothing voice was not that of Isabella, but Neela, now maturing into a comely young woman.

There was a good reason why his mother was not looking after the as yet un-christened boy. Tragedy and joy have a way of striking together as was the case with the baby, and his mother.

"Rockabye baby," sang Neela to the child until he feel asleep at last, soothed by the words sung in a language he did not yet understand.

After the night in which he had learned of his proposed fate at the hands of the Henderson family, Gilbert had returned to *High Wynd* and was greeted by Isabella. She had not gone to the event because it would have meant a long trip and she was now too far advanced in her pregnancy to be able to go that distance and back. Neela had stayed with her to act as her nurse.

On seeing him, she asked, "What happened?"

She had never been a robust woman and now looked pale and worried, though Gilbert believed it was mostly by her own thoughts.

"I'll tell you an amusing story. You remember Flint?"

Isabella nodded.

"He turned up at the Henderson's ranch. He said a lot of nonsense to me – " Gilbert did not want to burden her with an uncomfortable truth "Then he made quite a spectacular exit from the proceedings. Only one shot was fired, and not by him, which was the miracle of the thing." If he expected his young wife to be amused he was wrong. She sat up towards him.

"Flint! Did they harm him, is he hurt?"

"Damn him, he was fine the last time I saw him, although he deserved to have been shot dead for his cheek."

"Thank God he's all right," Isabella sank back down on her soft pillows.

That same night, when Gilbert was still sleeping, she had gone into labour. Neela, who had been with her all this time, woke up and tended to the distressed woman.

The baby boy was born without too much trouble, but afterwards Isabella seemed to be a broken woman. Within two days she developed post-partum fever. Neela tried her best with various concoctions made from herbs, but it was as if Isabella had no fight left.

On the fourth day she slipped into a deep sleep from which she never awoke.

*****

After Dr Etheridge had ridden out and signed the death certificate, Gilbert had some of his men dig the grave, and he buried Isabella alongside his mother and father, a simple wooden cross marking where she lay until he could get a memorial stone made in town.

The only other person present at the funeral, besides Thomas Kederline, the minister, was Neela, who kept the well-wrapped baby close to her body in case he, too, succumbed to some childhood illness.

They were not to know that a pair of keen eyes watched the burial from the shelter of a hill, close enough to see everything, but far enough away to remain completely unobserved.

When he returned home Gilbert immediately refused to have anything to do with the child who, despite Reverend Kederline's protestations, had still to be named and christened. Instead, the duty of caring for the child fell to Neela. She did not object to the imposition because in the event of Isabella having lived, Neela would have expected to become a more or less full-time nursemaid for the boy anyway.

In the meantime Gilbert retreated to his study with his favourite whisky, McQuade could deal with all the paperwork. Gilbert wanted to retreat from life and live inside the bottle.

Neela had a peculiar dread strong drink, possibly because of what she had seen alcohol do to her own people. She tried to reason with Gilbert, both face-to-face and then through the doors that increasingly closed on her. Of all the people he had known when he was growing up she had been one of the few to whom he would listen but now he treated her with a maddening indifference. Nothing mattered to him now, not even his own son.

Neela decided that time was the only course of action they could take, while she looked after the child. This was all very well, but Gilbert had sent everyone away from High Wynd in his grief, wanting to be as isolated as possible. In sealing them here like this she sensed that he had placed the three of them in some kind of terrible danger, but what was worse, he didn't seem to care, even seemed to desire the inevitable ending. Neela moved the child to the second floor of the house where she carried out most of her duties, hoping above all that her instincts were wrong.

*****

Unknown to her *High Wynd* had a formidable guardian in the form of Joe Flint. After his strategic retreat, Flint took to the woods he loved so dearly. He was not a thing of properties and enclosures, instead he needed the hills and valleys of the wild country around him. The days when he felt most free in the employ of William Shaw had been when he'd led the two women on the trail through the hill country, learning about where he was in ways not always obvious to some who had lived there the whole of their lives.

He had managed to keep hold of his Colt .44, and everything he needed for survival in the wilds. He would also sneak into the camp, avoiding attention.

Coggins had woken up one time to find Flint getting ready to go. The old man had not said anything to reproach Flint at all. They had tried to keep a wild animal indoors, so that animal had to finally leave or die, and he had made the sensible choice.

Coggins slipped him some food supplies and a Winchester rifle that was his own, along with a plentiful supply of ammunition.

"You deserve it," he said.

Flint realised that he was a symbol of freedom for some, they knew the injustices that had been done to him, would not blame him for escaping when he could.

"Tell McQuade I was thinking of him," he said before departing.

"That I will. Now head out before they comes to get ya."

In the early light of dawn Flint found the very place he was looking for. In the valley near *High Wynd*, was the cave of treasures that Catriona had shown him. He still had on his wrist the talisman she had made for him, with stones from this very place. Inside he laid down some moss and thick grass. With his bedroll on top, lush plant life shielding the entrance, he had a place to live and hide. He horse sheltered amidst a nearby clump of trees where there was plenty of grass for cropping. Then he slept soundly, safe in the knowledge that he was securely hidden from the world.

For the next few days he trapped and stored food for the days ahead, smoking the meat on a low fire that he promptly extinguished before leaving to hunt.

Then he started going back to *High Wynd*. He noted that the workhands were heading away. As far as he could see this left only Matthew Jacob, Gilbert and Neela. Why this should be happening he had no inkling, until on the fourth day he saw the funeral being held, immediately understanding that Gilbert wanted to shut the place off from the world.

He also noted Catriona was not at the funeral. She would have been there if she had known. This meant Catriona was still at *Eagle Cross* with Rawley.

Seeing the burial gave Flint a peculiar sensation. He'd not known Isabella well enough to really grieve over her passing, but just the same she had given him her love – no, it was lust really – giving him a fresh view on the world and women. The sight of her child, wriggling in the arms of his nursemaid gave him a peculiar sensation he could not identify.

He had been planning to go to Catriona at *Eagle Cross* after scouting the area. Once there he would ask her to make her choice. Stay, or leave with him and, if she chose to leave then they would bear all their hardships together.

Flint came back to the cave every day, now armed with gun and rifle.

He was waiting.

*****

The meeting between Old John and Rawley was not a comfortable one. John was in prophet mode, eyes blazing, beard waggling as they met in the ranch, safe in the knowledge that Catriona had gone out for her daily horse ride.

"I've heard the news, his wife is dead." said Old John.

"Who told you?"

"One of the men who left High Wynd in the last few days."

"Does Catriona know yet?" asked Rawley.

"I don't think so."

"Then she'll have to be told."

"She'll be furious her brother didn't let her attend. She'll insist that she goes back to pay her respects to Isabella. So we don't have much time."

"Time for what?" A terrible suspicion grew in Rawley.

"You have to kidnap and kill that child."

"I can't do that!" Rawley shrunk away from his father.

"When that child is out of our way we'll have a clear path to ownership."

"I want nothing to do with this."

"You will instruct three men you trust to do the job. I have already been informed that Gilbert has rejected his own son. They will head out, take the child, and leave a ransom note demanding money. That way it will look like a simple kidnap. The child will be found nearby, a day later, his brains dashed out. Then it will look as though the kidnappers quarrelled and killed him."

*****

Early in the morning Neela was downstairs feeding the baby. There was no denying he was turning out to be a big, robust lad. The larder was well stocked preserved meats, but she knew that the child had to eat greens too.

Keeping him close was easy, she wrapped him up as a papoose in a carrier on her back. She wasn't going to leave him alone in the same house as his deranged father. She knew Gilbert was insensible upstairs, but when he was roused he would be subject to fits of violent rage.

There was a pounding at the door, which surprised her. They rarely received visitors now, but hope rose in her that this would be Catriona, returning from the Henderson's out at *Eagle Cross*. Then she heard Matthew Jacob say:

"What do you fellas want?" Then she heard him cry out as he was summarily clubbed to the ground.

She knew better than to see what was going on. She simply gathered up the child and ran out the back way as three masked, black clad shapes, pushed into the main house hallway.

She screamed, trying to rouse Gilbert from upstairs, but the three men caught up with her and ripped the child from her arms, "Help! Mr Shaw, they're kidnapping your son!"

"Ain't no-one here except us." One of them pushed her to the ground and began to force her legs open while she desperately clawed at him. He was vastly superior in strength, but the leader pushed the man off her.

"No time fer that, come on."

The man grumbled that a few minutes wouldn't have made any difference, but he followed the other two as they ran off bearing the child, heedless of his high- pitched wails. Moments later there was the sound of galloping hooves.

Neela got up and went to where Matthew Jacob was lying. The old man had been hit pretty hard, though it seemed to be only one blow, which probably saved his life because he would have fought them to the end.

There, pinned on the door with a hunting knife was a roughly written note.

"We have the kid. Ransom to 10,000 dollars needing paid. We will tell you where and when."

Below this note was the imprint of a human hand done in red, whether dye or the blood of an animal it was hard to tell.

Neela freed the knife and took the note, then helped the dazed old man to his feet. She got him to sit down, then from the kitchen she brought a cold wet towel and got him to hold it against his forehead.

With the old man recovering, she went upstairs bearing the note to Gilbert, trembling at the thought of telling him what had happened to his son and heir.

*****

Up in the hills Flint did not see the start of the kidnap as he'd slept a little later that day. It was a delay he had reason to regret. As he rode towards *High Wynd* he heard Neela crying for help.

He quickly got off his mount and flattened himself on the brow of the hill, looking down at the ranch. He had a clear view as the men came running out of the main house clutching the wrapped and crying child. One of the men swung it over his shoulder like a quiver held in place with a strap.

Flint did not wait, he ran and remounted his horse, knowing that even a second's delay could mean the failure of his mission.

He followed the three of them fairly easily by the trail of dust and the sound of their horses pounding against the rocky soil of the hill country.

He had been practicing with his Colt during the long evenings, and now had much better accuracy on the draw – though he scarcely used any of his precious store of bullets.

In the leather sheath attached to his saddle was the Winchester Coggins had given him, not the easiest of weapons to use while riding but one that would have a devastating effect when used well. Also with him, attached by a sling over the pommel, was a weapon he had not used since he was a young boy. A kind of insurance against hand-to-hand fighting.

It wasn't long before Flint caught up with them at the mouth of the long valley where he had raced against Rawley what seemed like a lifetime ago. They were strung out in a row, the man on the left had the child across his back, secured in Neela's papoose carrier.

Flint reached into his boot and pulled out his hunting knife. He spurred his horse forward and caught up with the three before they even knew they had a pursuer.

Holding the knife in one hand, and steered only with his legs, he leaned over to one side and made two upward slashes at the outer rider. The man gave a great cry of surprise and fear, but he was not the target. With the two leather straps holding the doeskin pouch to the wooden frame now cut, Flint discarded the knife and grabbed the falling baby with both hands. Then, holding the child with one hand, he grabbed his reins with the other and spurred his mount forward.

He rode fast and well, rapidly losing the other three due to his intimate knowledge of the place he had chosen to live.

Five miles into the hills he hid the child in the shrubs safe in the shadow of a Texas oak that grew against the wall of the valley. Then he heeled his horse around, and went back down in pursuit of the three men.

This might have been a fatal mistake, but forewarned was forearmed, and Flint wasn't expecting it to be easy.

As he approached, all three started to shoot, but a speedy, moving target is notoriously hard to hit.

He rode low and fast, screaming at them in an unnerving manner, a wild man of the hills – a trick he knew would confuse and panic their horses.

Dodging returning fire, he swung wide, and fired the old Civil War Colt, watching as the rider slumped forward and his horse veer off, wide eyed and panicked.

Turning further around in his saddle, he got a clear shot off at the second rider, watching as the rider fell forwards then dropped from the horse, foot catching in the stirrup. With the body dragging alongside it, the horse slowed to an eventual stop.

Flint's own horse gave a snort of fear as the valley wall loomed upon them, then clattered to a sudden stop, almost throwing Flint, who had been busy looking back.

Flint heard the clatter of his Colt as it fell out of his hand and into a mass of rocks and dirt, and the thunder of hooves, as the third rider charged at him, gun in hand.

There was only one thing to do. Flint dismounted, snatched the Winchester from the saddle holster, cocked it then bent down on one knee.

He fired straight at the horse, hitting it between the eyes, all the while cursing that he had to shoot the animal to save his own life.

The horse threw its rider in its dying throes, but he was quick to get back on his feet. Flint pulled the trigger again, but the Winchester gave an empty click. Flint swiftly threw the weapon away and snatched his final line of defence from the side of the saddle.

The last rider drew a bead on Flint, who dived forward just as he fired, and Flint heard the bullet zing close to his head.

Rolling forwards, Flint was back on his feet, and barrelling into the shooter, knocking both of them onto the dirt. With a wild whoop Flint brought down the stone axe hard, splitting open the head of the man who had tried to kill him.

With the dead body beneath him, Flint pulled back, panting, bathed in dust and sweat, his axe dripping with blood, and surveyed the terrain around him.

All three were dead.

He cursed this, because he wanted to get a confession out of any of them in order to try and understand why they'd attempted the kidnapping.

He cleaned off the axe, gathered up his Colt, then mounted and headed back up into the hills to fetch the child from his hiding place.

When Flint gathered him back up, he looked into the child's dark brown eyes and felt they already held a wisdom beyond his age.

Putting the baby where he could see him, Flint went over to the men, one by one, to see if he could recognise them.

From the back of his memory he was able to put names to the now dead men.

Pete Tyler, Jake Burns and Ade Watkins. All three were Henderson's men. No use confronting Old John, Flint knew, because that patriarch would deny any knowledge of what had being on, would declaim loudly to all and sundry that 'the devil' must have got into his men and that they were after easy pickings.

He picked up the baby, turned his horse towards the ranch, and rode back to *High Wynd*. He met Neela on the way, a terrible look on her face. She was on her pinto, a robust little animal, intent on getting help from the men

Gilbert had sent away. When she saw Flint she dismounted and came to his side.

"Is it some kind of miracle?" She asked as he handed over the unharmed child.

"If it is, it's written in blood across that nearby valley," said Flint grimly.

"Come back with me, speak to Gilbert, he will forgive everything when he learns of this. When he learned his child was gone he realised how stupid he'd been to leave us defenceless. Yet he sent me to ride out and bring back some men from the outstation."

"Forgiveness does not count when no crime has been committed," said Flint. "I may come back when Catriona returns. Have Gilbert proclaim this kidnap to all and sundry so that word reaches the Henderson's. Have your men return to take care of the ranch. Hopefully Gilbert will take charge now. Goodbye

"Wait," said Neela. He turned back.

"What?" To his astonishment she kissed him fully on the mouth with her soft, expressive lips.

"Thank you, for saving us all." Neela left with the baby.

As a 'thank you' it wasn't the worst in the world.

His job with her was not finished, he trailed her home without her seeing what he was doing, and watched as she left the child in the charge of Matthew Jacob, who seemed to have recovered most of his hardened exterior.

Once this was done, Flint returned to the valley.

The two horses had wandered off, and they were of no real interest to him – more a hindrance than a help. He stripped the bodies of guns and ammunition, the dead horse of its saddle and provisions, then he roped and dragged the three riders to the edge of a near-by ravine and pushed each one over the edge. The vultures could have the dead horse, and the drag marks would show any tracker worth their salt as to where the bodies were.

Yet it gave him no satisfaction in the knowledge that he'd thwarted the attempted kidnapping. He felt it was only just the start.

Chapter Thirteen

Catriona was in the most comfortable circumstances of her life. *Eagle Cross* was a sprawling place that housed an extended family, where uncles, cousins, nieces and nephews all lived and worked for the Henderson Empire. She not only had plenty of company, Henderson was not averse to spending his wealth and Rawley splashed a great deal of money on clothes and jewellery.

She also ate the best of food, regularly enjoying choice cuts of meat, fresh vegetables and exotic fruits brought from south of the border.

She should have been happy and content, but something in her rebelled against the comforts. When she was with Rawley they seemed forever on the verge of arguing. It was as if she felt she had to find fault with him, no matter what or how slight.

Then she heard from one of the servants a piece of gossip she was not supposed to know.

Rawley was getting ready for work at the stables near the large paddock when she confronted him.

"Rawley, I need to see you about Isabella."

"What about her?" His smooth face betrayed no emotion.

"One of the servant girls, I heard her telling the cook that Isabella is *dead*." She looked steadily at him as she waited for an answer. "Well?"

"I was going to tell you…"

He hardly had the words out before she began to walk away, her face contorted in fury. He strode after her and grabbed her by the shoulder.

She turned around, her eyes blazing.

Rawley was taken aback by her anger and tried to soothe her. "Wait, I only knew a few hours ago. I was just waiting for the right time." His words sounded lame even to his own ears, and Catriona knew it for the lie it obviously was.

"Get my horse ready."

"Catriona."

"If you won't do it, then I'll find another stable hand to do it. I said get my horse ready, I have a motherless nephew and a mourning brother who await me."

He complied with her wishes, thankful that she had not stated, yet again, that she was breaking off their engagement.

"But we're to be married soon."

"I don't even want to think of that right now," she said. "Now get my horse."

Thirty minutes later Rawley watched as she ride off with a ranch hand with her to act as her protection. He would have offered to do that job himself, but he knew that at that moment Catriona could not stand to have him in her presence.

As he watched the two of them ride away he felt the prospect of owning *High Wynd* was steadily slipping from his father's grasp.

Then his mood brightened. By now the three 'kidnappers' should've done their work. Gilbert would have to try and put together a ransom that he would never need to pay.

*****

Perhaps the dining table was the wrong place for Rawley to break the news. His father was leaning back after a good meal when his son approached him. Old John had expected his three men to have reported back to him before now, only they a couple of days late. He was having dark thoughts about the missing men, yet knew if he were to ask about them he'd draw attention onto himself as well. So he contented himself to bide his time, and for now he seemed cheerful enough after eating.

"What's it that ails you son?"

"I need to discuss a matter with you father."

"What matter is that?"

"Catriona."

"You're to be married soon, that's all."

"I did as you asked and kept the death of Isabella from her."

"Good thing too. Best keep a lid on it until the marriage has taken place. If her brother doesn't turn up she will think it's because of his ill-will towards her."

"That's the problem sir. She has heard the news."

"What?" The huge man rose from behind the table, his beard quivering.

"Why would you tell her a thing like that?"

"I didn't, she learned it from somewhere else."

"Then you'll just have to reassure her. Tell her you'll take her to see her brother as soon as possible."

"It's too late,' said Rawley fearfully.

"What?" Old John's voice was a muted roar. "Where is she?"

"I am afraid she has ridden off to see her brother, and I fear that the marriage is off again."

"You let her go just like that?"

"I couldn't kidnap her."

"You could have kept her back in some way."

"I couldn't."

"Then you are a fool of the first order. Don't you realise what may happen now?"

"Nothing. She'll sympathise with her brother then return here, that's all."

"You really don't understand what's happening," raged Old John. "Once she finds out about the kidnapping she'll go over to her brother's side. And where is that renegade?"

"Flint? I suspect he's long gone. Nothing's been heard about him since the social."

"This has gone too far to stop. The child is dead and gone. If Gilbert has an ounce of sense he will have already sent for men to help defend High Wynd. Before that can happen you need to go there with our own. You'll take Thomas, the preacher with you. You'll take over that ranch which, with only two servants for defence, should be a trifling matter, even for you. And once you have the ranch secured, you can make her marry you."

"But won't Gilbert object to that kind of treatment?"

"What Gilbert wants doesn't matter. Once you and the girl are married they'll both have to take to the law to try and part you. That'll never happen. We'll pretend to Gilbert that she's played you like a fool, using the marriage as a tool to manipulate you, a behaviour witnessed by many. She'll have to comply. If she doesn't then tell that her brother will be a dead man."

Old John finished his speech by thudding his fist so heavily on the dining table the empty dishes jumped and rattled.

He had not figured on the reaction of his son.

"Sir, I can't believe what you're asking me to do. You're using naked force gain the property of another man."

"You know about the kidnapped baby."

"I'll swear otherwise. I'll say you had some absurd plan, and that I wanted nothing to do with."

"Too late for that, I've already sent three men to take the child from Gilbert. They should have left a ransom note for $10,000 for the child's return. With any luck the servant girl will find the dead child."

"Why?"

"The 'why' is self-evident, son. With his heir dead, on top of the demise of his wife, Gilbert will go mad and he'll forfeit his right to the ranch. His sister's wedding is going to be small beer over his grief at the loss of the child."

Rawley was white faced, his mouth a grim line. "What you're suggesting is madness! Catriona will fight against any kind of forced marriage. And should she find out it was you behind the child's murder, then there would be no reconciling her."

"Then you'll just have to do what I tell you." To his astonishment Rawley saw a gun in his father's hand, a Derringer he always carried with him. "I'll take the lead as you seem to much of a coward to do so! You'll go with me and I'll make her comply."

Rawley said nothing but the line of his mouth was even tighter. He wasn't prepared to take a bullet as a form of punishment, but he knew full well that he'd break free from this madness as soon as a chance was offered.

His father, looking at the set expression of his son, knew what the younger man was going to do, mainly because they were more like each other than either would admit.

Old John rubbed at his chest, as if Rawley's refusal to go along with his plans had caused him indigestion. Indicating the door with the small gun, he said, "Now get out of here."

Rawley had turned and had almost reached the doorframe when he heard a gasp from the old man. He turned back to find that his father's face shade of puce. The gun dropped from Old John's fingers as he clutched at his chest and left arm. He fell to his knees, clawed at the air for a brief second, and then pitched forward on to his face. He gave a massive, shuddering sigh, then lay still, as lifeless as the weapon that lay beside him.

*****

Flint was his usual post overlooking *High Wynd* when he saw Catriona arrive with one of Henderson's ranch hands. He could tell something was amiss as she was riding on her horse rather than in a carriage sent there by Rawley.

Her hair was wild, drifting out behind her, while her clothes were functional rather than decorative, so she'd obviously left *Eagle Cross* in a hurry. Perhaps she must have finally learned about the death of her sister-in-law.

Neela came out to greet her, Catriona's voice carried to where Flint had stationed himself.

"Neela! I've only just found out. I'm so sorry I wasn't at Isabella's funeral."

Neela tried to smile, but failed. "You're bother, he needs you. The child is safe, but I don't know how long for."

"Safe? Has something happened to him as well?"

"We were attacked, and the poor child was kidnapped. But he's back safely at the ranch." She left her explanation at that, not knowing how much she should tell about how Flint had rescued the boy.

On seeing Catriona Flint had wanted to shout out and make his presence known.

But here was a woman who had learned about the tragedy in her family. She was hardly going to greet him with open arms. Besides, seeing her like that suddenly reminded him of the great divide that existed between the two of them.

She was the true heir to the riches of her brother's ranch. He was a simple working cowhand who had won her friendship. He felt that she was too good for him.

Flint mounted his horse and rode away from the scene.

*****

After returning to his hideaway Flint had time to think and consider the situation.

He knew the so-called kidnappers had been sent Old John. Several days had passed since their disappearance, and no doubt the rancher would be getting anxious that no word had come from his men. He might even suspect that they'd decided to go for a genuine ransom, and made off with the money. After all, the amount demanded was more than most of them would ever see in their lives. If Catriona had learned the news about her brother, she would have come here on impulse, which might prompt Old John to send someone to bring her back.

Flint knew that the Henderson's planned to take the ranch through the girl, via marriage. But wasn't that marriage her choice? But she seemed to be continuously rebelling against it at the same time.

Hope rose in Flint's breast. He had already defeated Old John in one way, so perhaps he could do so in another. Flint rose and whistled to his horse. The window of opportunity would not be long open.

*****

In the meantime Neela and Catriona were together in the morning room with Gilbert. He was unshaven, sullen, but there was a glint in his eyes that had not been there since the death of his wife.

"I've sent word to the outstation that I'm going to need more men to be here at High Wynd. I was despondent when Isabella died, but the near loss of my boy has made me realise just what I have, and the need to protect it. I owe it to him to make this place prosperous again, to keep the business going. It was what my father and mother would have wanted."

The child, in his bassinet, gurgled and waved his arms and legs, evidently none the worse for his ordeal.

Gilbert continued, "I'll call him William after his grandfather. He's my pride and joy. Now take him and look after him. I have work to do."

Gilbert had not said anything to Catriona in regard to trying to make some kind of reconciliation between the two of them. But the look he gave her as she departed with Neela was enough for her to know that he was grateful for her return.

Catriona went out and after telling her travel guard he should head back to *Eagle Cross*, she took her own horse to the stables, closely followed by Neela.

While she was calming her steed down from his hard day's work, she fixed

Neela with a look that was at once both pleading and haughty. It was a look that Neela knew too well, the look of a woman who wanted several things at once.

"Neela, I need to talk to you about what has happened."

"Yes?"

"Who actually rescued William from the kidnappers?"

Neela looked reluctant to reveal the information.

Catriona tried again. "It doesn't matter who they are, I just want to know their name."

"It was Joe Flint. He saved the child from the three raiders. He is the one both you and your brother should be thankful to."

The revelation caught her by surprise. "Is he still here? If he is then I want to see him more than anything."

"That can be arranged, I'm sure he's still around these parts. You're the reason why he stayed."

"I think of him every day." Catriona suddenly felt that the stables were a good place for her to make her confession. "But I also feel that there is just too much that I do not want to give up."

"What do you mean?"

"I mean that Rawley dotes on me."

"So does Flint."

"I know that, and I have not been fair to him. I kept away deliberately, you see, not just because of the fight with Gilbert. Rawley is nothing like his father. He is a wonderful man who knows how to treat people. He is good-looking, fun to be with. He is even a kind man, kinder than his father will ever be. If I marry him I will have money, status, a true position in society. It isn't his fault his father is a scheming hell-hound."

"Then marry him and have done with it."

"Then I will have to give up my friendship with Flint, a friendship that is more, that is something I cannot express in words. He completes me in a way that Rawley does not. I don't know what it is, I just cannot explain what I mean."

"Then go with Flint and see where your journey takes you."

"Go with Flint? But don't you see? In society, Flint is the lowest of the low. He is nobody and he has nothing. If I go with him I will lose everything I have known or worked for."

"Then marry Rawley and see how your life goes."

"I don't want just Rawley, I want them both, Rawley for his position and power, Flint for who he is. I can't have either of them on their own. If Flint and I were together we would have to leave everything I have ever known, and I'm not strong enough for that. And what if Rawley refuses to take me back if it doesn't all work out?"

Both turned as they heard a noise that sounded almost human, a dry bark of despair.

"What was that?" asked Catriona.

"I don't know," said Neela. "Horses can make strange noises."

They heard no other sound like it.

After a moment of silence between them, Neela spoke, making her own feelings plain.

"If you cannot have him, leave him and let him get on with his life. Otherwise you would be committing a great evil. Neither man is ever going to be happy with the way you are behaving. And you know that one would die at the hand of the other, eventually. I am not a seer, but I can tell that much. Set one of them free."

"I can't! Without Flint there is an emptiness inside that could never be filled with a million treasures." Catriona paced up and down in her despair, tears edging from the corners of her eyes.

Neela, who knew her mistress well, said nothing and waited until the storm was over.

Finally Catriona took a small handkerchief from her skirt pocket and wiped away her tears. Her jaw was firm and she had a new resolve burning in her eyes.

"I have made my choice. Once I have fulfilled my task here you will take me to where Flint is hiding. I'll bring money and other supplies and I will go with him. We are young and this is a land of opportunity. I will write a letter to Rawley to let him know of my decision."

Neela said nothing for a second, and then they both embraced. The die had been cast.

*****

Just a few minutes earlier Flint had arrived at the stables. He'd decided to hide out there and, when the opportunity presented itself, he would speak to Catriona, cutting through any social niceties and simply ask her to go away with him, once and for all. He had a sneaking suspicion that Gilbert would not be too troubled if his sister left for good. The pair of them had never got on. As for the rescue of the child? All that meant to Gilbert was that he wouldn't actively pursue them. Neither he nor Flint would ever have any kind of friendship and both were wise enough to know this.

Once inside the stable he could hear Catriona talking to Neela, and as he came closer he realised what the subject was. It is said that an eavesdropper never hears good things about themselves and this was certainly the case with Flint. When he heard Catriona say that he was a nobody and that she might crumble and leave him, that was enough. He stole away from the sound of their voices and went back to the trees where he had hitched his horse, all the time aware of a dull ache inside. It was something he'd never experienced before and didn't know what to call it. Just that it was somewhere in the region of his heart.

He mounted and rode away without looking back.

Chapter Fourteen

Josh McQuade was not a man to give up easily.

He knew that John Henderson had just lost three of his men, and they were not ones McQuade had any particular liking for. He also knew they had vanished in what were possibly odd circumstances, if the outstation gossip was to be believed.

In his opinion the whole business had a lot to do with the disappearance of Joe Flint – something he'd sorely mourned at the time. His own sons had left the cattle business a long time ago and were out East now, both in banking and finance, so he didn't hear from them very often. Flint had become almost like another son to him.

Taking some time off, one of the few blessings that came with being in charge, McQuade decided he gone out looking around the hill country, to see if he could fathom what was going on.

After a few miles he stopped at the foothills so he could feed and water his horse. Looking back at the plain he could see for miles.

That was when he saw what appeared to be a posse of four men heading for the hill country. They were riding in the same direction, but he doubted he was their target. At that distance he couldn't make out their faces, but just from the horses and their general look, he could tell they came from the Henderson ranch.

They were moving along so rapidly that they hadn't even seen him. McQuade knew that he should go to them and find out what they were doing, but he held back where he was, beneath their notice.

*****

Flint rode out from the shelter of the hills. He had no idea of where he was heading. He'd just packed his supplies and was heading out south. As far away from everyone and everything as he could go. He'd long since ceased to feel the buckskin strap around his wrist, but as he rode, the sleeve of his jerkin rode up and he could see it before his eyes. He slowed his horse and undid the strings that held it together. For a second he was going to throw it away, but then stuffed it down his shirt, the memories too real for him to make that final gesture.

A mood had settled on him, one of bleakness, even despair. His world was drained of all colour and meaning. It was in this mood that he moved out of the tree line and encountered the four horsemen.

They immediately spotted him, heading in his direction, which wasn't that surprising since he had taken the widest road out, the one they would need to use.

Curly Logan was the leader, a tall man who wore his hair as long as Rawley's. It streamed out from beneath his hat as he rode.

"Well look who it is, the barnstormer." He slowed his horse down and halted, the other three spread out beside him. Flint could have tried to ride through them, but his own steed was laden, which would make it slow, so he wanted to size up the potential danger.

"You out to get me?" He said with deceptive mildness.

"That's for us to know."

In truth, Logan and his men had been sent by Rawley to let Catriona know about the death of Old John, and to get her to come back to *Eagle Cross*.

Rawley had sent four, mainly because he didn't know of the fate of the other three his father had sent out days before. Logan had specific orders to shoot Pete Tyler, Jake Burns and Ade Watkins on sight. Rawley hadn't given the order to kidnap the Shaw child, so as far as he was concerned the men involved were fair game.

He also didn't want Catriona finding out what his father had wanted to do with the child, or her.

The four men were already spoiling for a fight when they encountered Flint.

Logan said, "Have you seen three of our team riding out this way? And if'n you did, was there a kid with them?"

"I've not seen a living soul for over a week now, let alone anyone with a child in tow." Flint had no intention of incriminating himself, especially when he was outnumbered and with no witnesses. "Now you boys just let me be and I'll get on my way."

Logan shifted himself in his saddle. "Suppose I ain't in the mood to let you just ride off?"

Beside him, one of the other riders muttered, "We didn't come fer this."

"Shaddup," said Logan. He addressed Flint. "So you just ride out of here on your lonesome after all the trouble you caused?"

"I've done nothing to you boys. Now if you'll just let me be, I'll get on with my day." Flint eased his mount forward.

A gun appeared in Logan's hand. "How's about you wait here with one of my boys until we come back? Does that sound fair?"

Rawley could hardly deny that Flint would be a useful bargaining counter. They were to bring the girl back. If she knew they had Flint, she would be more likely to comply.

In Logan's head the whole matter was immediately settled. He had not reckoned on the force he was dealing with. After all, they were four to one. What was the lone horseman going to do? Logan didn't know that after what had happened with Catriona in the stables, Flint no longer had anything to lose.

Giving a whooping roar in reply, Flint rode forward so rapidly that Logan's one shot at him had no chance of connecting. Riding straight for Logan, the other three riders scattered away from the two of them, at the same time Flint lashed out with the stone axe he'd lifted from his saddle.

If the axe had connected directly it would have brained Logan. Instead the broad side of the stone blade caught him on the shoulder with a force that knocked him off his mount to the trail. Such was the force of the blow that it took Flint off his own horse, knocking him to the dusty ground.

For a second both men were winded, then they staggered to their feet, a yard or so from each other. They were both filled with a raw and intense anger that comes from the pure urge to survive at all costs. Seconds later they both attacked, while the other three riders moved back to give the two fighters space - none of them willing to draw their weapons, for fear of hitting the wrong man.

A rapid exchange of punches followed between the two, and it became obvious that Logan, despite his seeming hardiness, was not good at close-up combat. Flint, although smaller, was spare and wiry, and it soon became clear that he was beating Logan without too much effort.

One of the riders pulled out a pistol and aimed it at the two combatants. He tried to get his timing right so that he could hit Flint. There was a loud report and a muzzle flash as he fired, and the fighters immediately fell apart from each other.

Logan looked down at his front in stupefied amazement, seeing bright red blood seeping into the cotton of his shirt, just below his heart. His mouth opened to say something, but there was just silence as he pitched over on his face.

Flint staggered and rolled onto the ground, snatching up a fallen pistol – either his or Logan's, he didn't care which. His only priority was remaining alive at all costs.

The remaining three riders looked uneasily at Flint and the gun he was holding, then at the dead body of Logan.

The silence was broken by one of the riders.

"Look what you've done Bern. There ain't any way this can be fixed, that's for sure."

Bern, still in shock, threw his weapon onto the ground by Logan. "I didn't mean to kill him. I just wanted to give him an advantage, that's all."

Still with the upper hand, Flint said, "Tell you what, the three of you throw down your guns and ride off to wherever you were going. I won't say a thing about this if you just leave me alone."

"How do we know you won't shoot us," growled Bern.

"Because I ain't an idiot like this one," said Flint prodding the corpse with the toe of his boot. "There's already been enough killing round these parts. Now, if you two take your guns and throw them on the ground, then back aways so I can see to them."

Flint watched as two more Colt revolvers joined Bern's on the ground and the three riders backed off, giving Flint a safe distance.

Still keeping a wary eye on them, Flint stepped forward and kicked the weapons safely under some rocks.

"Now get going, and no circling back. If I see you heading this way then I won't hesitate to shoot." He didn't know that their mission was to bring Catriona back to *Eagle Cross*, nor that Old John was well and truly dead. He just wanted them away from him as quickly as possible.

They rode off, looking backwards several times, fearing that Flint would not keep his word.

But flint was beyond caring anymore. He simply remounted his horse and rode as fast as he could in the opposite direction.

Normally he would have been more observant, looking around to see if any other source of danger existed, but he had a feeling that they were the only cowboys he would encounter on that particular path. The chance encounter had settled his mind. He was going away from a place that had done nothing but bring him trouble. His one regret was Catriona. Silently he wished her well in her new life. He would make good and build himself a social status worthy of her.

Then he would be back.

*****

McQuade had seen the whole encounter from the spot where he rested with his horse. He could have intervened, but something in him said that Flint would be able to handle the situation. There was another reason he couldn't show his hand. He was in charge of an opposing camp, if he had appeared then Henderson's men might well have allied the trail leader with Flint, to the detriment of the fragile Shaw-Henderson relationship. It was cowardly, in one sense. But it would have been dangerous for him to be seen with such a person as Flint. If word got back to Old John, he might well end his alliance with *High Wynd* on the basis of what he would regard as an insult.

Yet McQuade was missing two vital pieces of information. He didn't know that Old John was dead, nor that the rancher had tried to implement an audacious plan to grab both land and property by murder and devious manipulation. If he had, then his reactions would have been very different.

Instead he waited until Flint had gone before mounting up and riding over to investigate Logan's corpse.

Logan's horse had wondered off, but the body was not a desirable thing to leave around. The foreman, despite the heat that prickled down his back, roped Logan's corpse and slowly dragged it well off the trail and into the bushes. The bugs and critters would quickly make short work of the body

That done, McQuade was about to get on with his original business when he saw something in the dust. It was a wrist-strap, lying on the ground. McQuade lifted the strap, saw the semi-precious stones embedded in the fabric, then placed the strap into his breast pocket.

When Flint had been ill – slipping in and out of consciousness – McQuade had come to see him and had seen the strap wrapped around Flint's wrist. It didn't take McQuade long to deduce where the bracelet had come from. If he was right then here was his chance to do well by the young rebel. McQuade turned his horse and trotted up the long trail to *High Wynd*, following along after Henderson's men.

Chapter Fifteen

McQuade had little intention, other than getting to *High Wynd* and seeing Catriona, but it wasn't long before he caught up with Henderson's men.

Bern, the newly elected group leader, addressed McQuade cautiously.

"Good to see you, Mister McQuade. The three of us are headed to High Wynd. Would you mind if I were to ask where you're headed?"

McQuade, unsure of what was going on, growled, "I have private business with Gilbert Shaw, not that that is any concern of yours."

"We've been sent by Rawley Henderson," said Bern. "We've been told to bring Ms Shaw back with us to Eagle Cross."

"Then you're making a mistake, and Rawley Henderson has sent all three of you on a fool's errand," said McQuade. "She certainly won't go back with you, and if you force her she'll no doubt kill another one of you."

"What do you mean another one?" Bern was suddenly on the defensive. "What do you know about this whole business?"

"I saw what happened out on the trail. I decided to keep out of the fight for good reason. One against four, and you were getting bested." McQuade thought for a moment. "Are you only going to High Wynd in order to settle up a lover's tiff?"

"No," growled Bern. "Old John Henderson has just died of a heart attack. Mister Rawley asked us to get his fiancé and return with her. He says she'll understand."

McQuade was staggered by the news of Old John Henderson's death. Those words changed everything.

But he also knew that Gilbert Shaw would not believe their story, and could well start a ranch feud now that news of the kidnap and return of the child had travelled fast in the area. Gilbert might well think this was an attempt to do more of the same.

McQuade leaned on his saddle. "Look, I'm pretty well in with Shaw. Let me go in and talk to him, then I'll escort the woman back along with you." He paused for a moment, then added, "But you have to do me a favour too."

He outlined his plan to them and they seemed more than happy to go along with it. With one of their companions dead they didn't want to become entangled in yet more conflict, and McQuade's plan provided them with what seemed like the perfect solution.

As they approached High Wynd, McQuade got them to hold back, so only he rode in through the gates, hitching his horse to a rail at the front of the building. Inside the house they were clearly being cautious, he saw a face checking him out from one of the windows before Matthew Jacob answered the door.

"I need to see Catriona," said McQuade.

Matthew thought this strange, but he complied with the request. "If you'll kindly follow me, sir." He turned and led McQuade into the kitchen. "If you'll take a seat, sir, I'll fetch Miss Catriona."

From somewhere in the building McQuade could hear a child crying. His heart lifted, at least that took away some of his problems. He didn't know how they'd got the child back, but he strongly suspected it had something to do with Flint.

Within minutes, Catriona appeared in the kitchen doorway, with Matthew behind her. She turned slightly to the servant. "Matthew, go and see if Mr Shaw needs anything. If he's asleep, then let him be."

When Matthew had departed she turned her attention to McQuade. "Hello Josh, what's this all about?"

She appeared bright and cheerful, more like her old self. Now that she'd made her decision about where she was going with her life, throwing in her lot with one man rather than the other, her mind was settled. She would go with Neela, find him that very day so that they could start their new life together as soon as possible.

"Does this mean anything to you?" McQuade held up the tanned, wristlet.

"Where did you get that?" The girl could not take her eyes off the object.

"I found it on the body of a man who had either been ambushed or thrown by his horse. Either way, he was stone-cold dead."

The girl took the band from him and nestled it in her hand.

"It can't be! Take me to him. I want to see him, let me see him!" It was clear that Catriona was genuinely distraught.

McQuade was quick to embroider the lie even more. "Too late, I'm afraid. I had him taken away and buried." He made a mental note to have the grave created as soon as he returned to the outstation.

From behind her came the sound of Gilbert Shaw bustling down the stairs. He was clean-shaven and there was a fire in his eyes that had not been there for a long time.

"McQuade, what are you doing here? Bringing good news I hope."

Catriona immediately broke in, "Flint is dead!"

"How? Where?" Gilbert was obviously confused by the news.

The foreman repeated his story, then added some truth in regard to his visit. "I have some of Rawley Henderson's men with me. They want to bring

Catriona back to Eagle Cross. He wants her by his side."

"What? I'm not going!." She jerked back her head and lifted her proud chin. "I had what I wanted, now it has been taken from me. I'll stay here and look after my nephew and grow to be an old maid, if that's what it takes."

"You don't understand," said McQuade. "Old John is dead. He died of a heart attack several days ago. Rawley is on his own. He needs you Catriona. That's why three of his men are waiting outside to escort you back to Eagle Cross."

Gilbert took the news of Old John's death calmly. There had been no love lost between him and John Henderson, but that didn't mean he should have any animosity against the remainder of his family.

To Matthew, he said, "Bring the Henderson men in and get them some food. Tell them there will be a delay while we get out the carriage. Catriona and I will drive out there in style once we have made our preparations. Though also tell them I will also have an escort made up of my own men."

"Very good sir, I will see to that now."

To McQuade he asked, "Will you be my right-hand man?"

"Yes," said the big foreman.

"Good. If this turns out to be a trap laid on by Old John for some strange reason then we'll be ready for him. If however it's as I suspect, and John Henderson has passed away, then Catriona, you should go be with Rawley. At a time like this he'll need you more than ever."

She looked at the rawhide band for a lingering moment then tucked it away in her the pocket of her dress..

"If he needs me I will go. I needed someone once and now I find he's left me for good." Her shoulders slumped as she headed to her room to start packing and to prepare for the journey.

McQuade remained in the kitchen as the Henderson men came in and sat at the pine wood table. Matthew busied himself at the cast iron range cooking up a quick meal.

Deep in his thoughts, McQuade felt no guilt about lying to Catriona and telling her that Flint was dead. He'd always believed that the two of them had never been right for each other, and they would've caused more conflict and death before they parted.

It was better this way.

*****

The sun was starting to fall below the horizon as Flint rode back to the cave entrance, illuminating him in blood-red light.

He'd returned via the same trail where he'd been confronted by Logan and the Henderson men, but saw that Logan's body was now gone. There were hoof, wagon and shoe tracks leading to and from the whole area, and he suspected someone had reported the body, and others had taken it back up the trail to the outstation. So far no one had been back to see if they could find anything more about the killing, but Flint knew that his luck wouldn't hold out for much longer.

There was no sign of the wristband he'd lost either, despite his searching. Maybe the others had picked it up when they came for Logan. Flint shook his head. It was gone, just like his old life. He'd discovered it missing barely an hour before, when he should have been riding out of the county. What was it anyway? A trinket? A token of a life that he might have had if the events of the last few years had unfolded differently.

Flint looked at his hideaway – still a little distance off.

After the incident at the stables he believed Catriona had chosen to be to be with Rawley, the man who could give her everything. He, on the other hand, had never been a man who needed much in the way of the material goods and possessions.

But if that was what was needed to make Catriona happy, then he would head off and try his best to get the things that she wanted. And when he had them, he'd come back to show her what he had done.

Yes, by then, it might be too late.

Either that or he could blow Rawley's brains out in a one-to-one confrontation.

A twitch tightened the corner of his mouth at the thought. But he knew such action would make her reject him completely; possibly get him labelled the biggest outlaw in the state, with a price on his head. Dead or alive.

No, the only way was to make his fortune, then return to claim her.

Habitually he rubbed his wrist where the band had been, then decided that the memory would be enough to treasure until he returned.

He turned his horse away from the cave mouth – the sun now so low that red rays made him a black outline as he rode out across the plains. He knew the old abandoned Cransfield homestead wasn't far, provided he kept a direct route, and just after moonrise he saw it as a dark shadow ahead.

Reaching it, he made sure his horse was out of sight, well fed, hitched up so it wouldn't stray, then went inside and slept soundly for the rest of the night.

The following morning, after he'd breakfasted, he packed up, mounted up, and continued to ride as far away from Eagle Cross and the Henderson family, and High Wynd and Catriona Shaw.

He was determined to become the kind of man who was worthy of her love. Rich, well-dressed, connected to those who mattered. And he would do it within two years or less.

She was going to be his and nothing was going to stand in his way.

He rode off across the plains to start his new life.

For the Honor of the Family
Jim Doherty

Hal Hachette could hardly believe his eyes.

He hadn't seen his brother in years, yet here he was big as life, casually guiding his horse up to the main building of the Jackson Ranch, where Hal was employed.

The last Hal had heard, Gus Hachette was fighting bandits along the border between Texas and Mexico as a sergeant in the Rangers.

Gus'd fallen into the profession of peacekeeping kind of accidentally, but once in it, he'd taken to it like a duck to water. He'd been punching cows for a ranch in Pecos County some ten years back. At the request of the local sheriff, he'd been deputized (over a party line phone) to track down a pair of horse thieves fleeing into the next county with their ill-gotten mounts, and had accomplished their apprehension with ease. The sheriff, favorably impressed, told Gus that if he ever thought of making a career as a peace officer, he'd put in a good word for him with the local company of Texas Rangers. A few weeks later, Gus was a rookie private in that fabled state constabulary, undergoing an apprenticeship that would give him a level of practical experience that many officers with twenty or more years on the Job couldn't match.

Two years later, at the age of 24, he'd been hired as the police chief of Aguaturbia, a wild and wooly town in East Texas. Two years after that, he'd been personally hired by the Mayor of Houston for a stint as a special investigator in that city's police force. That had been followed by a year as a deputy assigned to suppress livestock theft for the Kimble County Sheriff's Office, then by a return to the Rangers when the border started heating up as the Great War raged in Europe, followed by a short term of duty in the Army's Corps of Military Police after the US entered that conflict, and then by a return to the Rangers after his discharge.

Though not well-known to the general public, Gus had become quite famous within Texas law enforcement circles. Hal never realized just how famous until he'd started working as a part-time deputy for the Scurry County Sheriff's Office to supplement his income at the ranch.

"Gus!" he exclaimed. "Is that really you?"

Gus Hachette dismounted, and walked over to his younger brother, who enthusiastically gripped his outstretched hand and pumped it.

"Hal," he said quietly. Gus Hachette was not one to display emotion openly. The only sign of the real pleasure he took in seeing his younger brother was a tight smile and a gleam in his eyes.

"What brings you to this part of Texas?" asked Hal.

"Chasing some rustlers. Heard from the folks that you had a job around here, so I thought I'd stop for a quick visit."

"Back with the Rangers?"

"No. Not really. I'm working for the Lone Star Cattlemen's Association."

"Range detective?"

"Well, the Association prefers to call me a 'field inspector.'"

"You're done with the Rangers?"

"More or less. The Association pays a lot better. I was hoping, when I applied, that a better-paying position might persuade Miriam to consider giving me a second chance. But by the time I had the job in the bag, it was too late."

"I was real sorry to hear about that, Gus. She was a fine lady."

"She was that. Just wasn't cut out to be a lawman's wife."

Gus had successfully courted Miriam Campbell, a pretty schoolteacher, during his tenure as Aguaturbia's town marshal. They were married six months before he left that job to take the Houston position. Educated and cultured, she'd liked living in a big city, though she'd never accustomed herself to the uncertainties of being married to a policeman. By the time Gus had left the Houston job to take the deputy's position in Kimble County, they had separated. She'd filed for divorce by the time he returned to the Rangers, and it had been finalized after he'd gone for a soldier. He'd hoped the Association position might be the prelude to a reconciliation, but only a few days before his appointment was confirmed, he'd learned that Miriam had drowned in a boating accident at a church picnic.

"I'm kind of surprised you didn't stay in the Rangers," Hal said. "Thought you'd make your career there once you re-upped after the Armistice. Course, if you wanted to get back with Miriam, well, Rangering isn't the life for a family man."

"That's sure true. But I'm still Rangering, after a fashion. Once the Association had me on the payroll, they fixed it so I got a Special Ranger's commission, authorizing me to make arrests, and such."

"Sort of like my job here. Mr. Jackson pays me to protect his daughter, Mrs. Simmons. He arranged for me to get issued a county badge, so I'd have some police authority if it ever became necessary. When I'm not looking after Mrs. Simmons, I put in some time deputy sheriffing to make extra money."

"What's she need protecting from."

"Her husband."

"Bad marriage?"

"Bad as it gets. It's a long story. Let me introduce you around. I've been braggin' on you a lot, big brother. The Jacksons'll be glad to meet you in person."

*****

Hal lost no time introducing Gus to Will Jackson, the wealthy head of the family; his wife, Annie; their daughter, Mrs. Claudia Simmons; and their grandchildren, five-year-old Bea and three-year-old Leila. Claudia's older brother, Stephen, the eldest of the two Jackson siblings, was in the nearby town of Snyder, where he managed the bank the family owned.

Hal noticed an immediate spark between Gus and the beautiful Mrs. Simmons. And, like many shy bachelors, a lover of children, Gus quickly took to the two little girls.

Invited to dinner, Gus sat quietly while Hal regaled the family with thrilling stories of his brother's years in law enforcement, Gus only interjecting occasionally with corrections or to tone down Hal's exaggerations. All the Jacksons were drawn to the tall, soft-spoken lawman.

But none more than the soon-to-be-single Claudia Simmons.

Later, in Hal's room, where Gus was spending the night, the two brothers conversed about the family.

"That Mrs. Simmons is real easy on the eyes," said Gus.

"Very pretty," Hal agreed.

"Can't hardly believe she's got a five-year-old. Doesn't look like she's out of her teens yet."

"She turned 20 just a few weeks ago," said Hal. "Married at 14."

"Must be a story behind that."

"Tragic one. Remember that play we used to read in school? About them two Eye-talian families had a blood feud, but the son of one and the daughter of the other fell in love?"

"*Romeo and Juliet.*"

"That's the one. Well, this is that story in reverse. Two wealthy families, the Jacksons here in Scurry County, and the Simmonses over in Garza. Fred Simmons fell hard for Claudia, and she returned the compliment. Neither family was anxious to see 'em married so young, but other than that, they had no objections. When the two young folks were determined to have their way, the families decided uniting two wealthy lines could only be an advantage to both. So they thought."

"What happened?

"Fred's a ladies' man, and he ain't exactly discreet. Also can't hold his liquor, and he's mean when he's drunk. And Claudia's been raised around ranching hands her whole life. She can ride and shoot better'n most men. So she ain't the kind to take being cheated on and beaten on with ladylike forbearance. The fights between 'em were epic events. Finally, she got fed up, moved out, and came home with the two little ones."

"Ending a marriage is hard," said Gus, remembering his own split with Miriam, but also recalling that it was, for the most part, amicable. "Doesn't mean there have to be hard feelings."

"Miriam didn't call it off 'cause you beat her, or cheated on her. She just couldn't stand the work you did. Man raises a hand to his wife, he brings the hard feelings on. Right now both families are taking sides. Things could turn violent real easy. Funny thing is it'd be caused by the marriage, not in spite of the marriage, like in the play. Tempers are high on both sides. Wouldn't take much more'n a spark to set the whole keg o' powder off."

*****

Gus Hachette's "beat" as a Cattlemen's Association investigator covered twelve contiguous counties, so he only managed to get into Scurry when he had some time off, which was seldom, or when a case took him there. He spent at least as much time "dealing misery to cattle thieves," as he put it, in each of the other eleven counties in his assigned district, as he did in Scurry.

It happened that he was in Garza County, where the Simmonses were the most prominent family, in the town of Post, Garza's county seat, conferring with the Sheriff, E.W. Chandler, and Post's town marshal, P.O. Foxx, on a case. Which is why he happened to be on hand when the spark that would set off the blood feud Hal had predicted was struck.

It was late December, and, while the divorce hadn't been finalized, the court had decreed that Fred Simmons would have custody of his two daughters during the Christmas holidays. Claudia decided to drive them over herself, and had made arrangements to meet her husband in the town square at Post. Hal Hachette, her bodyguard, was down with a flu, which is probably why the exchange escalated into violence.

Gus Hachette recognized the machine Claudia drove up in as belonging to the Jackson ranch. His attention was drawn, when he saw Claudia, obviously full of resentment at having to give up her little girls at Christmastime, exit the vehicle. Simmons tried to coax the children out of the car, but they, having heard nothing but bad things about their father during their stay at the Jackson Ranch, were reluctant to exit.

Losing his temper, Simmons attempted to force the door open.

"You both have to come with me, now!" he shouted.

The girls slid over to the other side of the car, obviously terrified. Claudia, who routinely carried a .32 automatic wherever she went, drew it and threatened to shoot Simmons if he didn't stop frightening the girls. Simmons pulled back his jacket to show he was not carrying any weapons.

"Claudia, don't! I'm unarmed!" he cried.

Hachette crossed the street, followed by Chandler and Foxx, came up behind Claudia, pushed her gun hand up toward the sky, and disarmed her.

"This is none of your put-in, Mr. Hachette!" said the enraged mother.

"Pulling down on your husband isn't the way to handle this, Mrs. Simmons," said Hachette. "Do you really want the last memory your two daughters have of their father to be their mother gunning him down?

Especially when he's got the law on his side?"

Handing her pistol to the sheriff, Hachette walked over to the car, looked inside, and said to the two girls, "Bea, Leila, you slide on over to this side, and open that door right now. Your daddy's here to take you to your Grandpa and Grandma Simmons for Christmas. I know you want to stay with your mama, but your Simmons family loves you, too, and they got a right to some of your company, same as your Jackson family."

"OK, Mr. Hachette," said Bea, exiting the machine, with Leila following. Both Mr. and Mrs. Simmons looked a little embarrassed that their daughters minded Gus Hachette more than they minded either of their parents.

"As for you," said Hachette, turning to Fred Simmons, "you just make sure those little girls have themselves a real nice Christmas. Don't ruin it with any of this ugliness that's between you and Mrs. Simmons. That clear?"

Simmons glared at him, as if trying to make up his mind whether he should be grateful to the tall confident lawman for having saved his life saved, or angry at his interference in a private, family matter.

"Is that *clear*?" Hachette repeated.

Simmons finally nodded, and said, "Clear."

"Well, then, take your children and get on out of here."

*****

Hachette's intervention kept the powder keg from going off, but hadn't managed to extinguish the spark. It turned out that all he'd accomplished was to delay the inevitable explosion.

The following Saturday, Simmons was in a Post speakeasy, getting drunk and running down his "whore of a wife."

Stephen Jackson had spent the day deer hunting in Garza, and was still holding his double-barreled twelve gauge shotgun when he entered the establishment just in time to hear that particular description of his baby sister.

He walked up to Simmons, tapped him on the shoulder, and, when Simmons turned around, butt-stroked him with the shotgun, decking his drunken brother-in-law.

Bracing the stock of the twelve-gauge against his shoulder, he thumbed back both hammers, and said, "I'll teach you to say foul things about my sister in a place like this."

Before he could squeeze off the twin blasts, another of the patrons said, "You've made your point, Steve. Fred there's unarmed. You shoot him like this, it's murder."

Jackson lowered both hammers slowly, and said, "You got a lot of luck, Simmons. 'Cause I wanted to kill you *bad*. You see that you keep your mouth off my sister in places like this."

With that, he turned around and walked toward the speakeasy's exit.

Simmons, a regular customer, reached behind the bar where he knew a Colt revolver was kept for protection, thumbed back the hammer, and triggered off a shot. In his drunken state, he missed by a wide margin, but he'd given Jackson the legal excuse to kill him that had been lacking a few moments earlier.

Jackson recocked the two hammers of his twelve gauge, and let his brother-in-law have both barrels. Eighteen double ought pellets, each roughly the diameter of a .38 revolver slug, slammed into Simmons's chest, killing him instantly.

And beginning the last blood feud between families in Texas history.

He also made his sister a genuine widow, instead of a grass one, the final divorce decree having not yet been issued.

*****

Even in Garza County, even with all the pull that the Simmons family had, there was no way that Stephen Jackson could get convicted when there were multiple witnesses to testify that Fred Simmons not only fired first, but tried to shoot Jackson in the back as he was leaving the speak.

The Coroner's Jury declared it to be an act of justifiable homicide. The Grand Jury refused to indict, declaring that Jackson had clearly acted in self-defense. In light of this, the district attorney over in Dawson County, whose bailiwick included Garza, refused to even attempt a prosecution by bringing the case before a judge for a preliminary hearing.

Collin Higginson, a former judge who was representing Steve Jackson on the case, had almost nothing to do. It was, he said, the easiest legal fee he'd ever earned.

*****

In fact, it turned out to be the *hardest* legal fee he ever earned. Higginson, though not a member of either family, was about to become the next casualty of the Simmons-Jackson feud.

It was a Sunday in March, nearly three months after the death of Fred Simmons. Higginson had spent the morning teaching Sunday School at the Methodist church in Snyder he regularly attended, followed by worship services in that same church. Afterwards, he kissed his wife goodbye and headed to nearby Clairemont, where he would be representing several different clients at various cases due to be heard at the district court over the next week.

After checking into the town's only hotel, he attended another worship service that evening in Clairemont's Methodist church. He returned to the hotel, and sat down in the lobby to visit with a couple of acquaintances. His back was to a window that opened out onto the street. A man who had been on the lookout for Higginson lifted a shotgun he was carrying up to one of the window panes, punched out the glass, and triggered a shot through the backrest of the chair Higginson was relaxing in. Before anyone could apprehend him, the assassin had disappeared into the night.

Higginson did not die immediately. He was transported by motorcar to a hospital in the town of Spur, some twenty miles north. His wife, brought to the hospital from Snyder, was able to see her husband before he went into surgery. Five twelve gauge pellets were successfully removed during the operation, but it was found that the shotgun blast had caused serious damage to Higginson's intestines, which had become irreversibly infected. He died just before noon the day after being shot.

Investigation by local law enforcement, and by the Texas Ranger Company stationed in the area, failed to turn up the killer.

*****

A lawman who murders knows what procedures the law follows when a homicide's being investigated. And, as a consequence, he's probably got a better chance of avoiding detection.

John Meaney, who habitually signed his name "J. Meaney," and was, therefore, commonly known by the nickname "Jay," had been a Texas Ranger and a deputy sheriff, and he knew the tricks for keeping himself from being identified. That's why he'd used a shotgun (no ballistics from a smoothbore weapon), worn gloves (no fingerprints), and stayed in the shadows (no eyewitness descriptions if all they saw was a vague figure in the darkness).

He was never a particularly dedicated peace officer, but he was sharp enough to learn the craft, and, if his ethics couldn't stand an intense examination, there was one principle he followed with fervor.

Family ties trumped all other considerations.

Meaney was a shirttail "nephew" of Asa "Ace" Simmons, the patriarch of the Simmons clan, by virtue of Ace being the brother of Linda Meaney, Jay's aunt by marriage. Jay was also Ace's son-in-law, having married his daughter, Adele, around the same time Claudia and Fred had tied the knot. So, when Ace asked Meaney to take care of the attorney who'd gotten "the murderer of my son off by cheap lawyering tricks," he didn't hesitate, notwithstanding his knowing as well as anyone that Higginson not only didn't use any cheap lawyering tricks, but that he didn't even have to, since the facts were so self-evident.

When Meaney reported back to Ace Simmons the night following the shooting, Simmons nodded with satisfaction.

"You did just fine, Jay," he told his son-in-law. "But that's just the beginning. Now we gotta go after that murdering Steve Jackson, and that whoring daughter-in-law of mine."

Meaney wasn't so twisted by hate that he could convince himself that Steve Jackson was guilty of anything but defending himself, nor that Claudia had ever cheated on Fred. But that didn't matter. Her leaving Fred was what got this whole pot stirred, and Steve, however justified, had killed Fred.

That was all Meaney needed.

Family was family, and a man stood by family. Family came before God. Country. Law. Even a man's own sense of right and wrong.

But standing by family didn't mean being reckless.

"That might not be smart right now, Ace," he said.

"Smart's got nothing to do with it. It's gotta be done."

"It's gotta be done, but that don't mean we gotta take unnecessary risks. Before this whole thing blew up, Will Jackson hired a bodyguard for Claudia."

"So? The fella looking after Claudia's just a cowboy with a part-time deputy's badge. That shouldn't be all that much for a man with your experience to handle."

"Killing a lawman, even a part-time one, isn't smart. Peace officers regard each other as family. Kill one, and it's like starting a blood feud with every cop in the country. Can we pull some strings to get his badge revoked, then go after 'em?"

"Will Jackson holds all the sway in Scurry County."

"Then maybe we can hire it done, keep suspicion off of us. I know some people we can use who'll do it for the right price. In the meantime, suppose we focus on Will. No one's protecting him."

"Now that just might be an idea," said the old man. "Before we're finished, we have to wipe all of them Jacksons out. Even my own granddaughters. Got no choice. You understand that, don't you, Jay? You know why we have to do this. It's a matter of honor."

"Sure it is," replied Meaney. "The honor of the family."

*****

While Meaney was putting out feelers to various individuals known to be willing to murder for a fee, Will Jackson was talking to Gus Hachette about ways of firming up the protection of his family.

"Collin Higginson getting killed raises the stakes," he said. "I need to have my family looked after, and your brother can't do the job all by himself. Would you be willing to let me hire you as a bodyguard, at least 'til this thing with the Simmonses cools down?"

"You're sure that Higginson was killed because he represented Steve? He wasn't the only man Higginson had as a client. And he'd probably made some enemies when he was a judge, too."

"Ace Simmons threatened him several times. Course, he had an alibi for the time of the shooting, but he could've hired it done. And if he's got professionals murdering for him, I need professionals protecting me and mine. Would you be willing?"

"I'd have to take a leave of absence from the Association," said Hachette, "and my Ranger's commission would probably be suspended once I started that leave, so I wouldn't have any law enforcement authority."

"I'll pay you half again what the Association's paying you, and I've got enough pull that I'll be able to get you your job back once things settle down. In the meantime, I can get Sheriff Russell to deputize you, like he did Hal."

"I'd have to wind up some active cases I'm working, and give some reasonable notice."

"Take what time you need. But I want you to start looking after my family as soon as you can."

*****

About a week after Hachette's leave from the Cattlemen's Association, and his employment by Will Jackson, began, Meaney contacted a hardcase he knew from his lawman days named Luke Smith, who'd once been a Coryell County deputy sheriff, and who was currently that county's tax assessor, but who made the bulk of his income as a hired killer. Smith's sometime partner, Gerald W. Kent, "Jerry" to his friends and colleagues, had also spent a year or two wearing a badge 'til he decided the other side of the law was more lucrative.

Meaney, seated across a table from Smith and Kent in a quiet corner of a Callahan County road house, about halfway between Coryell and Garza Counties, handed each of them a hundred dollar bill.

"That's yours whether you take the job or not, just for coming here to listen," he said. "My father-in-law'll pay you four thousand dollars each for killing Will Jackson. A thousand each for his son, another thousand each for his daughter, and five hundred each for the two little girls."

"That comes to thirteen thousand dollars in total. Sixty-five hundred apiece. Though I don't think I cotton to the notion of killing two little girls," said Smith. "If he's that intent on wiping the family out, he can do for his granddaughters himself. That leaves six thousand apiece. Why such a high price for Jackson and his kids?"

"'Cause of who you'll have to kill to get to 'em."

"Who's that?"

"One of Jackson's hands is a fella named Hal Hachette. Crack shot. Enough that, instead of punching cows, he's a full-time bodyguard for the family, with a deputy sheriff's badge to give him legal authority. Just recently, Hachette's big brother has joined him, and he makes Hal, good as he is, look like an amateur. You may have heard of him, 'cause he's got quite a reputation."

"You're not talkin' about *Gus* Hachette, are you?" asked Kent

"That's exactly who I'm talking about."

"Not that we couldn't take him, if we had to, but I'd just as soon not have to. And if his kid brother's anywhere near his class, that's hell of a lot to bite off."

"You're getting paid for it."

"*If* we decide to take the job," said Smith. "Jerry's right. It's a lot to bite off. If we tried to pick 'em off one at a time, each subsequent kill would be that much harder, 'cause they'd increase the level of protection that much more. And the odds of getting all three of 'em together at the same time, at a place where we could kill 'em all and get away clean are pretty damned slim."

"And," said Kent, "that's leaving aside the fact that we'd have to kill at least one of the Hachette brothers to get to the target you really want dead. Killing Hal Hachette would be one thing. He's just a cowboy whose boss arranged for him to get a badge. But killing Hal would put his brother on the warpath, which would mean we'd probably have to kill him, too, eventually. And that's whole different ball of wax. Gus Hachette's a top professional, one of the most respected peace officers in Texas, and killing him would mean every cop's hand would be raised against whoever did for him. You tell your father-in-law we'll do it if both of us get five thousand. But he's got to decide who wants dead the most. You got that straight? One dead body for ten thousand total, but he gets to pick the body. We'll throw in, free of charge, whichever Hachette we might have to kill to make that body dead."

"I'll get back to you," said Meaney.

*****

Ace Simmons was not pleased at the deal Kent and Smith offered. He wanted a clean sweep of all the Jacksons made, and he was willing to pay for it.

"How much you're willing to pay," said Meaney, "has nothing to do with it if there's no one willing to accept it. And there's a point where the risk involved is too much no matter the amount. Kent and Smith are two of the hardest cases in Texas, but they won't kill more'n one Jackson, no matter how much more you offer, 'cause killing even one Jackson means killing a Hachette brother, and, like I told you, killing a cop's like starting a blood feud with every cop in America. They'll do one, and do it for ten grand. And the two kids are off the table."

"They all have to die!" insisted Simmons.

"Killing two little girls would turn every hand against you. Even folks who understand blood feuds stop short of killing babies. And killing their mother would only be a little bit less infuriating. As a practical matter, you've gotta decide between Will and Steve. Steve's the one actually killed your boy, but only after he tried to shoot Steve in the back, and that after his making a lot of dirty talk about Claudia."

"Well, then, which one of those two'd be easiest to kill?"

"Was it me, I'd go for Will. He's buying protection for his family, but not seeing so much to his own safety. And do it when Gus Hachette's around. If you'n and me've got alibis, they can make it look like Hachette was the target instead of Will."

"What would be the point of that?"

"Gus Hachette's made enough enemies that if he and Will both die, Will's death might be taken as unintended. People might not attribute the deaths to a feud at all if we're not even in the area."

"All right," said Simmons. "Tell 'em to make Will the target."

*****

Some weeks later, Luke Smith sat in a darkened third floor hotel room on Mesa Avenue in El Paso. Will Simmons and Gus Hachette were staying at another hotel across the street. Right now they were attending a cattle auction a few blocks away. Smith was staked out with a rifle waiting to gun them both down from ambush when they returned from the auction.

Smith was better with a rifle than Kent, so the labor had been divided to make Smith the triggerman, and Kent the public face. Kent had registered at the hotel then given the key to Smith, who'd entered the room without being seen. Kent was in a speakeasy a few blocks away, buying drinks for the house, and thus establishing an unbreakable alibi. Once the business was completed Kent would return to his room, and profess to be shocked that it had been used as an assassin's perch, while Smith unobtrusively drove off in the auto which had brought them to El Paso.

He was standing back far enough from the window that it would be difficult to see him, but close enough that he still had a clear shot at the entrance to the hotel across the street. He'd considered using a piece with a telescopic sight, but decided that the range was close enough that the Winchester '92 with aperture sights would suffice.

Keeping a close watch, he saw Simmons and Hachette, his distinctive Colt automatic pistol with the ivory grips holstered at his side, approaching the hotel entrance across the street. They stopped just outside the entrance, when a third party approached Simmons, his hand outstretched in greeting.

As Simmons stopped to shake hands with the newcomer, Smith cocked the rifle, lined up his sights on Hachette, and slowly started squeezing the trigger.

*****

"Just wanted to congratulate you, Will," said the man shaking Simmons's hand. "You clearly wanted that Durham bull more'n I did."

"You must not've wanted him at all, Ted," replied Simmons. "We both know that I could've bid my entire ranch, my bank, and every cent I have, and you still could've outbid me with the spare change in your pocket."

This was only a slight exaggeration. Will Simmons was a powerful cattle baron, true, but Ted Leonard, who owned one of the biggest ranches in the entire Southwest, the T&A Cattle Company in Gila, New Mexico, was a cattle *king*. Between Leonard and the likes of Will Jackson, there were a host of cattle dukes, marquesses, counts, and viscounts. Jackson was rich. Leonard was *fabulously* rich.

Leonard chuckled, and said, "You must've been carrying the price of that bull in cash to have a badge-toter standing guard over you."

"Sorry. Should've introduced you. This here's Gus Hachette. Late of the Texas Rangers. He's just working for me temporarily 'cause of a fracas that got stirred up back home. Once thing's settle down, he'll be returning to his regular job. His brother, Hal, is one of my regular hands."

"Gus Hachette," repeated Leonard. "Heard of you I think. Aren't you the one tracked that fella who killed that Houston policeman into Louisiana. Killed him when he made a gunfight."

"I've been in more'n my share of shootouts, Mr. Leonard," replied Hachette. "But that fella in Louisiana came along quietly. And it was a district constable he killed, not a Houston city cop."

Leonard stepped over to Hachette, his hand extended in greeting, when his head suddenly exploded, a sight followed almost immediately by the sound of a gun firing.

*****

God damn it!, thought Smith.

The hammer dropped just as that third fellow stepped in front of Hachette. Now he'd not only killed the wrong man, but both his actual targets were alerted.

He cocked the rifle again and triggered off another shot.

*****

Instinctively, Hachette knew the round must've been some kind of hollow point or exploding round, since Leonard's head was essentially disintegrated. That'd probably saved Hachette's life. A high-powered rifle round, even after penetrating the thick, hard bone of a skull, would've gone all the way through and hit whatever was behind the target, unless it was designed to come apart inside the target.

He quickly stepped toward Simmons, pushed him to the ground, and covered him with his body as the next shot was fired. He able to identify which window the shot came from, but could not see the gunman.

He rolled off Simmons, saying, "Stay down!" and drew his Colt .45 semiautomatic Government Model. He already had a round under the hammer. Quickly thumb-cocking the pistol, he cranked off five shots as quickly as he could squeeze the trigger. The slide mechanism automatically cocking the pistol after the first shot, making rapid fire possible, as if the pistol was fully automatic instead of needing a separate trigger squeeze for every shot.

*****

Smith shouted an obscenity as he felt one of Hachette's rounds penetrate his left upper arm.

All five shots came through the window, a testament to Hachette's marksmanship under stressful conditions, but only one actually connected with Smith.

Aside from the pain, which was considerable, Smith found himself chagrined and humiliated that Hachette had been more effective with a handgun than Kent had been with a rifle.

Maybe the stories Texas lawmen shared about Hachette's skill with a gun, stories Kent had always assumed were exaggerations, were actually true.

Unable to hold the Winchester any longer with one arm disabled, the rifle dropped onto the floor. Smith left it there as he hurriedly left the room and made his way to the ground floor.

At the rear exit, as previously arranged, Kent was waiting in an auto.

*****

"You'll have to drive," said Smith.

"What happened?"

"Somebody stepped into my line of fire just as I squeezed of my shot. Hachette returned fire and put one in my left arm."

"But if we both leave, they'll know I was part of the murder plot."

"Well, I can't drive, so you'll have to get me someplace where you can dig this slug out. Then we can figure out where to go from there."

Damn, thought Kent, as he put the machine in gear. This whole business of making a living by killing people had its drawbacks.

*****

Six hours later, Smith was dead drunk, lying on a bed in a modest hunting lodge in Hudspeth County, just east of El Paso County. Kent had spent the better part of those six hours, driving to the lodge, filling Smith with liquor, digging out the round with a knife he'd sterilized, first by moving the open flame of a match back and forth over the blade, then by pouring the same cheap whiskey that had inebriated Kent over that same blade.

Once he had the slug in the palm of his hand, he looked at it closely, then put it in an envelope he got from a desk in the bedroom, and sealed it. He didn't know why, but he had a notion that saving that slug might give him some kind of a way of getting out of this situation.

The ten thousand dollars they were going to split for killing Will Jackson was no longer available after the flubbed attempt. And there was a possibility, indeed a probability, that they might both be identified as the men behind that attempt. He had no idea what advantage keeping that round in his possession might give him, but his instincts told him to hold onto it.

*****

After making sure Will Jackson was uninjured, Hachette, pistol drawn, had entered the hotel across the street and made his way to the third floor room from which the rifle shots had come. The door had been left open. The rifle, dropped or abandoned, was still on the floor. A trail of blood drops from the window, to the door, down the hallway, to a stairwell, and out a side entrance, finally ending at the sidewalk curb, indicated that the sniper had escaped. Hachette went back into the hotel, and instructed a desk clerk to call the police, and have them meet him on the third floor.

*****

Two uniformed officers arrived at the hotel room a few minutes later. Hachette suggested that one stay outside the room, keeping people out, in order to preserve the integrity of the room, then showed the other the trail of blood that led to the sidewalk outside.

When they returned to the third floor hallway, Hachette asked, "Your department have a Bertillon man?"

"Sure," said the uniformed cop.

"He know about fingerprints, or does he just take mug shots and measurements?"

"He's got a print kit. And he knows how to use it."

"I know this is your territory, so I don't want you to get the notion I'm giving orders. But I'm going to suggest you go downstairs and phone your station and get your Bertillon man up here pronto. Have him print the entire room. Particularly that rifle. Also get a detective. Also a coroner for that body across the street."

"I'll do that right now," the cop said.

Turning to the other officer, Hachette said, "I'll stand guard here if you want me to. Why don't you go across the street and keep that body from getting interfered with."

*****

Hours later, the El Paso PD's Bertillon man had collected a fair number of prints from the room, including several off the rifle, and some clear partial thumbprints off the back off the rounds still in the rifle.

Meanwhile, Ted Leonard had been officially pronounced dead by a deputy coroner, who'd taken possession of the body.

Mrs. Leonard, also in El Paso for the auction, had, upon being informed of her husband's murder, contacted El Paso's three daily papers and every radio station in West Texas, and announced that she would pay fifteen thousand dollars for information leading to the arrest and conviction of Ted

Leonard's killer.

*****

While Smith slept it off in the only bedroom in the cabin, Kent sat in the outer room half-listening to the radio, while he tried to figure out a way to extricate himself from this mess.

At the top of the hour, the music stopped, and a short news bulletin began. About halfway through the bulletin, the announcer said, "This just in. Mrs. Ivy Leonard, the widow of New Mexico rancher Theodore Leonard, shot to death earlier today on the streets of El Paso, has announced that she will pay a fifteen thousand dollar reward for any information leading to the arrest and conviction of her husband's murderer. She was quoted as saying, 'Let me make it clear. Arrest and conviction! I will not pay a cent to anyone bringing in a dead body and claiming it's the corpse of my husband's killer. I want this murderer arrested, tried, and convicted in a court of law.'"

Kent padded the breast pocket of his shirt, where he'd placed the envelope containing the pistol slug. It occurred to him that he might just've been handed a way out of this predicament. And it also occurred to him that fifteen thousand dollars he didn't have to share, was a lot better than ten thousand dollars split two ways.

He went into the bedroom to rouse his partner, at least rouse him enough that he'd be able to get him into the machine without having to carry him. He could sleep all the way to the county sheriff's station.

*****

Hachette and Jackson were eating dinner in the hotel dining room, when one of the clerks approached him

"Mr. Hachette," he said, "phone call for you."

Hachette followed the clerk out of the dining room, and at the front desk, he picked up the proffered telephone and said, "This is Gus Hachette."

"Sergeant Hamilton, El Paso Police," came the response. "Sorry to interrupt your dinner, but we just got a call from Hank Morely, the Hudspeth County Sheriff. Seems he has a fellow in custody he thinks is your sniper."

"Already?"

"That bounty Mrs. Leonard offered must've had its effect. This fellow was turned in by his own partner. They're both known as hired killers, though nothing's ever been proven. The partner, Jerry Kent, is claiming that he had no idea that his partner was planning on making the kill today. The gunman, Luke Smith, has got a bullet wound in his arm, and Kent dug the slug out. It's a .45 from a semi-auto, just like your Colt."

"That sounds promising," said Hachette.

*****

By the next day, after Smith had been examined by a physician, and then allowed a night's rest, Sheriff Morely transported the putative sniper to El Paso County, where he was booked into the county jail.

The slug Kent had removed during his amateur surgery was turned over the El Paso Police, where it was booked into evidence. Four other slugs, found lodged in various places in the hotel room, all from a .45 semi-auto, all the same make as the one dug out of Kent, had already been booked into evidence.

Speaking with Captain Edward Payton, the head of El Paso PD's detective bureau, Hachette suggested that, if Payton was interested in proving, beyond any doubt, that those rounds were fired from Hachette's Colt, that he should contact Colonel Frank Goudard, a retired Army officer who was an expert in forensic ballistics.

"He's proven," said Hachette, "that no two guns leave the same markings on the rounds fired from it. Every gun's unique. Like fingerprints. You match the round removed from Smith with the rounds found in the hotel room, then match all of those with a round from 'Ol' Lucky,' here, the case becomes, not just solid, but damn near impossible to disprove."

"I dunno. I got a lot of respect for all these scientific advances, but it's hard to make juries even understand, let alone accept that kind of evidence. I know a lot of cops, not just ordinary citizens, but *cops*, who think fingerprints, which have been around for thirty or more years, are just a lot of 'new-fangled nonsense.' If cops are skeptical, jurors'll be even harder to convince."

"You might have a point," admitted Hachette.

"Anyway, even without that... what'd you call it... ballistic matching, four rounds fired from a .45 Colt semiautomatic, our Bertillon man's matching all those prints from the hotel room and from the rifle to Smith, Kent's testimony, yours and Jackson's testimony, I think we're probably on solid ground. But I'll mention this here Colonel Goudard to the chief and the prosecutor. Wouldn't need him for the preliminary hearing, in any case, but, if it comes to a jury trial, they might want some frosting on the cake."

*****

Some weeks after the conference, Gus Hachette and Will Jackson, accompanied by Hachette's brother, Hal, and Jackson's children, Steve Jackson and Claudia Simmons, returned to El Paso to testify at the preliminary hearing.

Will Jackson testified first, telling how they had been greeted by Ted Leonard in front of the hotel entrance, how Ted's head exploded just as he stepped over to Gus Hachette to shake hands, followed immediately by the sound of a rifle shot, how Gus had pushed him to the ground just before a second rifle shot was heard, and how Gus returned fire with his pistol.

The cross examination of Jackson was *pro forma*, simply asking for additional details on the points Jackson had testified about.

Hachette was called next. His testimony confirmed Jackson's. He was also able to give more details about from exactly which window the shots had come from, how many shots he'd fired in return, and how he had entered the building after the firing stopped, found the open room on the third floor, the rifle, and the trail of blood from that room to a side exit.

Russell Hardy, the prosecuting attorney, then asked Hachette to look closely at Luke Smith.

"Can you identify the defendant as the man who shot at you?" he asked.

"No, sir, I cannot."

"Can you state where you hit your attacker when you returned fire?"

"I can't say, as a matter of my direct knowledge, that I *did* hit him. I can say that I fired, and that I found a trail of blood leading from the room our attacker used to shoot at us to the side exit of the building. I can draw a reasonable inference from those circumstances, and come to reasonable conclusion, but that's all."

"Thank you Mr. Hachette."

Smith's lawyer, Pierce Carter, asked Hachette about his employment.

"Are you a police officer, Mr. Hachette?"

"I'm employed by Mr. Jackson as a bodyguard for him and other members of his family. He has arranged for me to be deputized by the Sheriff Hanlon of Scurry County to give me law enforcement authority. When I'm not performing my job for Mr. Jackson, I work part-time for the Sheriff's Office."

"Have you ever been a full-time police officer?"

"Yes, sir. Most of the last ten years I've been a lawman of one kind or another. Mostly for the Rangers, but I've also been a town marshal for a place called Aguaturbia in Grimes County, Texas, a detective for the Houston Police, a full-time sheriff's deputy in Kimble County, and a field investigator for the Lone Star Cattlemen's Association, in which capacity I was commissioned as a Special Ranger. I also served a short stint in the Army as a military policeman."

"You've moved around a lot, Mr. Hachette. Can't you hold a job?"

"Man wants to better himself in his profession if he possibly can. Being Aguaturbia's police chief paid better'n being a Ranger private, and I got to be my own boss. Being a special investigator in Houston paid better than being a small-town marshal. I resigned from that job when the mayor chose not to run for reelection, since he was my sponsor, and got hired as a deputy in Kimble County which paid as well as the Houston job did. I returned to the Rangers when the incumbent sheriff who hired me chose to retire. Didn't pay as well, but being a Ranger was the most exciting job I've ever had, and I was appointed a sergeant. Went into the Army 'cause there was a war on, and I felt soldiering was the duty of an able-bodied man. Went to work for the Cattlemen's Association 'cause it was the best paying job I'd had since entering law enforcement. Went to work for Mr. Jackson 'cause he paid even better."

"Was there any other reason you accepted Mr. Jackson's offer?"

"My brother, Harold Hachette, was already employed in that capacity. I wanted to support him."

"Was there any *other* reason you accepted Mr. Jackson's offer?" repeated the lawyer, this time allowing an insinuating tone to creep into his voice.

"I suspect you 're trying to get me to draw another one of those inferences we were talking about before. But I've already answered that question. If you have something else in mind besides what I've already said, maybe you should just ask me directly, 'stead of hoping I'll draw the... *correct* inference."

"I quite agree, Counselor," said the Honorable Neal Roberts, who was presiding over the hearing. "You've asked the question twice, and he answered it clearly and directly the first time. Merely emphasizing the word 'other' isn't likely to adduce a different response. If you have a specific question, ask it. If you don't, move on to something else."

"I was trying to ascertain the witness's feelings for Mr. Jackson's daughter, Mrs. Claudia Simmons."

"Was Mrs. Simmons present during the attack on her father and Mr. Hachette that led to the death of Mr. Leonard?"

"No, Your Honor."

"Then I fail to see the relevance of Mr. Hachette's feelings or lack of same, for his employer's daughter. Move on to something else."

"My apologies, Your Honor."

Frustrated that his attempt to imply that something indecent was going on between Hachette and Claudia Simmons had been thwarted, Carter ended his cross. Had this been an actual trial, the fact that the suggestion had even been made might have had some effect on the jury, even if the question never got officially asked or answered. But this was a preliminary hearing, and the decision whether or not to bind the defendant over for trial was solely the judge's.

And all Carter'd managed to do was annoy the judge.

*****

Following Hachette, Lee Pinker, the El Paso Police Department's Bertillon man took the stand, testified to the many prints he had lifted from the third floor hotel room that had been used as a sniper's perch, and particularly those from the rifle left behind, and how he had matched them to the defendant, Lucas R. Smith, aka Luke Smith, how he had dug four spent .45 rounds from various points in the room, how a fifth round, also a .45 from a Colt Government Model, and of the same brand and make as the other four, had been turned over to him by Smith's associate, Gerald W. Kent.

Carter began his cross with, "You stated that Gerald Kent turned the fifth slug over to you?"

"Yes, sir."

"And he had removed it from the defendant's upper left arm?"

"He *said* he removed it from the defendant's upper left arm. I wasn't there when he did it."

Damn, thought Carter. These witnesses had been well-briefed. None of them could be tricked into testifying to anything outside the boundaries of their own personal knowledge.

"Can you say to a certainty," asked Carter, "that all of these rounds were fired from Mr. Hachette's pistol?"

"I can't. I can say that they're all the same calibre and make as those Mr. Hachette still had in his weapon after the exchange of gunfire. It's very likely that such a determination *can* be made, but I don't have the training or expertise to make that assessment."

"What do you mean?" asked Carter, who then cursed himself silently for being drawn into the trap of asking a question to which he did not already know the answer.

"Firearms make distinctive marks on the rounds that are fired from them. And those marks are unique to each individual firearm. So, if I had the training, I could, theoretically, compare two slugs of the same calibre, and determine whether or not they'd been fired from the same weapon, or from two different weapons of the same make and model. Colonel Frank Goudard, who is a professor at Northwestern University in Illinois, has developed this form of identification. He has the expertise to make the assessment you're asking about, but I do not."

And they wouldn't, thought Carter, go to the trouble of getting such an expert for a prelim, but they might for an actual jury trial. Juries, Carter knew, were often skeptical of scientific evidence, but were becoming less so with each passing year. And with all the other evidence amassed against Smith, enough to convict by itself in Carter's estimation, this ballistics matching process might just be the tipping point.

Carter dismissed the witness with thanks.

*****

Hardy's last witness was his star, Jerry Kent, who testified that he and Smith had been hired by Jay Meaney, on behalf of Ace Simmons, to kill Will Jackson.

"I pretended to go along with it," said Kent. "But my intention was to warn Jackson before the murder came off. I thought Jackson might be grateful enough to give me a cash reward that would exceed what Ace Simmons was offering Luke and me to kill him. I didn't expect Luke to try to take a shot that afternoon. I intended to warn Jackson that evening at dinnertime."

"Where were you when the attempt was made?"

"Well, I'd prefer not to answer that with precision. I was at a speakeasy not too far from the two hotels. I don't want to give the exact location, but I can name several people who saw me there, 'cause I bought 'em all drinks!"

Continuing to respond to Hardy's questions, he described how he picked up Smith at the side entrance to their hotel, how they drove to a hunting lodge in Hudspeth County, how he dug the slug out of Smith's arm, and bandaged it up, getting him drunk as an improvised form of anesthetic, and, upon learning of the reward offered by Mrs. Leonard, decided to turn Smith in as an act of good faith to square himself with the law.

Carter bore down hard in his cross, but, since Kent was already a pretty disreputable character to begin with, couldn't really make him look any worse, and, more to the point, was not able to shake his testimony in the slightest.

When Carter was finished, Hardy rested, and Carter asked to defer his defense until after the recess.

*****

"Feel any tightness around your neck, Luke?" asked Carter after court adjourned.

"Tightness? No. Why?"

"You should. Because in a few months you'll be feeling it for real when they walk you up the stairs to the gallows."

"Why do you say that? This is just the preliminary hearing. The judge hasn't even bound me over for trial yet."

"That's the point. All Hardy has to do to get you bound over is prove that a crime was committed, and that there's probable cause to believe you committed that crime. That's miles south of proving a case beyond a reasonable doubt."

"So?"

"He's already presented enough evidence to convict you. Not a sure thing, mind you, but well beyond reasonable doubt for anyone with minimal intelligence. And, since this *is* only a preliminary, it's not likely that they've presented their whole case. They'll have a lot more to throw at you when it comes to a jury trial."

"What else could they have?"

"Who knows? Maybe they're planning on bringing that college professor colonel down from Chicago. Maybe they've got themselves an eyeball witness who can identify you as the sniper. All I know is if they can already convict just on what they've presented, they must have enough to completely smoke you off the Earth at the main event. Do you want to hang?"

"Course not!"

"Then I advise you to plead guilty in exchange for taking the death penalty off the table."

"You think the death penalty's worse than spending the rest of my life behind bars?"

"Where there's life there's hope. Jake MacFergus might be returning to the governor's mansion in a few years. He's always ready to give a fellow a full pardon in exchange for a hefty campaign contribution."

"He can't be returning to office. The State Senate convicted him of a dozen different charges and barred him from ever holding elective office in Texas again."

"Didn't say he was returning to office. Just that he was returning to the governor's mansion. His wife'll be the one running. She's *not* barred. And once she's in office, she'll be the one on stage. But he'll be the one holding her strings."

"Well, I might not live that long. I'm an ex-cop. You know what happens to lawmen in prison."

"I can see that you're protected. But if we try to fight this at a trial, the end result will be you getting hung by the neck until dead. Huntsville may be a terrible place, but death is final."

*****

After some more pointed persuasion on the part of Carter, Smith agreed to plead guilty if Carter could make the deal. Carter went to Hardy to discuss a possible bargain.

When court reconvened, the judge asked Carter if he planned to make a defense. Carter replied that he did not, and that, in fact, he and the prosecutor had come to an agreement.

"With the Court's approval, Your Honor," said Carter, "and with Mr.

Hardy's assurance that the prosecution will not seek the death penalty, my client would like to change his plea from 'not guilty' to 'guilty.'"

"Is this acceptable to the State?" Judge Roberts asked Hardy.

"It is, Your Honor," replied the prosecutor.

"I will take this under advisement, and announce my decision when we convene tomorrow morning at ten o'clock. In the meantime, the prisoner and the material witness, Mr. Kent, are both remanded to the custody of the sheriff. Until then, this court is adjourned."

*****

Hot damn! thought Kent. A guilty plea meant a conviction, and a conviction, following the arrest, would mean that the reward would be collectible as soon as sentence was passed. Mrs. Leonard might not be pleased, but, after all, the conditions she'd set down had been "arrest and conviction," not "arrest, conviction, and execution." If she'd wanted him dead, she should've made the terms "dead or alive."

A deputy came over to escort Kent back to his quarters. Kent noticed that the Will Jackson and his son and daughter were leaving the courtroom, under the watchful eyes of the Hachette brothers.

"Can you let me have a word with Gus Hachette?" asked Kent.

The deputy asked if Hachette had moment.

When Hachette came over, Kent held out his hand in greeting, and said, "Hello, Hachette."

*****

Hachette looked down at the extended hand, then at Kent, then back at the hand. His facial expression didn't change, except for his dark, piercing eyes, which seemed to burn angrily.

"What do you want, Kent?" said Hachette.

"Just thought we could congratulate each other on getting Smith convicted," replied Kent, slowly lowering his hand.

"Yeah. You taking the stand in the cause of justice was truly inspirational," replied Hachette. "You're really one for the books, Kent. Smith's a criminal, but at least he's consistent. You're just a backstabber, selling your partner out for a payoff."

"You think he could've been convicted without my testimony and the evidence I provided? He's paying the price for what he did, and I'm the reason he's going to pay that price. And if Mrs. Leonard wants to reward whoever brought her husband's killer to book, who am I to tell her how to spend her own money? But that's not really why I asked to see you."

"Then get to the point."

"You heading back to Snyder today, or staying for the payoff tomorrow?"

"My part's over. We're all leaving right now."

"Well, was I you, I'd go around Sweetwater, not through it."

"Why's that?"

"I have it on good authority than Jay Meaney and a few others are waiting there to ambush you."

"That so?"

"What I've been told."

"Well, I've always gone wherever I've chosen to go. And Sweetwater's the quickest route home."

"That's fine, Hachette, if that's your choice. But don't say I didn't warn you."

*****

Later, escorted to the hotel room where he was being confined as a material witness, Kent asked to make a private phone call.

"I'll pay for it," he said.

Having no reason to deny him, he was allowed to make a private call from a booth in the lobby.

Kent quickly made a connection to the Simmons Ranch, and asked to speak with Ace Simmons. When Simmons came on the line, Kent told him he had some valuable information for him.

"What information could you possibly have for me at this point, Kent? I've got no use for double-crossers like you."

"Now, Simmons, when Smith went and killed the wrong man, I was in a fix I couldn't get out of without selling Smith out. Only thing I had to bargain with was the truth. And, like it says in the Good Book, the truth set me free."

"Only you implicated *me* with that truth."

"You got caught up in the tide. But that's what happens when you get so intent on revenge you're willing to pay someone to get it. Nevertheless, though I imagine our business arrangement's at an end, I do feel I have a professional obligation to you. So, free of charge, I'm going to let you know that you may have another shot at Jackson and his two kids, but you'll have to kill both Hachette brothers to get it."

"What are you talking about?"

"Jackson, his son and daughter, and the Hachettes will be passing through Sweetwater, probably tomorrow, on their way home from the trial."

"And just how do you know that?"

"I don't absolutely know it. But I'd bet the entire fifteen grand I'm getting from Mrs. Leonard."

"Why?"

"'Cause I told Gus Hachette that Jay'll be there waiting to ambush him."

"How's that supposed to guarantee he'll go through Sweetwater? Warning him like that'll just make him go the long way 'round."

"Maybe. But Gus Hachette's a prideful man. Exactly the type to ignore a warning just so it won't look like he's afraid. If I hadn't've warned him, he might've decided to take a different route for one reason or another. But, now that he *has* been warned, his pride won't let him go any other way."

"If you've read him right."

"Nothing's a hundred per cent, Simmons. But what've you got to lose if Meaney and a couple of other men are waiting for him? If he doesn't come through, some other opportunity will present itself eventually. But if he does, you can end the whole thing in one concentrated attack."

*****

A few years earlier, Kent's assessment of Gus Hachette's likely reaction would've been spot on, but time and experience had mellowed the young lawman. With three people he was being paid to keep *out* of harm's way seated in the back seat of the spacious 1919 Pierce-Arrow that he and his brother were taking turns driving, going through Sweetwater instead of around seemed a pointless exhibition of bravado. Consequently, when they got up earlier that morning in Odessa, where they'd all spent the night after leaving El Paso yesterday, he and Hal had agreed to take a detour that would allow them to bypass Sweetwater altogether.

What finally forced the party to enter the town was a minor calamity that was all too common in an era where paved roads were a rarity, and most of the automotive thoroughfares connecting one part of Texas with another were dirt trails.

One of their tires went flat.

"Damn!" said Gus Hachette.

"Well, we've got no choice now, brother," said Hal Hachette. "We'll have to go into town. We won't be able to make it to Sylvester or Roby going the long way."

"God damn it!" said Gus Hachette. "OK, here's how we'll do it. I'll let you and the Jacksons out at the first public building we see once we get into town. You stay with the family, and I'll get the tire replaced."

"Don't know as I like that idea, Gus."

"One of use has to stay with the family. If the one getting the tire is attacked, the one getting the tire ought to be the one with the most experience in gunplay. And we both know that's me."

*****

Sweetwater, a booming town thanks to its being a hub where three different railroads met, had a bustling population in excess of 10,000. Moving slowly to minimize further damage to the wheel, Gus Hachette stopped at the Nolan County Courthouse, a red brick building with a row of pillars at the front entrance, and let the Jacksons and Hal Hachette out. The Jacksons, and particularly Claudia, were not pleased at the notion of Gus Hachette getting the car repaired on his own, but, in the end, acquiesced.

After staying long enough to make sure all four had entered the building, Gus Hachette continued down the road to a filling station a half block away.

*****

Farther down the road, Jay Meaney and one of Ace Simmons's hands, Ed Bartholomew, nicknamed "Brick" for his both his solid build and his shock of dark red hair, were parked at a curb in an open-topped Model T.

When Meaney saw the Pierce Arrow slowly pull into the filling station, and Gus Hachette exit the machine to go into the station office, he knew that that the showdown had finally come.

He turned to Bartholomew. He was a young kid. Good with a gun, like most Texans, but, by no means any kind of professional gun hand. Certainly he'd never killed anyone.

"You ready for this, son?" he asked the kid.

"I ride for the brand, Mr. Meaney."

"I know you do, Brick. But we're not punching cattle here. We're about to do murder. And one of the men we're trying to murder has survived more'n a dozen gunfights. Fights he didn't start, mind you. But he *finished* all of 'em. I won't think less of you if you decide to step away. And if ol' Jackson fires you, well you can always get another job, long as you're alive enough to look for one."

"Mr. Jackson said he'd pay extra."

"Extra pay won't mean a thing 'less you're alive to collect it."

Bartholomew hesitated a moment, then steeled himself, and repeated, with greater emphasis, "I ride for the brand."

Meaney turned on the machine, put it in gear and said, "Well, let's get to it, then."

*****

Gus Hachette stepped out of the filling station office to find Jay Meaney and another man waiting for him, guns out. Meaney, holding a Colt .45 Government Model in his right hand, cocked back the hammer and started to raise it. He and Hachette were less than two feet apart.

Hachette grabbed Meaney's right wrist in his left hand and pushed it down. The pistol went off. A .45 slug smashed into Hachette's right thigh, just above the knee.

"Now I've got you, Hachette!" Meaney exclaimed, wrenching his gun hand loose and raising it again.

This time Hachette put Meaney in a bear hug. A second shot went off, entering Hachette's left shoulder, coming apart and sending shards into his left lung.

His left arm now useless, Hachette grabbed at Meaney's pistol with his right hand, gripping the slide mechanism at the top of the barrel. Meaney wrenched it loose and tried to fire a third shot, but Hachette's vice-like grip on the slide mechanism had caused the piece to jam, rendering it useless.

*****

Brick Bartholomew had exited the Ford from the passenger side, armed with a semi-automatic shotgun. Crouched behind the hood of the machine, he trained his weapon on the two struggling combatants, but was unable to fire while they were clinched so closely together.

*****

When the sound of the gunfire exploded a half-block away from the courthouse, Claudia Simmons immediately reached into her shoulder bag and pulled out her ever-present Colt .32 Pocket Hammerless. She sprinted down the front stairs and covered the half-block between the courthouse and the filling station in less than fifteen seconds. Crouching behind the right front fender of the Pierce Arrow, she took aim at the shotgun-wielding attacker and fired three shots.

*****

Bartholomew felt the whiz of the three rounds as they went by him, missing but coming uncomfortably close, before he actually heard the shots.

He turned around and recognized the boss's daughter-in-law, Mrs. Simmons, holding some kind of pistol. He scooted around to the rear of the Model T, providing himself with cover from her attack.

Bringing the shotgun to his shoulder, he peeked around the corner of the Ford to try to draw a bead on his tiny attacker. He didn't feel comfortable shooting at a woman, but a threat was a threat. And, in any event, she was one of the targets he was getting paid to kill.

*****

Throwing the now useless Colt .45 Government Model away in frustration, Meaney ran to the back seat of the Ford, reached in, pulled out a pump action shotgun, and racked a round into the firing chamber.

Gus Hachette reached for the holster at his right hip, drew his own .45, and squeezed off three shots at Meaney just as the latter was shouldering his weapon to fire.

Meaney fell before he could trigger a round, dead by the time he hit the ground, all three of Hachette's shots having pierced his heart.

*****

As soon as Claudia ran out of the courthouse, Hal Hachette swore viciously, then turned to Will Jackson and his son, Steve, and said, "Both of you stay *right* here. You ought to be fine, surrounded by sheriff's deputies. *I've* got to see to your damned headstrong daughter."

He was approaching the filling station just as Claudia ran dry. She was crouching behind the Pierce-Arrow to reload.

Hal saw the red-headed shotgun wielder, apparently figuring that Claudia's pistol was empty, stand up and shoulder his weapon, bringing it to bear on his brother.

Hal brought his own revolver up and fired three shots.

*****

One of Hal Hachette's rounds cut a pretty fair chunk of meat out Brick's right shoulder, veered up a little as it exited, and tore a crease across the bottom of his chin. The sudden pain caused Brick to pull his shot a little to the right, just enough so that, instead of giving Gus Hachette a face full of double ought buck shot, it tore the entire left brim off of Hachette's Stetson.

*****

Claudia finally found the spare magazine in her shoulder bag, reloaded, and began sending more shots at the redheaded gunman.

*****

Gus Hachette triggered off two shots from his .45 at Brick Buchanan, but the blood loss was finally getting to him and both shots went wide.

*****

With his partner dead, and three different people throwing shots at him, it suddenly occurred to Brick Bartholomew that trying to kill folks he had nothing personal against, simply 'cause his boss bore them a grudge, wasn't all that good a reason to die. Instinctively, he threw down the shotgun and began to run.

Ironically, toward the courthouse.

*****

Gus Hachette sat down wearily on the running board of the Model T as Hal and Claudia ran up to him. Hal took aim at the fleeing Bartholomew.

"No, Hal" cried his brother from his seated position. "Not in the back."

Hal lowered his revolver.

*****

Gus Hachette's merciful impulse turned out to be wasted.

Nolan County Sheriff Jack Sothern himself, hearing the sound of gunfire, rushed toward the front entrance to the courthouse, exiting just as Brick Bartholomew was passing by the building.

Drawing his sidearm and aiming it at the apparently fleeing man, Benjamin yelled, "Stop right there, in the name of the law!"

Instead, Buchanan reached for a pistol he had shoved into the waistband of his trousers. As soon as he pulled it free, Sheriff Sothern emptied his revolver at him.

So much for the hallowed ethic of "riding for the brand."

*****

A few days later, while Gus Hachette recuperated in his hotel room, the Nolan County Grand Jury no-billed him, his brother, and Claudia Simmons. Indeed, this was almost a foregone conclusion since the Grand Jury had been convened on another case at the same time the shootout occurred and, when they heard the shots, the jurors all went to the windows to see what was going one. Thus, they knew very well that Hachette confronted Meaney and Bartholomew with empty hands, had sustained several wounds before he'd even drawn a firearm, and that his firing at Meaney and Bartholomew was, in consequence, thoroughly justified. That Hachette did not fire at Bartholomew when the latter threw down his shotgun and fled confirmed their view that he was acting only out of necessity, not vengeance. Mrs. Simmons and Hal Hachette, they concluded, were justified in supporting the outnumbered Gus Hachette when he was being attacked.

In the same session, they no-billed Sheriff Sothern, who didn't fire until Batholomew drew down on him, after having been ordered to surrender.

*****

And that was the end of the Jackson-Simmons feud, the last blood feud in Texas history. The only fatality on the Jackson side was Collin Higginson, the lawyer hired to represent Steve Jackson, who really did nothing in the case other than to stand by while the Grand Jury no-billed his client, the coroner's jury declared it justifiable homicide, and the DA refused to prosecute, all of which would've happened whether he'd been retained or not.

Ace Simmons had lost his son, his son-in-law, and would be denied contact with his grandchildren for the rest of his life. He was castigated by both his wife and his daughter, who both held him more responsible for the death of Fred Simmons and Jay Meaney than the people who actually killed them.

"You raised our son to be wife-beater and an adulterer," his wife would rail at him. "To say nothing of a coward. He's dead because he tried to shoot a man in the back, and, like the useless drunkard he was, couldn't even manage that."

His daughter was just as critical. "You were the one who insisted on this insane feud. All any of the Jacksons did is defend themselves when they were attacked. You were the one who ordered Jay to attack the Hachettes in Sweetwater. Now my husband, my children's father, is dead, killed in the very act of trying to murder a man, which means he's not just dead, but burning in Hell. All because you were too proud to admit that Fred had it coming."

From that point, he was a stranger not only to Claudia's children, but to the children of his own daughter, Adele.

Everybody in his family was either dead, or hated him.

Less than two years later, Ace Simmons also died. His doctor said it was cancer. But those who knew him said that it wasn't the cancer that ate him up, but the bitterness that had been building since the Sweetwater shootout.

*****

Three days after the Grand Jury handed down its decision, Gus Hachette was deemed well enough to travel to the Jackson Ranch and complete his convalescence there. Less than two weeks after the gun battle, thanks to both his iron constitution and his own grim determination, he was getting around on crutches. At the end of a month, he was walking, though with a noticeable limp, and still using a cane.

One night, as Hachette sat on the front porch reading by a gas lamp, Claudia came out and sat by him.

"What are you reading, Mr. Hachette?" she asked.

"*The Lone Star Ranger*," he answered. "Book by Zane Grey. Main character's supposed to be based on Captain Hughes. 'The Border Boss.' Always admired Captain Hughes. Met him a few times, but never got the chance to work under him."

"Are you enjoying it?"

"Man knows how to tell a story."

He marked his place with the dust jacket of the book, and turned to Claudia.

"Mrs. Simmons, it occurs to me that I haven't thanked you for saving my life."

"Didn't do anything of the kind. None of my shots even came close to hitting. I was just cranking them off without aiming, I was so nervous."

"But you kept him occupied. Only reason Bartholomew hadn't opened up on me was 'cause Meaney and I were clinched, and he couldn't cut loose with a shotgun without hitting both of us. But once Meaney broke free, Bartholomew had a clear shot. He'd've taken it if you hadn't've kept him occupied with that .32. You saved my life, and there's no two ways about that."

"Well, you're certainly welcome, Mr. Hachette."

She paused for moment, then continued, "May I ask you a question?"

"Sure."

"How do you feel about me?"

An awkward pause followed the unexpectedly frank query.

Finally, Hachette managed to stammer out, "Excuse me?"

"I said, how do you feel about me?"

Hachette looked away from her.

"Come on now, Mr. Hachette. You're an honest man. I've asked you a simple question. How do you feel about me?"

"Well, since you put it like that, Mrs. Simmons, I guess I love you."

"Enough to marry me?"

"Enough not to ask you. You deserve better than a two for a nickel lawdog drifting from job to job."

"So it's a question of money?"

"Partly, I guess. Partly just the nature of the work. It's what came between me and my late wife."

"Well, I've got enough money so that you'd never have to work again, unless you wanted to. I'm pretty sure you *would* want to, and I wouldn't keep you from that. You're the kind of man that gauges his worth by how well he does his job. And I know that, for you, being a policeman's the only job. What the Catholics call a 'vocation.' That takes care of the money issue. So what do you say?"

"About what?"

"About us getting married?"

"Mrs. Simmons, are you proposing?"

"I guess I am," she replied.

"Well, in that case, seeing as how I *am* in love you, it seems like it'd downright impolite to say no."

*****

A week later, after exchanging vows at First Presbyterian Church in nearby Kaufman, the newlywed Mr. and Mrs. Gus Hatchette were on a train bound for New Orleans, where they spent a month-long honeymoon.

By the time they arrived home, Hachette's wounds had healed considerably, but he was still well shy of being fully recovered. After a night at the ranch, they gathered up Claudia's two daughters, and drove out to California, where Will Jackson kept a vacation home just outside of Los Angeles.

When they returned to Texas, six months later, he was fully recovered and, though they didn't know it yet, Claudia was carrying the baby who'd become Augustine Francis Hachette, Jr.

By that time, the Volstead Act having been effect for nearly two years, bootlegging and liquor smuggling were going full throttle, and Hachette easily landed a job as an agent in the US Treasury Department's Prohibition Unit.

But that's another story.

Murder at Bullet Pass

Bruce Harris

CHAPTER 1 – The Anvil

Leadville was a misnomer. There hadn't been a shooting there in a year. Fact is there were no guns, rifles, weapons, bullets, or ammunition of any kind in Leadville. Not since Sheriff Ted Pitman pinned a badge to his vest. The town needed a lawman. People still got killed. Disease, old age, accidents, stabbings, and the occasional bludgeoning occurred, but no shootings. Not any more, not in Leadville under Sheriff Pitman's watch. So they changed the name. Leadville became Bullet Pass.

Things were different after the name change. Bullet Pass was like any other town or city in Kansas. Hardworking folk made their livings in farming, ranching, doctoring, preaching, blacksmithing, banking, working the railroads, politics, or in any one of the successful businesses that lined Bullet Pass' dirt roads. The town's three saloons opened at noontime and all were busy up to and including closing time. On Saturdays men stood three deep at the bars, tables all occupied.

"Folks are saying we need another saloon," said Bullet Pass' mayor Harley Reynolds. He placed two fat thumbs in shallow vest pockets, wiggled his exposed fingers, and continued. "I agree with them, Sheriff. Heck, it's hard enough for a man to get a drink around here ever since The Anvil closed down. And I don't mind telling you that some folks won't come live here for that very reason. And what's worse," he paused waiting for a reaction but received none. "Do you or don't you want to know what's worse?" he asked the sheriff.

Pitman yawned. "Sure. Sure Harley. Tell me, what's worse than folks not wanting to move to Bullet Pass?"

"That's more like it," said the now smiling mayor. "What's worse is folks are moving out of Bullet Pass. Just up and up leaving."

"Well now, those wouldn't happen to be people who voted for you, would they Mr. Mayor?"

A coughing fit followed nervous laughter. "I really couldn't say. I'm sure some of them voted for me. Like the Johnsons, and the Barber family, nice people all and they just up and left moved out."

"And you think it's because we only have three saloons? Or is it that we don't allow guns anymore in Bullet Pass? Or maybe they don't like the mayor? Ever think about that?"

"Well sure. I mean, no. This is serious sheriff. People are talking and that's what I hear. Fact is, a number of our good citizens asked me to see you so we can discuss things man to man."

"You go back and tell those same people that Sheriff Pitman is thinking about closing down one of the saloons. We have too much drinking and gambling in town now. I figure we could eliminate some of that non-Christian behavior by reducing the number of drinking establishments. What we need more than anything is another hotel."

What Mayor Reynolds lacked in height he made up for in girth. He stood, looked around the sheriff's office, stopped to read a number of Wanted posters tacked to the walls. He turned toward the sheriff, face serious. "Sheriff, we've known each other a long time. I consider us friends. But I've got to tell you, the men of this town are getting antsy and most of them aren't too happy." Harley Reynolds' father was a preacher, and the old man's oratory skills were not wasted on his son. His tone and demeanor changed. "Sheriff," his voice now raised, "It's my duty to declare before you that the people of this town are getting fed up and tired of a lot of things and one of them is your no gun policy."

"Wait," interrupted Sheriff Pitman, a smile crept across his face. "I thought you came here to tell me Bullet Pass needed another saloon? Now we're talking guns? Is that what you and everyone else want, more guns? It wasn't that long ago. Do I have to remind you about The Anvil?"

The Anvil sat on the outskirts of Leadville. Since the day it opened, the territory's most unsavory characters were drawn there. One of four Leadville saloons, most respectable citizens stayed away. According to legend, the owner, a man named Dan Black had won the saloon in a card game. Accused of cheating, Black had it out with the saloon's original owner. In front of a large crowd, Black was faster with the gun. After shooting the man, Black stood over him, lit a cigar, and dropped the still lit match on the dead man's body. To everyone's horror, they watched as the dead man burned. "That's what you can expect if you accuse me of cheating," he said to the gathered townsmen. He walked back into the saloon. No one said a word.

Leadville's sheriff was out of town at the time. He was ambushed upon his return. A U.S. Marshall appointed Ted Pitman sheriff. Pitman, an experienced lawman, had one thing in mind when he took the job, to shut down The Anvil and rid the town of Dan Black. It didn't take him long. Less than a week on the job...

Sheriff Ted Pitman heard two explosions, the second coming on the heels of the first. He grabbed a rifle off the wall rack and headed out of his office. People ran and screamed. Salty Wright, pointed a bent finger eastward. "Sounds like it come from The Anvil, sheriff," he shouted through tobacco stained lips. "I knows that place is no darn good. I done hope the whole place blow up. Serve 'em all right."

Pitman wasn't listening. In mid stride, he noticed a small commotion in front of The Anvil. He worked his way inside. There sat Dan Black, dressed like he was going to hear an opera or attend a high-end ball. His legs were crossed at the ankles, the unsoiled soles of his shiny boots caught Sheriff Pitman's gaze.

"What's going on here Black?" asked Pitman. "Is this some kind of a joke?"

"Welcome to The Anvil sheriff. First drink is on me." He craned his neck around and barked orders to the bartender. "Hank, a whiskey for the sheriff here. The best we got. He's my guest."

Pitman looked around. He didn't like what he saw. A number of Black's men surrounded him, hate in their faces and eyes. "Are you responsible for that explosion Black?"

Dan Black looked at his fingernails, satisfied, he answered. "Explosion? What explosion? I didn't hear anything. You gentlemen hear an explosion?"

"No" came the retort as the five men shook their heads.

"I'm closing this place down until I find out what exactly it is you're up to Black."

"On what grounds?" asked The Anvil's owner.

"On my say so is the only grounds I need."

"I don't think these gentlemen…er…my customers would take kindly to that sheriff." He addressed the five. "Would you, gentlemen?"

Again the five shook their heads. One man, slim with a hat a size too large, reached for his gun. Before he touched the handle, Sheriff Pitman whirled and fired. The man dropped. Black didn't budge, but the remaining four all made moves for their weapons.

"Don't try it!" commanded Pitman, "Or you'll wind up like your dead friend here."

The youngest of the group, his nose broken more times than he'd bathed in the last month, took a step toward Pitman. "You don't scare me none sheriff. Let's make this a fair fight. Just me and you. I think my friends and Mr. Black would enjoy a little show like that, watching me shoot you through the neck."

Pitman laughed. He faced Black. "What makes this tinhorn think he'd have a chance against me? Tell him to shut up or I'll shut him up for good."

"Why you…" were the last two words spoken by the flat-nosed one. The second bullet from Pitman's rifle shattered the man's Adam's apple and exited his body, striking a third member of the group in the chest. The youngster fell face forward, his nose now permanently pressed against his hairless upper lip. The third man dropped his weapon, clutched his chest and fell backward.

"Hold your fire boys!" instructed Dan Black. "Very nice work sheriff. Very nice. Yes sir. Two bullets, three bodies. Impressive. Problem is there is still three of us and only one of you."

"Look Black, I don't like the kind of place you run here. Every night someone is either getting shot at or being cheated at cards, or being swindled by one of your hostesses. And tonight, there's an explosion or two. I'm shutting this place down for good."

"Ha!" chuckled Black. "I'll tell you what sheriff. I'm a fair man, am I not boys?"

Both remaining bodyguards responded in unison. "Yes Mr. Black."

"I won this establishment in a card game, and I'm willing to put everything on the line with one draw of the deck. For a little change of pace, let's do low card wins. I'll wager that I pick the lower card than you, sheriff. If you win, you can shut down The Anvil as early as tonight and I'll pack up and get out of

Leadville. Forever. If you lose, the coroner carries you out of here. Agree?"

"Nothing doing Black. I don't mind putting my life on the line to see to it that you and your friends here are run out of town, but I'll be damned if I'm going to gamble with one of your crooked decks."

"Unfortunately for you sheriff, you aren't in a position to argue. I'm giving you a chance. Otherwise…"

The two outlaws aimed their weapons at Pitman.

"Tell you what Black. You pick first. That's not asking too much, is it?" asked Pitman.

Dan Black glanced at the two men who had pistols aimed at Pitman. He shrugged his shoulders. "Why not?" He called to one of the servers who promptly brought a fresh deck of cards. He shuffled and cut the deck.

"Just a minute Black," interrupted the sheriff. "Don't I get to cut it before you pick?"

"Of course sheriff. Where are my manners? I guess our little game has me rattled. A lot riding on it. Go ahead, cut." He sat back, a satisfied look on his freshly shaven face, while Pitman cut the deck.

Before Black picked, the sheriff asked if he could smoke. "Certainly," came the reply. "You're a guest here tonight. Smoking is always encouraged. It adds to the atmosphere."

Sheriff Pitman reached into his pocket, pulled a bag of tobacco and paper, and with one eye on Black, rolled himself a cigarette. He replaced the pouch, pulled a match from another pocket and lit up. He blew smoke and said, "What are you waiting for? Change your mind Black?"

The Anvil's owner said nothing. He reached for the cards, stopped midway in the deck and pulled. "Ah, a deuce. What do you know? That's going to be tough to beat," he said chuckling. "You're turn."

Pitman didn't hesitate. He reached over the deck, quickly displayed the two of diamonds. "Well, well," he said. "Looks like I just won myself a saloon. I want you and your friends out of Leadville by morning."

Black's jaw dropped. "Why you cheatin' little…"

"Hold on Black. This was fair and square." He stared into the man's eyes. "Wasn't it?"

Black looked from the deck to the sheriff and back again. "We draw again. We both pulled deuces. It's a tie. Let's do it again."

"Nothing doing Black, This was no tie. I won. Your bet was that you'd draw a lower card than me. Guess what? You didn't. I won!"

"You cheated!" shouted Dan Black, his right hand reaching downward beneath the table.

Sheriff Pitman twisted, dove behind Black and fired off two quick shots at the two outlaws. One of them got off a shot before hitting the floor. Unfortunately for Black, that shot struck him and he crumbled to the ground, blood dripped from his mouth. Black's eyes found Pitman. "How'd you do it Pitman?" the words struggling to come out.

Without sympathy or expression, the sheriff replied, "I didn't walk into this place without a few select playing cards in my pocket. Thanks for giving me the chance to reach into my pocket. I needed that deuce more than I needed that cigarette."

Whatever fire remained inside Dan Black raged. He wanted to strike Pitman, but he had nothing left. He croaked, "You might have got me sheriff...but we got the money. The bank..."

Pitman ran out of The Anvil and headed toward the bank. He found a group of townspeople there. Apparently, the second explosion occurred in the bank, but the robbery went badly. Instead of the safe, two of Dan Black's gang blew themselves up.

Within a day Leadville had three working saloons and The Anvil, like its owner Dan Black, was history. The town also had plans to change its name, build a wall surrounding it along with a new law. No firearms!

CHAPTER 2 – *Jenny Whitlock*

Mayor Reynolds shifted an unlit cigar from one side of his mouth to another, felt around his pockets for a match but before he could find one, Sheriff Pitman produced a lit match and held it an inch from the cigar's end. Harley Reynolds leaned forward. The flame jumped upward in spurts until the mayor had the cigar going to his satisfaction.

"Much obliged sheriff." He took two quick puffs. "No, you don't have to remind me of The Anvil. I remember it like it was yesterday. I'm not saying you shouldn't have closed that place down. But look at this," he explained, spreading his hands as if showing off artwork on the walls. "These are bad men sheriff. All of them. Sure, Dan Black and his crew are gone, thanks to you I might add, but there are plenty more ready to take his place." He walked over to one poster. "How about him?" Reynolds pointed to one of the Wanted posters. "Walter 'Water Moccasin' Montgomery wanted for multiple murders by U.S. Marshalls. What happens if this Water Moccasin fella happens to stop by into Bullet Pass? Then what?"

"Then," answered Ted Pitman, "Mr. Montgomery would be required to leave his guns and any ammunition he had with Willie and his crew at the head of town. Remember Harley, building the wall around our town wasn't to keep good folks out. Nope. It was so that we could control the number of firearms coming in. If this snake of a man Montgomery wants to come to Bullet Pass, then he'd have to surrender his guns and I'll place him under arrest the minute he steps foot within the town's lines."

Not pleased with the sheriff's answer, Mayor Reynolds pressed on. "Who says he'll give up his guns? Who says any of these outlaws," again he pointed to the posters on the wall, "Would stop and give up their guns? We're nothing but a bunch of sitting ducks here sheriff and no offense, but it isn't like you could save any of us unless you have a gun or a rifle stashed somewhere around here."

Pitman laughed. "I can assure you that's not the case. No one has breached our entrance yet."

"Yet," repeated Reynolds. "I'm worried about what could be. Just as we are attracting good folk looking for a peaceful way of life, word gets out to the outlaws and lawless as well and they'll try to take advantage of us sure as I'm standing here. I have no doubt in my mind. Not if, but when that happens, how are we going to protect ourselves?" asked Reynolds.

The question made Sheriff Pitman think. His brain went back again to the scene a year ago at The Anvil. A lot had happened in the twelve months since that day. Once word got out that there was a town prohibiting weapons, Bullet Pass' population had slowly increased. More families settled there and businesses opened, so much so that a few months prior they had to knock down the wall on the western border. This expanded the town's boundary lines and allowed for construction of a new bank, general store, and livery stable. There was talk about expanding northward as well if the population continued growing. Sure, there was still too much drinking and gambling occurring for Pitman's taste, but he wasn't about to do anything about that despite his threat to close another saloon. Ted Pitman was most proud of the new school currently occupying the structure once known as The Anvil. Education and smiling faces replaced debauchery and violence. He wasn't happy about the wall, but couldn't think of another way of controlling the weapons. Sure, there were a few who tried to break the law and sneak in a derringer or a pistol or two, but no one had succeeded. Sheriff Pitman placed Willie Sanchez in charge of the entrance. Sanchez had served as Leadville's deputy but gave up the job to scout for a wagon train. He returned to Leadville after taking two hostile Indians' arrows, one to his hip and the other his thigh. Near death, he swore to the good Lord that if he recovered from his wounds, he'd settle down again in the town in which he was born. Walking with a limp was a cheap price to pay, and Willie Sanchez, if nothing else was a man of his word. Upon his return, he worked as a ranch hand before helping to build Bullet Pass' wall and accepted the job as sentry to the sole gate leading into and out of Bullet Pass. Sanchez hired a couple of responsible people, those he personally knew and those he could trust. The men took shifts, working in pairs all day and night, seven days a week including Christmas. Sanchez was proud of his work. He didn't know of any other town or city that prohibited guns and rifles. He felt safe in Bullet Pass. Everyone depended on him and his team to ensure no weapons or ammunition of any kind found its way into Bullet Pass.

Sanchez kept separate locked wooden cases for guns, rifles, and ammunition. There were two keys to the cases. Sanchez kept one on his person at all times, even when sleeping. The other was kept in a desk in the small makeshift office constructed just outside Bullet Pass' entrance. The process was a simple one. Anyone requesting to enter Bullet Pass turned over their weapons, received a receipt, and upon exiting the town presented the receipt for return of their firearms. Sanchez and his men were heavily armed and they were not afraid to display their wares. They worked outside the town's border so they were within the law. The arsenal at Sanchez's disposal served as a deterrent to anyone with foolish ideas about bringing weapons into Bullet Pass. And there were those who tried. In fact, as Sheriff Pitman and Mayor Reynolds debated the issue, a father and son tried to outfox Sanchez. The boy faked illness, said he got stricken after sharing campfire food with a group Mexican outlaws. The father claimed the boy insulted their food and the woman who cooked it and barley escaped from the banditos with his life. The father said the Mexicans swore revenge and were only an hour's ride behind. The father pleaded with Sanchez, begging Willie to bring the boy into Bullet Pass to see a doctor, but as the boy's parent and guardian, he would have to remain armed in order to protect his son.

Sanchez balked. For whatever reason, he didn't trust the man. He'd seen him before but couldn't place the face. Something about the man's right eye. He looked the two over.

"I'm Sanchez. You got a name?"

A warm smile. Too politely, "Williams. Chester Williams. That's my son Chester Junior. You do have a doctor in this town, yes?"

"We do," snapped Sanchez.

"Good. Normally, I wouldn't think about asking you to violate your local laws but this is a special circumstance. I fear there could be danger and my boy is the only thing I have left in this life and I need to protect him at all costs." The man's deadeye fixated on the boy as he spoke to Sanchez.

"You have nothing to fear inside Bullet Pass Mr. Williams. The town is completely safe. We don't make exceptions to our laws. I'm afraid you'll have to surrender your guns before seeing Doc Carter."

Chester Williams looked down, raised his head, right eye lagging. "I assure you sir that it'll be perfectly safe for everyone in town if I were allowed to carry this weapon." The sickly smile followed.

"Out of the question, Mr. Williams."

"Well, if that's the way its gotta be, then I won't argue further. I can't afford to waste any more time. How far is this Doc Carter?" Williams asked, handing his gun belt to Sanchez.

Sanchez reached out for the weapons without taking his gaze off Chester Junior. "Just up the trail, follow it to the Triple B Ranch, you'll see the sign. It's a quick ride into town from there. You can ask Billy Browner or one of his ranch hands when you get there."

"Much obliged Sanchez. Let's go Junior. The sooner we get to see this Doc Carter the sooner you'll be feeling better."

Before father and son could take a step, Sanchez held up his hand and stopped them. "Curtis!" he screamed to his partner at the checkpoint. Curtis snapped to attention. He read Sanchez's tone and knew what to do. Without further instruction he pulled his colt and aimed it at Chester Williams Sr..

"Over there, pops," Curtis said, pointing his gun toward the side. "Don't make any quick moves. That's it, nice and easy."

"What's the meaning of this?" asked a bewildered Chester Williams.

Sanchez ignored the senior Williams. "You, boy. Put your hands in the air."

"I demand to know…"

"Shut up!" screamed Curtis. "What's up Willie?" His gun steady, Curtis didn't take his eyes off the father.

"Seems to me this young fellow here has some real peculiar bumps under his clothing." Sanchez limped over to the boy and the youngster dropped his arms, struck Sanchez with a right fist, sending Willie backward."

Chester senior began moving toward the fight but was stopped by Curtis. "Another step and your good eye stops seeing." The elder Williams froze.

The youngster reached under his shirt where a .45 resided. Sanchez recovered, jumped the boy, tackled him, the gun fell to the ground. Williams Junior spit a mouthful of dirt, spit, and rolled over. Before he could get to his feet Sanchez tackled him again. Willie, no stranger to fistfights, having won a few saloon bare-knuckle bouts in his prime, landed three quick rights to the boy's face. Junior's left jaw reddened and swelled like a puff pastry ready to be pulled from a brick oven. The kid was no pushover. He managed to get his hands around Sanchez's neck and began choking Willie. Sanchez's suspicions that this so-called sick boy was neither sick nor a boy were confirmed. He clasped his hands underneath Junior's elbows and with all the force he could muster, crashed into his opponent's boney joints. The strangle hold broken, Sanchez landed a left-right combination to the boy's chin. The latter went down a few feet from his colt .45. With leopard-like speed he rolled toward the weapon, grabbed it and fired at Sanchez. Thanks to Curtis, the shot missed badly. Curtis fired at the boy a split-second before the kid got off his shot. Curtis' bullet found a home in Chester Junior's right shoulder causing the wayward shot at Sanchez and a groan from the boy's mouth that sounded like a rabid coyote giving birth. Bleeding, the boy dropped the gun, applied pressure to his wound. Willie Sanchez kicked the weapon away.

"Thanks Curtis," said Sanchez. "You think you could manage these two while I go fetch Sheriff Pitman?"

Curtis grinned. "Yup. I just hope one or both try to make a run for it. I haven't killed a man, or two for that matter, since last week." He winked at Sanchez. "Say, who are these two? Do you know?"

Sanchez flexed sore fists. "I'm gettin' old or out of shape or both. Time was I would've whipped a youngin' like this in one, maybe two punches at most." He examined reddening knuckles and fingers. "Felt good, though. I gotta say it felt good." Sanchez walked over to the discarded pistol, picked it up and stuck it in his belt. "I'll have this thing disabled in town. It'll be a pleasure watchin' LaGrange take a sledgehammer to it." He had a faraway look, "What was yer question?"

Curtis shook his head. "Gab, gab, gab. I asked you who in blazes are these two and you go off on a…"

Sanchez held up a hand. "Sorry. Robbers is what they are. Stagecoaches, trains, and who knows what else. My guess is they were after the money in our bank, figuring if they could sneak a weapon into town they'd have an easy time of it."

"But how'd you know?"

"The eye. The old man's eye. I knew there was something familiar about him, and then I remembered a story Mrs. Adams told me while back before she took the stage to New Mexico. She was concerned 'bout a pair a thieves that had been hitting up stagecoaches. The two men, one small and one large wore masks. The only description other than the difference in their sizes was the man's deadeye. I'm sure their names ain't Williams. We'll let the sheriff take care of that part when he locks 'em up.

After Willie Sanchez watched the blacksmith LaGrange crush the colt .45, he joined Sheriff Ted Pitman and Mayor Harley Reynolds in the sheriff's office. He explained the situation to both men, said he doubted Williams was their names but maybe they could find out for sure by looking at the 'Wanted' posters.

"See what I'm saying?" said Reynolds, addressing the sheriff. There's always someone trying to get in and do us harm. The voters in this town want change. We need to bring weapons back so that we can at the very least defend our properties and families."

"That's why we have Sanchez and his men," answered Sheriff Pitman. "No one's gotten past them yet. The colt was destroyed?" he asked Sanchez.

"Saw it with my own two eyes," answered Sanchez. "LaGrange had a good ole' time destroyin' it. He still got whatever's left of the thing if you want to see it."

"Not necessary," assured Pitman. "Good work Willie." He turned to face Reynolds. "You have nothing to worry about mayor. This town is safe. Now, if you gentlemen will excuse me, I'll take a ride out to the checkpoint and arrest those two…"

The door swung open with a thud. Jenny Whitlock couldn't contain herself. "Ted, it's…" she stopped, looked around, and blushed. "Oh, Mr. Reynolds. And Mr. Sanchez. I'm…I…didn't see you. I'm sorry."

"What is it Jenny?" asked Pitman.

Paleness replaced crimson. She looked shaky on her feet.

"Are you okay? What happened?" questioned the sheriff.

"Sheriff Pitman…It's Pete McBride at the hotel…he's dead!"

"Dead?" repeated Mayor Reynolds.

"Murdered!" shrieked Jenny.

CHAPTER 3 – Crown House

The Crown House, Bullet Pass' sole hostelry, was a two-story wooden structure built decades earlier. Situated roughly 2,000-feet from the sheriff's office, the inn was owned and run by Pete McBride. Pete and his wife, an Indian woman Pete affectionately had called Beautiful Feather, bought the place from a small company that did business with the railroads and Wells Fargo. The company had bigger ideas and wanted out of the hotel business. Following his wife's death, Pete ran the place by himself. He worked the front desk, cleaned the rooms, and cooked the meals. He seldom ventured outside the hotel's confines and was well liked by the townspeople and guests. Pete McBride was one of the more vocal Bullet Pass residents making it known that he wasn't too happy with Sheriff Pitman's gun restriction laws. He felt unsafe that he couldn't be armed, especially since he typically had large amounts of cash on hand. Sheriff Pitman used to tell him that he had a nice selection of kitchen knives from which to choose should some, and he'd stress unarmed man or woman, attempt to rob the hotel.

Eight numbered rooms and one closet comprised the hotel's second level. Rooms one through four on one side of the hallway and five through eight the other. Fifteen steps led up to the second floor. Once on the landing, patrons could turn left (room numbers one, two, five, and six or right (rooms three, four, seven, and eight). An unnumbered storage closet, located opposite the staircase was between rooms two and three.

A small crowd that had gathered around Pete McBride's body greeted Sheriff Pitman, Mayor Reynolds, Willie Sanchez, and Jenny Whitlock.

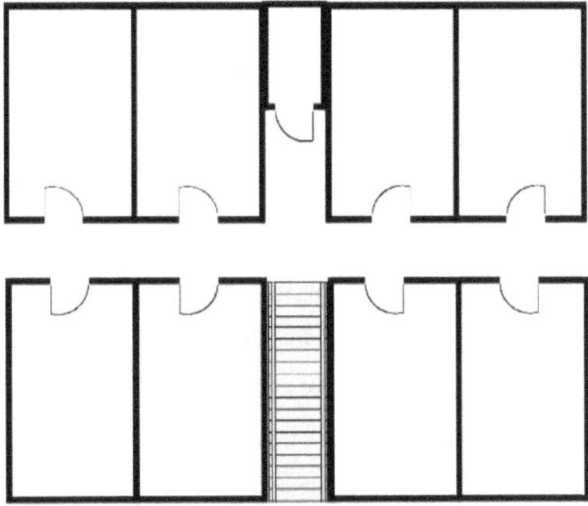

McBride's head had been smashed. A cast iron skillet, presumably the murder weapon, lay nearby. Pitman pushed his way through and knelt down next to the dead man. "Someone fetch Doc Carter."

"Ain't gonna do him no good sheriff," a voice from the crowd said. "Not with his brains spilled all over the rug."

Pitman looked up. "Anyone see anything?" The sheriff saw several heads shake and heard murmurs of 'No,' 'Nope,' 'Not a thing,' and 'No sir.'"

"Who found the body?" asked Pitman.

"I did sheriff." It was Jenny Whitlock. For the past several months, Jenny Whitlock had lived at the hotel, room number 4. Her home had burnt down a little more than a year prior. Rumor had it that one of Dan Black's gang, on a drunken rampage after a night of heavy drinking at The Anvil, got careless with a match and destroyed Jenny's home. Fortunately, she was able to escape unharmed. Thanks to Pete McBride, he gave her a place to stay until her house could be rebuilt, a case of neighbor helping neighbor.

"Tell us what you seen," ordered Pitman.

She hesitated, took a deep breath. "Well, I came downstairs to have coffee and one of Mr. McBride's homemade corn muffins."

"Did you see anyone else?" asked the sheriff.

"No, no one. I didn't see Mr. McBride either. He wasn't behind the desk, so I rang the bell but he didn't respond. I rang again, but still nothing." She paused.

"Take your time," said Pitman.

"I called out his name but he didn't answer. I decided to go over to the café myself and see if he was in there." She stopped again. "Oh my…this is so…so difficult," she choked, stifling tears.

"Would you like to sit down?" asked Mayor Reynolds.

"No. No thank you." Jenny wiped her eyes and nose with a white fabric she pulled from underneath her blouse sleeve. She steadied herself. "I walked toward the table over there," she pointed. "And that's when I saw his boots, lying on the floor, so still. I just knew something was wrong. I called his name again and then moved a little closer. That's when I knew…" she broke down and collapsed.

"You're just in time doc," said Mayor Reynolds. "The body is over there," he pointed. "Miss Whitlock needs your immediate attention."

Doctor Carter wasn't a typical doctor, at least not his background. Once a gunslinger, he found God after one of his victim's widows forgave him following the shootout. He then devoted his life to removing bullets from men rather than injecting them. Carter, refused to talk about his checkered past. He rarely smiled and although a medical man, was not pleased with Bullet Pass' no-gun policy. "Makes it difficult for me to make a decent living," he'd tell anyone within listening distance. He bent down over Jenny Whitlock, cradled her head in his hand and asked someone to fetch a glass of water and a cold, wet cloth. He propped up the fallen woman. "You'll be fine in a moment or two," he said.

Sheriff Pitman turned his gaze from Carter and Whitlock and addressed Reynolds and Sanchez. "Let's have a look at the hotel register and guest list."

The threesome approached the front desk. Pitman opened a drawer and looked at the cashbox. "Money still here," he declared. "This wasn't a robbery." He turned and examined the small safe behind the desk. "Still locked. This is cold-blooded murder," he said. He opened the guest book and ran a finger down the list of names.

"Sorry to interrupt sheriff but remember we got us two outlaws on the outskirts a town being watched by Curtis and one of 'em is wounded," interjected Sanchez. "I'm certain they're wanted men and need some locking up."

Before Sheriff Pitman spoke, Mayor Reynolds chimed in. "Go get those two and lock them up Ted. Willie and I will begin the investigation here. We'll gather the names and start talking to everyone until you get back. Heck, it won't take you all that long and this way we'll save time and maybe find us a murderer. Whaddya say?"

"I don't know..."

"Nonsense," responded Reynolds. "Go. The sooner you leave the quicker you're back to help us. That's right, isn't it Willie?" Sanchez nodded agreement.

"I suppose so. Okay, get started on this register. I'll ride out and bring those two Williams or whatever their names are in and lock them up."

"Let's get started," said Mayor Reynolds. He opened the large register, wet a fingertip and flipped pages. He grabbed a pen from its holder. "Is there paper around here Willie?"

Sanchez limped over to what looked like a file drawer and extracted a sheaf of papers. The two men stared down. Handwritten names varied immensely in style.

"We'll go from the bottom up. Hopefully, these people are still around," said Reynolds.

"That'll be telling, now won't it Mayor?" said a smiling Sanchez.

"How's that?"

"Easy. If one of them ain't here no more after just checking in, doesn't that mean they took off sort of unexpected and in a hurry? Like maybe they killed McBride and then ran? Makes sense to me."

Mayor Reynolds gave it thought. "Could be. Doesn't necessarily mean that, but could be."

"What else could it mean Harley?"

"Any number of things. Maybe they finished their business in Bullet Pass and took off. Maybe they had an emergency of some type and were forced to go. Could be they only needed a few hours sleep before heading off somewhere else. Could be…"

"Okay. Okay. I get the message," interrupted Sanchez.

"Let's wait and see what we find before we make any conclusions. This is murder Willie. Serious business. Start reading and I'll write. Give me the name and the room number."

Reynolds dipped the pen into the ink as Willie Sanchez began reading the names from the bottom up. He wrote:

Fred Hilson – 6

"I can't read this first name," said Sanchez. "Last name looks like Solomon. Room 2."

Reynolds jotted:

??? Solomon – 2

Sanchez continued reading and Reynolds continued writing:

Mr. and Mrs. Wallace – 1

Wyatt Lemon – 3

Oscar Blessington – 5

Ty Stoner – 8

"That's it. All the other names going back have check marks next to them. I'm guessing that means they have checked out." Sanchez stared at the register. "Looks like rooms 4 and 7 are empty."

"No," said Reynolds. "Jenny Whitlock stays in room 4. Remember?"

"Right."

The two men headed up the stairs and turned left on the landing.

"Might as well begin with room 1." Reynolds knocked.

"Just a minute," a man's voice. Seconds later the door opened. Reynolds and Sanchez faced a short man in mid shave. One chubby cheek was lather-covered, the other cheek smooth. A towel was wrapped around his neck and he held a razor in his hand. Shirtless, the man's ample stomach hung over expensive looking slacks. Suspenders hung down his legs. "Can I help you gentlemen?"

"Mr. Wallace?" asked Mayor Reynolds.

"Yes." His eyebrows rose. "I'm Mr. Wallace. Please, excuse my appearance. I was just shaving."

"We can see that," blurted Sanchez. "Have you left your room recently?"

"I beg your pardon?" questioned Wallace.

Harley Reynolds gave Sanchez a stern look. "We're sorry to disturb you sir. We are seeking some information. Unfortunately, there has been some bad business downstairs at this hotel and Mr. Sanchez and I are investigating. My name is Harley Reynolds. I'm Bullet Pass' mayor."

Wallace wiped his chin with the towel. "Nice to meet you. What sort of bad business?"

"A man was…" began Sanchez but Reynolds cut him off.

"I'm sure you have nothing to worry about but we'd like to ask you a couple of questions if we may." Wallace didn't respond so the mayor continued. "Are you here with your wife? Is Mrs. Wallace here?"

"Yes and no," answered Wallace. "My wife, Mimi is with me on this trip, but she's out doing a little shopping at the moment. What is this about anyway?" asked the man.

"Just a few more questions Mr. Wallace. What is your business here in Bullet Pass? Why are you and your wife here?"

"Now just a minute," cried an annoyed Wallace. "You didn't answer my question. What's this all about?"

Calmly, Reynolds explained. "A man's been murdered. Pete McBride is…was his name. He's the one who checked in you and your wife. Mr. Sanchez and I are working for the sheriff in his absence. We're simply trying to rule out the hotel's current guests as suspects. We have no reason to believe either you or your wife were mixed up in this, but we'd like to know why you are here in Bullet Pass."

"That's awful. Yes, this Mr. McBride checked us in yesterday. Seemed like such a nice gentleman. Fact is we're on a little vacation. I'm a lawyer back in Missouri. Haven't taken a vacation in years so the missus convinced me to take some time off and we're heading west to California. We're taking our time, you know, rail and stage, stopping along the way here and there. Bullet Pass is just one of our stops. Mimi's doing a good job of spending my money! She loves shopping. I don't begrudge her. She's a good woman. We're planning on taking the afternoon stage out of Bullet Pass today. I'm sorry about your friend, but I assure you neither my wife nor myself had anything to do with this unfortunate affair."

The two men listened carefully. "We'll have to ask you and Mrs. Wallace to stay in Bullet Pass until this matter is cleared up. I'm sure you understand." Reynolds paused. "What part of Missouri are you from?"

"Saint Joe, along the Missouri River. Lots of fur traders, a lot of business and where there's a lot of business there is need for attorneys. I do okay for myself, but I guess I work too hard and could stand some time off. Mimi is right about that. Anyway, now that I'm out and travelling, I know I made the correct decision. By the way, you know about Jesse James, right? Killed right there in St. Joe. Not far from our home." Wallace said it with pride.

"I see Mr. Wallace. Well, thank you for your time. We won't bother you any longer. Thanks for stopping here and enjoy the remainder of your vacation. Safe travels."

Wallace smiled, bowed and closed the door.

Willie Sanchez wasted no time. "What do you mean by letting him go like that? How do we know what he's telling us is true? He could be lying. We didn't even see his so-called wife. Does she exist? We should question her too. I think we need to hold him in jail until we find out who killed McBride."

"Slow down Willie. If we find out he might be involved, we'll hold him. As for his wife, she exists. Did you see the newly purchased hat boxes in the room? Or the dresses?"

"No," responded Sanchez.

"I did," answered Reynolds. "And I asked him about Missouri. His answers ring true. No, I'm certain Mr. Wallace and Mimi Wallace had nothing to do with Pete's murder. Let's see who occupies room 2."

Resigned, Sanchez limped over to the next door and wrapped on it.

"Yes?" came a voice from within.

Sanchez, about to respond, stopped when Reynolds placed his hand on

Sanchez's shoulder.

"My name's Mayor Harley Reynolds. Mr. Solomon? Is that you?"

The door opened. A large man dressed in black looked out at Reynolds and Sanchez. He wore an oversized black hat and held a worn black leather book in his left hand. "Rabbi Solomon. What is the nature of your visit gentlemen?"

"Rabbi?" questioned Sanchez. "Is that your first name?"

The man chuckled. "No, of course not. My first name is Max. I'm a rabbi. Most people just call me Rabbi Solomon. Are you Mayor Reynolds?" the question addressed to Sanchez.

Taken aback, Sanchez didn't answer so Reynolds jumped in. "I'm Mayor Reynolds. Harley Reynolds. This here is Willie Sanchez." The men shook hands. "A rabbi. A religious man," said Reynolds. "What brings you to Bullet Pass?"

Solomon stepped aside and with a sweep of the hand welcomed Reynolds and Sanchez into his room. "Come in gentlemen, come in. I have a little food to offer you. I eat kosher food, so I travel with my own sustenance. Can I interest you in something?"

The two men looked at each other, entered room 2, and looked around.

"No, thank you sir. I'm not hungry," said Reynolds.

"Nothing for me either," said Sanchez.

"If you change your minds, let me know. Now, what brings you to my humble room at this fine establishment?"

The two visitors glanced around the sparse room. Mayor Reynolds began, "We'd like to know why you are here." He paused. "Not here in this room necessarily, but why here in Bullet Pass?"

"I know very well what you meant. The town's reputation has brought me here. As you said Mr. Reynolds, I'm a religious man. My congregation and myself believe in the word of God, not the sound of guns. Bullet Pass has itself a nice reputation. I'm correct in saying no weapons of any kind are permitted within the town limits?"

"No firearms of any kind are a more accurate way to say it. Yes."

"As a man of peace, I'm thinking about starting a congregation here in Bullet Pass."

A small look of concern crept across Reynolds' face. Sanchez's expression was blank. "You might have trouble with that," began the mayor. "We don't have any Jewish people in this town at least to my knowledge. Are you aware of any Willie?"

Sanchez snapped out of his stupor. "Nope. Not me I don't."

Rabbi Solomon flipped through pages of his book. He read silently, then snapped shut the little volume. "My people will come. We'll begin our own modest community. A peaceful town like this has many attractions and benefits."

Reynolds cleared his throat. "Um, well that's what we want to speak to you about. Isn't it Willie?" After a brief pause to collect himself Sanchez agreed. Reynolds continued. "Sheriff Pitman is away on an errand. He'll be back shortly. In his absence, Willie and I are investigating the murd…um…the death of Pete McBride. He's the man who runs…um…ran this hotel. Would you know anything about that rabbi?"

A forlorn expression covered Solomon's face. "Death? That's awful. Would you like for me to say a special prayer?"

Sanchez jumped in. "No, we'd like for you to answer us if you know anything 'bout this or when or if you left this here room since you checked in?"

Harley Reynolds looked annoyed, but Solomon calmly responded. "I'm afraid I don't know anything about this poor man's death. I assume it is the same gentleman who registered me yesterday upon my arrival. God has plans for us all. Such a shame. Did he have a family?"

The mayor answered before Sanchez could assert himself. "No family. He lived alone downstairs in a small room behind the check-in desk. The Crown House was his life." He waited. "And his death."

"What about it rabbi?" jumped in Sanchez. "Did you leave this room since you arrived? You didn't answer that question."

The rabbi looked from one to the other. "I did. I walked around the town, you know, just seeing the sights. I stopped and got a haircut. Nice man the barber, his name is Perry. I'm the first rabbi who ever sat in his chair. I returned to my room, studied the bible some and went to sleep."

"Did you see Mr. McBride last night before you came up to your room?" asked Mayor Reynolds.

"Yes. He was at the front desk writing something. I said hello and goodnight. He said the same back. He seemed in good spirits. Such a shame. How did you say he died?"

"We didn't," answered Sanchez.

CHAPTER 4 – An Arrest

Sheriff Pitman's voice rose to the second floor. "Reynolds. Sanchez. You up there?"

The two men turned and headed downstairs toward the voice. Pitman stood at the bottom of the stairs with Doctor Carter. "Glad to see you sheriff," said Mayor Reynolds. "Willie and I have been questioning some of the guests. But first, how'd you make out sheriff?" He turned and faced Carter. "How's Miss Whitlock, Doc?"

"She'll be fine Harley. Just a little shook up is all. Terrible thing stumbling upon a dead man. She's resting in my office for the time being. I don't think she's in any rush to return to her room here."

Sheriff Pitman seemed focused on the doc's every word. It was no secret Sheriff Ted Pitman and Jenny Whitlock were fond of each other. They'd been to several dances together and every now and then were seen dining or simply walking around town with little distance between them. Unconsciously, Pitman smiled. He addressed Reynolds and Sanchez. "Those two Williams fellows…you were right about them Willie. They are father and son for sure, but their name is Ford and they're wanted for robberies from California to Kansas. One of the U.S. Marshals was hot on their trail and met up with me shortly after Curtis handed them over to me as I escorted them back to town. Now, what have you two discovered? Make any arrests yet?" he chuckled.

"No, but I'm not sure Willie here isn't ready to arrest everyone at the hotel," said Reynolds.

Willie Sanchez had bitten his tongue long enough. "Sheriff, we just begun our investigation but we already have us a couple of suspects. Don't we Harley?" He didn't wait for a response. "We spoke to a Mr. Wallace in room one."

"Does this Mr. Wallace have a first name?" questioned Pitman.

Reynolds and Sanchez looked at each other. Sanchez continued speaking.

"Um…not sure sheriff. Not sure that we caught that. Don't matter much though. He says him and his wife…"

"Mimi is his wife's name," interrupted a smug Mayor Reynolds.

"Right," said Sanchez. "Mimi. They are travelling from Missouri to California. Just happened to stop in Bullet Pass. Imagine that sheriff, the couple just happens to stop in a hotel in a town at the same time the hotel's operator is murdered. What do you think about that?"

The sheriff shrugged. "I don't think anything about it. Did this Mimi Wallace have anything to add?"

Looking downward, Sanchez admitted he and Sanchez hadn't met her. His spirits promptly perked up. "But you should see the guest in room two sheriff. Now there's a suspicious character if I ever seen one."

"How's that?" asked Pitman.

"Better let me fill in the sheriff," said Reynolds. "Fellow in number two, he's a rabbi."

"A what?" asked Pitman.

"You know sheriff, a preacher man for the Jewish people. A rabbi," said Sanchez proudly.

Harley Reynolds continued. "He's right sheriff. Rabbi Max Solomon is his full name. He's a religious man. Carries a bible and all."

"That don't mean he didn't murder McBride," spat Sanchez.

Reynolds shot him an annoyed look. "Said he heard about our town, likes the idea of our laws prohibiting firearms and such, and he might be interested in settling here and maybe forming some sort of church…what term did he say…congregation I think in Bullet Pass."

"Sounds innocent enough," chimed in Doc Carter.

"What do you know Doc?" asked Sanchez. "You wasn't there when we questioned him.

"I was just saying…"

"Enough," interrupted the sheriff. "Did you find out anything else about this Solomon or any of the other guests?"

"The rabbi said he left his room and got a haircut. We haven't spoken to Perry about it yet. That's something we still need to do. Other than that, he didn't do much else or so he says. He mentioned that he saw McBride alive last night writing something. That was the last time he saw him. We were about to knock on door three." He referred to his handwritten guest list. "Man by the name of Wyatt Lemon. That's when we heard you calling and came down here."

"Good work. I'll make you deputies someday," he joked. Sheriff Pitman turned to Doc Carter. "Notice anything on McBride's body that might help us?"

"Follow me," ordered Carter. Pete McBride's prostrate body appeared smaller and more ghastly to the three spectators. The dried blood took on a brownish hue. The violence to which McBride had been subjected was evident in the skull pieces and fragments that dotted the floor. Reynolds had to look away and steady himself. "Someone wanted him dead, that's for sure. If you look closely…"

"No thanks," said Mayor Reynolds.

Carter ignored him. "…You'll see he was struck twice by that skillet. It was as if the killer wanted to make fully certain just in case McBride survived the first blow. What's this?" he asked, bending lower, his face inches from the floor. "I missed this before. Strange."

That got the attention of the other three men. Sheriff Pitman took a step closer. "Find something important?"

"This." He held up something.

"I don't see…"

"It's a hair," said Carter, holding it up between thumb and forefinger. He squinted and held it out toward Pitman, Reynolds, and Sanchez. "It's black. A black hair."

"And McBride's got red hair!" shouted Sanchez.

"Gentleman, I believe this hair belongs to our killer."

"That rabbi!" an excited Sanchez bellowed. "I knew it. Let's go up there and arrest him!"

"Just hold on Willie," cautioned Pitman. "Lots of people have black hair. Fact is most folks in Bullet Pass are suspects. You, me, the mayor here, doc, Miss Whitlock…" he paused, a faraway look in his eyes before continuing…"I'm afraid this clue isn't much of a help to us. What about the other guests? How about this Mr. Wallace you spoke to? What color is his hair?"

Sanchez thought for a moment. "Black. But only one of us had a haircut yesterday! We have our man sheriff. And he's a stranger."

Harley Reynolds put his face next to the hair. "I don't know Willie. This hair is fairly long. The rabbi has much shorter hair. I don't think…"

"Then this hair is from his beard!" shouted Sanchez. "He's our man sheriff."

Sanchez took the stairs two at a time. The others followed. He knocked on door two and confronted Rabbi Solomon again. "Tell these gentlemen what you told me and Mayor Reynolds."

A confused and slightly annoyed Solomon said, "About what?"

"You know, the haircut."

"I did. Yes. So?"

"So the doc found a black hair next to Pete McBride's body and it looks to me like the hair matches your beard."

The rabbi looked from one to the other. "I said I got my hair cut, not my beard. I don't see what this has to do with me."

Sheriff Pitman interceded. "Sorry to bother you." After a quick introduction, "Let's go," he said to Sanchez.

Willie Sanchez took off down the stairs, leaving Pitman, Reynolds, and Carter with open mouths. "Where's he going?" asked Reynolds. The men shrugged. "Might as well continue our questioning. Let's resume with Mr. Lemon in room three. He knocked once, twice, but no one responded. "Must be out," said Reynolds. He looked around. "Room four is where Miss Whitlock lives, at least for now." Just as his fist was about to make contact the door to room number five opened.

"I thought I heard noises out here," said an elderly man. Longish gray hair could be seen under a newly purchased Stetson. He noticed Pitman's badge. "Is there something wrong sheriff?"

The sheriff smiled. "No, not at all. Nice hat you have there…Mr…" he let the words hang.

"Blessington. Oscar Blessington from Texas. Friends call me Sticks." He patted his stomach. "Yessir, I lost me a good deal of weight over the years."

He removed the hat. "It's a beaut. Got it just the other day in San Antonio. Here, have a looksee."

Sticks Blessington was gray all over. "That's quality," Pitman said, barely looking at the hat. "Are you planning to be in Bullet Pass long Mr…I mean Sticks?"

"Depends. I'm a horse trader. I'm meetin' up with a nearby rancher by the name of Paul Palmer. Know him?"

"Sure do," said Pitman.

"I hope to conclude my business with Mr. Palmer within a day or two at the most and head back home."

"That's fine. Nice meeting you Sticks. Enjoy your stay here." The man smiled and closed the door.

"Well, we can strike him from the list," said Doc Carter.

The men received no response in room six. "Someone named Fred Hilson," said Reynolds. "Oh well, let's see if the fellow in room eight is in."

"What about seven?" asked Doc Carter.

"No one registered there," said Reynolds. He wrapped on door eight.

"None of your damn business!" shouted the man greeting Reynolds, Pitman, and Carter. "I don't care if you are the President of these United States. I know my rights and I'm not telling you a thing. Not a word. There's no law stating I have to. Now isn't that right sheriff?"

Everyone's eyes focused on Pitman. "I can arrest you," he said.

"For what?" asked the man. "I paid good money for this room."

Sheriff Pitman kept calm. "There's a dead man downstairs. Murdered." He watched the man's reaction but he couldn't detect one. "Everyone in this hotel is a suspect." The man had long black hair. "That includes you…"

"Ty Stoner," interjected Mayor Reynolds.

Stoner ignored Reynolds. "If you think I committed a murder then arrest me. Otherwise, beat it. I haven't done anything wrong."

"Mind if we come inside and have a look around?" asked Pitman.

"I most certainly do mind! And I'll tell you something else, I don't like for one minute this crazy law you have around here about having to give up my pistol. I never heard of such a thing. I'm already planning to speak to a lawyer about this."

"The law is for everyone," said Pitman. "No exceptions."

"Oh, I get it. You take everyone's weapons so that they are defenseless and then you harass law-abiding citizens. Some racket you got going here. I for one…"

Ty Stoner's diatribe was interrupted by an out of breath Willie Sanchez. Perry Oliver, Bullet Pass' barber accompanied Sanchez.

"Tell 'em Perry. Tell 'em what you told me! Go ahead!"

"Sheriff, I got to get back to my shop. Mr. Foreman is sittin' in the chair right now with a half-shaved face. I got me a business to run."

"Oh for God's sake, tell 'em!" shouted Sanchez.

The barber, still holding a straight razor, said, "Okay, okay. Willie here wants me to tell you that I cut a stranger's hair, fellow with a beard. Said he was of the Jewish religion. Nice man and all. He wanted…"

Sanchez couldn't contain himself. "He started to cut the rabbi's beard before the rabbi stopped him! Ain't that right Perry?"

"Yes. I don't know why Willie thinks that is so important, but he rushed me here to tell you that. I figured the man wanted me to trim his beard, but he stopped me and…"

"That's enough Perry. Thanks!"

"Can I go back now?" asked the barber.

"Sure. Sure." Sanchez, about to shake Perry's hand, stopped short when he noticed the razor.

The barber saw Sanchez balk. He held up the razor. "Funny thing this razor."

"How's that?" asked Sheriff Pitman.

"It's a new one. I seemed to have lost my favorite one. You know, the one with my initials on the handle? The one I won at the fair's shaving contest a few years back?"

"We all know that razor Perry. What happened?"

"Beats me. It just up and disappeared. I know I had it when the rabbi stranger got his haircut. I used it on him to trim his hairline on the back of his neck. When I finished with him, I flipped the OPEN sign to CLOSED and took my normal lunch out back. Best I figure, someone came in and took it while I ate."

"Maybe you misplaced it?" asked the sheriff.

"Don't think so," answered the barber. "I think someone walked off with it. Shouldn't be too hard to find though, not with my initials on the handle."

"Everyone in town knows you close for lunch the same time every day Perry," said Mayor Reynolds.

"Not the strangers," chimed in Sanchez. "Maybe the rabbi took it. Let's search him and his room."

"Don't think so. He paid and walked out and then I closed." The barber thought for a moment. "I guess he could have come back in and taken it, but that don't make no sense really. Anyway, I got to get back to the shop. I've been here far too long as it is." Perry Oliver scurried down the stairs.

"Good God!" snapped the man in room eight. "Beards. Razors. This whole town is crazy!" he said, slamming the door shut.

"Don't you see?" asked Sanchez. "It's the rabbi. He lied to us. Perry cut his beard. One of the hairs must have fallen loose when he struck McBride with the skillet. And I'll wager he stole Perry's razor. Let's go back and search him."

"Wait a minute," said Harley Reynolds. "Didn't that fellow, Mr. Wallace have a razor in his hand when he opened the door? Maybe we should arrest him too? What do you say Willie?" He laughed along with Sheriff Pitman.

"Knock it off Harley," said Sanchez. "Sheriff, you have a duty and a responsibility to lock that man up. A hair was found next to Pete McBride. It looks to be a match to that of the rabbi's beard. The rabbi told us…"

"Enough Willie. I think you're wrong, but before rumors start flying around town and things get out of hand, I'll do as you suggest." Reluctantly, Sheriff Ted Pitman arrested Rabbi Max Solomon on a murder charge and locked him up. "Rabbi, we're still looking into possible suspects, but for now this is the way it'll have to be."

The rabbi took it remarkably well. He explained to Pitman and the others that although the barber did not cut his beard, it was possible that some hairs nevertheless fell out and that he had no intention of lying to them. "It is written in Proverbs, *The Lord detests lying lips, but He delights in people who are trustworthy.* God will guide us and show us the truth. I'm not worried."

CHAPTER 5 – *An Envelope*

Sheriff Pitman sat in his office with Willie Sanchez. Mayor Reynolds and Doc Carter had both returned to their respective offices. Pitman smoked a cigarette. Sanchez drank coffee.

"Is this slop from yesterday?" Sanchez asked. "It tastes terrible."

Pitman thought for a moment. "Two days, maybe three." He smiled but the grin didn't last long. "I don't like this business one bit Willie. I'm not so sure this rabbi we got locked up murdered Pete."

Sanchez swallowed and winced. He took a few steps outside and dumped the remainder of the coffee. He set the cup down and pulled up a chair next to the sheriff. "Why not? We have us one of his beard hairs."

"We don't know for sure that it's a match. Like I said, almost everyone around here has the same color hair. This fellow don't seem like the murdering type. Besides, what motive could he possibly have to kill Pete McBride? Not robbery. It doesn't add up."

Lost in thought, Sanchez snapped his fingers. "Maybe it has something to do with his religion?"

"Now you're making less sense than normal Willie. What religion kills for the sake of killing? No, this man is innocent. I'm sure of it."

"But he didn't even put up a fight when you locked him up," argued Sanchez.

"Exactly," countered Pitman. "Do you think a guilty man would behave that way? I don't. He seems confident that God will show us the truth and he'll be set free."

"Well, now that you put it that way, maybe you got you a point. Say, what about that ornery fellow in room number eight. What was his name?"

"Ty Stoner."

"Yup, Stoner. What about him? He's got something to hide sure as that coffee I just drunk was no better than a cupful of thick mud. Why don't you arrest him?" asked Sanchez.

"And release the rabbi?"

"Well…why don't you lock them both up? They both could have committed the murder. Two strangers. One with a hair at the murder location and the other refusing to answer questions."

"Willie, I can't go around locking up every stranger that comes into town. Besides, we don't know it was a stranger that killed Pete. Could be anyone, including me I guess. And you, Willie."

Sanchez stood and paced around the office. "Okay, let's say for a moment that this rabbi is innocent. I'm not sayin' that he is, I'm just sayin' we'll pretend that he is for the time being. We still haven't spoken to the other two fellows who weren't in their rooms. I forget their names."

Mayor Reynolds had left the hotel's guest list with Pitman. The sheriff pulled it from his shirt pocket and flattened it on the table. "You mean Wyatt Lemon in room three and Fred Hilson in room six?"

"Yup, that's exactly who I mean. Maybe one of 'em did it? Maybe they've already left town and are miles away? I should check with Curtis at the checkpoint and see if either man retrieved their weapons and beat it outta town."

"You might want to check on the Wallace woman too."

"Huh?" a bewildered Sanchez asked.

"Mrs. Wallace. Mimi. Didn't you say she wasn't in the room when you spoke to Mr. Wallace?"

"Oh right. Yes, Mimi Wallace too. I'll be back as soon as I can and let you know." With that, Willie Sanchez hopped onto his horse and sped to see Curtis at the edge of town.

Sheriff Pitman's concentration was broken after an envelope was tossed onto the table in front of him. Startled, he looked up.

"Get a load of that," said Mayor Reynolds, pointing to the envelope. "Go ahead, open it."

Reluctant to grab the envelope, the lawman stared at it as if it were some sort of poisonous reptile. He looked up at Reynolds, the latter nodded. Pitman counted, "One hundred, two hundred, three hundred, four hundred, five hundred dollars! Five hundred dollars! Harley, where did you get this?"

"Look at the note," said Reynolds.

The letters were cut from a newspaper, pasted on Crown House logo stationery. It read:

MEET ME ALONE AT 6 AT POKE

"Where did you get this Harley?"

"Damndest thing. Someone slipped it under my office door. Who do you suppose did it?"

"Did what?" the voice feminine, inquisitive. Jenny Whitlock's smile turned to an oval after seeing the five hundred dollars on the table. "Have a good day playing Faro mayor? Or is that someone's contribution to your next campaign?"

"How you feeling Jenny?" asked Sheriff Pitman. "You gave us a bit of a scare you know."

She blushed. "Better, I think. I still can't get over poor Pete McBride. Have you had any luck finding out who did it? And why?"

"No on both accounts," Reynolds chimed in.

"Do you think it was one of the hotel guests?" she asked.

"Hard to say. We locked up one of them, but I'm not sure he committed the crime," said Pitman.

"It's horrible. I'm going to have trouble spending the night in my room after something as gruesome as that. I wish that fire to my beautiful home never happened. And now this."

"You can stay over my place," offered Mayor Reynolds. "Me and the missus have extra space. Be no trouble at all."

"Thank you, but I could never impose on your generosity." She looked at Ted Pitman with lustful eyes. The sheriff said nothing. Whitlock returned her gaze to the table and the money. "Where did that money come from?"

"And this note." Pitman handed her the strange note. "Someone wants to meet with the mayor at six o'clock at the Poke. This same someone wants us to believe they are staying at the Crown House, or at least visited there."

"Do you think this is tied into Pete's murder?" asked Jenny.

Sheriff Pitman rubbed his chin. "I don't know. Could be. Then again…"

Harley Reynolds pulled a gold watch from his vest pocket. "One hour until six. I'll meet this fellow and find out what it's about."

"I'll be there to back you up Harley," assured Pitman.

"No thanks sheriff. The note said, alone. I don't want to scare him off. This could be our first lead."

"What about the hair we found next to McBride?"

"What hair?" asked Jenny.

Reynolds waived his hand in the air. "Ah, I forgot about that. Okay, our second lead in Pete's death. I'm gonna run." He scooped up the letter and the money and headed out. "I'll let you know what I find out this evening sheriff." He turned to Miss Whitlock and tipped his hat. "Ma'am."

Ted Pitman and Jenny Whitlock stared at each other for a full minute before either spoke. Jenny broke the silence. "What were you two talking about a hair? You found a human hair near the dead body?"

"We did. Apparently, it's a match to one of the hotel's guests, man by the name of Max Solomon. He's a rabbi."

"Rabbi? What's a rabbi doing in Bullet Pass?"

"According to him, he likes the fact that we've outlawed guns and ammunition and he's thinking about starting a congregation here. Seems genuine and nice enough. He's locked up in the jail cell." Pitman pointed behind a partially closed door.

"You arrested him but you don't think he did it?" questioned Jenny.

"I'm not sure. Willie Sanchez has no doubts about it, but then again, Willie is a quick one to accuse."

"But the hair belongs to this Rabbi Solomon? It's a match?"

"Apparently so. I'm not totally convinced. Even if it is from the rabbi's beard, it seems too convenient. You know, like the letter Harley Reynolds just received, written on Crown House stationery. But, let's wait and see what Harley has to say about his little meeting tonight with the letter's author."

"I'm gonna make coffee," said Jenny, changing the subject and the mood with four words. "Want some?"

Momentarily taken aback, Pitman agreed. He stood, peeked through the door to check on his prisoner. "How you doing in there, rabbi? Comfortable? Can I get you anything? Coffee?"

Jenny heard Rabbi Solomon answer that he was fine and not in need of anything at the moment. She poured two cups of coffee. Pitman wrapped two large fists around his cup, watching the smoke rise. He liked the smell of fresh coffee and wondered how many days it had been since he had made a fresh pot.

"Ted, about night before last," she said softly, "You aren't regretting it are you? Because I'm not. It was overdue. You mustn't think less of yourself or of me. I can tell you stories about people in this town Sheriff Pitman that would make your spurs spin!" She laughed.

Sheriff Pitman felt uncomfortable. He took a sip of the coffee and burned his tongue. The physical hurt was easier to deal with than the emotional ride Jenny Whitlock had strapped him into. Ted looked aimlessly around the office, stalling. He took another sip, cleared his throat and said, "I don't know. I don't care about other people in town. I was raised a certain way and I don't think it right for two…"

She held up a hand and stopped him. "Don't be silly. We're adults. And besides, no one saw us."

Pitman was about to correct her, but stopped. He was relieved when he heard Rabbi Solomon's voice. "If you don't mind sheriff, I think I'd like a cup of coffee after all." But, he wondered, did the rabbi overhear their conversation?

CHAPTER 6 – Wyatt Lemon

The Poke was three-quarters full when Mayor Harley Reynolds walked through the wooden doors. The place wouldn't fill up for another hour or so. Small by saloon standards, the Poke was popular with an older, better behaved, and more under control crowd. An oversized piano sat unaccompanied against the far wall. No one could figure out how anyone was able to get the large wooden instrument into the place. It was almost as if the Poke was built around the piano. Reynolds scanned the interior. He recognized most everyone. A few acknowledged him as he approached the bar.

"Howdy mayor. What'll it be?"

"Beer. Anyone asking for me Cliff?" reaching for the mug.

"Can't say anyone has mayor." The bartender wiped the bar although Reynolds saw no need for it. He figured it was just habit, Cliff automatically wiped off the bar hundreds of times a night whether it was warranted or not. He turned and again surveyed the customers. Any one of them could have sent him the letter and the money. He wondered which one? His eyes shifted to the door as a stranger walked in and headed his way. Mayor Reynolds stiffened. The man removed his hat revealing a cleanly shaven head. Eyes wide apart and a pointy nose gave him an almost comical, yet sinister appearance. His spur-less boots appeared new. The man looked from Reynolds to the bartender. The stranger spoke, his voice deep.

"Glad you made it mayor," the man began, "I'm the one who sent you that letter. Oh, and the five hundred enticing reasons for you to wet your whistle at the Poke. Nice place they have here. In fact, when you get down to it this is a real nice town too. Friendly people. Good shopping here in Bullet Pass as well. Got my eye on a nice silver belt buckle I seen at McDougal's store. Ornate carving on it. Saw one like it in Denver once. Regretted not buying it then. I don't intend to make the same mistake this go around. No sir. Before I leave your fine town, I'll own that belt buckle. That's a promise." The man's eyes never blinked. As he spoke he sized up Reynolds and realized this might be one of his tougher sales. He felt up to the challenge.

Mayor Reynolds' expression didn't change. He listened without interrupting. When the man finally stopped speaking, he asked, "You got a name mister?" Before the man answered, Reynolds noticed the uncooperative Ty Stoner, from room number eight at the Crown House, walk into the Poke. Stoner, still scowling, positioned himself at a table about 30-feet from the bar.

"Forgive me Harley. You don't mind if I call you Harley, do you?" The mayor's looks answered the question. "Okay, that's fine. Mayor Reynolds it is. I'm usually not this forward or rude, but I figured that since you already have five hundred of my dollars we should be on a first name basis."

Reynolds had enough. "Listen to me mister. You and I are not friends. Got it? And as for your money, I haven't accepted it and if you don't tell me who you are or what you're doing in this town or what you want from me, I'm going straight to Sheriff Pitman and I'll let him deal with you. We've just had a murder here in town and frankly you sir, are a stranger behaving very strangely. And, I might add you interacted with the murdered man and we know you were at the murder scene. And, so was your buddy sitting behind you."

The man with the baldhead, strange eyes and pointy nose spun his head around. He swiftly turned back to Mayor Reynolds. The look on his face had switched from one of arrogant confidence to one of genuine fear.

"Look Mister…I mean Mayor Reynolds. I don't know anything about no murder. I don't know anyone in this town and that includes the gentleman behind me. I swear it."

Annoyed, Reynolds responded, "Who are you and what do you want?"

The man cleared his throat. "Wyatt Lemon at your service." He held out his right hand. Harley Reynolds shook it, "I'm a gun salesman. Work for Smith and Wesson Company going on nine years now. Like I was saying before, you got you a real nice town here. From what I can see, it's got just about everything a man needs except one thing, and that one thing is guns."

"That's the law here in Bullet Pass, Mr. Lemon."

"Please, call me Wyatt."

"That's the law here in Bullet Pass, Mr. Lemon," continued Reynolds. "That's the way the sheriff wants it and that's the way it's gonna be."

Lemon nodded. "I understand that's what Sheriff Ted Pitman wants. But, is it what the townspeople want? Is it what you want, Mayor Reynolds?"

"The law is the law Mr. Lemon. We have no reason to change it. What's this all about?"

"I told you. I sell guns. I'm trying to make a living."

Reynolds' eyebrows rose. "And the five hundred dollars?"

Lemon grinned. "An investment. I needed a way to meet with you alone, one on one, to pitch my offer."

"And just what is your offer Mr. Lemon," a skeptical Reynolds asked.

Wyatt Lemon ran a hand over his smooth head. "Look here, it's just a matter of time before everyone, including your sheriff, realizes this little no-weapons policy is a mistake, a big mistake. When that happens, some lucky gun salesman is going to make a killing." Lemon saw Reynolds' eyes narrow and continued. "Sorry, bad choice of words. Someone is going to clean up. How's that, better?" He didn't wait for an answer. "I'm just trying to make sure that I'm that salesman who is going to get rich when this town comes to its collective senses. Nothing wrong with that, is there mayor?"

"And the money?" Reynolds asked again. "Five hundred dollars is a lot of money."

Lemon nodded. "Sure is. Thing is, it's just the beginning. I been around these parts a long time. I know politicians like mayors have a lot of influence on things. Your word carries weight. All I'm saying is that if you help me get the laws changed…well…there'd be a certain percentage of every sale…negotiable of course…going back to you."

"That's blackmail!" said Reynolds.

"I like to look at it as a business proposition mayor. Everyone wins. The townspeople get their weapons back and you and me make ourselves a little profit. No one gets hurt."

Mayor Reynolds reached into his pocket, withdrew the five hundred dollars from an etched leather wallet and tossed them at Wyatt Lemon. "Mr. Lemon, take back your money. And hear me out. I'm going to do you a favor. If you're cleared of Pete McBride's murder, I'm not going to mention our conversation today. You'll be free to go. If that were the case, I'd ask you to go and never return to Bullet Pass. Am I clear?"

Wyatt Lemon wasn't accustomed to being turned down. He gathered himself. "I had nothing to do with your murder, mayor."

"That'll be determined. Again, I'll ask, who is your friend that followed you in here?"

Lemon swung his body around. The seated man appeared not to be paying attention to Lemon's conversation with Reynolds. "I don't know. Never seen him before in my life."

"What if I told you he's also staying at Crown House? What if I told you this murder I've been speaking about occurred at the Crown House?"

Lemon swallowed hard. "I explained my business to you mayor. I don't know the man and I certainly don't know anything about a murdered man. Look, I just want to…"

The Poke's wooden doors exploded open. Sheriff Ted Pitman blew in followed closely by Willie Sanchez. The sheriff spotted Harley Reynolds. "It's Curtis. At the checkpoint. He's dead. Murdered!" blurted out Pitman.

CHAPTER 7 – A Clue

Mayor Reynolds' jaw dropped. Words stuck deep in his gut. Wyatt Lemon jammed the money into his shirt and scrambled toward the door. Ty Stoner rose from his seat at the corner table, his eyes focused on Lemon. Lemon didn't get far. Sheriff Pitman grabbed him by the arm and thrust him back toward Reynolds.

"Get in there," a stern Pitman demanded. Strain showed on the sheriff's face.

"What happened?" Reynolds managed to ask.

Sanchez piped in. "He was stabbed. A knife stuck in his chest. A knife from the Crown House! It was one of them skinny blade knives that poor old Pete used all the time."

"I didn't do it!" yelled Wyatt Lemon. "I was right here. You can't blame this one on me too." He looked back and forth from Reynolds to Pitman.

"You're being right here now doesn't prove a damn thing," said Reynolds. "No one except you knows where you were or what you were doing before you got here. You could have easily killed Curtis just as easily as you could have murdered Pete McBride!"

"It's not true!" shouted Lemon.

Sheriff Pitman approached Reynolds and Lemon. "I take it this is the man you met here Harley? The one who sent you the letter and the five hundred dollars?"

The seriousness of the situation wasn't wasted on Wyatt Lemon. After all, he was a stranger in this town and he had offered the mayor a bribe. Now, two men had been murdered and Lemon had no doubt that this sheriff would be anxious to make an arrest. He addressed Pitman. "That's between me and the mayor. A business deal between the two of us. Nothing more. It didn't work out for reasons I don't want to get into, so if it is all the same to you, I'll be on my way."

Pitman chuckled. "You're not going anywhere. No one is." Lost in thought, he began thinking out loud. "Fact of the matter is, the only one who has an alibi for Curtis' murder is the rabbi. Solomon. Of course, we could be dealing with two different killers."

"I didn't do either one," reiterated Lemon. "I don't even know…"

"Shut up!" said Reynolds.

"Everything goes back to the Crown House," continued Pitman. "Pete's murder, the weapon one of his skillets. Curtis gets stabbed, the knife comes from the Crown House." He scratched his chin. "One of the hotel's guests is responsible. I'm convinced of it. Unless, someone is trying to make it look like a Crown House guest is responsible."

Sanchez burst out, "Sheriff, can I tell them the rest of it?"

Pitman looked annoyed. "What rest? What is it Willie?" asked Harley Reynolds.

"Sorry sheriff," said Sanchez. "I couldn't help it. I know you told me not to…"

"Not to what?" asked a frustrated Mayor Reynolds.

Pitman thought about things. He decided it best to share the information Sanchez discovered at the murder scene with the mayor. He motioned Reynolds over, away from the others. "Willie, keep an eye on him while I speak to Harley."

Sanchez nodded. "He ain't goin' nowhere sheriff. I'll see to that."

"Don't forget that one," Reynolds said, pointing at Ty Stoner. "He's the big mouth who didn't want to talk to us back at the hotel. Make sure he stays put too." Stoner stared at Reynolds. About to say something, he thought better of it and remained silent.

"What happened?" asked Reynolds when he and the sheriff were off to the side, out of ear shot from the others. "What did Willie find at the check point?"

Sheriff Pitman looked serious. "Two things, Harley. First, Curtis was still alive when Willie found him."

"Alive?"

"Yes, but barely. According to Sanchez, Curtis managed, just before he died, to scrawl something in blood with his finger." He paused. Reynolds waited. "I'm not sure what it means Harley, but my guess is Curtis was trying to identify his killer."

"What he write?" asked the mayor.

"It looked something like:

IM IM

"You saw it too?" asked Reynolds.

"Yes," confirmed Pitman. "The blood had dried some by the time I arrived, but it was still clear enough. Willie agrees, but neither of us can make sense of it."

Harley Reynolds gave it thought. "It appears to me that he was trying to say, I'm something or other, but that he couldn't finish. He must have seen his killer. What a terrible thing."

"That's not all," said Pitman. "I told you there were two things. The other is a gun was taken from the checkpoint."

"A gun? Stolen?"

Pitman nodded. "Afraid so. Sanchez confirmed it. The chest was open. One pistol was removed."

"So, someone is walking around Bullet Pass right now with a loaded weapon," said Reynolds. "Maybe this Wyatt Lemon is right."

"What?" asked Pitman. "Say, what was that letter and the money all about anyway?"

The mayor knew nothing would come of it, but he pressed Pitman again. "Lemon is a gun salesman for Smith and Wesson. I don't know if he's a murderer or not, but he tried to bribe me with the money and promises of future payments if I could influence you and the town council to reverse the existing laws prohibiting guns. I'm sure I'm not the first one he's tried to bribe. He probably deserves to be in jail, but with two murders and a stolen gun, I don't think I would bother with him at the moment."

"Unless he's responsible for either Pete's or Curtis' murder, said Pitman.

"Or both," added Reynolds. He went on, "I know we've discussed this numerous times before Ted, but I don't think it's going away. Things are beginning to spiral out of control and I fear they may only get worse. Maybe this little experiment isn't working out. Did you ever think about that?"

"Every day," answered Pitman. "We can't give up now Harley. I know this is a safer town, a better town now in which to live and raise a family. I'm sure we can enforce the law without weapons and the sooner we all get used to the fact the happier we'll all be. Besides, I'm not about to give into an outlaw or two that's trying to change who we are. We all made a tough choice to change. We knew there would be some difficult times and challenges, but we'll face them and eventually root out evil." He stopped, thought about Rabbi Solomon. This second murder helped convince him more so of the religious man's innocence. And, the rabbi was proof that a town without guns and ammunition was the humane way to proceed. He thought about enlisting the rabbi's help. A religious leader generally has keen insights into the human soul, and although unfamiliar with the Jewish religion, Pitman was intrigued with the thought. He mentioned it to Reynolds.

"I have nothing against this Rabbi Solomon, but we don't have any reason to trust him over anyone else staying at the Crown House. If you want to get so-called religious help, why not ask Preacher Watkins to assist?"

Pitman shook his head. "Nothing against Watkins, but he's one of us. I think an outsider, one who was drawn to our town for the very reason of our gun laws, would be more effective. My concern now is that gun floating around. I'm afraid there's going to be another killing, Harley."

"Hmm. Maybe we should arm up, at least temporarily, until the stolen weapon is found?"

"No," answered Pitman sternly.

"What do you suggest?"

The question had no right answer. Things flew around the sheriff's mind. One killer? Two? A hotel guest? A Bullet Pass resident? He didn't know. How could he know? Where did this Rabbi Solomon fit in? Was he part of the problem? Or someone sent by the Lord to offer assistance? Ever since his childhood, Ted Pitman discovered that gut decisions were usually the right ones. He couldn't afford to be wrong this time, not with two people murdered and a stolen pistol somewhere in Bullet Pass. He let his gut guide him.

"Everything points to the Crown House," he told Reynolds. "I say we gather all the guests together, including the ones we haven't met yet."

"Like the man in room number six, I believe it was, who wasn't in his room at the time."

"Right. And Mrs. Wallace in room one. We haven't seen or spoken to her. I'm curious about her and her husband."

"And don't forget that Ty Stoner fellow, the one who just happened to show up here during my meeting with Wyatt Lemon. We still haven't gotten him to say who he is or what he's doing here."

"Let's start with him," said Pitman. The two men joined the others.

"You didn't have a thing to worry about sheriff," said Willie Sanchez. "I've had my eyes on both of them and neither one ain't goin' nowhere."

"Thanks Willie." He faced Lemon. "You're in enough trouble friend. Trying to bribe a mayor is against the law. I have every reason to lock you up right now."

"How many times do I have to tell you I didn't kill anyone?"

Pitman then addressed Ty Stoner. "Okay you, enough games. You're gonna talk and tell us what you're doing in Bullet Pass or I'll toss you in jail until you do speak. Your choice."

The once belligerent Stoner stood. "I'll talk. I'll say this sheriff. It wasn't him!" pointing at Wyatt Lemon. "He wasn't near the checkpoint when that man Curtis was stabbed."

CHAPTER 8 – An Alibi

"Sit back down Stoner," commanded Pitman as he, Willie Sanchez, Reynolds, and Lemon moved closer to the table. Pitman glanced at Lemon. The stranger appeared just as confused and intrigued as everyone else. "What do you know about this?" Pitman asked Stoner.

"I know he isn't guilty of the murder of this man Curtis." Stoner pulled a long, thin cigar from his pocket and lit it. He pulled a card out of another pocket and dropped it on the table. No one reached for it, their eyes still focused on Stoner. Amused, Ty Stoner said, "Well, aren't you going to look at the card sheriff?"

Ted Pitman took the card and without taking his eyes off Stoner placed it in his back pocket. "No."

For a brief moment Stoner thought about not cooperating, but decided against it. "You already know my name. I'm a detective hired by Mr. Elmer Fisher. He's a big shot at Smith and Wesson to…"

"You little…" began Wyatt Lemon, but he was promptly stopped by Sheriff Pitman. "Go on, Mr. Stoner." Pitman looked at Lemon. "Keep your mouth shut."

Stoner nodded his appreciation. "As I was saying, Mr. Fisher hired me to keep an eye on this gentleman, Wyatt Lemon. Mr. Fisher had heard rumors that Wyatt Lemon had been engaging in let's just say, less than savory business practices. Mr. Fisher demands the utmost integrity from the people who represent the Smith and Wesson name. He was deeply concerned about some of the things involving Wyatt Lemon. If nothing else, Mr. Fisher is a fair man. He needed to know for certain if the accusations against Lemon were valid and accurate. He hired me. I've been following Mr. Lemon for several weeks now and I trailed him to Bullet Pass and the Crown House. I'm sure you gentlemen could see why I was so rude back in my room. I didn't want word to get out to Mr. Lemon that a detective had been following him. My sincere apologies about that."

"Arrest that man sheriff," implored Lemon. I came to Bullet Pass with a simple business proposition for the mayor and this man is spreading false rumors about me. What kind of town are you running here? I'm a guest in this town and I'm being accused of being a common criminal."

Sheriff Pitman glared at Wyatt Lemon. "You don't know how lucky you are friend. At the least you're guilty of bribery of a town official. This man has done you a tremendous favor by providing you with an alibi. You should be thanking him." He turned and faced Stoner. "You can swear this man Lemon was nowhere near the town's checkpoint since he arrived in Bullet Pass?"

"That's right sheriff. He was never out of my sight." He paused and then added, "Except of course when he was in his room, but I kept my door open a bit. I had a good viewpoint of Mr. Lemon's room across the way. He didn't leave his room without my knowing about it."

"I resent this!" cried Lemon.

"I'm not telling you again Lemon. Shut up!" ordered Sheriff Pitman.

"How do we know the two of 'em ain't in it together Ted?" asked Sanchez. "We don't know neither of these two people. Maybe they killed Curtis together. Ever think about that?"

Ty Stoner didn't wait for the sheriff to respond. He jumped right in. "That's nonsense. But, he has a point. You don't know either one of us. I suggest you get a wire to Mr. Elmer Fisher himself and ask him to verify that he hired me to do a job and that's what I'm doing."

"Sheriff?" asked Sanchez. Pitman nodded and Willie Sanchez took off for the telegram office.

"Once Mr. Fisher confirms that I am who I say I am, that will clear both myself and Mr. Lemon of this Curtis murder. Still, there are bribery laws and this isn't Mr. Lemon's first offense. A month back I trailed him to Amarillo. He spent a lot of time in a place called The Armadillo. He got real friendly with one of the performers, a painted-faced dancer who went by the name Sage. I couldn't figure his angle at first. He spent good money on her for a couple of weeks before I figured things out. I wised up one night and decided to follow this Sage woman instead of Lemon. And what do you fellows think

I found out?"

"Keep talking," said Mayor Reynolds. "We're listening."

"I followed Sage to Ernie Miller's gun shop. Ernie owned and ran the biggest and most successful gun store in Amarillo. I waited a few minutes for Sage to come out, but she never emerged. After a while I went in and guess what I saw?"

"What?" asked an eager Mayor Reynolds.

"Nothing," He paused for affect, and then continued. "They weren't there. No sign of Sage or Ernie Miller. I walked through to the back and that's when I saw the two of them in well…I'm a discreet man…let's just say a compromising position. This little routine went on for days, until Mr. Lemon began showing up more and more at Ernie Miller's shop. From my vantage point, their relationship appeared cordial enough at first, but it didn't take long for things to deteriorate. Sage stopped showing her face around Miller. Miller did his best to avoid Lemon, but our friend here," he pointed at Wyatt Lemon, "Wouldn't let Miller alone and eventually he broke the poor man. Lemon had first paid off Sage. Despite the fact that Miller was a married man, he succumbed to Sage's flirtations and advances. Lemon moved in after that and threatened Miller that he would expose the gun shop owner's indiscretions. Miller closed up shop and Wyatt Lemon filled the void. He sold an awful lot of guns to the good people of Amarillo. I have more similar stories if you're interested to hear them."

"That isn't necessary," said Pitman.

"Wyatt Lemon may be a despicable human being who belongs behind bars, but as far as I can tell he isn't a murderer," declared Detective Ty Stoner. "At least, he didn't have anything to do with the death of Curtis. I can't help you there."

The men listened to Stoner's tale. Willie Sanchez, back from the telegram office joined them. Like cannon shots on Fort Sumter, several thoughts and questions bombarded Sheriff Pitman. Two murders. Were they related? Did the same person commit them? A beard hair perhaps linking a man to one of the murders, or not? A cryptic message, IM IM, written in blood. Unaccounted-for hotel guests. A stolen razor. A gun taken from the checkpoint. A man, a religious leader no less, locked behind bars. A man Pitman knew in his heart was innocent. And whether he wanted to admit it or not, a growing romantic relationship with Jenny Whitlock. Pitman pined for a deputy's help, but a town without weapons could not justify two lawmen. Willie Sanchez was the closest thing to a deputy and he provided some relief and comfort to Ted. Sheriff Pitman steadied himself and took charge. "There are too many loose ends. We need to find out exactly what's going on here and put a stop to it."

The Mayor nodded. "I agree with that," said Sanchez. "What do you suppose we do sheriff?"

"I want everyone gathered at the Crown House, and that includes the guests we haven't met yet. Willie, work with a few of the men and round everyone up. But before that, make sure the checkpoint is secured. No one goes in or out. Who is stationed there now?"

Sanchez said, "Wilson and Garcia."

"Good. We'll get together tomorrow morning at seven o'clock sharp at the Crown House. By that time, we should have an answer to your telegram verifying Ty Stoner's claim. Until then, you come with me," Pitman's comments were directed at Wyatt Lemon."

CHAPTER 9 – *Gathering at Crown House*

A young boy ran into the sheriff's office and handed Pitman a telegram. The sheriff thanked him and gave him a tip. The boy bowed and ran out to spend his newly found fortune. With paper in hand, Pitman stopped next to the jail cell. "Do I have to tell you what this says?" he asked Wyatt Lemon. "The response from Elmer Fisher of Smith and Wesson."

Lemon, who had been standing, fingers wrapped around the bars, said nothing. His shoulders dropped, he backed up and sat on a wooden bench that doubled as a bed. Rabbi Solomon stood outside the bars, having been released by the sheriff.

"Are you certain?" asked the rabbi. "I don't mind waiting here until this murder is solved."

"Two murders," corrected Pitman.

The rabbi's eyes looked downward. "So sorry. Man can't seem to avoid violence, no matter the time nor the place. Those who kill will pay the ultimate price. Genesis says, *Whoever sheds human blood, by humans shall their blood be shed; for in the image of God has God made mankind.*

"I don't know about that rabbi," said Pitman, "But I know a man of your demeanor and knowledge could be beneficial to me and our town. If you're willing to assist, I'd welcome your help."

"Very well. I don't have much experience with this sort of thing, but a town without weapons is a town worth saving." He looked at the sheriff's expression. "What's wrong sheriff? Is there something else going on?"

Pitman wasn't ready to go into his personal feelings involving Jenny Whitlock, but he confided in the rabbi about the stolen gun and the enigmatic IM IM blood-written message. "I'm afraid it's only a matter of time before that stolen gun becomes another murder weapon. We've got to find it and stop whoever it is that killed Curtis and took it."

"Assuming of course that the same individual murdered Curtis and took the gun," said the rabbi. "Let me ask you about those letters, IM IM."

"What?"

"Do you think he was trying to write, I'm? Was there an apostrophe between the letters?"

"No," answered Sheriff Pitman.

"You're sure?" Pitman nodded. "Interesting," murmured Solomon.

"Why is that interesting? We all just figure that with his life bleeding out from him, he didn't have time or care much about adding the apostrophe. Wouldn't you agree?"

Solomon gazed thoughtfully. "Perhaps. Perhaps not."

At seven o'clock next morning, a gathering had arrived at the Crown House. Mayor Reynolds stood alongside Sheriff Pitman and Willie Sanchez. Rabbi Solomon, dressed in black, sat alone at a table silently reading scripture, his lips moving faster than a hummingbird's wings. Mr. Wallace from room number one drank coffee. Sheriff Pitman couldn't tell if Wallace's sour look was due to the coffee taste or the inconvenience of the seven o'clock request. Next to him sat a rather attractive woman who Pitman assumed was Mrs. Wallace, although she appeared years younger than her husband. Sitting two seats from Mrs. Wallace was a man in his early to mid-thirties, thin, jet black hair combed straight back, and a devious looking smile. His eyes, directed toward Mrs. Wallace, were wide. A pencil rested between his right ear and the side of his head. Two others sat together at a separate table, the horse trader Oscar Sticks Blessington from room number five and Bullet Pass ranch owner Paul Palmer.

"Where is everybody?" asked Sanchez. "It's past seven o'clock by now."

Ted Pitman surveyed the group. "Let's see now, Wyatt Lemon is in jail at the moment." He looked around again. "I don't see Ty Stoner or Jenn…Miss Whitlock." He turned toward Paul Palmer and smiled. "Morning Paul, good seeing you. What brings you here this morning? I don't believe you were…"

"I invited him sheriff if you don't mind," interjected Oscar Blessington. "If this here is some sort of accusatory proceeding, I figured the next best thing to having a lawyer at my side is to have the man who can vouch for me. The man I come to see to conduct business. He's one of you. I hope you don't mind."

"I certainly mind," the unexpected response from Mr. Wallace. "Why is he permitted to have someone speak on his behalf while no one else here is? What kind of trial are you running here sheriff?"

Pitman glared. "This isn't a trial," he said. "And what are you afraid of that you need a lawyer, Mr. Wallace?"

"This is outrageous. I'm not afraid or guilty of anything. How dare you…"

"That'll be enough Mr. Wallace," Reynolds chimed in. "By the way, I didn't catch your first name."

"That's because I didn't give it," a defiant Wallace declared. "My wife and I have no intention of sitting here listening to a lot of nonsense and answering questions for things we know nothing about. As I explained to you before, we are merely travelers minding our own business and the sooner we get to California the better."

Wallace's wife placed a hand on his cheek and patted it. "Now, dear, I don't see what the problem is if they want to ask us some questions. After all, we have nothing to hide. Do we?"

"Of course not!" rapped Wallace. "It's just that…"

"Enough!" shouted Pitman. "You're going to stay here until I let you go and there's nothing you can do about it. Just settle down there, both of you." No matter how hard he tried, Pitman still couldn't picture this pair as husband and wife. He continued. "How's anyone seen Ty Stoner or…Miss

Whitlock?"

"I'll go check on them if you'd like." It was the thin young man with the pencil stuck behind his ear. "Happy to assist."

"That's might friendly stranger," said Mayor Reynolds. "I don't believe we've met? I'm Harley Reynolds, mayor of Bullet Pass."

"Fred Hilson, reporter for the *Cheyenne Wells Record*, out of Colorado. Nice to meet you."

All eyes focused on the man. Then, Sheriff Pitman turned and addressed rancher Paul Palmer. "Paul, I'm afraid I have to ask you to leave. This is an official investigation we're conducting and the only people I want here right now are those who are staying at the Crown House. Nothing personal you understand, but I want to be fair to everyone."

Paul Palmer stood. "No offense taken Ted. But, I'm more than happy to vouch for this man Blessington. He's in Bullet Pass to buy some horses from me. I'm certain that he doesn't have anything to do with these terrible happenings around town."

"I appreciate that Paul. But again, this isn't a trial. We aren't calling witnesses to tell their stories. I'm going to ask you to leave. If we need additional information we'll certainly come out and visit you. And, maybe Mrs. Palmer could bake one of her delicious apple pies?"

"Of all the ridiculous…" began Oscar Blessington. He stopped, more in control of himself, continued, "In that case, I'd like to be given permission to leave as well." He began standing.

"Sit down Sticks," demanded Pitman. He shook hands with Paul Palmer and the latter departed.

"Where were we?" asked Pitman. "Oh yes," he faced the young Fred Hilson. "Colorado? Newspaper? Please explain to us…"

All heads turned toward the room's entrance as a frail and pale Jenny Whitlock slowly walked toward an empty table. She tried to manage a smile. It came off as a sneer. Sheriff Pitman rushed to her side and grabbed her by arm.

"Jenny. What happened? Are you okay?"

"Yes. I suppose so. I'm so sorry for being late. I know the importance of this meeting. I tried to be here on time. It's just that…I felt so sick this morning…I don't know what's come over me."

"Would you like some coffee?" offered Sanchez.

Whitlock smiled. "Yes, please. That would be very nice Willie."

Color slowly returned to her cheeks as she finished the drink. "Can I get you another coffee ma'am?" asked Rabbi Solomon. He had sat down next Whitlock. Still carrying his small leather bible, he stared directly into Jenny's eyes. It seemed to Jenny as if he were looking through her and she felt uncomfortable. She declined, looking up at Sheriff Pitman as if pleading with him to intercede. The lawman got the message.

"Rabbi, please return to your seat. Thank you." He ordered Willie Sanchez to go upstairs and to check on Ty Stoner in room eight and then turned his attention back to Fred Hilson.

"Please continue Mr. Hilson. You were saying?"

A large smile creased the newspaperman's face. "You might say I hit the jackpot sheriff."

"Oh?"

"My editor, a Mr. Porterfield back in Colorado, heard about your little town here and the fact that you've outlawed weapons and ammunition of all kinds. Frankly, he didn't believe it. He sent me out here to do a story about you and Bullet Pass. So here I am."

"What's this about a jackpot?" asked Harley Reynolds.

The smile broadened. Fred Hilson displayed straight, white teeth. "Murder, of course. And, times two! How lucky can one reporter get? This will be a sure promotion for me once I report back to Mr. Porterfield. I can see the byline now. Yessir, just a real lucky break for me. Wait until Huggins gets a load of this. Huggins is a reporter too. My competition you might say. Old man Porterfield promised to promote one of us. He sent Huggins out to New Mexico to cover a story about some sick cows! Can you imagine? Huggins knee deep in dung and me, Fred Hilson reporting on a town with no guns and two murders!"

Pitman looked annoyed. "Maybe in Colorado you think murder is such a great thing, but I reckon violence is violence no matter where you come from and I don't mind saying that your words insult every law-abiding citizen in this county."

An awkward silence enveloped the room. The reporter looked embarrassed. "I'm sorry sheriff. Guess I just got carried away with myself. It won't happen again. If there is anything I can do to help you just let me know." He pulled the pencil from his ear and jotted down words in a notebook.

Willie Sanchez entered the room limping followed by Ty Stoner, the latter tightening a bolo tie. "He overslept," announced Sanchez, flipping a thumb at Stoner.

"What did I miss?" asked the detective, the question rhetorical. "This has never happened to me before. I guess all this travel and running around finally caught up with me. I must apologize to you and everyone else here for my inexcusable behavior. I'll take a seat and fully cooperate with your investigation sheriff."

"Excuse us a moment," said Pitman as he, the mayor and Willie Sanchez huddled together. After a brief discussion he said, "Whoever murdered Curtis at the checkpoint also stole a gun." The admission was met with a collective breath intake and frightened sighs. "It is my…our belief that one of you in this room has that weapon. We're going to search everyone here first. Frankly, I don't expect anyone to have the weapon on their person. After that, we plan to search everyone's room upstairs, beginning with room number one."

"I object!" shouted Mr. Wallace. "No man is going to search my wife! I won't stand for it."

Sheriff Pitman scratched his chin and turned toward Jenny Whitlock. "Would you mind helping with Mrs. Wallace?" he asked.

"And who's going to search Miss Whitlock?" asked an outraged Mr. Wallace.

"That's enough from you Mr. Wallace. Jenny, are you feeling better? Are you willing to help us search Mrs. Wallace?"

"Yes, I think so." She looked at the Wallaces. "I'm sorry. We're all a little on edge and shaken up here. The quicker we do this the quicker we will all be free to be on our way." She managed a smile and then looked at Pitman for confirmation. "And I don't mind agreeing to being searched." She looked at the sheriff, a twinkle in her eye.

Ty Stoner laughed. "Ha! This is going to be real interesting sheriff."

"How's that?" asked Pitman.

"Miss Whitlock's impending search of Mrs. Wallace. I wouldn't miss this for the world."

"I ought to pop you one!" shouted Mr. Wallace. "Sheriff, I demand an apology from this man!"

"Please Mr. Wallace, I'll handle this. And you Stoner. You show up late and interrupt us with these crude comments. I wouldn't blame Mr. Wallace here for being upset and wanting to slug you. What's wrong with you?"

"There's nothing wrong with me sheriff. Especially my eyes. I got real good vision." The detective laughed again. "And these peepers are looking at Mrs. Wallace over there. Or should I say Sage, late of The Armadillo saloon in Amarillo, Texas!"

CHAPTER 10 – Murder Accusation

"That man's a liar!" shouted Wallace."

"Am I?" asked Stoner. "Why don't you ask Ernie Miller, that poor gunsmith back in Amarillo? Or better yet, you don't have to travel to Texas. Just walk over to your jail cell sheriff. Have Wyatt Lemon identify her. No one forgets a pretty, little poisonous face like that. You'd do well to lock her up and that so-called husband of hers."

Wallace clearly looked nervous. Of all the rotten luck, two men from Sage's past in the same town who could identify her. Wallace knew she'd be trouble from the start. His cocksure demeanor morphed into one of a schoolboy getting ready to ask a cute girl to his first dance. He wasn't happy with the fact that Sage had killed Curtis in the process of stealing a gun. The original plan called for Sage to seduce Curtis and to convince him to 'look away' while she removed a weapon from the stockpile. There was nothing in their plan that called for murder. He didn't stab Curtis, but Wallace knew enough that the sheriff would consider him an accessory to murder. Still, he figured, what proof did they have that Sage murdered Curtis? No one saw her. It was almost as if Sage were reading his mind.

"I'm afraid you can't prove a thing sheriff," said Sage. "You have this man's word that my name is Sage. You have two people, myself and Mr. Wallace saying otherwise. We are a couple travelling to California and we just happened to stop in Bullet Pass. I'll take it as a compliment that this vile man said he'd never forget a pretty face like mine, but until you have a shred of hard evidence, I suggest you continue your investigation, or whatever you call this annoying circus, and leave us law-abiding citizens alone."

"Then you won't mind if we search you first?" asked Pitman.

"I object," interrupted Fred Hilson, the reporter from Colorado." He promptly apologized and corrected himself. "I'm sorry. What I meant to say is I'd appreciate it if you would search me and my room first sheriff."

With raised eyebrows, "Oh? Why's that?"

"I need you to clear my name as quickly as possible. You know, rule me out as a suspect so that I'm free to come and go as I please and get all the facts of this story. This is a once-in-a-lifetime opportunity…robbery…murder…times two! And with your permission, after I'm cleared that is, I can follow you around as you investigate. That's what some of the boys do in Cheyenne Wells. 'Course we haven't had a murder there since I can remember. Mostly neighbor squabbles and bar brawls but nothing like…"

It was Stick Blessington's turn. "Why him? I think I should be the first one searched, cleared, and let go free. After all, I was the one who brought in Mr. Palmer to speak on my behalf. That should account for something."

Sheriff Pitman slammed a fist. "We're starting with you Mrs. Mimi Wallace, or Sage, or whatever your name is. He ordered Willie Sanchez to pat-down Mr. Wallace. He made eye contact with Jenny Whitlock. Despite regaining some of her color, she still didn't appear totally well to Pitman. "Stand up ma'am," addressing Mrs. Wallace, "We're going to search you."

Sanchez froze in his tracks. Sheriff Pitman hadn't taken his first step when Mrs. Wallace grabbed a pistol from her handbag and stood. "No one moves!" she said. "You can't pin a murder on me. Robbery? That's a different story. Everyone slowly put your hands in your pockets and remove any cash. That includes you Chubby," she said, addressing Mr. Wallace. She walked around the room waiving the pistol around. "You," she said to Ty Stoner, "The smart one. You collect all of the money and hand it over to me. If anyone tries anything stupid they are going to get shot."

"Ma'am," began Rabbi Solomon, "At this point, all that we know is that you have a gun in a town that does not permit such things. As far as we know, the gun belongs to you and would have been given back to you once you departed this town."

Sage looked at him with amusement. "What are you getting at?"

All eyes were on Rabbi Solomon. Pitman studied the religious leader. The more he observed him and heard him speak the more impressed he became. "I'm trying to tell you that technically, you didn't steal. One can't steal their own property. I assume that is the same gun you…and your partner…Mr. Wallace…checked before entering Bullet Pass. If so?" he waited and Sage nodded for him to continue. "If so, and if you didn't commit the murder as you stated, you're guilty of nothing more than violating a local law in Bullet Pass. I'm not certain what the penalty is for such an infraction, but I can assure you it is a lot less then for robbery."

The words weren't lost on Sage. She thought about them as Ty Stoner gathered the money. "What about murder? The sheriff here and the rest of them think I killed this Curtis man when I took the gun. I say I didn't. Now what?" Stoner had everyone's cash but Sage made no movement toward getting it.

"The sheriff is investigating the murder. If there is no evidence against you, you will be free to go. Turn over the weapon. We must bring it back to the checkpoint so as not to violate the local law."

"What about the other dead guy?" she asked, clearly intrigued by the rabbi' words.

"Mr. McBride? I myself was under suspicion for Mr. McBride's murder, but as you see, I am here and not in a jail cell. Give yourself a chance. If you take our money and try to run away, you will be a wanted fugitive and it will be a matter of time before you are caught. You'll be looking over your shoulder wherever you go, worrying that you'll be caught. What kind of existence is that for one of God's children? You are at a crossroads in your young life. Please, let me help guide you to take the righteous path."

Willie Sanchez was not a betting man, but if he gambled, he would place money in favor of the rabbi. The man was persuasive. Willie lacked formal education, but he appreciated it in others. He wondered if Rabbi Solomon could even be a genius. It appeared to him as if the woman was coming to her senses. Jenny Whitlock, deep in thought, sat motionless. Concerned that this out of town rabbi seemed to be taking over the investigation from Sheriff Pitman, she thought it best to not say anything or get involved in any way.

Ty Stoner had other ideas. "Are you kidding rabbi? This woman is a known con artist. Someone needs to speak to Wyatt Lemon to corroborate what I'm saying. Heck, just ask him," pointing to Mr. Wallace. "He was taken in by her as well. She's guilty. I guarantee it."

"Guilty of exactly what, Mr. Stoner?" questioned the rabbi.

The detective thought for a moment. "Something. Anything. Tell him Wallace. She conned you. Tell him!" demanded Stoner.

Mr. Wallace rubbed his chin, digesting Stoner's words. He stared at the money now in Ty Stoner's possession. Wallace stood to lose over two hundred dollars if Sage took off with the money. He was afraid of her. "Umm…I can't agree with Mr. Stoner. Okay, maybe we aren't legally married, but I went into this wide-eyed. She in no way pulled the wool over my eyes. I wasn't born yesterday sir, and to suggest the same is downright insulting. She's free to go on her own way. I wouldn't stop her."

Stoner shook his head and pumped a fist full of dollars. "Fool! You're a yellow, cowardly fool Mr. Wallace. No backbone!" He looked at the money in his hand. "You have the most to lose here. You know that? I hope she takes the money and is never caught. What do you think of that?"

"Ah, but if she took the money now and tried running she would get caught," said Rabbi Solomon, his voice calm, even. "Let us not confuse what's going on here. There have been two murders in Bullet Pass. It isn't clear why either murder occurred, if they are related, or if the same person committed them. That's for Sheriff Pitman, Mr. Sanchez, and Mayor Reynolds to determine."

"What about you?" Jenny Whitlock couldn't help herself. The words blurted out.

Solomon smiled. "*Judge not, that you be not judged.* If I can assist these gentlemen, it will be my honor. God wants to see justice. Man is on earth to carry out God's deeds. The guilty must be punished. But," he added, "They must be caught first."

"Of course," came Whitlock's response.

"It's your decision ma'am," Max Solomon said to Sage. "What will it be? You can hand over the gun to me or the sheriff, or you can take our money and try to run."

"Give everyone their money back," Sage ordered Stoner. "Here." She walked a few steps closer to Sheriff Pitman and handed him the gun. "I didn't kill Curtis and you can't prove otherwise," she said.

"Sheriff Pitman, this woman is not telling the truth. Arrest her for the murder of Curtis. She's guilty!" cried Rabbi Solomon.

CHAPTER 11 – *Rabbi Solomon Explains*

The words startled everyone. "Rabbi, please repeat what you just said," requested Sheriff Pitman.

Teeth peeked through partially covered lips. Rabbi Solomon wiped his mouth. "We have evidence that Miss Sage, or Mrs. Mimi Wallace, or whomever she is murdered Curtis. Curtis told us as much before he died."

"Are you going to pay any attention to what this crazy nut has to say?" asked Sage. "Words from a dead man?"

"'Fraid so ma'am," answered Pitman. "If he says there is evidence against you, I want to hear him. And, so might a judge and jury."

"Wait," said Sage. She faced Solomon. "You're supposed to be a man of God?" The rabbi nodded. "What kind of religion allows you to tell falsehoods and make false accusations against me?"

"The accusation is not false. You murdered Curtis."

She moved closer to the rabbi. "You said just a few minutes ago that if I didn't run off with everyone's money, that I wasn't guilty of anything except possession of a gun inside Bullet Pass."

Solomon shook his head. "No, my exact words were if you didn't commit the murder as you stated, you're guilty of nothing more than violating a local law in Bullet Pass. However, you did commit the murder despite your false claim."

Sage spit but the rabbi shifted away, the filthy saliva mixture fell harmlessly to the ground. Grabbed tightly by the sheriff, she squirmed and clawed like a rabid dog. "Leave me alone! Get your hands off of me. You can't prove a thing against me!" she shouted.

Mayor Reynolds watched everyone's reactions as the sheriff struggled with Sage. Rabbi Solomon stood steadfast, detached, almost machine-like and without feeling. Jenny Whitlock looked like she was ready to say something, but thought better of it and remained silent, her eyes glued on Sheriff Pitman. Horse trader Oscar Sticks Blessington appeared worried. Reynolds didn't think he showed concern for Sage, rather for the business deal he was trying to transact. The murders had derailed what should have been a routine transaction. The most worrisome look belonged to that of Mr. Wallace. His head shifted constantly, his unfocused eyes rolling around like a pair of dice. Reynolds almost felt badly for him, except for the fact that he might have had something to do with Curtis' murder or even Pete McBride's death for that matter. Detective Ty Stoner had an amused look on his face, as if he was being entertained by the entire proceedings. The last person in the room, Fred Hilson, was determined to capture everything on paper. The newspaperman rarely looked up, his hand writing with speed rivaling the quickest gunslingers. Reynolds didn't like Hilson, or anyone else in the newspaper business. Fact was he had nothing personal against any of them, except for the fact that one of them was probably a murderer.

While Mayor Reynolds observed the room, Willie Sanchez assisted Sheriff Pitman in controlling Sage. Struggling with the woman's legs, he looked up and said, "Go ahead rabbi. Tell us what you mean. How do you know for certain she killed Curtis? What's the evidence against her?"

Rabbi Solomon walked over to Mr. Wallace. "Did Curtis check your gun and hand you a receipt for it at the checkpoint?"

With a look of annoyance, Wallace said, "Yes. Why?"

"May I see it please?"

Wallace dug into a couple of pockets before producing the receipt. He unfolded it and handed it to Solomon. "What of it? I want it back."

"You'll get it back," a large smile emerged. He had second thoughts about disturbing Fred Hilson so he moved toward Oscar Blessington. "And you? Did Curtis give you a receipt for your weapon?"

"No sir. It was him," pointing at Willie Sanchez. "He checked me in."

"Curtis checked me in." interjected Ty Stoner. "Got the receipt right here."

"Can I see it?" asked Solomon.

"Sure. But what in the world does this have to do with evidence against Sage?"

"Did you look at the receipt?" asked Solomon.

A perplexed look covered Stoner's face. "Sure."

"I should have asked you, did you read it?" questioned Solomon.

"Umm…not really. Why should I? I handed him my revolver and he gave me the receipt. How was I supposed to know the poor guy would get murdered? I had no reason to read it. What's it say that's so important?"

The rabbi handed the paper back to Stoner. "Take a close look."

"That's funny," said Stoner. He wrote my name backwards. YT instead of TY. It says, YT S."

Solomon smiled. "And you, Mr. Wallace. It's time for you to reveal your first name."

Wallace looked at Solomon and shrugged. "Sure. It's really no mystery. Ed. Ed Wallace at your service."

Handing back the receipt to Wallace, Solomon said, "And would you mind reading out loud to everyone what it says on your receipt?"

Wallace looked at it, said nothing. He glanced up and then looked back down at the paper. "That is strange," he said, "Curtis wrote DE W instead of ED W. Is this some kind of coincidence? And why is it so important?"

Keeping oneself educated and abreast of the latest medical advances was as important to Rabbi Solomon as was his Jewish heritage. "Strange how God works," he began, "He must have known I'd be solving a murder mystery. I'm certain the name Rudolf Berlin has no meaning to anyone here. Am I correct?" He looked around the room. Blank stares returned his gaze. Solomon continued, "Dr. Berlin is an ophthalmologist and…"

"A what?" asked Sanchez.

"Eye doctor," answered Solomon. "He's also a professor in Stuttgart, Germany. It's a slightly long story, but I'll do my best to keep it short and to the point. Two of my congregants, the parents of a 10-year old boy came to me for help. They were frustrated with their son's inability to read. They had the boy's vision checked but there was nothing wrong with his eyes. Yet, he continued struggling with the written word. Why they came to me I can only guess. A religious leader is faced with many challenges. More times than not, the person in need simply wants someone that they can talk to and who will listen. I'm not a doctor, but I read a lot, and that's how I came to know of this Dr. Berlin in Germany. Apparently, he had been engaged in research with adults suffering the same reading problems as our 10-year old boy. Eventually, Dr. Berlin came to the conclusion that the problem was caused by some physical change in the brain. He coined the term dyslexia to explain the phenomena." Max Solomon paused. "Have I lost everyone?"

Sheriff Pitman scratched his head. "I can't speak for the others rabbi, but you lost me back at opthth…or whatever that word is."

"Ophthalmologist. Eye doctor. I'm sorry."

"What's the point to all this?" asked Ty Stoner.

The rabbi grinned. "The point is that in some extreme instances, people inflicted with dyslexia reverse letters. In your case Mr. Stoner, he reversed the T and the Y." He turned to Wallace. "And you sir, he reversed the E and the D."

"Wait a minute," jumped in Harley Reynolds. "I'm beginning to see what's going on here. Curtis, bleeding to death, made a last-ditch effort to write his killer's name in blood." Rabbi Solomon nodded, encouraging the mayor to continue. Reynolds stared at Sage. "As far as we knew at the time, your name was Mimi. At least that's what you had told us and I'm certain that's how you introduced yourself to Curtis."

"You don't know what you're talking about," spat Sage.

"I think I do," answered Reynolds. "Curtis was trying to write MIMI in his own blood before dying. Instead, he reversed the letters, and we all thought he was trying to say I'M something or other. That's it, isn't it rabbi?"

"My guess is she took a knife from the Crow House here. When her attempts to seduce Curtis failed, she stabbed him and then took a gun," said a beaming Sanchez.

Before Sheriff Pitman could place Sage under arrest for Curtis' murder and slap her in handcuffs, she wheeled around quicker than a polecat and pulled the pistol from the lawman.

"Nobody moves!" she shouted. "This time I won't be so foolish as to listen to this sorcerer's lies," referring to Solomon.

"Don't be foolish," said Pitman. "We've been through this before. You're in enough trouble now ma'am. Don't make it worse for yourself. Hand over the gun."

"Nothin' doin'," she spat. "Murder is murder. I can only hang once. I got nothin' to lose by killing another one of you or the whole bunch for that matter. In fact, that might make the most sense, seeins' as that's my best chance of getting away from here. And I'd be much obliged if you'd hand me back the money again." Sage giggled. "This is kind of funny, ain't it? We just went through this performance. This time, it's the final curtain."

"She must have killed Pete McBride as well, either her or her fake husband, Mr. Wallace," said Jenny Whitlock.

"Shut up!" said Sage. "I killed one man and one man only. I don't mind taking credit for that, but I'll be damned if I'm blamed for a killing I didn't commit."

Ed Wallace chimed in. "How do we know you didn't kill this McBride, ma'am?" he asked of Jenny Whitlock.

"You can't convince me it isn't the rabbi who killed Mr. McBride," said Fred Hilson, looking up from his notebook for the first time. He seemed strangely unfazed by the goings on in the room, worried only about the story he was writing. "Remember that hair that was found with the body. I'm no judge, but that seems like enough evidence as far as I'm concerned."

"Enough!" shouted Sheriff Pitman.

Sage waived the gun around. "Okay, listen up. Everyone back up against that wall, nice and easy. No quick moves. I'm going to walk out of here, get on a horse and ride out of this joke of a town. If anyone makes a move to stop me or follow me they're going to get shot. Don't test me. That includes you Mr. Rabbi. I'll shoot you down just as easy as a rabbit."

"Do something sheriff," implored Sticks Blessington. "You can't let her get away with this."

"Let her go," said Rabbi Solomon. "No sense anyone else getting hurt. She won't get far. Proverbs says, *Be assured, an evil person will not go unpunished.*

"Better listen to this religious fool this time," said Sage. She took two steps back and was about to turn and leave when she was blindsided by Bullet Pass' barber Perry Oliver. The two tumbled to the floor, the gun knocked loose from Sage's hand. Sheriff Pitman picked up the pistol and yanked Sage to her feet. He put the confused and shaken murderer in handcuffs. Oliver slowly got to his feet. His hand was wrapped in a handkerchief heavily stained with blood. Temporarily dazed, he found a chair and sat down. Sage let out a curse.

"Perry, what on earth happened? What's going on?" asked Mayor Reynolds.

"A messenger from God," said Rabbi Solomon. "A prophet, like Aaron."

"Will you please shut up with that mumbo jumbo," said Ed Wallace.

"Are you okay? What happened to your hand?" asked Pitman.

The barber stared at his wrapped paw like an unattached appendage, something foreign to his body, something unexplainable. He was pale, clearly shaken. Then he fainted.

CHAPTER 12 – Another Lie

Jenny Whitlock rushed to the fallen barber. She pulled a silk handkerchief from her breast, found a pitcher of water and applied the wet cloth to Perry Oliver's forehead. Slowly, Oliver came to.

"Are you okay Perry?" asked Pitman.

"Don't worry about me sheriff." He licked dry lips. "It's Doc Carter." Oliver went silent.

"What about him? What Perry?"

"He's dead! Doc Carter's been shot!"

The shock of it all muted everyone in the room. There was no movement, save for Fred Hilson, whose writing speed intensified. The reporter never looked up. "Hot damn!" he yelled. "A third murder! This is too good to be true. Who would have thought an assignment to cover a town that forbids guns and ammunitions would turn into a triple killing bonanza? I know reporters who've gone an entire career without getting a chance at something like this. Latman, he's our most senior reporter, has covered hangings and face-to-face shootouts, but no one has seen anything like this." He seemed to be speaking to himself, and he wasn't listening to his own words as he continued scribbling at a furious pace.

"Dear God help us all!" shouted Sanchez. He glanced over at the rabbi but he wasn't sure why.

"Tell us what happened Perry," said Mayor Reynolds. "And your hand…it's bleeding badly."

Oliver held up the wounded hand and stared it. "I was sharpening a pair of scissors and the darn thing slipped and sliced a 5-inch opening in my hand big enough to stick a tobacco chaw into it. I rushed over to see Doc Carter. I didn't knock or nothing, I just rushed into his office and there he was on the floor, dead, gunshot wound in his chest."

"Did you see anyone around?" asked Sheriff Pitman. "Anyone nearby his office?"

"No. No one."

"Did you hear a shot?" asked Mayor Reynolds.

"No. Nothing. I nearly fainted in doc's office, but managed to scramble out of there as quick as I could and raced over here. That's all I can tell you."

Pitman's eyes were on Sage. So were those of Reynolds, Sanchez, and Solomon. She responded. "I know what you're thinking but you'd be wrong. I didn't shoot this doctor of yours. Never even laid eyes on him. What do you think of that?"

"He's been shot," said Mayor Reynolds.

"And you're the only one in town with a gun," added Sanchez.

"That don't prove nothing. You think I'd deny killing this doctor if I had done it? Really? After you already arrested me and practically convicted me of murdering that Curtis fellow at the checkpoint."

"You done lied to us before, ma'am, and I have no doubt you'd lie to us again," said Sanchez.

Sage thought for a moment. "Well, maybe you're right at that. Maybe I wouldn't tell you the truth. That's true enough." She laughed. "But in this case, I ain't lying none. I didn't shoot no one."

"Gentlemen, if I may," interjected Ty Stoner. "May I see the gun for a moment?"

Sheriff Pitman hesitated, but agreed after seeing Reynolds nod his approval. "Just don't try anything funny Stoner. I'll lock you up faster than a blinking eye."

"You have my word sheriff." Stoner reached out for the gun and Pitman handed it to him. The detective examined it closely. He smelled it, opened it, and with a look of satisfaction declared, "This gun has never been fired."

"What? You're sure of that?" asked Mayor Reynolds.

"Positive. At least not within the last 24 hours. No empty chambers, no powder marks, no odor, no nothing. This gun has not been fired. Of course, if you don't want to take my word for it, you can go to the jail and ask Wyatt Lemon. He deals in guns and he's the real expert, but I'm around them enough to tell you Doctor Carter didn't die from a bullet shot from this pistol."

"If that's the case…" wondered Harley Reynolds, "Then,,," his voice trailed off.

Sheriff Pitman finished the sentence,"…There's a second gun in Bullet Pass!"

"Ha!" yelled Sage. "I told you I didn't shoot him!"

Willie Sanchez jumped in. "That don't mean you didn't kill him. Heck, it only means you didn't shoot him with this gun. How do we know you didn't use another gun to shoot him?"

"I guess you don't," said a smug Sage.

"No one leaves town," ordered Sheriff Pitman. He led Sage back to his office and locked her up. He released Wyatt Lemon. Lemon confirmed what Stoner had said, that the gun in Sage's possession had not fired a single bullet within the last 24 hours.

Pitman sat with Mayor Reynolds, Willie Sanchez, and Rabbi Solomon. "I'm open for ideas fellas," he said. "Damn situation has me accusing everyone I know and no one I know." He scratched his head.

"Who would have it in for Doc Carter?" asked Mayor Reynolds. "Man didn't have an enemy in the world."

"That's where you are wrong mayor," said Rabbi Solomon.

"Huh?"

"Someone hated him enough to want him dead," interjected Willie Sanchez.

"Not necessarily," responded Solomon.

This time it was Sanchez's turn to respond, "Huh?"

"What are you trying to say rabbi?" asked Pitman.

"Human behavior is difficult to predict. Surely, it is easier to figure out how groups of people might act under specific situations but when it comes to an individual…well…that's a different story. Why would anyone want to kill Doctor Carter? A number of reasons come to mind. Something might have happened a long time ago that just now caused such violent behavior. Was it a planned killing or something spur of the moment? Did the doctor know or see something that caused his untimely death? Again, as was the case with Pete McBride, what was the motive? Many unanswered questions. You ask me sheriff, what I'm trying to say? I wish I knew. Ever since Exodus, after the Israelites escaped from Egypt, they wandered in the desert for forty years. Frustrated with their predicament, the Israelites built a golden idol in the absence of any other sign that Yahweh, the Lord was still on their side. To punish them, Moses commanded the Levites to take their swords and ambush the people. There's nothing new under the sun. Since the beginning of time, man has committed brutality against man. Unfortunately, it's nothing new and it won't end in with Doctor Carter's murder in Bullet Pass."

"I don't know nothin' about any of that," said Sanchez. Only thing I know is that you," he pointed at Solomon, "Didn't kill poor old Curtis and that gun salesman…what's his name…"

"Wyatt Lemon," interjected Mayor Reynolds.

"Right. Wyatt Lemon. He ain't responsible for killing Doc Carter. Rabbi here was in jail when Curtis was stabbed and that Lemon fella was behind bars when Doc got shot. Got any ideas sheriff?"

"I won't speculate Willie. The only thing I will say is that we've got to find the killer…"

"Or killers," interrupted the rabbi.

The lawman appeared frustrated. "True. We don't even know at this point if we're dealing with one or more than one killer."

"If anyone is interested in my opinion," chimed in Reynolds, "I suspect that Blessington fellow."

"Why him?" asked Sanchez.

"First off, I don't believe any of our Bullet Pass townspeople are capable of these murderous acts. Why was he so anxious to bring Paul Palmer to vouch for him? How do we know he didn't use a so-called business deal with Palmer as an excuse to come here and begin murdering our friends? I don't trust him."

The three men listened to Reynolds. "What's Mr. Blessington's motive?" asked Rabbi Solomon. "A man…or woman for that matter…generally doesn't kill without a motive."

Harley Reynolds slammed a fist on the table. "I don't know. It could be anything. Maybe he tried to get McBride to provide information about Palmer's ranch? You know, inside stuff that could help him negotiate a better deal. Or, maybe he tried to involve McBride in some kind of illegal scheme and McBride threatened to turn him in? I don't trust him, that's all."

"And Doctor Carter? And if he did shoot the doctor, where did he get the gun?"

The mayor shook his head. "I don't know. I wish I did."

"Wait a minute," said Willie Sanchez. "How about the newspaper fella Fred Hilson? A couple a things. First, have we checked with the newspaper in Colorado that he says he works for? Did anyone send a telegram to the *Cheyenne Wells Record*?" He paused, looked at Pitman.

"No. But that's a good idea Willie." He gestured to Reynolds. "Harley, would you mind going to…"

"On it." The mayor departed.

Sanchez smiled. "And if you are looking for some kind of motive, I'll give you one. He's writing a story about murder, right? I don't believe for a minute that these murders occurred just by coincidence while this fellow just happens to be in town covering a story about a gun-less town. I don't claim to be no great judge of character, but this young man strikes me as very competitive, and he would stop at nothing to get ahead. And that includes murder! And why stop at one? The more killings he writes about the better for him. And that's if he is who he says he is. Also, he seems to keep to himself in a funny way. The more I think about it, the more I think he's our man."

"And do you think he's connected in any way with Sage? We know she killed Curtis. If Mr. Hilson wanted to write about murder, why would he kill Doctor Carter after the Curtis murder? That doesn't make sense to me," said Rabbi Solomon.

Sanchez didn't hesitate. "Remember, the first killing was McBride. Even if we give Hilson the benefit of the doubt about Doc Carter's murder, he's still the number one suspect in my book for McBride's death. I can't wait to get an answer to our telegram to that newspaper he claims to write for."

"I'm sure you could make a case for any of the Crown House guests," said Solomon. He hesitated.

"Go on," chided Harley Reynolds, back from his trip to the telegraph office.

"Take the detective, Ty Stoner for example. He had the same opportunity as Blessington or Hilson or anyone else and is probably more skilled at committing murder than the others. Remember how belligerent he was when we first met him? He said it was because he didn't want to blow his cover while following Wyatt Lemon. I wonder."

"Motive, rabbi," said Sanchez smugly. "You preach there's no murder without motive. Why would Stoner want to kill McBride? Or Doc Carter?"

Solomon grinned. He had these men thinking correctly. "You're right Willie. Let's assume that Stoner had some type of argument with McBride. It might have been about his blown cover. Maybe Stoner found out that McBride told Lemon that there was a detective staying at the hotel? Or, perhaps McBride saw something he should not have seen?"

"Like?" asked Sanchez.

"Like Stoner following Lemon and then threatened to expose Stoner."

"Ah, that don't sound like Pete McBride none. I can't imagine old Pete threatening anyone about anything."

"I'm not saying it happened that way. I'm just saying it's a possibility, same as your Hilson reasoning and Harley's Blessington theory. What do you really know about Mr. McBride? Was he having personal trouble? Money problems? He might have been trying to shake down Stoner and the latter snapped in the moment, grabbed the skillet, the first thing he saw and committed the murder. It's plausible."

"Possible. Maybe. Not plausible," interjected Mayor Reynolds.

"I stand corrected," Solomon concurred. "But among Stoner, Blessington, and Hilson, I contend that the detective is most likely, once having committed the murder, to think about planting evidence at the scene that would implicate someone else."

"You mean the beard hair?" asked Reynolds.

"I do. None of the others strike me as the types. Although it's hard to know exactly what that type is." Solomon shifted gears. "But if you really think about it, it was probably one of the locals who killed McBride and Doctor Carter. Bullet Pass residents are much more likely to have reasons, or motives, to do away with two of their own."

"That didn't apply to Curtis, now did it rabbi" asked a skeptical Sanchez.

"No, it didn't. Then again, Curtis is for lack of a better term…um was…the town's keeper of the weapons. In his case, the more probable suspect would be an outsider. I offer this explanation as an alternative to blaming Mr. Ty Stoner. It's a strange little puzzle and we can't be sure that the killings will stop. I'm not certain Judaism has the answers."

"At least you're here in case someone confesses," said Sanchez with laughter in his voice.

Throughout the discussion, Sheriff Pitman remained quiet, lost in thought. Rabbi Solomon took notice and questioned him. "There's something on your mind sheriff. What is it? Do you pay creed to any one of these theories?"

Pitman looked up. He suddenly appeared older; his face creased with lines engraved by life's burdens. The office never felt spacious, but at this time Pitman felt as though the walls had inched closer to the room's center. Embarrassed because he hadn't been paying attention to the conversation, he caught only the last two words of Solomon's question.

"I'm sorry rabbi. I wasn't..."

"Just like Zechariah," said Solomon.

"Huh? Who?"

"John the Baptist's father. Never mind, it's not a fair comparison."

The sheriff shrugged his shoulders. "It's just that..."

"No need for explanations," Solomon said, like a father comforting a son. "Something you'd like to share? Perhaps one of us could help?"

Pitman managed a weak smile. "No, no thank you. I just need a little time to myself, to think things through. Mind if I take a little walk?"

"It's your town sheriff. We'll wait here for you, if you have no objections that is."

"Stay as long as you like," Pitman said as he turned and exited the office.

The air felt warm and comforting, blanketing his skin. He walked slowly. His heels made deep indentations into the soft brown dirt. Pitman's mind formed its own solution to the mysteries, but like a nightmare he didn't like it and tried repressing it. He regretted not having listened more closely to Sanchez, Reynolds, and Solomon. Especially Solomon. The rabbi impressed Pitman as knowledgeable, someone educated on many topics and who seemed to possess keener insights into others' behaviors. He couldn't put a finger on it, but Pitman believed Rabbi Solomon was sent to Bullet Pass by a higher authority at this time of crisis. Right or wrong, he trusted the rabbi, and was thankful the man was willing to help. Pitman turned by the bank and walked through the narrow alley between the bank and Potter's Seed Store. Bullet Pass was quiet. The silence belied the recent savage killings. The juxtaposition was not lost on the lawman. If he didn't bring the killer to justice within a reasonable time, he'd call for assistance from a U.S. Marshal. Loathe doing that, Pitman had pride. He was a man of conviction who had witnessed too much death. He was convinced that a town could thrive without weapons or ammunition. Pitman knew it was a controversial position, not for everyone or every city, but he believed if he could pull it off others would follow. He never expected things to be easy, but then again, he didn't anticipate multiple murders in a short period of time. A gun was stolen and a man was shot, yet upon inspection it was determined that the gun had not been fired. That meant a second gun, its whereabouts unknown, remained somewhere in Bullet Pass. His thoughts were interrupted by the sound of footsteps, initially soft, but becoming louder as they approached Pitman. He felt like a stranger in his own town. The normally close-knit community had been replaced by one of suspicion and accusatory stares. Reflexively, he reached for his holster that wasn't there, smiled, and turned to face the person behind him, Jenny Whitlock.

"Oh Ted," she said, shivering despite the mild temperature. "I'm so scared. What's happening here? No one feels safe anymore. I don't feel safe."

The two embraced, his strong grip providing relief, comfort. "It'll be okay Jenny," Pitman said. "We'll find out whoever's doing this and get them behind bars."

She managed a smile. "Are you sure?"

"No question about it," he said, but inwardly he wasn't certain. He placed two fingers under Jenny's chin and gently lifted up. "Come come," he said, "Things will be fine."

She dabbed her eyes with a handkerchief and asked, "What about us Ted? I know you said you aren't comfortable talking about marriage, but neither of us are getting any younger and so many terrible things have been happening here lately that well…I think it's time we face the future. The other night was special. I don't regret it. I just know it was the right thing. I was so happy, but now with all these horrible things taking place in Bullet Pass. I'd feel so much safer and happier knowing we'll always be together. Just thinking about the fact that I'm living under the same roof at the Crown House as a killer has me beyond jumpy."

Sheriff Pitman seemed to shrink from the weight of Jenny's words. He'd rather have taken a punch to the face or gut then to be on the receiving end of a word barrage, especially one delivered by Jenny Whitlock on the subjects of murder and matrimony. He had to stall her somehow, but wasn't skilled in communicating with women.

"About that night," he stammered. "I…I just can't focus on that right now Jenny. You understand?" By her look, she didn't. "We have a serious situation here and a lot of people are counting on me to catch whoever is responsible. I took an oath to uphold the law and that's what I plan to do." Pitman did his best to sound firm and confident.

Whitlock pouted. "I don't understand why you can't do both?"

"Jenny, please try to understand. If…" and he quickly corrected himself, "When things are settled here and the killer is caught then I'll be able to focus more intently on us."

"Well…I…never, Sheriff Pitman!" she said in frustration. "Of course I want you to find the murderer and put him behind bars. I just thought our relationship shouldn't play second fiddle to your job. We're not getting any younger Ted!" and with that she stormed off.

One minute she shivered in fear, and the next she gave Pitman a tongue-lashing. The sheriff shook his head, more confused than ever. He needed to speak frankly with Rabbi Solomon. He couldn't face Harley Reynolds or Willie Sanchez with his innermost thoughts, but Max Solomon was different. The religious leader had a knack for listening and Sheriff Ted Pitman was ready to talk. He headed back toward his office.

Solomon, Reynolds, and Sanchez looked up when Pitman walked in. "Tell us, have you solved this mystery?" asked the rabbi.

Pitman shook his head. "I just went out to clear my head. I'm not sure if I'm any closer or father away from figuring out this mess. I'm almost afraid to ask, but have you three come to any new conclusions?" Three heads shook in unison. "In that case, there's something I'd like to speak to Rabbi Solomon about."

"Go ahead!" blurted Sanchez.

"In private, if you two gentlemen don't mind." Pitman directed his words at Reynolds and Sanchez.

"Of all the…"

Mayor Reynolds cut Sanchez off, grabbed him at the elbow, and said, "We were just leaving. Let's go Willie."

Both men stood. The telegram delivery boy ran into the office waving an envelope in his hand. He headed straight to Harley Reynolds. "Here you go mayor," he said, handing him the note. The boy took his tip and departed.

"An answer to our question about Fred Hilson's employment at the *Cheyenne Wells Record.* Hmm, now that is interesting," he declared.

"What? What?" repeated Sanchez.

"It appears as though our reporter friend is not currently employed by the *Cheyenne Wells Record.* Mr. Hilson lied to us!"

CHAPTER 13 -- *Theories*

"I knew it!" shouted Willie Sanchez. "I knew it! He's our man. Arrest him sheriff. Newspaperman…in a pig's eye. I spotted him as a phony from the first time I laid eyes on him. He couldn't fool me. I know the type. The quicker you arrest him sheriff the faster this town will sleep easy again,"

"Slow down Willie," cautioned Pitman.

"Slow down nothing. He's our man!"

"What does the telegram say Harley?"

Harley Reynolds read out loud to Pitman, Sanchez, and Rabbi Solomon. "We'll need to question him Ted. I'm interested in knowing why Mr. Hilson lied to us about his employment."

The three men made their way to the Crown House, ascended the stairs and knocked on door number six.

"Who's there?" came Hilson's voice.

The men didn't wait for an invite. As soon as Hilson began opening the door, Pitman, Reynolds, and Sanchez burst into the room.

"What's the meaning of this? You have no right to barge in here like this," said Hilson.

"Who are you and what do you do for a living?" blurted Sanchez. He saw

Pitman's and Solomon's looks and decided he had better stay quiet and let them do the questioning.

"Mr. Hilson," began Sheriff Pitman, "Is that your real name?"

The startled man looked from one to the other. "Of course. Why wouldn't it be? What's this all about sheriff?"

The sheriff answered not with words, but by handing Hilson the telegraph message. The latter read it and turned pale. He handed the paper back to Pitman.

"Okay, so what? You found out I'm not actually a reporter for the *Cheyenne Wells Record*. That doesn't mean I'm guilty of murder. Besides, I have my reasons why I said what I said. I may not be a reporter, but I am a writer and I'm researching Bullet Pass. Like I said before, the murders, although unfortunate, are an added bonus for me. That's the truth."

Rabbi Solomon spoke. Proverbs is full of interesting text. *The righteous hate what is false, but the wicked make themselves a stench and bring shame on themselves.* It will only serve you well to come clean and tell the truth. You can see lying to us in the midst of murder doesn't portend well for you Mr. Hilson."

Hilson knew the time for him to be truthful had arrived. "It's nothing nefarious gentlemen, I'll tell you that from the start."

"Lying to a sheriff when he's trying to find a killer or killers is nothing nefarious, as you put it? I disagree with you Mr. Hilson. As far as I'm concerned, you are in a heap of trouble. I'll leave it to Sheriff Pitman. It's not for me to arrest you, but if I had the authority, rest assured you'd be behind bars as we speak," said Mayor Reynolds.

"Then I'm happy you don't have the authority," Hilson responded, smiling. "What I did wasn't right. I admit that. But think about things if you were in my boots. I'm a stranger in town, a couple of murders are committed, and I have no real reason to be here, other than to say I'm interested in Bullet Pass. The reason Bullet Pass fascinates me is twofold. First the ban on guns and ammunition like I originally said, but the other and more important reasons is the root cause of the ban."

The men listened. Sanchez asked, "What do you mean by this root cause?"

"I'm talking about The Anvil, the saloon you shut down before beginning this new law of yours."

"What's your connection to The Anvil?" asked Sanchez.

Six skeptical eyes were on Fred Hilson. Sheriff Pitman tried not to think about The Anvil, but thanks to Hilson its memories had moved front and center on his brain. He winced as he relived the violence and un-Sunday-like behaviors that were commonplace. Pitman couldn't imagine what possible connection this man could have to The Anvil. Mayor Reynolds on the other hand saw nothing but red when he looked at Hilson. The man had lied when asked direct questions about a murder. Reynolds had a general bias anyway toward the press, having fought them over the years for misquoting him and as he had put it, stretching the true story in order to sensationalize the news. He had no interest in hearing out Hilson. Why should he believe what this liar had to say now? Willie Sanchez didn't know what to make of Fred Hilson. He didn't trust him. Then again Sanchez didn't trust any of the strangers staying at the Crown House. Sanchez preferred that Pitman lock the man up for a spell while they sorted things out. He knew the sheriff wouldn't go for that, but that's what he would do if he were running things. Sanchez relied on gut feelings and his gut told him that Fred Hilson was no good. The third man waiting for Fred Hilson's explanation, Rabbi Max Solomon, wasn't as eager to hear Hilson's story as the others. Everyone lied. That didn't mean they were killers. Whereas the focus seemed to be centered on the Crown House guests, Rabbi Solomon was more concerned about the townspeople. Something troubled Sheriff Pitman. The lawman was about to get something off his chest when the telegram delivery announcing that Hilson didn't work for the *Cheyenne Wells Record* interrupted him. What was it that Pitman was about to say? Why did he need to tell it privately? Solomon had great respect for the sheriff. He appreciated the lawman's patience and sense of fairness. Pitman wasn't one to fly off the trigger. He impressed Solomon for going about the investigation in a methodical manner. The murders were complicated. Solomon realized that from the start and he also feared unless the killer or killers was caught, there would be more murder. Sage's arrest for killing Curtis was independent of the murders taking place in Bullet Pass. Pete McBride and Doc Carter's killings were different. No matter how hard he tried, Rabbi Solomon couldn't figure why a stranger in town would want to kill either of these two. Motive. It always came back to motive for Solomon. Could it be Jenny Whitlock? What about the barber, Perry Oliver, the one who claimed his straight razor went missing? There was Paul Palmer, the ranch owner doing business with Oscar Blessington. He could have committed the murders. Solomon thought about Palmer. The ranch owner had sort of disappeared during the investigation. Was he hiding something? Many questions. Few answers.

Hilson's voice broke the silence. "My brother is…was Dan Black." The self-professed newspaperman stopped, watched the dumbfounded expressions on everyone's faces, and then added, "My half-brother. Same mother. Different fathers."

Sanchez blurted, "Dan Black? That no-good, murderin', theivin', drunkin', son-of-a-…"

Pitman held up a hand. "Stop it Willie." He addressed Hilson. "I still don't get why you didn't tell us the truth about the reason you're here. The fact that Black is your half-brother as you say…well…so what?"

"You killed him sheriff."

All heads turned to face Pitman. "I did at that. He had it coming. I'd do it again given the chance."

A sneer creased Hilson's mouth. He appeared ready to explode, but quickly recovered and in complete control of his emotions, said, "Well, what's done is done. I'm not going to hold that against you sheriff."

"Then what on earth are you doing here Hilson?" asked Sanchez.

With an annoyed look, Hilson responded, "I've already explained that to you. Want to hear it again?" He didn't wait for an answer. "When word travelled about my brother and what you had turned this town into, I admit I was curious, and furious. I'm a writer, not for a newspaper as you found out, but for a publishing house in New York. They had heard about Bullet Pass and were looking for someone to do an article about them. I jumped at the chance. I not only wanted to see what this town was all about, but also to come face-to-face with the man who killed my brother. My brother and I are very different people. He chose his path. I mine. As far as meeting you sheriff, I don't fault you for doing your job. My publisher had a hard time believing that Bullet Pass hadn't become lawless since you banned weapons. I too had my doubts. So, when these murders began happening, I was more than happy to document all that I'd seen and experienced."

"Excuse me for interrupting, but why deceive us with your story about writing for a newspaper?" asked Rabbi Solomon.

"Fair question. The publishing business, especially back in New York is highly competitive. I'm from Colorado. The *Cheyenne Wells Record* had turned me down on several occasions. I wanted to be a reporter ever since I was a child. I submitted local stories to them but all were rejected. When I heard about this New York opportunity, I jumped at it. They didn't want me to announce that they had financed this trip. They wanted to keep it a secret. Once word gets out that a story is being researched, competitors flood the same area and it becomes a contest as to who can get the story out first. I just thought it a bit of sweet personal justice to tell you that I was associated with the newspaper when in fact I was not."

"What do you think sheriff?" asked Willie Sanchez. "I say lock him up. The way I figure it, poor Pete McBride must have found out who he really worked for and threatened to expose him. In a fit of rage, this fellow did in poor Pete. And then, once Curtis got it, he," pointing to Hilson, "Decided to kill again. He figured he got away with it once so why not try again? Doc Carter's office is off away from everyone, sort of private, so that there'd be no witnesses. This Hilson figured the more murders he wrote about, the more his publisher would like it. That's why he didn't stop at McBride's murder and I have me no doubts he wouldn't have stopped with Carter's murder if we hadn't found out he was a fraud."

"That's absurd," countered Hilson. "I didn't kill a sole. Just so happens I was in the right place at the right time, if you were writing a story about a town, that is. Nothing more than that." He thought for a moment. "I guess you could say my brother Dan Black, although in the same town as where I now stand, was in the wrong place at the wrong time. Ironic, isn't it gentlemen?"

With a nod toward Hilson, Harley Reynolds declared, "This one's a little too smug for me sheriff. Something doesn't ring true about him."

"I'll have to disagree with you mayor," said Rabbi Solomon. "I think Mr. Hilson's story makes perfect sense."

Reynolds frowned. "But what about Willie's theory and Hilson's killing Pete McBride? You're always preaching about a motive, and Willie came up with a valid motive for killing both McBride and Doctor Carter. Besides, you're a stranger in these parts no different than Hilson, Lemon, or any of them. Why should we take you in our confidence?" He turned to Pitman. "And what about that beard hair that was found where McBride was killed? I know you released the rabbi from jail, but I'm still not one hundred percent convinced that he wasn't mixed up in McBride's death somehow. A beard hair just doesn't fall off a face at a murder scene without placing the person at that murder scene. Do we really know who this man is, Ted?"

"Now let's all calm down and stop making accusations against everyone and anyone. As far as I'm concerned, Rabbi Solomon has had nothing to do with any of these killings and I find him to be helpful as we try to figure things out. I realize we are all under a lot of strain right now and that's probably what the killer is counting on, for each of us to turn against one another, accusing each other and pointing fingers, so that nothing gets accomplished. I think Mr. Hilson has explained himself and whether or not you accept what he says now as truthful is up to you. I tend to believe him. Rabbi," the sheriff turned to Solomon, "You were about to tell us why you thought Mr. Hilson's story makes perfect sense. As I said, I'm inclined to believe him now as well, but what were you going to say?"

The rabbi bowed to Pitman, showing his appreciation and gratitude. "I forgive Mayor Reynolds. Like Sheriff Pitman stated, we are all tense given the horrendous violence that has occurred in Bullet Pass. God knows that when we are under stress we are liable to say things we don't mean and which we later regret. Who among us has not sinned? As for Mr. Sanchez's theories, they are not farfetched. It's certainly possible, although not probable that Pete McBride threatened to expose Mr. Hilson. How could McBride possibly know that Hilson didn't work for the *Cheyenne Wells Record*? And for that matter, did Hilson even mention that fact to Pete McBride?" Solomon paused and stared at Fred Hilson.

"Come to think of it, no I didn't. I just signed the register with my name and the state I'm from, Colorado. My occupation or the newspaper wasn't discussed at all."

"Do we have to believe everything this man tells us?" barked Sanchez. "For all we know, he told McBride his life story when checking in."

Solomon grinned. "Again possible, but unlikely. I think Mr. Hilson's recollection of events makes more sense. There is no likely, or should I say apparent motive for Mr. Hilson murdering Mr. McBride."

"That's what you say," said Sanchez.

"Yes, that's my opinion," responded Solomon. "As for Doctor Carter's murder, your explanation Mr. Sanchez, and correct me if I'm wrong, was that after he killed Pete McBride, his own personal good fortune rose when Curtis was murdered. He therefore took it upon himself to kill Doctor Carter, for no apparent reason other than to give himself further grist for his story. Do I have that correct?"

Willie Sanchez shuffled his feet. "Well yeah, sort of." He paused, and then, "That's right!" he said with conviction. "That's exactly what he done. Why not? He figured he got away with Pete's murder so why not try it again so that he'd really have something to write about. I wouldn't put it past him, not for a single second I wouldn't."

Acting as judge, Sheriff Pitman weighed in. "You all make good points, but standing around jawing about this isn't going to find us a killer or a gun that we know is somewhere in Bullet Pass and it probably isn't going to prevent another murder from occurring."

"What do you suggest," asked Reynolds.

Pitman rubbed his chin. "I don't know. I do know that it wouldn't be fair to lock up Fred Hilson for lying to us. I don't believe he's our killer any more than anyone else staying at the Crown House or any of our townspeople for that matter."

"If I may," chimed in Rabbi Solomon, "I think the answer may lie with one of the townspeople. Perhaps questioning some of them could prove fruitful?"

"I resent that," said Mayor Reynolds. "I've known these people all my life and each and every one of them is trustworthy and God-fearing as the day is long. We should focus on the strangers. All of them!" he added with emphasis. "We'd just be wasting our time questioning the fine folks of Bullet Pass."

"I agree with the mayor," shot back Sanchez.

Pitman looked at Solomon. Neither man said a word, but it was if they were holding a private conversation between themselves. There was something Pitman needed to tell Solomon, but the wise, insightful religious leader was beginning to understand what troubled the lawman. Solving these two murders was something more than simply doing the job of a sheriff, and having enough pride to bring the killer or killers to justice without asking for outside help from a U.S. Marshal. It was personal for Sheriff Ted Pitman.

Rabbi Solomon could see it in the sheriff's eyes, in his demeanor, in the words he chose to express his opinions. The rabbi had seen conflicted men before. But God was not unjust and had a way of helping those in most need. At this moment, Rabbi Solomon realized that his coming to Bullet Pass was more than an opportunity to simply scout out a town and begin a new congregation. It was God's will. It was the rabbi's duty to save a man, a good man from himself and to save a town trying to do the right thing. He knew it wasn't going to be easy. Nothing worthwhile is. But some things are worth saving, even if preventing their destruction causes hardship and pain.

Solomon broke the silence. "I won't insist, of course. If you gentlemen feel that strongly against questioning some of the townsfolk, then we won't. Is that okay with you sheriff?"

The wear and tear of the recent events continued taking their toll on Ted Pitman. He sighed. "I think in order to conduct a thorough and complete investigation, we'll have to talk to everyone and that includes some citizens of Bullet Pass." The rabbi looked pleased, but Reynolds and Sanchez showed their annoyance.

"Then why not start with me Ted?" asked a sarcastic Harley Reynolds. "After all, I'm just as likely to have killed old Pete McBride and Doc Carter as any of these strangers in town. Of all the nerve, I never…"

"Harley, this is nothing personal. You know that. The law is the law. Just because someone stays at the Crown House does not mean that they are any more likely or unlikely to commit crimes than someone from Bullet Pass."

"Including murder?" asked Willie Sanchez.

"Including murder," said the sheriff. No one is more upset about this than me. But I…we all got a job to do and that is to find out who killed Pete and Doc…whoever it is. Now, are you two clear on this and willing to assist? If not, then that's fine too. The rabbi and I will continue investigating."

Mayor Reynolds looked down at his boots. "I suppose so," he sheepishly said. "I'll assist in whatever way I can. How about you Willie?"

"I don't like it. I don't like it one little old bit," replied Sanchez.

"No one likes it Willie," said Pitman, "Not a damn bit. Are you in or not?"

"In," was Willie Sanchez's one word answer.

Pitman turned toward Rabbi Solomon. "You're an outsider. Who would you want to question at this point?"

Honored by the question, the rabbi thought about it for a moment. He not only wanted to, but also needed to speak in private with Sheriff Pitman, but he felt the timing wasn't right. He feared that Reynolds and Sanchez would both take offense and resent him more than they currently did if he didn't include the two in the discussion.

"I think a good place to begin is with the barber, Perry Oliver."

Harley Reynolds exploded. "That's ridiculous! Perry is as solid a citizen as they come. I've known…we've all known Perry for decades. He's the last person I'd suspect as having committed these murders. No, I don't think we need to question Perry Oliver. Who's next on your list of suspects rabbi?"

"Harley, calm down." Sheriff Pitman walked closer to the mayor and put his hand on the mayor's shoulder. "You agreed that we needed to speak to the town's citizens. We can't start eliminating people just because they are our friends or because we like them. The law is blind. Let's let the facts take us wherever the truth lies. I'm sure Perry will have no objections to our asking him some questions. In fact, he'll probably welcome it. Perry wants the killer or killers found as much as anyone else."

"But why start with him sheriff?" asked Sanchez.

"Why not? He's as good a person as any. Besides, he might be better than some others."

"Oh?"

"Sure. Wasn't his straight razor taken from his shop? I'd say he's an excellent person to begin asking questions," said Sheriff Pitman.

The time was late but the four men walked to Perry Oliver's barbershop. Sheriff Pitman and Rabbi Solomon led the way, Willie Sanchez and Mayor Reynolds, side-by-side, a few steps behind.

"Did you notice anything, anything at all when you got your haircut?" Pitman asked Solomon. "Especially Perry's special razor. Did he use the razor on you?"

Solomon shuffled his feet and thought about the experience. "He used that razor on me."

"You're sure?"

"One hundred percent. I commented on it. I'd never seen such a fancy razor…and with initials…it's quite a shame that its disappeared. Who would want to take something with such personal significance to the owner?"

"That's what we need to find out," said Pitman.

"Of course, the person who took Mr. Oliver's razor isn't necessarily the same person…or persons…that killed Mr. McBride or Doctor Carter."

Sheriff Pitman hadn't thought about that possibility. "Hmm…that's a good point rabbi. What's your feeling about that?"

"It's difficult to say. It could well be the killer and he or she could be planning another murder using the razor as a weapon. Or, it could be the killer and he…or she…has no intention of using the razor."

"Then why take it?" interrupted Pitman.

"Perhaps to throw us off the scent? Or, to plant on some innocent person so that we'll accuse that person?"

"Like the beard hair?" asked the sheriff.

"Exactly. The possibility also exists that the razor theft has no connection to either murder."

The men walked in silence before Pitman asked the rabbi, "Did you see Perry put the razor away before he closed for lunch?"

"No. I paid him and walked out. I didn't even notice that he had closed the shop after he finished with me. There really was nothing remarkable about the experience. I found Mr. Oliver friendly enough. He asked me the reason for my being in town and I told him. He seemed interested, and a bit confused. I'm convinced I'm the first Jewish person he's met."

Sheriff Pitman chuckled. "I think that description applies to a lot of us here in Bullet Pass, myself included."

I'm used to that," replied Solomon. Solomon wanted to ask Pitman about the important things the sheriff wanted to get off his chest, but didn't feel it was the appropriate time, not with Sanchez and Reynolds a few steps behind. "Tell me sheriff, you've been in this town long enough. Is there any reason why Mr. Oliver would have any hostility or reason for disagreements with either of the deceased?"

Pitman stared into the religious leader's eyes. "Are you some sort of gypsy or fortune teller?"

"Excuse me?" Solomon looked bewildered.

"It's just that at times, your intuition makes you almost clairvoyant."

"Are you suggesting there is some friction between Mr. Oliver and either Mr. McBride or Doctor Carter, or both?"

"I don't think it fair for me to inject my feelings into this. As a lawman, I follow the facts, wherever they lead." Again, Solomon thought he detected worry and concern on the sheriff's face. Pitman continued, "Let's let Perry tell his own story and we'll all judge."

CHAPTER 14 – Perry Oliver

The four men, Ted Pitman, Harley Reynolds, Willie Sanchez, and Max Solomon found Perry Oliver in his shop, alone, smoking a pipe. "Howdy Perry," Pitman greeted them. "New tobacco?"

"I declare," began Willie Sanchez, "You're right about that sheriff. That ain't yer regular blend of burnt rope Perry. This stuff actually smells kind a pleasant."

The barber removed the briar from his mouth. Smoke dripped from his nostrils, the pipe's bowl, and the amber stem mouthpiece. "I'm not so sure I like it." He puffed again. "Slade got in this new shipment all the way from Virginia and he wanted me to give it a whirl. 'Fraid this stuff is gonna ruin my good pipe."

"Nonsense!" said Sanchez. "This is the first time I come into this shop and can breathe through my nose. Whatever Jake Slade gave you is a big improvement over yer regular blend and that's a fact."

"I'm guessing you gentlemen didn't come to see me so late in the day just to talk about my pipe tobacco. Must be this murder business. Horrible thing. Folks are gettin' so that they're afraid to leave their homes. That ain't good for business. Or maybe you got news on my stolen razor?" he added hopefully. "What's on yer minds?"

"First, how's your hand?" asked Mayor Reynolds.

Oliver smiled. "Healing. Thanks."

"You remember the rabbi here?" asked Sheriff Pitman.

"Yessir," said Perry Oliver. "Sure do."

"He's helping us with the murders and also with your missing razor. We have a couple of questions Perry."

"Fire away. I've nothin' to hide. And it ain't like I'm cuttin' anyone's hair at the moment."

"Good. On the day you gave Rabbi Solomon his haircut, the same day your personal razor went missing, did you take a normal lunch break?"

The barber shifted in his chair. Rabbi Solomon detected a bit of discomfort in Oliver's posture. "What do you mean by normal lunch break Ted? Sure, I closed the shop at noon, had my lunch and when I finished I went back to work."

"You see, there's nothing we can gain by questioning Perry," interjected Willie Sanchez. "The man was just doing his work. Someone stole his favorite razor." He glared at the rabbi. "He has nothing to do with any of this except for the fact that his razor was stole."

Sheriff Pitman ignored Sanchez's outburst. "I mean was your lunch break that day any shorter or perhaps longer than usual? Did you see or meet anyone during your break? Did you go anywhere other than behind your shop?"

The barber hesitated. He looked at each man separately and felt pressure. "I didn't go nowhere. Stayed right back there the whole time just as I do every day when I take my lunch. Took thirty minutes like always. Can't run a business if folks don't know when or not the barber is around. Everyone in town knows that."

Rabbi Solomon looked at Sheriff Pitman. Pitman continued questioning. "Did anyone come to see you during your break that day?"

More squirming. Oliver puffed on his pipe, but the flame had gone it. "Dang it," he said, rapping the pipe's bowl against a leg of the chair, spilling burnt tobacco ash onto the floor. "Well, now that you mention it, just so happens Doc Carter stopped by to see me. So what? That don't mean nothin'," Oliver said, his voice defiant.

Once again Willie Sanchez came to his defense. "He's right sheriff. That don't mean nothin'. We're wasting time here."

Sheriff Pitman treated Sanchez as if he wasn't present. He again ignored Willie's words. Harley Reynolds had been silent the entire time, listening to the exchange with keen interest. Rabbi Solomon's eyebrows rose. Perry Oliver stuck the pipe in his shirt pocket.

"What did doc want to speak to you about?" asked Pitman.

"That's sort of personal sheriff," Oliver said, looking around at the others. He prayed that a customer would walk into the shop, but his prayers went unanswered.

"I'm afraid you're gonna have to tell us Perry, even if it is embarrassing. The information may prove helpful to us. Think of the town Perry. If you have something to say, please tell us."

"Go ahead Perry," added Mayor Reynolds. "We're all friends here. I'm certain anything you have to say will in no way implicate you in any of these horrific events. We've been through tough times together before. We'll get through this one too."

Perry Oliver swallowed hard. "Like I said, it's personal. He come by to see me, that's all. Nothin' unusual about that. He'd come and visit me during lunch lots of times. Lots of people did that. This time it happened to be Doc Carter is all. Don't mean a thing."

"What did he want with you Perry? What did he say? What did you two talk about?" asked Sheriff Pitman. The lawman had put personal feelings aside, focused on the business at hand. "You understand I'm just doing my job, right?"

The barber frowned. "It's just that…"

Rabbi Solomon jumped in. "Rest assured Mr. Oliver, you are no more a suspect in these killings than any one of us or anyone else in town. You were the victim of a theft, an item that has personal meaning to you and you alone. That's the main reason we are questioning you now. We think the theft of your razor and the killings are probably related. Please don't take this as an attack on you in any shape or form. It's merely an information gathering session and as a group we feel that you might have seen or heard something that could help us in our information quest."

The rabbi's words had a calming effect on Perry Oliver. "Well, if you must know, and I can't see how this can help, but Doc Carter came to see me about money." He stopped, hoping no one would follow up. He was wrong.

"Money?" questioned Pitman. "What about money Perry? Please don't make this more difficult than it needs to be."

"Okay, I owe…um…owed doc some money is all," a sheepish Perry Oliver admitted.

"How much?" asked Pitman.

Rabbi Solomon jumped in before Oliver humiliated himself further. "I'm not so sure the exact amount is important sheriff. I'm sure in a town like this, providing services or selling items on credit is quite common, especially among friends."

With sudden respect for Solomon, Willie Sanchez added his two cents. "That's right! The rabbi is right about that. Heck, that happens all the time in Bullet Pass. Ain't nothin' strange or peculiar 'bout that. No sir. Fact is I owe Jake Slade twenty-five cents for a bunch a cigars I picked up the other day. Just happened to be short on cash at the time. Friends takin' care of friends. I'll pay him back. Jake knows that. And I'm sure Perry will pay Doc Cart…" he stopped, realizing what he was about to say. "Ah shucks."

Perry Oliver volunteered additional information. "Business ain't been great of late," he began. "Lots of folks cuttin' their own hair these days. Can't blame 'em, tryin' to save money wherever they can. Anyway, I've had some kind of stomach ailment for the last few months and Doc Carter was seeing me on a regular basis. He had been trying out different medications that he thought would help, but they really didn't. I liked Doc Carter. Heck, everyone liked Doc Carter. He kept trying and trying to help me. Remember when he took a trip to Crest Rock 'bout a month or two ago?" Pitman, Reynolds, and Sanchez nodded. "He went to see the doc at Crest Rock to ask him 'bout medicines for stomach problems. That's the kind of man he was. He had me trying a couple of new concoctions and combinations of a few different things. He never said it, but I got the impression that he was becoming more and more concerned with me on account of I wasn't gettin' no better. First couple a visits I paid him in cash. Full. But as the visits piled up, I just couldn't pay it all. Doc wouldn't hear 'bout me not coming back while I still owed him money. He insisted I keep coming and not to worry 'bout the money."

"Go on," said Pitman. "Was doc asking you to pay him?"

Oliver shuddered. "That's the part I'd rather not talk 'bout Ted."

"Haven't we bothered Perry enough Ted?" asked Mayor Reynolds. "I think he's told us enough so that he's not a suspect in these killings. I'm satisfied."

"Me too," added Sanchez. "Thanks for your help Perry. We won't be bothering you again about this business."

"Just a minute." Rabbi Solomon took charge. "With all due respect. We've spoken about motive in the past. I don't mean to be rude or forward, but there seems to be a clear motive for doing away with Doctor Carter. Money. Money is a powerful motive. It's broken families and friendships since the beginning of time. Proverbs says, *Precious treasure and oil are in a wise man's dwelling, but a foolish man devours it.*"

"How dare you?" shouted Sanchez, his newly found respect for the rabbi gone as quickly as it had appeared. "I demand you take back that statement and right now."

Sheriff Pitman came to Solomon's defense. "What the rabbi said is true, Willie. You, Harley, Perry, and me might not like it, but his statement is fact. Money is a motive for murder. Perhaps only love is a stronger reason for man's violence against man."

Rabbi Solomon smiled, nodded. "Unfortunately, I can tell you stories."

"That won't be necessary," said Perry Oliver. "What you say is truth tellin'. But the fact is, Doc Carter came to see me 'bout the money, but he said he didn't want me payin' none of it back."

"How's that?" asked Pitman.

"He said that since he ain't been much help to me, there was no reason why I should pay him. He said he was wiping out my debt and that when he found the right medicine for me to take, then I could pay him for that."

"Is that the first time he mentioned eliminating your debt?" asked Solomon.

"Yup. Generally, it was somethin' neither of us discussed. I guess he wanted to put me at ease, but it kind of had the opposite effect on me."

"How's that?" this time Mayor Reynolds.

Oliver took a deep breath. "Sort of made me more uncomfortable. I always pay my debts. I ain't one of those types to take advantage of folks, especially friends or someone who is trying to help. No matter what the doc said, I had every intention of paying him back, every cent of it."

"Did you tell him that?" asked Solomon.

"I sure did."

"What was his reaction?" asked Pitman.

"He laughed. Said he figured I'd say that, but that he meant it and that if I insisted on paying him back, he'd be fine with it as long as I took my time paying it back. He said he didn't need no more money than what he already had and that he'd rather be helpin' folks doctoring than making money at this point in his life. Jeez, who knew it was near the end of his life?" He paused. "That's the kind of guy doc was. I can't imagine why anyone would want to do him in. I ain't aiming to point fingers, but if you ask me, it had to be a stranger in town responsible for his murder. Everyone in Bullet Pass knows what kind of straight shooter doc was."

"That's what I think too," shouted Sanchez. "Nobody in town would hurt old doc. No one."

"I think that's all for now Perry. We appreciate your honesty and help. If we have any further questions we'll let you know," said Sheriff Pitman.

Perry Oliver stood and nodded. "Anytime sheriff. I just hope you find out who is responsible for this."

"We will. Hope your stomach feels better Perry," said Pitman. "And we'll find your razor. You can count on that."

It appeared as if Perry Oliver had aged during the short time the men were questioning him. He looked down, sullen. "Thanks. I don't suppose it matters much anymore. Not with Doc, Curtis, and Pete dead. A razor don't seem so important." He removed his apron. "I guess it's time to close up for the day." He escorted the men out and shuffled away from his shop, looking smaller and slower after confessing his personal business.

Back at the sheriff's office, the four men sat drinking coffee, smoking. "Well, I think we can rule Perry out," said Mayor Reynolds. "If you ask me, he wasn't acting like a guilty man."

"And what does a guilty man act like?" asked Rabbi Solomon.

Through squinted, suspicious eyes, Reynolds answered. "That's an odd question to ask rabbi. A guilty man acts nervous, fidgety. Someone who has something to hide doesn't look the person who questions him in the eyes. Perry was direct. I made it my business to watch his eyes. And guess what? He looked directly at you and Ted when you asked questions."

"Yes, he did. I was aware of that too. Frankly, it doesn't mean he isn't guilty," said Solomon.

"Well, that's not the sole reason," continued Reynolds. "He told us that Doc Carter wanted to forgive his debts. That right there eliminates the money motive for killing him."

"Does it?" asked the rabbi.

"It does in my book," answered the mayor. "We all saw it. It was harder for Perry to admit to us that doc wanted to relieve him of the debt than to admit he owed the doc money. That tells me a lot. That tells me he's a proud man and he had every intention of paying back the money he owed. I find that convincing. We should turn our attention to someone else. Perry Oliver is an innocent man and you'll never convince me otherwise."

"I agree with you," said Solomon.

Shocked, Reynolds and Sanchez simultaneously said, "You do?" Sanchez chomped down hard on a thin cigar. "Then why are you askin' all these questions?"

"The more we talk, the more things illuminate."

"Huh?" a confused Sanchez asked.

"The more we question things and the more we express our opinions the better. Communication helps things become clearer. Questions are the foundation of knowledge."

Sanchez still didn't understand. He was just happy that the rabbi didn't think Perry Oliver was guilty. "How 'bout you sheriff? What do you think?"

Lost in thought, Sheriff Pitman focused. "I don't think Perry had anything to do with the murders. At least I hope not. It doesn't add up. Besides, what reason would he have for killing Pete McBride?"

"Exactly!" said Sanchez.

"You are assuming the same person that killed Doc Carter also killed Pete McBride?"

"I don't know what to assume anymore," said Pitman. "I'm tired. What do you say we all sleep on it tonight and meet back here first thing in the morning?"

The sheriff departed, leaving Reynolds, Sanchez, and Solomon behind. "Time to go," said the mayor, sipping the last of his coffee. Sanchez, still smoking, stood and headed for the door. Rabbi Solomon sat alone for a few minutes, regretting another lost opportunity to speak one-on-one with Sheriff Pitman. The morning was a few hours away.

CHAPTER 15 – Sheriff Ted Pitman

The day broke sunny. Rabbi Solomon, first to arrive at Sheriff Pitman's office, pulled the leather bible from his pocket and said the Shacharit, or morning prayers. He relished the freshness of the day, the stillness, the peace and tranquility. God's beauty was in direct contrast to man's evil ways. He shook his head, thinking about the day ahead. Mayor Reynolds, next to arrive, his usual smiling face replaced by one of concern.

"Morning rabbi," he said. "Beautiful day."

"Good morning mayor. Yes indeed. Splendid." He pulled a watch from his vest pocket. "I'm surprised the sheriff isn't here yet."

Harley Reynolds looked up the street. "Me too. He's rarely late to anything. Still, these killings have been tough on him and I'm sure he could use the extra sleep. Wait, I see someone coming." He craned his neck. "Never mind, it's Willie."

Willie Sanchez joined the two men in front of Sheriff Pitman's office. "Ted ain't here yet?" he said. He didn't wait for a response. "Should we wait inside or stand out here?"

"I'd just as soon wait for the sheriff outside and enjoy this sunshine we're having. You fellows feel free to go on ahead inside if you prefer."

"I think I'll do just that," said Sanchez. "I'll start us a fresh pot a coffee."

"Good idea Willie. I'll help you with that," said Reynolds as the two men entered the sheriff's office.

The minutes ticked by. Rabbi Solomon didn't like the growing feeling inside his gut. He checked his watch again, waited. Mayor Reynolds poked his head out of the office to ask the rabbi if he'd seen any sign of the sheriff. After another thirty minutes, Reynolds and Sanchez left their cups on a wooden table and joined Solomon outside.

"Dang it. Where is he?" asked Sanchez.

"Something's wrong," declared Reynolds. "This isn't like Ted. I think we should check on him."

"Lead the way," said Rabbi Solomon.

Sheriff Pitman's home, located a few thousand yards from his office, stood quiet and neatly kept. The three men looked at each other after seeing the front door ajar.

"I don't like the looks of this one little bit," said Harley Reynolds. "You two wait here, I'm going in."

"I think we should all go in," suggested Solomon. "There's strength in numbers."

"I agree!" snapped Sanchez. "I ain't fixin' to standing out here and waiting, especially if something's wrong and Ted needs help. Let's go."

The three men entered in single file, led by Reynolds, Sanchez behind him, and Rabbi Solomon bringing up the rear.

"Hello! Ted? Hello! Are you here Ted?" shouted Mayor Reynolds. "Ted? Can you hear me?"

The place was eerily still. Reynolds inched his way forward, the two men behind him. The kitchen was clean. All cups, dishes, and napkins properly in their respective places. Harley Reynolds made his way toward the bedroom but then stopped short. He saw the bottoms of the sheriff's feet!

"Oh my God!" he shouted, rushing into the bedroom. The grizzly sight that greeted him made him sick. Without another word, the mayor of Bullet Pass rushed out of the room, past Sanchez and Solomon, and outside the front door and then dropped to his knees and vomited.

Sanchez and Solomon moved forward. Sheriff Ted Pitman lay on the dried-blood drenched floor, his throat cut from one end to the other, a straight razor inches from his face. Sanchez sucked in his breath and took a closer look.

"P.O. inscribed on the handle. We found Perry Oliver's razor," he said.

The two men walked outside to join Harley Reynolds. The mayor had gotten to his feet, but he was white and stood on shaky legs. Again the rabbi pulled out his bible and said a prayer. When he finished he addressed Sanchez and Reynolds.

"I was afraid of this," he said, snapping the bible shut.

"Enough of this no gun policy!" screamed Sanchez. "There's been too much killin' and now poor Ted…it's just too much. I say we take this town back and we're going to need weapons and ammunition and we're gonna need them both right quick!"

"I don't think…" began Rabbi Solomon, but he was cut off my Harley Reynolds.

"Willie's right. We need weapons. Remember, there's still a gun loose in

Bullet Pass in the hands of our killer. We have got to stop whoever is doing this before they kill again. No one will blame us…not even Ted…God rest his soul…for bringing back our weapons."

"If the killer was so intent on using the gun, why did he…or she…use Mr. Oliver's razor on the sheriff?"

"Because he…yes he…this wasn't done by a woman…is crazy, that's why," said Reynolds. "A crazy man does things that don't make sense. Killing Ted Pitman doesn't make sense."

Rabbi Solomon stiffened. "Or, it makes perfect sense."

Both Reynolds and Sanchez glared at Max Solomon. "What in the name of hell do you mean by that?" questioned Sanchez.

"Sheriff Pitman knew the risks. If the killer felt that he was getting closer to making an arrest, the killer would strike at the sheriff. There's something you two men don't know."

"Oh? And what is that?" asked Mayor Reynolds.

"Something was bothering the sheriff."

Willie Sanchez cut him off. "Well if that don't beat all. 'Cause he was bothered. There been a bunch of murders in his town right under his own nose. Whaddya expect him to be like? Of all the silly things to say."

"I understand your frustration Mr. Sanchez. When I say the sheriff was bothered, I mean on a personal level as well as on a professional level."

"How do you know that?" asked Reynolds.

"Because he wanted to tell me something in private. The other day, when we were at his office, but we were interrupted by the telegram delivery boy and he never got around to telling me what it was."

"And why would he confide in a complete stranger, when his friends were around and available?"

Rabbi Solomon shook his head. "Unfortunately, I cannot answer that question. I can only say that I believe that Sheriff Pitman was about to tell me who he thought might be responsible for the killings."

"Now what?" asked a frustrated Willie Sanchez. "Without Ted, we're doomed."

"Not necessarily," said Solomon. "I have an idea." He waited for the mayor's and Sanchez's reaction before proceeding. The two Bullet Pass residents, resigned, shook their shoulders.

"Okay rabbi, we'll listen," a wearied Harley Reynolds said. "What do you think we should do?"

"Go back to the Crown House," he replied. "We'll find our killer there."

"I knew it!" blurted out Sanchez. "I knew it had to be one of them strangers. I should have just gone with my initial hunch and have the sheriff arrest the lot of 'em until the killer confessed."

"I don't think that would have been a wise course to take."

"Oh? And why not? We could have save Ted's life if we done that."

"That's just my opinion," quipped Rabbi Solomon.

"Enough banter!" shouted Reynolds. "What's your solution rabbi?"

CHAPTER 16 – *The Killer*

Rabbi Max Solomon explained his plan. Willie Sanchez took off for the sheriff's office while Solomon and Mayor Reynolds headed for the Crown House. The two men ascended the stairs, stopped in front of room number four, and knocked on the door. No response. They knocked again, harder. This time they heard murmurings from within.

"What? Who's there?" the voice weak, confused. "I'm not feeling very well. Come back later."

"I'm afraid our business can't wait Miss Whitlock," said Mayor Reynolds. "Please open the door ma'am. We need to speak to you."

"I really am sick this morning mayor. Can we talk later?"

Rabbi Solomon shook his head. "No ma'am," said Reynolds. "I'm afraid we have some bad news for you that simply cannot wait for another time." Reynolds whispered something to the rabbi and the latter nodded his agreement. "Take a few minutes to collect yourself. We'll wait right here outside your door. We aren't going anywhere until you open up. Is that agreeable?" asked Reynolds.

"Who is with you? Um…is that Sheriff Pitman with you?"

Again the mayor checked with Rabbi Solomon for confirmation on how to respond. "No ma'am, it's Rabbi Solomon."

"Um, where's Sheriff Pitman? Is he with you?" asked Jenny Whitlock.

"That's what we'd like to speak to you about," answered Reynolds, and then he added, "When you are ready."

The two men heard rustling in Jenny Whitlock's room. They patiently waited for nearly twenty minutes before the door slowly opened. Jenny Whitlock did her best to present a positive image, but she looked thin and pale, her skin a chalky hue.

"What is it Harley?" she asked, her head peered out, both hands gripped the door's edge.

"May we come in?" asked Reynolds.

Whitlock spun her head around and then back. "I don't think that's proper, especially at this hour. Besides, I already explained to you that I'm not feeling well and I want to lie back down. Now, what's this about Ted…Sheriff Pitman?"

Reynolds backed off and Rabbi Solomon stepped forward. "As a religious leader, it is my honor to deliver pleasant news, but it is also my burden and responsibility to hear and to communicate sad news. I'm afraid we are here for the latter reason."

A confused Jenny Whitlock turned to Reynolds. "What's he talking about Harley?" she asked.

Rabbi Solomon said, "I'm afraid Sheriff Pitman is dead." He watched closely her expression before continuing. "He was killed last night in his home. We found his body this morning."

Jenny Whitlock covered her mouth. "No. No. It can't be. What? How?"

Solomon didn't mince words. "His throat was slit. The killer cut it with the straight razor taken from Perry Oliver's shop. The razor's handle sported Perry's initials."

Whitlock turned away, faced inside her room. "I think I'm going to be sick again. This is so horrible. Just awful. I don't believe it."

"I'm afraid it's true Jenny," said Mayor Reynolds.

"Forgive me for asking," began Solomon, "But where were you last night Miss Whitlock?"

"I beg your pardon?"

"Please do not take offense to this or any other questions we might ask you. We seek information about a third murder that has taken place in Bullet

Pass. No one is above suspicion. I repeat, where were you last night?" the rabbi's voice firm.

She glanced toward the mayor again seeking relief, but he urged her to answer the question. "I…was…right here last night. In my room. That's right. I wasn't feeling well yesterday evening either so I decided to stay here and get to sleep early. Does that answer your question Mr. Rabbi?" she venomously asked.

"I guess the extra sleep didn't help very much," responded Solomon. Her expression showed she didn't understand, so he continued. "You mentioned that you were still ill this morning, so I'm simply stating the obvious." He smiled, but the grin quickly dissipated. "Miss Whitlock, I have every reason to believe that you did not spend last night in your room as you stated. In fact, it's my belief that you are responsible for Sheriff Pitman's murder!"

Harley Reynolds sucked air in rapid spurts. It took him a moment to process what he had just heard. If he wanted to speak he couldn't. He was too shocked. At this point, Reynolds knew this was the rabbi's show and he had no intention of intervening.

"What? That's the most ridiculous thing I've ever heard. Such nonsense! Harley, are you just going to stand there and let this strange man accuse me of murdering Ted? Do something!" demanded Whitlock.

"Um…well…" the mayor stuttered. "Um…I'm sure if the rabbi here has made such an accusation, he has proof. Isn't that so rabbi? You have proof of the charge?" Sweat beads formed on the mayor's forehead.

Solomon didn't take his eyes off of Jenny Whitlock. "Yes, I expect to have all the evidence I need shortly. And I'll go a step further Miss Whitlock. I'm also accusing you of murdering Pete McBride."

Reynolds grabbed a handkerchief from his pocket and wiped his face. He needed water, something to drink. His mouth felt desert dry. He couldn't believe what he heard. He hoped the rabbi had evidence. Otherwise things would go from a dark hell to a place the Devil himself would be afraid to reside in. Despite not knowing what to say, Harley couldn't remain silent. He was a politician, and no one ever heard of a reticent mayor.

"For the sake of Bullet Pass and yourself, it's best to come clean Miss Whitlock." It was if the words uncontrollably poured from his mouth. "Surely, you didn't think that you'd be able to get away with something as awful as this?" Reynolds couldn't stop speaking. He didn't believe his own words. For the first time in his life he felt like a helpless puppet, being manipulated by a puppeteer. The mayor prayed that this stranger who claimed to have come to town to begin a congregation of Jewish worshippers knew something he didn't. Where was Willie Sanchez? What was he doing? He should be here helping out. He dismissed those thoughts and said, "It's no use ma'am. He…we have the goods on you. We'll bring in another sheriff or a U.S. Marshall and place you under arrest. For now, let's just take a walk to the sheriff's office." He mopped more sweat off his face.

"You're all crazy! You know that? Why on earth would I want to kill Ted…Sheriff Pitman? It don't make sense. I loved him! Besides, him and me had plans to get married. Bet you two smart guys didn't know that, did ya?"

Rabbi Solomon gave Whitlock's comments some thought. Was that the message Sheriff Pitman wanted to tell him in private? It didn't make sense to the religious leader. Why would Pitman want to keep a happy announcement like that private? Surely, he'd want to share it with his friends. Her words didn't add up. Everything pointed to her guilt. Solomon admitted to himself that his theory was built on conjecture, not hard evidence at this point, but he was confident enough to continue to push forward. Certain Jenny Whitlock would overplay her hand and incriminate herself, he continued.

"Strange, that's not what Sheriff Pitman told me," he said. "Fact is, he never said a word about marriage to me. Did he to you, Mayor Reynolds?"

Robotically, Harley Reynolds responded, "Not a word. No. Not to me."

"So what does that mean?" asked an angry Jenny Whitlock. "Don't mean nothin'. I'm tellin' ya both we was to be married. I loved him and he loved me back."

"From all indications, I'm afraid that's not exactly the case Miss Whitlock." The rabbi paused before continuing. "You see, Sheriff Pitman was upset and not himself before his untimely death. He had a lot on his mind. And do you know what one of those things was that was on his mind?" The question rhetorical, he continued. "Your pregnancy. I believe that explains your frequent morning sicknesses. My dear wife Sarah had similar symptoms after becoming pregnant with our two children."

This time Harley Reynolds was speechless. Jenny Whitlock was not.

"That's a lie!"

"Are you denying you're pregnant? And that the man who impregnated you was Sheriff Ted Pitman?"

Whitlock's cheeks turned redder than a rare steak. She glanced into the hallway, toward the door next to her room, bit her lip, and then smiled.

"You can't prove a thing mister. Besides, you said I killed Pete McBride too? Now why on earth would I want to do that? Pete was my friend. He let me stay here after my house fire. It doesn't make sense that I'd kill him. And, I suppose you're going to try to pin Doc Carter's murder on me as well? This is a farce. I'm going back to sleep." She attempted to shut the door, but Rabbi Solomon stuck his boot out and blocked her.

"As a matter of fact, yes. You killed Mr. McBride and Doctor Carter as well ma'am. God is forgiving, but for the sin of murder…multiple murders…may He have mercy on your soul."

"Oh why don't you just shuddup with that religious mumbo jumbo. I don't believe in your religion anyways. It don't mean nothin' to me."

Harley Reynolds stood stone-faced, taking it all in. "McBride and Doc too?" was all he could manage to utter.

"That's right mayor. Miss Whitlock killed all three. The way I see it, she was in love with Sheriff Pitman, but it was an obsessive love. The two had a relationship and a few nights ago it went too far. Unfortunately for the sheriff and Miss Whitlock, Pete McBride witnessed Sheriff Pitman sneak up to Miss Whitlock's room and leave in the middle of the night."

"You mean, unfortunately for poor old Pete McBride," interjected Mayor Reynolds.

"How true," agreed Solomon. "Sad, but true. Mr. McBride must have confronted Miss Whitlock about it and told her he wouldn't stand for that kind of behavior in his establishment. My guess is he either threatened to expel her from the hotel or go public with what he saw. I know something heavy was weighing on Sheriff Pitman's mind. Miss Whitlock saw an opportunity to silence Mr. McBride, grabbed the first thing she saw which happened to be the metal skillet discovered at the murder sight and struck him."

The mayor looked at Jenny Whitlock in disbelief. "How could you?" he asked. "After all that Pete did for you."

"Ah, he don't know what he's talking about. He has no proof of anything he's saying."

Reynolds addressed Solomon. "What about Doc Carter? How does he fit in? Why should she want to kill him as well?"

The rabbi nodded. "The morning sickness. Miss Whitlock is pregnant. She went to see Doctor Carter and he confirmed it. That unfortunately became his death sentence. She shot him in cold blood. I wouldn't know for certain, but after killing Mr. McBride, I assume killing the doctor became easier. Sheriff Pitman is the father."

"Where on earth did she manage to get a gun?" asked Reynolds.

The rabbi turned to Jenny Whitlock. "Do you want to answer that one? Where did the gun come from?"

Jenny sneered. "What gun? I don't know anything about a gun. That kind of spoils your little explanation, don't it rabbi man?"

"We'll see," said Solomon coyly. "With McBride out of the way, Miss Whitlock was forced to silence Doctor Carter as well. He became a witness to her pregnancy."

"And Ted?" asked the mayor. "Why?"

"Miss Whitlock didn't spend the night here last night as she claims. She visited Sheriff Pitman, no doubt making a last ditch effort to convince him, now that she carried his baby, to marry him. He refused. He wanted to clear up the murders in Bullet Pass first before committing to such an important decision. By that time, Sheriff Pitman no doubt suspected Jenny Whitlock of the murders and played it cautious, too cautious for his own good. I doubt he suspected she would slit his throat."

"So she took Perry Oliver's razor?"

"Yes," confirmed the rabbi. "I figured only a Bullet Pass resident would be familiar with Mr. Oliver's lunch hours and that he never locked his door. It stretched coincidence that a stranger in town just happened to walk in with a CLOSED sign displayed during Mr. Oliver's regular break. I'm sure Sheriff Pitman reasoned similarly. Therefore, my search concentrated on one of the regular townspeople. It was also Miss Whitlock's little plan, after seeing me get a haircut, to plant one of the hairs she removed from the barbershop at the sight of Mr. McBride's death. Her little scheme almost paid off." He spoke to Jenny Whitlock. "Let's go ma'am. I'm afraid it's time we walked you down and over to the jail cell."

Mayor Reynolds scratched his chin. "And Curtis' death?"

"What about it?" asked Solomon.

"That's what I'm asking you? Miss Whitlock had nothing to do with that? No connection?"

"No. The unfortunate Mr. Curtis met his death at the hand of another woman, the woman first introduced to us as Mimi Wallace in room number one, whom we now know goes by the name, Sage. His death was independent of Miss Whitlock. Sage was interested in obtaining a weapon and murdered Mr. Curtis in the process. For a brief period of time, it muddled things up for our investigation but no doubt helped Miss Whitlock, who must have been surprised as the rest of us when Mr. Curtis' body was discovered."

"You still haven't explained where she got the gun from," stressed Reynolds.

Solomon ignored the mayor. "Are you coming willingly, or must we force you into the jail cell Miss Whitlock? If you're innocent, a judge will hear your case and you'll go free. If not..."

Resigned, Jenny Whitlock said, "Sure, I'll come. I have nothing to fear. But allow a lady to gather a few personal things first?" The men nodded. "Fine. Please take a few steps away from the door so that I may have my privacy. You have my word I'll be right with you."

Rabbi Solomon smiled, nodded to Mayor Reynolds that she should be permitted this request. The two men stepped back a few feet. After several minutes, Jenny Whitlock emerged from her room.

"Oh, just one more thing gentlemen. Please bear with me."

The two men watched as Jenny Whitlock closed her door. She turned right, moved toward the stairs, then pivoted and swung open the door to the unnumbered closet.

"Quick! Stop her!" shouted Rabbi Solomon, but he was too late.

Jenny Whitlock reached down and had sprung up with such alacrity that neither man had time to take a step closer. She held a Colt .45, the weapon looked like a canon in her small hand.

"Don't move. Don't try anything or I'll shoot you where you stand," she said.

"Jenny, this is outrageous. Hand over that weapon before you do something you'll regret," said Reynolds.

She laughed. "Ha! That's a joke, right mayor? I've already killed three people, adding two more to the total won't change a thing except to buy me my freedom now."

"I guess now we know where she got the gun from," said Rabbi Solomon. He was calm, in control. "Is that the weapon you used to kill Doctor Carter?" he asked her.

"Aren't we the smart rabbi today. Yes, I killed him with this gun. I knew it would come in handy someday. Had it hidden inside that closet ever since I moved into this place after my house fire. Of course, I didn't break any laws at the time. It was perfectly legal to own weapons when I moved in here. I guess I must have forgotten all about it when the late Sheriff Ted Pitman changed the laws in Bullet Pass, forbidding all weapons." She let out a sinister laugh. "My memory isn't what it used to be." Again she laughed and took steps toward the staircase. She paused at the landing. "You two don't believe for a moment that I plan to let you live, do you?" More laughter. "Because I don't!" She aimed the weapon at Rabbi Solomon.

BANG! BANG! Two shots split the silence. A shocked expression covered Jenny Whitlock's face as she dropped to the ground and spilled down the stairs onto the same floor where Pete McBride's body was found days prior. She had two bullet holes in her chest.

"You cut that might close, Mr. Sanchez. Might close indeed," said Rabbi Solomon.

Willie Sanchez stood inside the previously vacant room number seven, a gun with two spent bullets at his side.

"Nice shooting Willie. Don't you agree mayor?" asked Solomon.

Mayor Reynolds didn't respond. He had fainted.

Later, the three men shared drinks in the sheriff's office. They toasted Sheriff Pitman, Pete McBride, Doc Carter, and Curtis. Then, they toasted to a weapon-free future for Bullet Pass.

"One thing gets me," said Mayor Reynolds. "Where did Willie get that gun?"

"This old thing?" responded Sanchez, holding the pistol in the air. "This is the same gun that Sage had, the same one that not had previously been fired."

Rabbi Solomon added, "Sheriff Pitman knew there was a loaded weapon somewhere in Bullet Pass that had been used to murder Doctor Carter. Instead of returning the weapon Sage had stolen to the checkpoint, the sheriff hid this gun in his office. He told me its whereabouts in the event of an emergency. I informed Mr. Sanchez to get it and to hide out in the one unoccupied room, room number seven at the Crown House. He then wait for Jenny Whitlock to make her move. I knew Miss Whitlock had a weapon but I did not know where it was located. That was the one piece of physical evidence we needed and she led us directly to it. I just wish Mr. Sanchez hadn't waited so long to shoot Miss Whitlock."

"You can say that again rabbi!" chuckled Mayor Reynolds. "I'll drink to that!"

"Cheers!" shouted Reynolds and Sanchez.

"L'Chaim!" trumpeted Rabbi Solomon.

Wild Yellow
Brandon Barrows

A lone buzzard circled above, silently and patiently winging its way through the glassy sky, biding its time, but keeping me always in sight. Something stirred in my chest, something telling me that I should shout my defiance, scream my rage, spit my disgust – do *something* to prove that I was still alive, that there was fight left in me yet. But shuffling along, feet barely clearing the dry, clinging sand of this desert hell, was all I could do. I tried to curse, but my swollen tongue only stirred numbly in my bone-dry mouth. I discovered that my rage was the only thing I could still swallow.

I turned my eyes from the buzzard, risking a glance at the huge, burning sun that had just barely passed mid-day. I knew it wouldn't have moved much since the last time I'd checked, but anything was better than staring at that damned bird – or at the limitless miles of desert that spread out in every direction. I saw nothing but sand and scrub from here to the horizon, taunting me, telling me without words that this would be my grave.

Inwardly, I damned the Great Western Railway for the job they'd given me and myself for being fool enough to take it. I damned Arizona and I damned the desert. I damned Bill Atherton for his train-robbing and all outlaws everywhere for doing things that made law-men chase them. Most of all, I damned myself for falling into the bushwhacking that had killed my horse and would probably kill me.

I was trying to think of other things to damn when my dragging foot hit some snag in the uneven sand and sent me stumbling. The feeble excuse for strength I still had wasn't enough to catch my balance or break my fall and I struck the earth like a dead weight. The buzzard, excited by the sight, swooped in low for a better look. *Damn bird*, I thought before my vision grew fuzzy and blackness closed in.

When the first, weak stirring of consciousness returned, the first thing I was aware of was a pleasant coolness. When drops of moisture began to splatter my face, I decided I must be dreaming. Even so, I raised a hand to investigate, rubbing knuckles across my dry eyes and sun-peeled cheeks, and when they, too, reported feeling water, I opened my eyes in astonishment.

Standing over me, seeming to fill the entire sky, was a tall, well-muscled man of fifty or more years. "Bet you never thought you'd feel a drop of water again, eh?" his voice boomed. After the silence of the desert, it seemed the loudest thing I'd ever heard.

The big man fell to one knee beside me, propping my head up with one hand. In the other, he held a tin cup, filled with the water he'd been sprinkling me with, and brought it to my lips. "Here now, drink up – but slowly, mind." I sipped and his whiskered face, weathered by age and elements, crinkled into a smile. "That's a lad."

For some minutes, the stranger continued to dribble water into my mouth, refilling the cup from a leather canteen as needed. While he did, I studied his face and decided it was a good one: wholesome and good-natured, the kind of man you'd expect to drag a stranger out of the desert and nurse him with water like a baby with a bottle. By and by, my swollen tongue seemed to shrivel back to its original size, my parched throat grew moist again, and I croaked out my thanks.

"No need, son. A good turn is its own reward."

I struggled into a sitting position, drank some more water and rasped, "Thank God you found me."

"God may have played a hand in it," the older man's eyes twinkled as he spoke, "but your own good sense is the reason you're alive. Your back-trail was plain as day and I could tell you used your strength slow and steady instead of burning it up like a fool, trying to rush across all in one go. That's how I find most of the desert's victims, you know," he finished.

"If I had any sense," I replied, "I'd have stayed out of the damned desert in the first place."

The other man's eyes searched mine for a moment, then he stood. "Bet you're hungry." He moved towards a small fire I hadn't before noticed and squatted down, removing things from a pack and setting to the business of making a meal.

I drew myself up on wobbly legs and took a look around. Sunset was in the sky, filtered through the junipers that surrounded the clearing. A short distance from where I stood, a pair of horses were hobbled and grazing on sparse grass. I walked over to the animals, set my hand on the withers of the nearest, a buckskin, who replied with a friendly sound then returned to its supper. Among the tackle piled nearby, I spotted my own bedroll, bags and saddle. Another thing to thank my rescuer for.

I strolled a little further, regaining the feel of my own legs and stopped where the circle of junipers did. I could see now that we were above the desert, which spread out to the east. Laid out below me, seen through the crisp, rapidly-cooling air, it looked as clear as a map. I hadn't even been able to see these foothills from where I'd collapsed. I wondered how far my savior had brought me.

I wandered back over to where the other man still squatted, holding a long-handled frying pan over his little fire. Delicious smells made my mouth water and my belly grumble. I hadn't really been hungry until then, but I realized now that it must have been more than day since I'd eaten. With that thought, suddenly, I was ravenous. I guess I was finally fully back to life.

After a few minutes, the big man filled a tin plate with bacon and beans and dry biscuits and passed it over to me. "Eat," was all he said before filling up, and then digging into, his own plate.

We ate in companionable silence for a time and then, when the meal was finished, my host said, "So, I guess you're the one I been waitin' for. Not who I expected when I sent for law, but I'm grateful all the same. One of these days, Sanctuary will need its own lawman, I suppose, but for now, we'll take any help we can get." He gestured to himself. "I'm Emmitt Powell, by the way, mayor of Sanctuary. And a man named Atherton is the one I wrote about, the one I suspect's been stealing from the mine that keeps Sanctuary afloat. We haven't had any luck catchin' 'im on our own. We run 'im and some crony off when they tried rustling steer from a neighbor of mine's spread a couple months or so back, but right afterwards, silver started disappearing from the mine. Haven't had any other strangers in these parts for a spell, so I suppose it must be him. Frankly, though, I suspect an inside man among my people, too. There's no way an outsider could get the ore out without help."

"You got it all wrong. I'm no lawman," I said, maybe a little too strongly. Powell's story was more words than I'd heard all at once in days. It was a wonder his lungs held so much breath and it was almost more than I could take in. Even in my jangled state, though, his story set my nerves afire. Atherton was the man I'd set out into the desert after, sure enough, but it was the railroad and the bounty they'd promised that had sent me, not Powell's request for help. I'd never heard of him or Sanctuary before. Atherton was hot in New Mexico, where I'd first picked up his trail, and the Great Western probably wasn't the only rail company after his hide, so maybe a change of "career" made sense. The whole situation seemed an incredible coincidence, but someone had shot my horse out from under me, out there in the desert, expecting me to die, and Atherton was the logical candidate.

"You aren't?" Powell asked, holding something up to the light of the fire. It was the seven-pointed badge that marked me as a railroad detective for the Great Western. I'd thrown it as far as I could manage, out into the desert sands, somewhere along my foot-dragging march. Guess it wasn't far enough.

Anger and shame rose to my face, hotter than the fire. "I came into the desert after someone, it's true," I admitted, "but that's all done with now. It's settled and I'm through."

"Is that so?" The words were said mildly, but it was like a slap in the face.

"Yes, damn it!" My embarrassment grew, but I forged on. "I'm through with the law. All I want now is the kind of life where a man can do honest work for honest pay, without being bothered by problems that aren't his own." Even to my own ears, it sounded false, but the other man said nothing, simply staring across the fire at me. Somehow, it was worse. I was sure it sounded like cowardice to him. It sure enough sounded like it to me, though I wouldn't have admitted it.

Finally, Powell said, "What do I call you, anyway?"

"Clint," I said. "Clint Hagar."

Powell nodded. "Clint Hagar. That's fine. Let's get some sleep, Clint." He drew the blanket he'd been sitting on up around his shoulders, laid down and rolled over. I did the same, but it was a long time before sleep came.

*****

The sun was rising, painting the sky above the desert pink and orange and blue as we left it behind, riding westward into a jumble of foothills that skirted the base of the true mountains to the north. Riding the borrowed horse Powell had provided, I followed him along a trail that sometimes looked well-used and at others, seemed to disappear altogether. First we went up, climbing higher until evergreens appeared and the air grew nearly chill, then down the other side into a valley that was green and fertile. The sun had passed noon, but was still high in the sky, when we reined up at the edge of a thick swath of forest that clung to the gently-rolling side of the valley.

Powell turned in the saddle, looking back at me. "This is the boundary, you might say. Want to go on?"

I didn't know what he expected me to say. Where else was there for me to go? I only nodded. Powell looked satisfied and led the way forward, weaving his horse between the trees, following a trail that was once again invisible to my eyes. When we came out through the other side, sooner than I would have expected, he paused again and waved a hand, beckoning me forward.

I pulled my horse up even with Powell's and saw a wide, sheltered valley of rich meadows, bordered to the west by more gentle, forested hills and to the north by rugged-looking mountains. The trail was now plain as day, obviously well-traveled, and in the distance, I could see the settlement that must be the town. Powell, a solemn sort of smile on his face, watched me taking it all in then said, "Welcome to Sanctuary, Mr. Hagar."

After a while, we were in the town itself, riding past long rows of houses from which curious children ran out to greet us. Dogs raced and yapped at the horses' heels. Powell greeted each one, child and dog alike, by name, and got smiles and happy noises in return. At the end of what I took to be the main street, we stopped before a long, freshly-painted livery building and dismounted. Two teenaged boys came forward to the take the horses, each earning thanks and a bit tip from Powell. Before the boys and horses had disappeared inside, a beefy man of thirty-some-odd years stepped out of the building and approached us, giving me the gimlet eye in a way I didn't care for at all.

"Found another desert stray, huh, Mr. Mayor?" he said, chuckling at his own wit. To me, the fellow said, "Where you headed and how soon you startin' out, boy?'

"What the hell business is it of yours?" I snapped. We hadn't even been introduced yet, but this smirking, loudmouthed shanny had already earned my ire.

The other man opened his mouth to make some retort, but before he could, Powell put a hand between us and said, "Mr. Hagar, this is Otis Bonney, he's sort of the foreman for the community. He manages one of the shifts up at the mine for me and he looks out for the young men who run several different outfits' cattle in the meadowlands. He likes his little jokes, but he don't mean nothing by them."

Bonney ignored Powell and said, over the older man's hand, "That mouth of yours has cost you, boy. You get yourself together and get out of this town before I decide to teach you some manners. From the looks of you, the desert gave you a licking, but it won't be nothing compared to what I aim to give you if you hang around here too long."

"You leave him alone, Otis, you big bully!" a high-register voice called. I turned and saw a small, lithe figure dash up, adding as it approached, "You ain't the boss of the whole town and you don't have a notion as to how to give someone a welcome!" The figure resolved itself into that of a young girl, eighteen or nineteen years old, her chestnut hair in twin tails and wearing a plaid shirt, faded Levis and small, rawhide boots splattered with mud. "Now you go on and get! I'm sure you've got something to do besides bother this fellow."

Bonney's eyes flashed with fury, but he held his tongue. Something about the girl had rendered him speechless and strangely cowed. He turned on his heel and stomped off down the dusty street.

Emmitt Powell sighed, hand to his forehead, and said, "You shouldn't have done that, Delia. You know how Otis is. He'll just take it out on the men." He turned to me, lowering his hand in a gesture towards the girl. "Clint, this is my daughter, Delia. Our town's foremost tomboy."

"Phooey, papa! Otis'll bully those boys no matter what anyone says or does to him. It's just who he is. And who, may I ask, are *you*?" she said, the last directed to me.

"This is Clint Hagar," Powell answered for me. "He'll be staying with us for a spell. Show him to the house, make him comfortable and give him a chance to rest, Delia."

The girl quirked a smile, making something dance and sparkle behind her eyes. "I'd be glad to," she said, offering me her arm. I took it and allowed her to lead the way.

We walked back down the street in the direction Powell and I had come from, then turned off onto a side-street that led north. Secretly, I studied the girl, marveling at the smooth, sure movements and the light in her eyes. I'd already seen the spunk in her, but it was more than that: there was in her a kind of liveliness that spoke of a love of life itself. It wasn't the sort of thing you see every day and it did strangely pleasant things to my head.

After a few more moments' walking, I could see where we were headed: a spacious, two-story house that was set apart from the rest of the town on a little rise. It looked out of place in the gentle, pastoral setting of the little valley town, as if it had been plucked from some well-to-do place back east or maybe one of the coastal cities in California.

I was impressed and I supposed it must have shown on my face, because Delia said, "Papa built it for mama." Coming to a halt by the waist-high, ornamental fence surrounding the property, she turned away and added, "But it's just him and me now." She opened the little gate in the fence and started up the gentle incline towards the house.

"Sorry to hear," I said, not knowing what else there was to say.

Over her shoulder she said, "It's all right. Mama's been gone for years. I just wish she'd gotten to see the place. Papa and Benjy were out here a long time before we came to join them." She shrugged. "It was a long, hard trip here."

"Benjy?" I asked.

Delia stopped and looked back. "My older brother." For just a moment, something dark passed across her face. Just as quickly, it disappeared and in its place, came something different. There was a twinkle in her eye as she said, "You seem a lot like him, you know. My heart did a little skip when I first saw you," she admitted, color touching her cheeks. "I think papa sees it, too."

I smiled, amused at the girl's sudden shyness. "Is Benjy one of those cowpunchers of Bonney's that your father mentioned?"

Any traces of amusement disappeared as Delia's eyes clouded and the look I'd glimpsed a moment before returned. "Otis worked for *Benjy*. Otis was only deputy foreman and never would have the job he does now if Benjy hadn't been shot down by rustlers back in the spring." The mention of rustlers made me think again of Bill Atherton, the man I'd entered the desert to find, the man who, if Powell was to be believed, was lurking somewhere in this country. I hadn't forgotten that Atherton was also likely the man who'd bushwhacked me, leaving me afoot in the desert and as good as dead. I said another, silent, thanks to my savior, Emmitt Powell.

We reached the house and passed into a long hallway. Delia led me to a door near the back of the first floor, stepped inside and moved quickly around the room, straightening this and that until she was satisfied.

"Well," she said, looking out a window that showed a wide view of the mountains that towered above the valley, "someday, some man or other will bring my brother's killer to justice." She turned then and looked me square in the eye, suddenly serious. "And when he does, I'd be happy to make myself his wife. This valley is peaceful enough most of the time, but now there's trouble, and it needs someone who can bring a little law and order." Her mood shifted again and she let out a little giggle. "Listen to me go on. Papa thinks I'm awful and foolish the way I prattle."

"Not at all," I said, meaning it.

Delia Powell moved to the door, brushing past me. "Well, Mr. Hagar, you feel free to get some rest. I'll bring around something to eat in a little while." She drew the door closed and disappeared behind it.

I moved to the window Delia had stood by and gaze up at the mountain, then turned to the east-facing window and looked out on the town. A feeling settled inside me that I couldn't quite name. Even with the threat of Atherton, and whatever accomplices he had, hanging over Sanctuary, something radiated throughout the valley that brought a kind of peace I'd never before known. This was a place a man could find a new life, leaving behind the troubles of his past.

I thought, too, of the life I'd led these past three years: the trails I'd ridden and the men I'd ridden them with, both good and bad – other lawmen and the outlaws we pursued. The duty I'd decided to abandon loomed large in my thoughts. Was it really just coincidence that here, in this place where I was thinking to build a new life, I had found Bill Atherton already waiting?

*****

In the morning, I shared a silent breakfast with Powell. Delia had served us and then disappeared without a word. I figured it was at her father's say so. It was fine with me, I didn't much feel like talking. Despite sleeping in a bed for the first time in weeks, I hadn't slept well and it wasn't just my bruised, burned body that was bothering me. The thoughts that had been rattling around in my head took up too much space to leave room for much else.

When we'd both finished eating, Powell pushed aside his plate, looked across the table at me and said, "Mr. Hagar, I've been thinking some about what Otis said to you yesterday."

The food I'd eaten turned to stone in my belly. This was one of the possibilities I'd been thinking about. "It's your town, sir, and I owe you a great debt. If you want me gone, I'll—"

Powell raised a hand, his head tilted slightly in a gesture I was already coming to know well. "That's not it. Now, listen: I don't pry into a man's affairs that don't concern me, so if you *want* to ride on out in a day or so, we'll speak no more, but if you plan to stay around…"

The significance of the pause wasn't lost on me.

I thought about the last few days, about why I'd come into this country and how I'd almost left it. I'd been after Bill Atherton, never thinking of myself as anything but a hunter, never dreaming I'd be the one caught in another man's sights.

The sounds of a shot from an unseen rifle, and the pitiable noises of a belly-punctured horse, dying in agony, echoed in my ears. I could feel the drag of the sand against my boots, never meant for walking distances, and the ache in my legs. The heat of a furiously-blazing disc high overhead leeched all the water from my body, leaving me nothing more than a shell. Sitting at the breakfast table in Emmitt Powell's fine home, dampness broke out across my chest. It wasn't heat I felt, though, it was a chill running down my spine. In that moment, thoughts of the desert loomed so large in my mind that the weight of them crushed any idea I might have had of leaving that town.

I didn't know how long I'd left Powell waiting for a response. If he knew what I was thinking, he had the courtesy to keep it to himself.

"I understand your meaning, sir," I told him, "and if you'll let me, I think I'd like to stay a while."

"All right." Powell nodded, but added nothing more. The look in his eyes said it all. He knew. He'd probably known all along. I'd have sworn he could hear my very thoughts.

Shame surged inside me, but the fear of the desert was stronger. Admitting what Powell already knew almost didn't seem so bad in comparison.

I swallowed, wetting my throat, then continued: "You found that badge, so you already know I was a lawman, and I already told you I come into the desert after someone. Well, he found me first and my horse was dead by the time he was through with me and I'd have been, too, if it wasn't for you. But before you found me, I had a lot of time to think and I realized something: I wore that badge, but it was never really in me, if you know what I mean. Some men carry the badge on their shirts and in their souls, too, but to me, it was just a job. I swore to myself that if I ever made it out of that desert, I'd find a new one. A new job, I mean. I don't figure I was ever really cut out to be a lawman, anyway."

That sounded all right, I told myself, but even as I did, I knew it was a lie. It sounded like cowardice.

It must have sounded the same way to Powell, because he said, "Son, there's a difference between quitting a job and letting it beat you, just like there's a difference between walking towards something and running away from it. Once you start running, you never stop."

Anger flared inside me, though I knew I had no right to it. What Powell said was true. Pride is foolish, though, and I told him, "The only thing on this Earth that's ever beaten me is that damned desert and I don't aim to go up against it ever again if I can help it."

Emmitt Powell, silent and expressionless, studied my face a moment, then said, "Is that so? Well, then, Mr. Hagar, I have a job for you, if you're interested." He stood up. "Are you?"

I stood, too, saying, "Yes, sir."

"Almost ten years ago," Powell explained, "my boy and I were blessed with the discovery of a vein of silver up in the mountain north of this valley. A nice, rich one, the kind folks dream about finding. Well, sir, we worked that vein ourselves until we'd made enough money to bring in a few others and build ourselves a stamp-mill."

He moved to the dining room window, from which he could see both the mountain, on his right, and part of the meadowlands to the west on his left. "With what we pulled from the ground, we built Sanctuary, brought in cattle and more folks and all of us together have made a life here. As much as we've pulled from the mine, though, there's still plenty of silver up there and once or twice a year, we put together enough ore to make a pack-train through the desert worthwhile."

He turned from the window and looked at me. "I am the owner, on paper, of that mine, but it really belongs to the men who work it. It's helped build this town and it's been a great blessing. It seems, though, that the devil has his own blessings to hand out to his followers. I told you that we run Bill Atherton off a while back after he tried to rustle some cattle. What I didn't tell you is that he killed my boy, Benjamin. Benjy wasn't quite gone when the other boys found him, though, and he named Atherton as his killer." Powell, grimacing at the memory, made a fist. "We don't get mail often out here, but we get the circulars when we do. Atherton's had more than one the last few years." Powell composed himself, the anger fading from his expression and said, "At any rate, not long after that, ore we'd had packed up for shipping disappeared from the mine storeroom and I just can't see how the two things aren't connected."

When Delia had told me about her brother, I had wondered at a connection. Now I knew for sure.

"I'm very sorry."

"So am I," Powell said, "but life goes on, and I am responsible for many others. That mine means money and money means life in this world, sad as that may be. I aim to see that no more of that ore is stolen. Can I trust you, Mr. Hagar?"

If the sudden change in subject was meant to catch me off guard, it failed. "Yes," I answered.

Powell nodded as if satisfied, turned on his heel and strode quickly from the room, through an outside door and into the sunlight beyond. From the window where I still stood, I watched him disappear around the corner of the house. A small sound turned my head and I saw Delia entering the room from the kitchen door.

"Good morning," I said.

"Where's papa?"

I nodded towards the outside door. "Just left. Gone to arrange a job for me, I guess. He needs a guard at the mine, I gather."

A small smile tugged at the corner of Delia's pretty mouth. "I knew you'd take the job."

I couldn't hide my surprise. "You already knew about it?'

"Of course," she said casually. "Papa tells me everything. A man needs someone to talk to and it's just the two of us since Benjy – " She broke off abruptly. Her expression and tone changed and she said, "I'm glad you're taking the job, Mr. Hagar. I hope you get that Bill Atherton."

"Call me Clint," I told her. Then, with a teasing grin, I added, "So does that mean you'd be pleased if I was the one who brought him to justice?"

The girl blushed and my grin grew wider as we both thought of the promise she'd made the day before. "You're just teasing me… Clint," she said finally.

I liked the way my name sounded, coming from her lips. I didn't get a chance to say so, though, before a heavy tread sounded on the gravel outside and the side-door burst open. Otis Bonney appeared in the doorway. "So! Already dipping into the sugar sack, are you, boy?" he growled.

"Otis! The very idea!" Delia cried, but took a step away from me all the same.

I let the anger I felt show on my face as I stared the heavier man down. "Mister, you better knock before you open the door to someone else's house when you haven't been invited. I get jumpy when I'm surprised and when I'm surprised, I tend to shoot first and ask questions later."

"Goes double for me," Bonney snarled. "But I got to wonder, *boy*," he emphasized the word like it was a curse, "if you're as fast with your hands as you are with your mouth." Then his own hand stabbed downwards to the gun riding his thigh. He was faster than some I'd seen, but he'd declared his intentions loudly, and I'd had more than enough warning. My lead clipped a chunk from the tip of his boot before his iron had even cleared leather.

Roaring in rage and surprise, Bonney leapt backwards with agility admirable in so beefy a man. He caught himself quickly, though, pushing away from the wall and stomping back towards me, ready to fight. The anger thrumming through his body was so great that his lips quivered and his breath came in gasps.

"Clear out of here, Otis Bonney!" Delia shouted. "Papa isn't here and you aren't welcome."

Bonney's eyes turned from me towards the girl. "Better tell your new friend to clear out," he spat, "or one day soon, I'll catch him without that gun of his and blast him into little pieces."

I stepped forward and shoved the big man towards the door. "You heard the lady. Get your hide moving or I'll show you how good I am with my fists, too."

Bonney puckered his lips as if he was going to spit for real, then apparently thought better of it, turned on his heel and clattered out the way he'd come, every line of his big body showing the rage he felt.

"I'm sorry you had to see that," I said, turning back to Delia.

Delia shrugged and said, "It's nothing to me. He shouldn't have been here to begin with. You just saved me some trouble getting rid of him myself." She wrinkled up her nose in disgust. "He comes around whenever papa isn't here, trying to get his paws on me, but I want nothing to do with that man." Her expression clouded as she added, "You better watch out for him, though, Clint. He meant what he said."

"If he's all I have to worry about," I smirked, "then I don't have to worry at all."

She looked thoughtful as she dug a small hand into the pocket of her Levi's. "I don't think that's all, Clint." Her hand came up and in it was my badge. Powell must have given it to her. "I've seen now just how fast you are on the draw, and it makes me wonder all the more. I'm glad you've taken the job at the mine, and I really do hope you're up to it. I'd like nothing more than to see you bring Atherton to justice." The girl lay the badge on the dining table, gave me a look and then stepped lightly out of the room, letting the door swing shut behind her.

Suddenly, I felt like I'd taken a punch to the back of the head. Delia knew. She'd known my shame all along. I supposed her father really did tell her everything. Maybe the whole incident with Bonney was nothing more than a test. Was it really only coincidence that Bonny had shown up just after Powell had left? I wondered and as I did, I bitterly cursed the things I'd said to Emmitt Powell and the streak of yellow that I'd painted myself with.

✳✳✳✳✳

I didn't see Delia or her father again until the afternoon. When I did, it was an effort just to keep civil to my hosts and we ended up sharing another silent meal. I hated the way I felt, but a sudden dislike for the both of them had sprung up in me. Their knowledge of my shame, and the possibility that they'd been playing some kind of game with me all along, made it impossible to feel the same warmth for them that I had only a few hours earlier.

Part of me knew that neither of the Powells was at fault, but Delia's speaking of my "worries" led me to more deep thinking and, finally, to the acceptance of what my real problem was: I was afraid and not of the desert. I had faced down the open danger of guns pointed at me and the crashing fists of men bigger and stronger than me, all without batting an eye and more times than I could count. But Bill Atherton, or whoever it was that had bushwhacked me, had gotten the better of me without my even being aware of their presence, leaving me to die alone in the vastness of the desert, and it had broken something inside of me. Even so, that fear was my own, my darkest secret, and having other people know it felt damning and shameful.

I didn't have much of an appetite and so just pushed food around my plate for a while before excusing myself. When I stood to leave, though, Powell said, "Let's ride up to the mine, son. You'll be working the late guard tonight—midnight 'til morning—so I'd like to show you around some during the daylight."

Powell's choice of words, calling me "son," reminded me of what Delia had said about my similarities to her brother. I no longer liked the comparison, but saying so wouldn't have done me any good. "Sure thing," was my only reply.

The older man finished the last scraps on his plate, thanked his daughter for the food then joined me at the door leading to the hallway towards the front of the house. "I have a few little errands to run around town before we go," he said. "I won't be long, though, so why don't we meet at the livery?"

"Sounds fine," I told him and headed out.

When I reached the livery building, Otis Bonney and a handful of young men were lounging in the shade. There was a heavy coating of trail dust over the younger men's clothing. Some were sweaty, even in the cooling shade, and all looked ready for a rest. Only Bonney seemed fresh and I surmised that the riders had just come in from the range and were giving him some manner of report on their morning's work.

"Well, look at this!" Bonney cried when he noticed my approach. "Here's Powell's little desert foundling! Don't think you boys have met yet." The young cowboys looked me over; a couple of them cracked smiles.

Bonney pushed away from the wall of the livery, making to put himself in my pathway. We both stopped, eight or ten feet apart, and Bonney declared, "You know something, boys – if I ever catch this one without that gun he packs, I'll show him just how low he really is."

"You looking to get another boot clipped?" I asked.

Anger colored Bonney's cheeks and he spat in the dirt between us. "Try it. You can't pull your fancy gun tricks on me here – not in front of witnesses! We hang folks for murder around these parts."

I had no intention of killing Bonney, but he was right about the witnesses. A glance at the young men, still relaxing in the shade of the big building, showed that all wore six-shooters. I was better than Bonney any day of the week, but I wasn't good enough to face six guns by my lonesome.

"Get out of my way," I growled, making to move around Bonney. He sidestepped, putting himself into my path again and said, "Where you think you're going? You think you're good enough for one of our horses?" He looked at his cohorts and laughed, but it sounded painfully forced.

I let the frustration and anger I'd been feeling all day show in my eyes. "Move."

Bonney's red, beefy face split into a sneer. "Make me."

Whatever Delia and Emmitt Powell's intentions for me, one thing was clear to me then: Bonny's hatred for me wasn't faked or any sort of test. I didn't know why he hated me so, but a showdown was inevitable now.

When Bonney first started his needling, his riders had paid only passing attention, but now the prospect of a fight—and some entertainment—drew their full interest. They moved away from the livery, forming a loose circle around Bonny and me. From the corner of my eye, I saw more men appearing from several directions. I'd faced mobs before, but knew that here, Bonney would be my only opponent; from what Delia had said, and what I'd witnessed, of the man, I figured at least half of the crowd would be rooting for me to put Sanctuary's town foreman in his place. I had no issue with giving them what they wanted.

"You've cut yourself a hunk of trouble, Bonney," I said, calmly as I could manage, putting ice into my voice. "And just so you don't get any ideas of what kind of fight this'll be—" My hands went to my gun-belt, undoing the buckle, snaking the loop from around my waist and snapping the leather end of it straight towards Bonney's face. "There's the iron you were so afraid of, now come and get the trouble you've been asking for!"

The weighted belt flew the short distance between us and glanced off of Bonney's cheek, surprising him, but doing no real harm. The unexpectedness and the way it made Bonney look foolish, however, stoked his anger higher than ever and he roared like a wild beast, put his head down and charged me.

I stood my ground, waited until the last moment and then pivoted, bringing the edge of one boot around to sweep Bonney's feet from under him while, at the same time, slamming an elbow against the back of his neck to hurry him along on his trip to the hard-packed ground. Bonney plunged face-first into the dirt, sending up a little cloud of dust and a half-choked string of curses. His pistol flew from its holster and skidded through the dirt towards the circle of onlookers, ensuring fists would be the only weapon in our fight.

A groan went through the assembled crowd and someone yelled "Foul!" but no one moved to interfere or help Bonney up. Bonney threw angry glances all around him as he rolled over and lurched heavily to his feet. Then, without pause, he was after me again, lunging forward, huge hands outstretched in an attempt to grab and crush me.

Bonney was big and I was sure he was strong, but I had no aims of finding out firsthand – and he made that an easy prospect to avoid. He'd roared like an animal and he fought like one, too: all anger and instinct, but without a scrap of thought or skill. I dodged and wove around his blows again and again, jabbing with fists that found his ribs over and over, and his left eye twice in a row. The most Bonney could manage in return was an occasional glancing blow off my shoulder or the side of my head.

The fight went on, seconds dragging out to minutes, and we fell into a sort of rhythm. I became aware of the tense silence of the onlookers all around us. It was like they collectively held their breath in expectancy, even though there was no doubt in my mind as to what the final outcome would be. Brute strength had won Otis Bonney a position of leadership over the younger men in a quiet, peaceful town –a town where I'm sure few had ever really challenged him before. But dozens of cow-town brawls had given me a wealth of experience fighting men who relied on nothing more than size and strength, many of them bigger and faster than Bonney, and I was able to step and sway around the other man, carefully aiming blows where they'd do the most damage, the way a skilled *toreador* does to an enraged bull.

Even so, Bonney kept on coming, driving in time and again, long after his face was swollen and his eyes nearly closed, hoping in desperation to land a blow that'd finally put me down. His arms had grown tired and flailing, but still he struggled. We both knew that failure here, in front of half the town, meant losing everything his strength had won him.

I left him no openings for lucky blows, though, and more than that, I was coming to enjoy the ease with which I could toy with the other man. There was a savage joy in punishing the blowhard who'd tried to cut me down without even knowing me and during the minutes of that fight, I didn't have to think about anything but how good it felt.

I don't know how long the fight went on, but after a time, a strong grip trapped my arm from behind and a pleading voice said, "He's had plenty, mister. Ease up, will you?" I turned and saw that a slim young man, dressed in the chaps of a cowpuncher, had hold of my elbow.

I jerked my arm from his grasp, then used it to push the interloper back into the circle of onlookers, growling, "He asked for this." I took another swing at Bonney, connecting with his already-pulped lips. "And I'll decide when he's had enough!"

Bonney fell forward then and I stepped backwards to get up the momentum for a heavy body-blow, but never got the chance to throw it. The darting form of Delia Powell flashed in under my guard, threw a grip around my middle and cried, "Stop it! Stop it! Otis is an oaf and a brute, but he ain't half the bully you are!" Into my chest, the girl panted, low-voiced, "You keep on like this and you really will kill him. And if you do, then the folks around here'll drive you right back into that desert you're so scared of." She looked up. There were tears in her eyes. "Is that what you want ... Mr. Hagar?"

The use of my formal name snapped some piece of my brain back into place. The fighting madness was gone and all that was left was exhaustion and shame. A shame deeper than the girl's knowing my innermost fear had brought.

Delia released her hold on me and I took a look around us. I found the whole crowd to be judging me with silent, solemn expressions. In some faces, I saw anger, even hatred. In others, fear. A few showed what I thought might be pity; pity for Otis Bonney, beaten so badly, or pity for the savage broken by the desert, I wondered. Whatever it was, the realization that I might well have destroyed any chance of a peaceful life in this idyllic town was upon me.

I turned from the crowd, snatched up my gun-belt, then pushed my way through the mass of bodies and on into the livery building. At the far end of the cavernous building lay a watering trough. I dunked my head then washed the blood—both mine and Bonney's—from my hands. I buckled my gun back on then I found the horse I'd ridden in on the day before, saddled it and led the animal towards the door of the livery.

When I reached the sunlight, the crowd had dispersed. The only people left were Otis Bonney, sitting on the ground, sipping from a cup held by Delia Powell, and her father, who locked me in place with a sad look.

"You were a mite severe, Mr. Hagar," the elder Powell said.

I cast a glance at Bonney, who studiously avoided turning my way, though I doubted he could have seen me anyway. "I just wanted to shut that big mouth of his up."

"Well," Powell drawled. "You may just have made your own night longer. Otis won't be able to take his shift guarding the mine this evening, the way you've left him."

"The hell I won't!" Bonney declared through split, swollen lips. He began to struggle to his feet, ignoring Delia's protestations. "I'll stand my guard if it kills me before I accept *his* help!"

Powell took a breath, glancing from Bonney to me, then said, "Have it your way."

*****

The ride to the mine took us from the valley floor up into wooded hills that grew rugged and became real mountain, then into a small canyon, invisible from the town below, where the mine lay snugged away from the world. Powell didn't say a word to me until we reached the mine and I figured we were both thinking about the repercussions of my fight with Otis Bonney. Pulsing pain in my knuckles kept those shameful moments foremost in my thoughts. I wanted to say something to my benefactor, but I knew there was nothing to be said. I supposed by his muteness that Emmitt Powell felt the same way.

We passed through a wooden gate, built more for show than security. Before Atherton, I supposed, security hadn't been an issue. Powell reined up his mount and said, "Well, here we are," breaking the silence at last.

I didn't know much about mining, but surveying the layout, it seemed impressive for such a small outfit. The main structure, made of split logs, was built right up against the wall of the canyon, next to where the mine drift opened. On the opposite side of the structure, a stream of water poured from a fissure in the rocks, feeding a water-wheel, before tumbling down a steep embankment. Powell explained to me that the stamp-mill was housed there in the building and about how the machine worked, crushing the loads of rock hauled up from under the earth to then be sorted into ore and waste. Early on, Powell said, he and his miners had blasted a channel into the very rock of the mountain to divert a stream to power the wheel, impressing me with his drive and ingenuity. After the ore was separated out, it was placed into sacks and kept in a storeroom. A third room held supplies, including a stockpile of dynamite, used for blasting new shafts. I'd never been around the stuff, and the thought of a room full of it made me uneasy, but Powell assured me it was all perfectly safe. I decided I'd have to take his word for it.

As Powell gave me the bit tour, he introduced me to the men we came across. It was too soon for any of them to have heard about what had happened in town, but even so, I got a distinct impression of suspicion from several of them. With Powell speaking for me, I had to be accepted, it seemed, but they'd still make up their own minds about me.

When Powell was satisfied that I'd seen all there was to see, he walked me back to where we'd left the horses and pointed towards a small shack a little further up the canyon. "Up there's where you'll be staying for the time being," he told me. "After the way you handled Bonney earlier, I don't feel it'd be a good idea for you stay in my home any longer." He turned somber eyes on me. "I'm sorry it has to be that way, but Bonney's a member of the community and you're still an outsider, Mr. Hagar. As the leader of Sanctuary, I must take the people's feelings into consideration and—"

"I understand," I said, cutting off what might have turned into another of Powell's speeches. I felt I already knew everything he would say and I didn't need to hear it aloud.

Powell looked askance at me, then nodded. "Fine. At any rate, there's supplies up there. Should be food enough for a few days, anyway. If you need anything else, ask one of the men and they'll get word to me." He mounted his horse, swinging up into the saddle with admirable agility for a man his age. Looking down at me, he continued: "You'll go to work at midnight. I suggest you get some rest this afternoon." He wheeled the horse around and headed back towards the town.

With nothing else to do, I climbed into my own saddle and turned towards my new quarters, taking a slightly roundabout approach so as to get a better sense of the canyon. After a few minutes, I was approaching the shack and saw a saddled horse hitched to a post in the yard. Wary, I hopped from my horse, one hand on the six-gun at my hip, and stepped lightly through the door. I found Delia Powell inside, stacking canned goods in a small cupboard.

"What are you doing?" I asked.

"What does it look like?" the girl asked, without turning my way.

I frowned at her back. "After what happened, I thought you'd be whipping up your neighbors' blood, making ready to chase me back out into the desert."

Delia whirled, eyes flashing. "What a miserable thing to say! You know very well I'd never do any such thing! You're awful to even suggest it."

The anger melted from her fine features and in its place came a perplexed look. She sighed deeply. "I know I should leave a man like you to his own devices, let you sink or swim all on your own, but I can't somehow. I guess it's just a woman's way."

I couldn't help but grin. "The town's foremost tomboy talking about a 'woman's way'?"

My little joke fell flat. Delia's frown returned and she went back to her work, removing cans from a burlap sack and placing them into neat stacks in the cupboard.

I tried again. "Even after what I did, you're worried about me?"

"I just might be," she said over her shoulder. Putting the final can in its place, Delia turned back towards me. "It gets awful dark and lonely out here at night and there's an awful lot of silver over there in the mill-house. Bill Atherton's come before and unless he's caught first, he'll be back again one of these nights. You got shot at once already, out there in the desert, and this time you won't be on horseback. Are you lucky enough that Atherton'll miss you twice?"

I could feel the tenseness in my jaw, but I still managed to get out, "What are you trying to say, Delia? Do you think I'm scared of him?"

"I've been watching you, Clint," she said, her voice strangely soft. "You *are* scared but you're trying so desperately to prove to yourself that you're not. I'm no lawman and Lord knows I'm no kind of gunfighter, but it seems to me—"

I moved without thinking, caught her up in my arms and pressed my lips to hers. There was something, not in the words, but in the way she said them – something soft and longing that touched me in a way no other woman ever had. I think, somehow, the combination of Delia Powell and Clint Hagar and the situation in Sanctuary had created something in both of us that couldn't have existed anywhere else. And so I kissed her and for the first heartbeat, she was yielding and leaned into me and something sparked between us. Then she resisted and tore away from me, a low cry catching in her throat.

"What did you do that for?" she wanted to know, wiping her mouth with the back of her hand. "You're worse than Otis Bonney. Even he never tried that!"

"Delia…" I reached for her, but it was too late. She whirled on her heel and raced through the doorway of the shack and to her horse. Something bitter welled up inside me as I heard the sounds of hoof-beats retreating down the canyon.

*****

Never in my life had I made so many mistakes in one day, I reflected as I stabled my borrowed horse in the lean-to built against the rear of the shack for just that purpose. I stripped the harness and saddle and as I rubbed down the horse, the same buckskin I'd first seen upon waking up in Powell's camp the day before, all I could think about was what a mess I'd made.

It was true that Otis Bonney had been looking for a fight, but if I'd been content just to defend myself, putting him in the dirt as quickly and as painlessly as possible, I could have called it self-defense. Nobody would have argued different, probably not even Bonney. Instead, I'd kept him on his feet as long as I could, punishing him, I'd told myself, but really just enjoying being able to do it, thrilling in the power that I possessed. The chance to destroy something had felt good for a little while, but remembering the fear I'd seen in the eyes of some of the townsmen, I now felt nothing but shame.

I finished with the horse, went into the little shack and flopped down onto the edge of the bunk built into the wall. Looking around, I found the place to be Spartan, furnished with nothing more than the built-in bunk, a tiny cook stove, the cupboard Delia had been stocking when I'd arrived, a rickety table just big enough for a single man to sit at and a chair that matched it. If I hadn't taken Bonney apart, I wondered, would I be sitting here, alone in this shack? Or would I be in town, preparing for supper with Delia and her father?

The thought of Delia pained me almost as badly as what I'd done to Bonney. Even after seeing the brutality I was capable of, she'd still come all the way up into the canyon to make sure I was taken care of – and I had repaid that kindness by forcing my affections on her. I lay back on the bunk, stretching out and staring at the low ceiling. Maybe Delia *had* seen something in me, something she liked or was even attracted to, but I had no doubt that if she still felt anything at all towards me, it was only disgust – disgust, and maybe pity, for the man who had run from his fear and in his haste knocked down anyone who got in his way.

I rolled over on the bunk, face turned to the wall, but sleep would not come. By and by, night closed in and the darkness became like a void in the unfamiliar space, but even so it would not swallow me up the way I wished it would. Time had little meaning during those hours, but some while after moonrise, a series of unfamiliar sounds drifted in on the night air and something about them set off warning bells in my brain. I couldn't identify those sounds, but they sparked a thought and it occurred to me that Powell had said he suspected some member of his own work crew had a hand in aiding Atherton's plundering the mine. As I sat up in the darkness and swung my feet to the floor, I realized how easily that person would be able to frame me, a newcomer and an outsider, as Atherton's accomplice. Having rescued me from the desert, and knowing what he did about me, Powell was unlikely to believe it, but that wouldn't matter if everyone else in Sanctuary thought it to be true. The danger of my situation suddenly seemed very real.

In the faint light of a half-moon, I checked my holster as I strode outside and back to the makeshift stable. Within minutes, I was headed for the mine. I promised myself that before this time tomorrow, I would be long gone from Sanctuary. Tonight, though, I had a job to do. In accepting the guard job, I'd made Powell a promise and I intended to make sure that there would be no thievery on my watch.

I raced the horse down the moonlit trail as fast as I dared; though it angled slightly downward, the trail was wide and fairly smooth and I trusted the horse's sure footing. Before we'd quite reached the mine, we slowed to a walk and when the horse began to softly nicker at the scent of other animals, I brought it to a complete standstill. Dismounting, I tied off the reins to a convenient sapling and moved through the darkness on foot.

Coming up on the mine building from the side facing up-canyon, I heard quiet animal sounds from behind a stand of low trees. Parting the branches, I saw a team of four mules hitched to a wagon, shuffling their feet anxiously in the darkness, waiting for their driver to return. The discovery sent ice down my spine that spread through my limbs and settled in them like lead. My instincts about the frame-up had been right: whoever Atherton's accomplice was, they were taking advantage of my presence to strike that very night.

I grit my teeth and bit back the anger, stronger now than the fear. I'd never wanted to come to Sanctuary, had never even known it existed until Emmitt Powell had brought me. I owed him my life and for that, despite everything else, I felt immensely grateful to him – but it didn't erase the fact that I'd had nothing but trouble since arriving in this valley. Some of it was my own making, true, but now, finally, it was time to settle a piece of it.

Quietly, I crept the rest of the way to the building. A light burned in the front room, the large space that housed the stamp-mill, but the door was locked. Moving around to the side of the building in a low crouch, I caught the faint murmur of voices coming through the wall of the storage room where the blasting materials were kept. The voices were too muffled by the wall and the sounds of the water nearby to pick up on words, but the urgency in one of the voices came through clearly. Whatever conference was taking place inside did not seem to be going well for at least that party. I planned to make their night much worse in order to secure that silver. To do that, though, I first needed to find a way inside.

Keeping low, I found my way to the rear of the structure, where it abutted the almost-sheer rise of the rock above the entrance to the mine. I discovered that the rough-built structure, functional more than anything else, was not entirely sealed – the back of the building, fitted right against the mountain, had no rear wall, using the mountain itself in its place, and that gave me access. The fit was tight, but using a little force, I was able to squeeze myself between the split log walls and the night-cold stone and squirm my way inside. On hands and knees in the deep shadows between stacks of crates, I paused to listen, praying that my entrance hadn't been heard or noticed.

The muffled conversation I'd heard before was louder now, almost as loud as the racing beat of my heart. After a tense moment of waiting and listening, I decided that the men's own voices, combined with the sound of the rushing water outside, had covered the noise of my entrance. I got to my feet and stole forward, keeping the piles of crates between me and the sound of voices until I was close enough to hear clearly. Otis Bonney's booming voice cried, "Like hell that's my cut, Atherton! I'm the one taking all the risk!"

"You're damned mouthy for a man who can't do even the simplest jobs," a calm, steely voice responded. "You'd better be thankful for whatever I decide to give you, Bonney. I can get along just fine without you – I did it before without your help and I can do it again, if need be."

I crept forward as far as I dared, shifting positions until I found a space between two crates that was large enough to peek through. In the light of an oil lamp, Bonney, leaning heavily against a stack of boxes, with eyes still swollen enough to make seeing difficult, did his best to glare at a slim, hard blade of a man. Between them lay a stack of canvas sacks that I knew would soon be filled with silver. The stranger shifted his weight and turned slightly and by the low light I saw a profile I recognized from the paper out on him: Bill Atherton.

"That ain't fair," Bonney protested, but Atherton cut in. "I gave you one job, fatty – stop that lawman your boss sent for. You told me he was good as dead and the next damned day he shows up in town and he's hired to guard this place! Then he beats the stuffing out of you on top of it! Either you're a liar or you're just plain incompetent. Whichever one it is, I don't need either, so just take your thousand and keep your mouth shut."

I should not have been surprised, but still it came as something of a shock. The man I'd entered the desert to find, the man who I thought had nearly killed me, was standing there with the man who had actually pulled the trigger – the same man who'd done his level best to make my life miserable since the moment we'd met. I'd come a long way to find Atherton and in just a short time, I'd gone through a lot of hell with Bonney. Now, the pieces of the puzzle fell into place and the picture they formed made the kind of sense that couldn't be argued with.

Rage hotter than the sun began to boil in my belly, but I kept my peace, watching and listening and waiting.

With a characteristic sneer in his voice, Bonney said, "Fine. I'll take my pittance, and I'll keep my plan to myself since I'm so damned useless to you. You know he'll be up here in an hour or so for guard duty so what're you gonna do then?"

Atherton laughed. "He'll never make it. Not if I'm outside of the door to his shack when he comes out. I'm not gonna make the same mistake you did, out there in the desert – I'll put my barrel right up against the back of his head before I pull the trigger. You just worry about filling up those sacks with ore then help Lee load the mule-wagon."

I heard Bonney gasp, then cry, "You mean you're gonna bushwhack him right here and leave me with no alibi? The hell you will! I still got to live here, Bill!"

"Well, what do you propose then?" Atherton asked.

I decided I'd heard enough. Slipping around a stack of crates, I pushed myself against the wall and crept into the corner opposite from where the other two men argued, the corner nearest the door to the main room. With the half-open door partially hiding me and the corner against my back, I was in about the best position I could hope for in the confined space. Bonney's back was to me, but if Atherton looked, he would see me. There was no helping it, I could only hope he wouldn't notice until there was nothing he could do about it.

"Easy," Bonney replied. "When he comes in here for guard duty, I'll knock him on the head as he comes through the door, then leave him to take the rap for the theft."

"You're a damned fool," Atherton spat. "If he's still here, who's gonna believe he's the one who took the silver?" Suddenly, his narrow-lidded eyes grew wide and his hand went to the iron on his thigh. From between thin lips, he growled, "God damn! He's right behind you, you blind idiot! Lee, get your hide in here!"

Atherton leapt to one side, putting Bonney between us, as the door flew wide open and a hard-looking, hatless redhead raced in, gun already in hand. In the position I held, though, Lee's arrival did him no good; I already had my gun at the ready and he was covered when he entered. "Drop it and get your hands in the air – fast!"

Bonney dropped to his hands and knees and crawled away, seeking shelter from the line of fire, while squealing, "Don't make him sling lead! He's as hellish with that six-gun as he is with his fists!"

"I'm going to drop the man who doesn't get his hands up," I warned, "so if you want to walk out of here alive, do as you're told."

Atherton's voice rose to a pitch as he shrieked, "No lousy badge-toter's ever gotten the best of me!" and drew his gun, side-stepping as he raised his arm to fire. His partner, Lee, mimicked the movement, falling back and moving in the opposite direction, separating to make me choose my target and leave me vulnerable to the other man's fire. It worked. I couldn't track both at once and my arm, still stiff from the beating I'd given Otis Bonney hours early, was slower than I was used to. The outlaws, however, wasted no time and lead was flying in my direction before I could get off a shot of my own. All I could do was dive for cover. The stacks of wooden crates between us saved me from taking a bullet, but in the dim light, it must have looked as if I'd fallen rather than ducked because when I popped back up, gun raised, I saw the surprise in the eyes of the man called Lee before I put a bullet between them. He fell backwards, convulsing grotesquely, leaving a smear of blood on the crate he fell against in his slide towards the floor.

Otis Bonney took that moment to make his break, dashing out of the shadows on the far side of the room. Careening off obstacles in his half-blind state, he knocked the lantern from its perch on an upturned crate in his charge towards the door and escape. There was a moment of darkness, filled with the sounds of Bonney's confused, frantic footsteps, then the door slammed shut. The draft it created whipped through the enclosed space, stirring to life some tiny flame left in the lamp and igniting the oil spreading across the floor among the stacks of boxes and piles of sacks.

Lead crashed into the place where I'd been and I snapped off a return shot at the muzzle-flash, but heard only the smashing of wood for my efforts. Atherton and I had both been in countless gunfights and we both knew not to stay in one place more than an instant. Only luck—good or bad, depending on your perspective—would reward either of us a solid hit.

The flames were growing higher and the light they shed was already enough to bring the room from darkness to flickering gloom. A rustling sound caught my attention and I turned and flung a round in the direction of the door just as a shadow appeared there. A sharp groan went up and then Atherton appeared, charging right at me, blood streaming from a hole high in his chest, a terrible ferocity twisting his features. Surrounded by the alternating shadows thrown by the growing flames, roaring in rage and pain, he seemed less like the outlaw I'd been hunting and more like a demon straight from the pits of hell, determined to drag me down with him.

Quick as I could, I brought my gun up, but the hammer clicked on an empty chamber and then Atherton was on me, driving me back, keeping me off balance with wild, swinging fists and clawing fingers aimed at my eyes. The heel of my boot caught on something and I went down, flat on my back, and Atherton followed, locking his clutching hands around my throat. Around us, the fire roared and began to rage and as I rolled, trying to free myself from the wounded man's grasp, I caught sight of the word painted on the nearest crate: DYNAMITE. Atherton had no need to kill me himself; in another few moments, we'd both be blown to hell.

The thought gave me wild strength and I twisted to one side, bringing a knee up into the pit of Atherton's belly. Again and again, I drove my knee into him and when he gave a little slack, I took advantage of it, kicking my leg full out, catching him in the middle with the heel of my boot, tearing the dying killer away from my throat and sending him sprawling into the flames crawling across the wooden floor.

Atherton hit with a *thud!* and instantly leapt back to his feet, screeching horribly as the fire bit his flesh, the burning oil soaking into his clothing and skin, clinging to him like death itself. He flailed and whirled, throwing off flames from his hands, setting more boxes alight, and then collapsed, a rattling gurgle his final earthly sounds.

The entire sequence took only a second and I had no time to register what had happened before I was on my feet and running. I snatched up the nearest burning crate, raced madly through the door and hurled it straight through the down-canyon-facing window of the main room, then turned and went back for another, not even waiting to see what had happened to the first. I heard the thunderous explosion of the first burning box as the dynamite touched off, somewhere down in the artificial river channel, but it hardly registered. Twice more, I repeated the process, and the explosions that sounded came so close together that they sounded like echoes of the first. I pushed aside the rest of the boxes, keeping them from the now-dwindling flame, and only when I was certain no more of the boxes were in any danger did I snatch up one of the canvas sacks and beat out what remained of the fire, thanking the Lord that much of the remaining oil had soaked into Atherton's clothing before reaching any more of the stacked crates. It was a terrible way for a man to die, but there was still justice in it somehow.

When the danger was finally passed, I staggered outside, groggy from the smoke and exertion but relishing the cool night air on my heat-blasted skin and sweat-soaked clothes. It was only then that I realized: I had not been afraid. At no point during the last few minutes, during the fight with Atherton and his compadre, Lee, nor during the desperate battle against the spreading flames, had there been even a twinge of fear in me. I'd spent the last day thinking of myself as a coward, a useless, broken man who would no longer be of use to anyone. At first, my thoughts were only of my promise to Powell and the duty it entailed, but then, in executing it, I'd had no doubts, no hesitation. The only thing I'd thought of was that I couldn't let Atherton or Bonney get away with stealing from the hard-working people of Sanctuary. As Powell had said, this mine was the town's lifeblood and I had made myself its first and last line of defense.

Sore, sweaty and exhausted, I still cracked a smile as I staggered through the darkness towards where I'd tied the buckskin. I needed to ride into town and tell Emmitt Powell what had happened. Maybe it was my fatigue, or maybe it was because I was occupied by thoughts of a future that was beginning to look bright once again, but I didn't notice the movement in the brush until Otis Bonney stepped into my path holding a scattergun leveled at my midsection. "You damned meddler," Bonney whined.

For an instant, the fear—the gnawing, damning thing deep inside me that had eaten up any self-confidence I might have had, that had turned me into a savage, selfish shadow of a man—leapt up, making my palms cold and clammy in the night air. And I laughed right in its face, right in the face of the quivering, half-blind man before me who, even holding a weapon he couldn't possibly miss me with, was shaking in his boots at the sight of me. I had beaten Otis Bonney twice, once with my gun and again with my fists, and he was scared of me – terrified, even. There was no reason that I should be afraid of him. I'd faced down Bill Atherton and his partner and come out unharmed. This sad little man was no terror for me.

As I realized that, I knew, too, that this was something every lawman had to come to terms with. Each of us suffered from the same ravenous fear that chased at our heels, knowing that each time we walked past a darkened alleyway or rode into a narrow canyon, there might be someone lying in ambush, trying to get revenge for some imagined wrong or simply to take one of us down in order to add to his own outlaw legend. And you can't be a good lawman without it – that tingling coldness down your spine keeps you alive, keeps you on your toes when there's danger around. It's no enemy; it's the best friend a lawman can have.

I lunged forward, diving into the brush at the side of the trail, at the same instant that Bonney's scattergun roared, sending a double-barreled load of buckshot into the spot where I'd just stood, ripping the foliage into shreds. Bonney knew he'd missed and, frantic, he broke the weapon, fumbling the empty shells out of the barrels to reload, but it was too late – I was already on him. Smashing fists that had already pulverized the man once did so again, but this time, I knew when to stop. Two blows knocked Bonney unconscious and then his own belt secured his hands. With effort, I dragged him back to the mine building and sat down on its wooden steps. I breathed deeply of the cool night air. Despite the night's events, my heart was singing. It held no more doubt or fear. That moment was the first pure joy I'd experienced in a long time.

*****

I didn't need to worry about returning to town. The explosions had been heard in the valley and before I was ready to make my way down, Emmitt Powell and a group of his men had found their way up.

When Powell arrived, he found me sitting, smoking Bonney's tobacco, as the trussed up man stared sullenly off into the distance. From his saddle, he looked down at Bonney, who stubbornly refused to acknowledge the older man. Powell did not show any emotion on his face, but there was satisfaction in his voice when he said, "I knew it." He turned to me and said, "And I knew you were the right man for the job."

I stood. "Guess you did. Thank you for that." I told Powell about what had happened, about Atherton and his crony, about Bonney's complicity, about the shootout and the fire.

When I was finished, Powell said, "I see." A smile spread across his lips and he added, "Remember what I said, when we first met?"

I wracked my brain, but I was too tired and it was no use. I shook my head.

"One of these days," Powell continued, "Sanctuary will need its own lawman. You know anybody who might be interested?"

It was my turn to smile. "I can think of someone, sure."

Powell climbed down from his horse, saying, "This town has a lot to offer the right candidate, but don't say yes or no until you've made up your mind. Think on it."

I had – I'd done nothing but think on it the whole time I sat there, waiting with my silent, brooding captive. What Powell had said was true: Sanctuary had a lot to offer. It was a beautiful, fertile land and it held the kind of promise that hard-working people could turn into something truly amazing, something approaching Heaven on Earth. But there was another promise I was more concerned with, a promise made by a girl named Delia, about the reward she'd offered for bringing her brother's killer to justice. It was news I'd be glad to bring her.

"Mr. Powell," I said. "When can I start?"

The Usual Unusual Suspects

John M. Floyd's work has appeared in more than 300 different publications, including *Alfred Hitchcock's Mystery Magazine*, *Ellery Queen's Mystery Magazine*, *Strand Magazine*, *The Saturday Evening Post*, and three editions of *The Best American Mystery Stories*. A former Air Force captain and IBM systems engineer, John is also an Edgar Award finalist, a four-time Derringer Award winner, and the author of nine books. His short story—**The Judge's Wife**—appeared in the Murderous Ink Press anthology series, CRIMEUCOPIA – *The Cosy Nostra*, and **Saving Mrs. Hapwell** in CRIMEUCOPIA – *As In Funny Ha-Ha, Or Just Peculair*.

Alexander Frew comes from farming and mining stock in the county of Ayrshire, Scotland. He went to the same Academy as Sir Alexander Fleming, the man who discovered penicillin, but it is fair to say that on leaving at the age of fifteen he failed to make the same societal impact. He wrote poetry and short stories in the 80s, then joined Borderline Theatre in the 90s and had several plays performed in an old church in Ayr. He also started South West Writers, and had three books for children published at the turn of the century. This led exactly nowhere, and after a fallow period he started self-publishing and produced a series of poetry booklets, CD's and performances in conjunction with the group.

After having an adventure story accepted by Hale in 2012, Alex has published some twenty books in the Western genre. He has also had a science fiction book published this March *by Mocha Memoirs Press*. His first, and greatest love, is the short story and he is trying to get better because it is harder to write a short story than a short book. His short story, **Darkness Before Noon**, appeared in CRIMEUCOPIA – *The Cosy Nostra*.

Jim Doherty is an American police officer, who has had a fairly peripatetic career, working as everything from a reserve cop for a municipal police force (roughly the equivalent of a British *Special Constable*), to a federal officer, to a small-town chief of police. His first novel, *An Obscure Grave*, was a finalist for a *CWA Debut Dagger* and a *Silver Falchion* in the category of *Best Police Procedural* at the *Killer Nashville* crime fiction conference. His Sherlock

Holmes pastiche, *The Adventure of the Manhunting Marshal*, was finalist for a Derringer Award, given by the *Short Mystery Fiction Society*, in the category of *Best Novelette*. His true crime article, *Blood for Oil*, won a Spur from the *Western Writers of America* for Best Short Non-Fiction.

Bruce Harris writes Crime, Mystery, and Western stories. He is the author of *Sherlock Holmes and Doctor Watson: About Type* (2006) and *Anticipations* in D. Martin Dakin's *A Sherlock Holmes Commentary* (2021).

Brandon Barrows is the author of the novels *Burn Me Out*, *This Rough Old World*, *Nervosa*, and has over 50 published stories, a selection of which are collected in the books *The Altar in the Hills* and *The Castle Town Tradgedy*. His short story, **Don't You See?**, appears in CRIMEUCOPIA – *We're All Animals Under the Skin*. He is an active member of the Private Eye Writers of America and International Thriller Writers.

16 stories ranging from the 14th to the 21st Century, all from women authors whose forte is crime.

Featuring *Karen Skinner, Hilary Davidson, Pauline Gostling, Linda Kerr, Kate Miller, Tiffany Lindfield, Lena Ng, Ginny Swart, Sandrine Bergèss, Michelle Ann King, Amanda Steel, Kelly Lewis, Paulene Turner, Claire Leng, Madeleine McDonald and Joan Hall Hovey.*

**Paperback Edition ISBN:
9781909498198
eBook Edition ISBN:
9781909498204**

18 authors take time to look under the skin of the people who sometimes inhabit their heads, and put what they find down on paper.

Featuring John Gerard Fagan, Nick Boldock, Weldon Burge, Chris Phillips, Dan Meyers, Jeff Dosser, Eve Fisher, Emilian Wojnowski, Fabiyas M V, Lamont A. Turner, Edward Ahern, Robert Petyo, Al Hagan, Caroline Tuohey, Steve Carr, Bobby Mathews, Michael Bracken, and June Lorraine Roberts.

Paperback Edition ISBN:
9781909498235
eBook Edition ISBN:
9781909498228

17 writers take us on Cosy journeys - some more traditional, while others are very much up to date.

Eve Fisher, Alexander Frew, Tom Johnstone, John M.Floyd, Andrew Humphrey, Joan Leotta, Gary Thomson, Eamonn Murphey, Matias Travieso-Diaz, Madeline McEwen, Lyn Fraser, Ella Moon, Gina L. Grandi, Louise Taylor, Judy Penz Sheluk, Joan Hall Hovey and Judy Upton.

Paperback Edition ISBN: 9781909498242
eBook Edition ISBN: 9781909498259

CRIMEUCOPIA

As In Funny Ha-Ha

Or Just Peculiar

Putting the Outré back into OMG are
Jesse Hilson, Gabriel Stevenson, Maddi Davidson,
Brandon Barrows, Robb T. White, Regina Clarke,
Martin Zeigler, K. G. Anderson, Andrew Hook,
Ed Nobody, Jody Smith, Michael Grimala,
W. T. Paterson, James Blakey, Emilian Wojnowski,
Andrew Darlington, Lawrence Allan, Ricky Sprague,
Bethany Maines, John M. Floyd and Julie Richards

Paperback Edition ISBN: 9781909498266
eBook Edition ISBN: 9781909498273